Novels by Lisa Silverthorne

A Game of Lost Souls series:
Contemporary Romantasy
THE CINDERELLA HOUR
THE PRINCE CHARMING HOUR
THE EVER AFTER HOUR
THE FALLEN HEARTS SEASON
THE RISING SPIRITS SEASON
THE ETERNAL SOULS SEASON
THE ROYAL WEDDING HOUR
THE HEAVENLY HONEYMOON HOUR
THE DIVINE NEWLYWEDS SHOW
THE CELESTIAL COUPLES SHOW
THE ENOCHIAN APOCALYPSE SHOW
THE ANGELIC ANNIVERSARY SHOW
THE PERDITION PICTURE SHOW
Complete Series!

Curse and Crown series:
Epic Court Intrigue Romantasy
THORN & BLADE
STORM & STEEL

The Spiral series:
Dark Contemporary Fantasy
BETWEEN
REPRISE
AVENGE

The Resurrectionist Papers
Supernatural Romystery
GRAVE RECKONING

Science Fiction Writing as L.S. Silverthorne

Experiencing True Purple series:
RECOMBINANT, Book 1
HELIX, Book 2
SPLICE, Book 3

Standalones:
REDISCOVERY

FORTHCOMING BY LISA SILVERTHORNE

FORTHCOMING!

Curse and Crown series:

Flame & Dagger, Book Three

Frost & Foil, Book Four

Curse & Crown, Book Five (Series End)

The Spiral series:

Ruin, Book 4

Descent, Book 5 (Series End)

The Resurrectionist Papers:

Corpses Delicti

Stiffed Again

SCIENCE FICTION WRITING AS **L.S.** SILVERTHORNE

Experiencing True Purple series:

Cipher, Book 4

Renascence, Book 5 (Series End)

THORN & BLADE

CURSE AND CROWN
BOOK ONE

LISA SILVERTHORNE

Book 1: Curse and Crown

Thorn & Blade

Lisa Silverthorne

Everyone wants me dead.
So, my mother, the queen, hired this terrifying outlaw as my
bodyguard.
The Butcher of Badriyah.

As a princess and a sorceress, I'm forced to marry an enemy prince.
Only one thing stands between me and certain death—my devilishly
handsome prick-of-a-bodyguard.

He's a scorching hot blademaster.
Thinks he owns me.
Sometimes, I want to end him in his sleep.
Sometimes, I want him to touch me—and more...

Can the two of us survive this long carriage ride?
Without falling in love? And letting the world burn?

An Enemies-to-Lovers Forced Proximity Romantasy Suspense

Map of Kambria

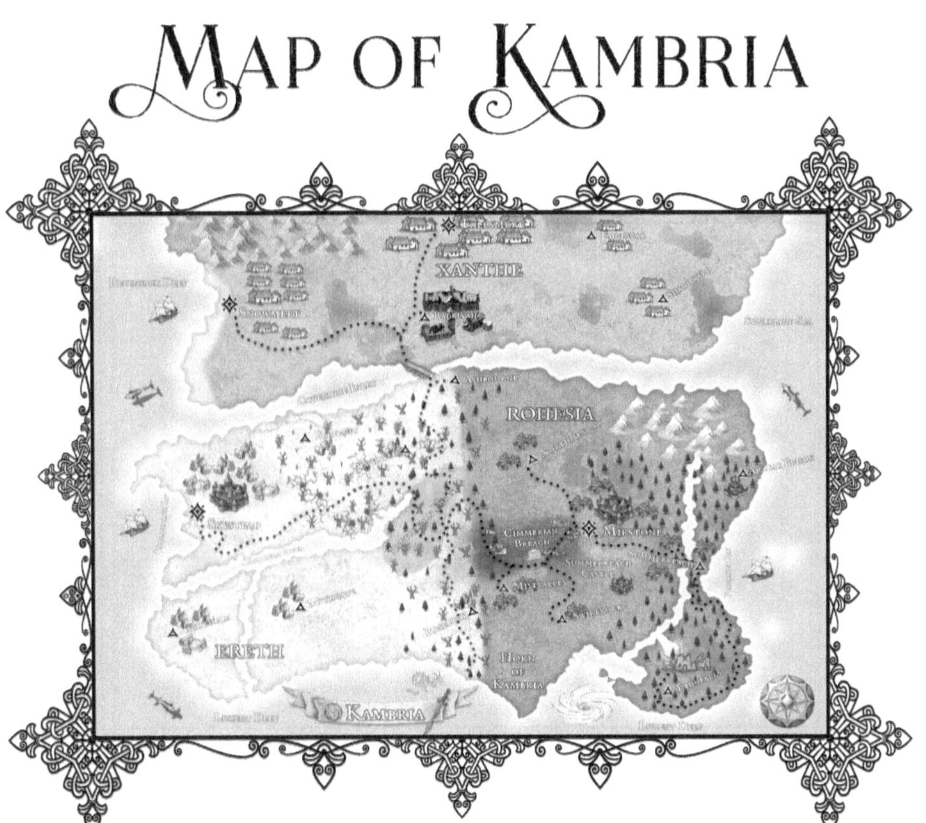

I

Shadows from Ereth's perpetual dusk eddied in the corners and pooled along the pocked grey stone castle walls battered and scarred from the Hundred-Year Sundering. A century of war with Rohesia to the east. A clash of magic against blade. A hundred years of fading sunlight and growing twilight.

Of dying crops and invading darkness.

Smell of ozone and wood smoke hung thick in the charged air as mages in royal purple silk robes and archers in grey tunics and trousers lined Castle Skystead's ramparts. Magic glowed amethyst and cyan at fingertips and the points of arrows. It felt like all of Ereth held its breath.

Waiting. Waiting for the enemy's arrival from the east under a banner of truce.

Fingers of pallid sunlight withered and receded as torches guttered in the painful silence, thrum of magic rumbling against the castle walls. Filling my heart with trepidation.

Standing alongside the elite magical guard in my violet purple Erethian betrothal gown, pulse racing, I watched the Rohesian convoy's carriages coalesce like an apparition out of the mists and gathering shadows. Toward Skystead. Without swords drawn. Without magic burning the air.

For the first time in a century, Rohesians stood on Erethian soil in the most tenuous truce ever seen in Ereth. The first I'd ever witnessed in all my eighteen years.

I'd never felt warm sunlight on my face—only this tepid glow. And with every passing day, the sunlight receded more, unable to penetrate the mists and shadows that cursed my mother's magic realm of Ereth. And the kingdom of Rohesia, those vile sword-mongering monsters to the east.

Ereth's bitter enemy.

Instead, the blanched, sickly sun rays cast an illusion of warmth in their fading gold hues, more the color of piss than sunlight. Crops died in the fields and leaves fell from the trees in a perpetual autumn.

Either way, this curse had been my doom. It fated me to wed Prince Arence Siridean of Rohesia—and my sisters to marry his brothers. To fulfill the prophecy that would break this curse and save Ereth. Save the world of Kambria. And Rohesia, too—not that I cared.

My life was over.

I held my breath as I watched the royal Rohesian carriage slide out of the mist, carved from dark grey ironwood by the sharpest blades in Kambria, and led by six stocky black Merced roans the color of midnight, coats ticked grey, manes wrapped in red and orange silks that undulated like flames in the wind. The scent of new leather and sweaty horses hung above magic's burnt lightning smell.

Whiffs of sulfur and lime from the torches burning above the gate made me move up wind to keep the smell out of my blond hair as I watched my doom unfold at Skystead's gates. The Rohesian royal red standard bearing crossed swords flew above the carriage. Fluttering like my heart.

It took all my courage to hold back the tears burning in my eyes, a golden hazel as Lady Laurel described them.

Lady Laurel, my lady-in-waiting, stood beside me, dressed in Ereth's long, royal purple mage robes with long raglan sleeves and silky drape. Magical symbols danced with ethereal light across the fabric, brightening and fading as twilight darkened. Already, she was casting. Wards. Protection. Calm.

She slid her arm around my waist and held me close. My blond hair mixed with long strands of her warm brown locks that had begun to cloud with silver and white. She smelled like magic and rosewater.

More mother to me than my own, Lady Laurel had helped me dress in the magnificent royal purple betrothal gown with its beaded lace bodice, off-the shoulder straps, and a delicate purple chiffon cape that floated into a royal train three feet behind me.

Conjured with air magic and finished by the finest Erethian tailors and seamstresses, the dress was a statement to Rohesia. That Ereth was still a rich and flourishing realm (despite this curse that would soon destroy everything). That its firstborn princess was borne of deep and powerful magical lines—and one of the most priceless gifts from Earth.

But I couldn't get past the fact that I was expendable.

I was one of four prices the realm must pay to save the world. My happiness and dreams had been taken from me and gift-wrapped into this visionary and alluring gown meant to enrapture a barbaric prince into marrying me. Where I would exist in a loveless marriage, in a foreign place I would never love, so that the world survived. I had just turned eighteen and my chest ached with the weight and depth of this sacrifice I was forced to make. Even though certain factions of Kambria wanted me—and my three other sisters—dead and this prophecy left unfulfilled.

This marriage was forever. I would never return to my beloved realm of Ereth.

"Chin up, princess," Lady Laurel whispered against my ear. "You are the bravest young woman I have ever met. Both Ereth and

Rohesia will make certain you are well-guarded. You will be safe and I will be with you. You won't be alone in Rohesia."

Lady Laurel knew about the threats to my life from across Kambria. It seemed incomprehensible to me that some didn't want this union of realms to take place. And they had pledged to stop it at all costs. To murder me before I ever reached the border between the countries.

Right now, I almost considered that a kindness.

"Your mother chose me as your lady-in-waiting because of my air sorcery's prowess. You will be safe. The hopes of Kambria go with you this day. And all the love Ereth can muster for our beautiful sacrifice."

She was leaving Ereth, too. Making the same sacrifice. Except that she wouldn't be forced to marry a man she didn't love and would probably despise. Prince Arence. Oldest son of Rohesian King Daegal Siridean. I had heard he was at least thirty and as barbaric and bloodthirsty as his father. In a kingdom that despised magic, mages, and sorceresses. The thought of their blades terrified me.

But Lady Laurel's gracious acceptance of her fate was a model I needed to emulate. Hold my head high no matter what.

"My sisters weren't allowed to watch me leave," I said, trying so hard not to let my voice crack or catch in my throat. "To tell me goodbye."

My mother, the queen, wouldn't allow them to witness my departure from Ereth and the only life I had ever known. Because it was their future. Genevieve would leave next spring. Carysana two years later. And finally, Arianwen two years after Carys.

"Even I can feel the heat and comfort of your sisters' magics swirling around you, Annarissa," said Lady Laurel as the creak of carriage wheels echoed in the quiet.

She was right.

I felt their love and magic supporting me. Wrapping around me like a blanket warmed by hearth fires. Gen with her explosive air magic (a fierce warrior princess and assault sorceress). Carys' fiery magic and fascination with daggers (Carys hated magic, a secret she'd kept from Mother—along with the daggers.) And beautiful white-haired Arianwen, blessed with powerful water magic. My sisters' combined magics kept me upright and moving right now when I wanted to collapse against the stone floor. I felt their magic.

And their fear—for me. For their futures.

Following me into Rohesia's dark, wild expanse. Forced to marry our enemies' sons. All princes of Rohesia.

Our freedom—and our love—was the price of peace. But having even one of my sisters near me in Rohesia was a comfort I clung to right now. And Lady Laurel's strength.

It had to be enough.

Besides, the Prophecy of Magics and Blades demanded it. A price dictated after Queen Maelena Thorn and King Onyx Siridean killed each other on a battlefield at Ereth's eastern border. In the aftermath, Lady Ambren Thorn (my mother) and Lord Daegal Siridean were crowned new rulers of Ereth and Rohesia. As the Kambrian peace delegation read the prophecy right there on the bloody, body-strewn battlefield, the newly crowned queen and king were given two choices.

Blood or death.

By blood or death, a sacrifice was demanded of both realms. Queen and king must sacrifice their children. Either they wed Rohesian blades with Erethian elemental magics or face the total annihilation of both realms.

To lift the curse and save the world of Kambria.

That very day, Queen Ambren Thorn put down her wand and staff, pledging the hands of her four young daughters when they came of age. To four princes of Rohesia. King Daegal Siridean put down his sword across wand and stave, pledging the hands of his sons to the sorceresses of Ereth.

It had been the only way to halt the curse stealing Kambria's sunlight and killing all its crops and livestock. Only Xanthe across Covendrie Inlet to the north, a neutral kingdom, still had full sunlight

—and could grow most crops. Without the Thorn sisters' and Siridean princes' sacrifices, all of Kambria's people would soon perish when the sun's light went dark across Kambria. And in Xanthe.

As the firstborn sorceress of Ereth, named for legendary ice sorceress Anna Thorn and her fire mage lady-in-waiting Rissa Thorn (my grandmothers), I became Ereth's first great hope. As the heir apparent to the throne, with three sisters in line behind me, I had been trained in battle magic since I could read the family grimoire. But I knew that after my magical confirmation, a ceremony where one (or more) of the elemental magics binds itself to a sorceress, my mother had been so disappointed in my magical inheritance.

And me.

In a moment that couldn't be taken back, I, Princess Annarissa Thorn, the first great hope of Ereth, had become...just an earth sorceress.

Considered the weakest of the four elemental magics, my magical inheritance had been a portent of doom to my mother. But it didn't matter. As firstborn, I had to make the first great sacrifice.

Part of me wanted to die. To escape this banishment and isolation to the west. A barbaric place I had never even seen before.

"Annarissa, it's time," said the stolid, icy voice of my mother who had materialized behind me in the finest royal purple gown in Ereth. Fit for a sorceress queen. A form-fitting color-changing silk, covered in iridescent beading, that flowed around her like smoke, shoulders bare, sleeves dripping with beads and the sheerest lace.

Made for the occasion of giving away her firstborn daughter in marriage. Bet Mother hadn't expected it to happen in this way. I know I didn't.

I wondered how long ago her ice sorcery had frozen her heart. She seemed indifferent to the fact that I was leaving her and everything I loved behind. Forever. That she would never see me—her firstborn—in person again.

Pulling in a deep breath, I squeezed Lady Laurel's hand and

reached up to adjust the gold and amethyst Erethian crown I wore. Delicate. Ethereal. Magical as the violet gems floated along the band and elemental symbols gleamed up and down the crown's myriad spikes of raw gems—like sun's rays. A smaller version of the queen's grand crown.

I gritted my teeth. I was a sorceress of Ereth. I would hold my head high and bury my heart this day.

Along with my hopes and dreams—and my love.

I reached for my earth magic. My hand sparkled with purple light as I conjured a handful of stark black soil that smelled rich and loamy like peat. In my other hand I conjured a delicate porcelain white pearl, a symbol of my wish for true love and the prince of my dreams that I had carefully nurtured and protected since I was a small child.

Inhaling sharply, I dropped the pearl into the soil and waved my hand across it. Burying my last hope of marrying for love. Letting it go.

The soil hardened and crumbled to dust.

I blew the remnants of the life I would never have over the rampart and it brushed across the massive, ornate Rohesian carriage that halted at the castle drawbridge.

The three wagons carrying a complement of hired swords behind the polished ironwood carriage creaked to a stop. Using wagons gave the procession a more innocuous appearance than a company of the king's soldiers on horseback riding the roads. The large, sleek roans nickered and fidgeted, stomping, snorting, tossing their long black manes and flame-like silks.

"Open the gate!"

A gruff, stocky man with black and silver hair, dressed in dark trousers and leather armor, climbed down from the carriage, longsword unsheathed, and waved toward the mages stationed above the gate entrance. The heavy wooden and iron gate glowed indigo with magical protection.

The Rohesian blademaster. My bodyguard on the long journey to Rohesia.

Like a rope stretched too tight, I felt the tension intensify in the magic that permeated the castle and the realm. At the approach of sword wielders invading my world. Enemies. Monsters that had slaughtered my people for over a century. The truce had been uneasy at best and having these marauders inside the castle—my home—made my anger spark and my heart race.

Chains rattled. Wood creaked and moaned.

With a loud thump, the massive wooden gate that led into the inner sanctum of Ereth's royal castle, Skystead, began to lower. The castle stood high on a hill, its five towers touching the clouds. The village of Skystead nestled behind its protection. The ramparts shook as the gate groaned and lifted, allowing narrow passage across the dark, murky moat that circled the castle. A moat filled with dangerous water spirits and deadly magics that could drown an enemy fast.

Feeling nauseated, I gripped Lady Laurel's arm and turned away from the convoy.

But the flash of fire made me turn back again.

A hail of arrows burning with fire magic rained down from the surrounding forest that covered the castle's northeastern edge. Killing the man in leather armor, sword still in his hand, and everyone in the carriage. Including the horses.

2

Ereth's mage captain, a tall, toned, dark-haired woman with a gold glow at her fingertips appeared in front of me, projecting a gleaming barrier that spilled onto Mother, Lady Laurel, and me.

A squad of four mages in robes the color of night materialized around the three of us. Wrapping us in a smoky screen as the guard hustled us into the castle and down dim-lit stone stairs toward the protective might of Mother's elite sorceresses that protected queen and crown. And her heirs.

Directing us toward the safe room off the throne room.

I ran, shrouded in light and mist down the long, high-ceiling knave lined with dark windows near the ceiling and swaying royal purple pennants. Past pairs of braziers trailing smoke and the scent of burning lavender wax, our footsteps muffled by magic and the royal purple carpet runner that stretched toward the golden throne ahead that glimmered with ethereal gold light.

Orbs of gold and purple and teal orbited the throne where my mother, Queen Ambren halted.

Royal sorceresses and mages immediately surrounded her, Lady

Laurel, and me. Casting a smoke spell around us. I could barely see Mother's crown of amethyst and gold burning in the massive dim-lit room that swallowed the light like an approaching storm.

"Annarissa!" Mother shouted through the force of sorceresses and mages surrounding us. "Stay behind the guard!"

Chandeliers burned with a warm magical glow overhead, dripping with crystals that cast rivulets of light like confetti along the carpet runner and grey stone floor as I turned toward the foot of the throne.

The crystals began to vibrate like wind chimes as the throne room went completely dark and then burned with white light, braziers and chandeliers guttering back to life throughout the huge cathedral-like expanse.

"Your Majesty!" shouted Captain Nevayna Otirys in a commanding alto voice from the throne room doorway.

The captain of the guard surged down the carpet runner toward Mother.

The tall, leanly muscled brunette had some magical talent, Nevayna had been chosen by Mother as captain of the castle guard because of her battle prowess, not the strength of her magic. She wore the midnight blue robes of the guard, the magical symbols of Ereth a shade lighter than the fabric, gold braid at the shoulders. The purple and gold signet captain's pin, shaped like a spiral, gleamed on the fold of her robe's left lapel. The pin was inset with a rare sunburst gem that shifted from gold to amethyst. It had a deep glow within, indicating it held absorbed magic inside the gem.

Sunburst gems absorbed residual magic from casting, giving each stone a unique burst of colors. The gold and amethyst hue was the most coveted of its myriad shades because it held the strongest and most magic. Its absorbed magic gave battle mages and assault sorceresses a reserve of magic attuned to their elements. A simple reversal spell sent the magic back to the gem's owner, a practice every sorceress knew to perform regularly—especially after battles.

Mother insisted that her crown and the crowns of her daughters be adorned with gold and amethyst sunburst gems.

As an added protection.

"The threat has been neutralized, my queen," Nevayna announced from the doorway. "The castle is secure."

The captain of the guard traversed the room in two magical fades, appearing a foot in front of Mother, hands on her hips, the glow of magical symbols on her robes shifting as she spoke. Until she waved her hand and they went dark.

"Thank you, captain," said Mother, casting an additional magical ward in the throne room.

As the sorceress guard took a step back, Mother lifted her arms into the air and closed her eyes until a white glow engulfed her. Pulsing as it oscillated and finally dissipated into smoke.

"It was a Xanthan force," Mother said finally, opening her eyes. "That group calling itself the Kambrian Equalizers. I can see them crossing Ereth's northern border back into Xanthe, cheering at their victory. They've killed the Rohesian blademaster and his delegation."

"And all the delegation horses," said Lady Laurel with a moan.

Mother sighed, her oval face pale, sapphire blue eyes bright against her light brown hair draped and braided into an intricate weave beneath her oversized gold and amethyst crown. Her royal dress shimmered with iridescence, silky train stretched four feet behind her as she leaned against the throne. Her train floated just above the floor with a soft gold sheen of magic. She'd been ready to receive the Rohesian delegation. Until they were assassinated.

Apparently, not all of Xanthe to the north believed in Kambria's curse.

Nevayna's big brown eyes widened.

"Breck Laurant? The finest blademaster in all of Rohesia? He was hired to guard Annarissa." Her face began to flush, hands in motion as she paced. "And all of those roans—intrepids—dead? They were a special, hearty breed of Rohesian horse...bred for such long journeys.

This is a disaster. Much too dangerous for the princess. We should reconsider this entire marriage arrangement, my queen."

"What?" Mother cried, eyes wide, mouth agape. "Reconsider the marriage? Ignore the prophecy? Forget this tenuous truce after a hundred years of killing each other? Nevayna, we can barely feed ourselves in Ereth. And neither can Rohesia." Mother frowned. "We would condemn all of Kambria to death."

Nevayna motioned toward me.

"Delay it, my queen," said the captain of the guard, hands on her hips. "Until our seaports are operating again. Rohesia's port at Summerreach is nearly rebuilt and ready to berth ships again."

"That will take months, Nevayna. We cannot risk this truce crumbling," said Mother, folding her arms against her chest as she glared at Nevayna. "This war has destroyed so much of our infrastructure and the curse nearly everything else. We cannot delay this marriage, captain. We will not!"

The captain pulled in a breath and began to pace in front of Mother again.

"The princess is no longer safe, Your Majesty. And the truce forbids us from sending a magical force to Rohesia to protect her. Magic is illegal there."

I hated when they talked about me in the third person. Like I was a child. Or absent from the room.

"Even long enough to protect their future princess?" I asked.

"Unfortunately, yes, princess," said Captain Nevayna with a nod to me, halting in front of Mother. "They made special allowance for only you, princess—and your lady-in-waiting. No other mages or sorceresses may cross Rohesia's borders."

Mother stepped in a circle around the captain and me, heels clicking as she looked up at Nevayna who was about six feet tall. At five foot eight, I was a little taller than Mother, but Nevayna towered over both of us.

"Yes, it's true, I'm afraid," said Mother, glancing back at me, her sapphire blue eyes hardening, pushing away from her role as mother and back into the role of monarch.

Daughter came second to the realm.

I saw the shift gleaming in her eyes. This wedding had to take place or the people of Ereth would die along with Rohesia and the world of Kambria. There was no other choice.

I looked just like my mother. Same delicate facial features. Same oval face and same gently curving regal nose. But I had wider set eyes with the golden hazel of my father. His fuller lips and light blond hair. But unmistakably the firstborn daughter of Ambren Thorn. She could never deny she was my mother.

And assassins would recognize me instantly.

Magical intervention of any kind—to ward my carriage or hide my looks—would offend the Rohesian people at best or lead to an attack at worst. Rohesians despised magic. Besides the politics, a ward gleaming in Kambria's grey light would shine a beacon on the carriage. Without any protective magic, I had to gamble my life on sharp metal sticks that were only as good as the people wielding them.

"We must hire a new blademaster, Nevayna," said Mother, her gaze not leaving my face. "Immediately." She sighed. "And the horses are another matter."

Nevayna's long face scrunched with anger and shock.

"A new blademaster? Here? In Ereth?" Her tone was dark and acidic. "We gave up inferior weapons centuries ago! Where would we find such a master blade wielder, Your Majesty? And so quickly?"

"Time is of the essence," said Mother, continuing to pace around the captain of the guard and me as mages relit the throne room braziers and chandeliers with soft gold magic.

"It's impossible, Your Majesty!" Nevayna insisted.

"We *will* get this wedding convoy back on schedule," Mother demanded, fixing the captain of the guard with her unblinking gaze. "Daegal will suspect foul play and we will be back at war by morning.

And the curse will intensify." She glanced up at the windows. "With the sunlight almost gone, we can no longer feed ourselves, captain. Xanthe—in its proclaimed neutrality—will bleed us dry of coin and resources for food until they cut us off to save themselves."

"Your Majesty," said Lady Laurel with a deep courtesy, royal purple mage robes rustling. "Why not hold a contest?"

"That's absurd!" Captain Nevayna cried.

Looking intrigued, Mother turned to Lady Laurel, the hint of a smile at the corners of her mouth.

"A contest? Explain."

Lady Laurel cast a frown at Captain Nevayna. "With the truce in place, we've already got Xanthans and even Rohesians crowding into Skystead to see if the convoy will really leave Ereth. Why not take advantage of the crowds and find a new champion to guard Princess Annarissa among them? Grant him or her a royal boon in exchange for getting Annarissa safely to Mirstone Castle in Rohesia."

Nevayna glared at Lady Laurel and then turned back to Mother.

Mother always said that Nevayna was one of the best guard captains she had ever employed. Nevayna looked at every angle and considered every possibility. But the trepidation churning in the captain's brown eyes and magic sparking at her fingertips worried me.

"Even if it's the Butcher of Badriyah, Your Highness?" Nevayna asked, looking almost smug as she shot a glare back at Lady Laurel.

A chill shot down my back and I couldn't hold in my gasp.

An entire border village that touched all three realms slaughtered in the dead of night by a band of hired swords. Led by a Xanthan they called the Butcher. I'd heard all the stories.

Rumors said that Badriyah was a ghost town now, considered cursed with death and blood magic. It was southeast of the Xanthan seaport they called Snowmelt, a lawless haven on the western coast. At the foot of Kirval's Shards, a mountain range north of Snowmelt. The area that the Butcher of Badriyah called home.

A flicker of worry passed across Mother's eyes as that familiar, unaffected stare of duty returned.

"As long as the hired blade we select gets my daughter safely to Rohesia, I don't care if it's the Butcher of Badriyah or King Daegal himself, Nevayna."

Nevayna bowed her head, stepping back and I couldn't see her expression.

Mother turned toward Lady Laurel. "I like this idea, Lady Laurel. Work with Captain Nevayna to make it happen. In two hours. In the castle courtyard. That convoy must depart on time."

"What of the horses, Your Majesty?" Nevayna asked, her brown eyes intense. "It will take a herd to pull that massive carriage—and those wagons. Even then, the distance would kill them faster than flaming arrows."

No team of Erethian horses could pull that carriage. Without the Rohesian intrepids, they had no convoy.

Lady Laurel's gaze narrowed as she studied Nevayna a moment. The two of them rarely saw eye to eye.

"We'll conjure teams using air magic," said Lady Laurel. "And the Rohesians have no choice but to put up with it. Combining earth and air will give these elemental horses the stamina and endurance to reach Mirstone Castle."

"Magic!" Nevayna scoffed at Lady Laurel. "Are you trying to get the princess burned at the stake, Lady Laurel?"

Risky? Yes. Dangerous? Yes. Choice? None. Lady Laurel was right.

"It's the only option, Mother," I replied with a nod toward Lady Laurel.

Her gaze flattened as it turned toward me again. Like I was an afterthought. And I was.

"Elemental horses then," Mother ordered. "And Annarissa, you will attend the contest under the guard's highest level of protection. As extra incentive to the winner. I want the world to see that gown you wear. To see the priceless worth of the princess who wears it. And the magnitude of the gift we are giving Rohesia."

Spoken like a monarch not a mother, but I knew she did not have that luxury right now.

Mother turned to Nevayna, pointing a finger at the captain of the guard and the other mages that had gathered behind her.

"Captain, I want a quick, expert choice made and then I want that convoy in motion. Make sure the contest is well guarded. Mages, get all of the princess' things loaded and ready to travel. On schedule. And captain, get that monstrously sized carriage reinforced with Ereth's best non-magical protection for the long, dangerous journey to Mirstone Castle." She sighed, eyes turning watery. "I hate sending my daughter into such danger, but it is the only way to save Kambria."

She glanced back to me

"Forgive me, Annarissa. I do this because I have no other choice. Now, all of you, go. Protect my daughter."

With the poise of a cat, Mother turned away. And hurried past the throne toward the corner door leading into her inner chambers.

I was moved by the emotion she had displayed. It was the first time I had seen her show any motherly compassion for a long time.

But with her departure came the end of any discussion. The matter was closed. We all had our marching orders. And our duties —no matter how soul-breaking.

"Yes, your majesty," said Nevayna, sounding almost defeated.

Nevayna motioned Lady Laurel and me alongside her as the guard broke into two forces, one following Mother through the purple door in the far-right corner of the throne room into her inner chamber. The other half of the guard surrounded Lady Laurel and me.

"Lady Laurel, send an entourage of court mages out into the village," said Nevayna. "Get the town criers announcing this contest and its prize. I'll get the cart and wheel wrights working on the carriage."

Lady Laurel looked concerned. "Captain, will the Queen truly grant a royal boon to this sword champion for getting Annarissa safely to Rohesia?"

Glancing over her shoulder, Nevayna nodded at Lady Laurel.

"You heard Her Majesty. If she says that is the prize for beating all comers, then that is the prize. When has she ever not said exactly what she means?"

"Never," I replied. "My Mother knows her mind and her decisions are final."

"Time is short," said Captain Nevayna, her brown hair shifting around her shoulders as she led Lady Laurel and me into the hallway and turned right. "We all have our marching orders."

We entered the drafty main hallway, chilly despite the guttering lanterns lining the walls, scent of warm lavender lamp oil soothing.

The other half of the guard flooded around us like a wave of sea water, keeping Lady Laurel and me in the center as we passed each guttering lantern, flames dancing as we passed, warm lavender tinging the air.

"This contest must start in two hours and be over in three." said Captain Nevayna, gritting her teeth. "And the entire delegation must be on the road before midnight. The safety of the convoy—and your life, princess—will rest with the new blademaster and their hired swords."

Midnight. Hired swords. A new blademaster. Getting a skilled one would be impossible on such short notice. At this hour.

Some dark-natured, unscrupulous sword wielder would become my champion and bodyguard all the way to Rohesia. And hand me off to some barbarian's son that also wielded a blade. Or maybe a club?

Or worse. I'd wind up with the Butcher of Badriyah as my bodyguard—a terrifying thought.

Maybe I would get lucky and take an arrow to the heart before ever reaching Rohesia?

3

Even from the castle courtyard, I heard the town criers' anxious shouts filling Skystead's streets, along with the court mages' royal call to arms regarding the sword contest. Both criers and mages emphasized the prize of a royal boon granted upon proof of the safe delivery of Ereth's heir apparent to Rohesia. To be wed to Prince Arence Siridean.

Captain Nevayna and the other mages had helped the stable hands and groundskeepers stack bales of hay and mark the boundaries of the contest in the courtyard. Behind the small, squat stone building that was part armory and part storage. Where the guard held meetings and training. It was just past the main gate beside the moat and faced the shielded courtyard, so it was the perfect place to screen contestants.

After the courtyard had been prepared, braziers set up all around it, the fragrant lavender oil masking the putrid scent of horse dung from the nearby stables. Royal purple Erethian banners on tall poles encircled the grounds, flapping in the wind like birds taking flight. Hay bales, stacked three high, defined the contest space and its boundaries. And kept the contestants in view of the guard towers—in case there was trouble.

Nevayna and the guard led Lady Laurel and me into the long, narrow storage building, mostly empty now. It smelled like old leather and dried hay. We walked past shelving filled with small wooden crates on both long walls to the back where stable hands had placed a wooden throne on a riser that lifted it two feet above the stone floor. Mother's orders. A regular chair stood to the right for Lady Laurel.

Ten feet in front of the throne stood a wooden table with a lantern at each end. A palace scribe with short sandy hair sat in a wooden chair behind the table. His dark green robes rustled as he laid out a few sheets of tan paper on a brown leather blotter and arranged an ink well and some quill pens around the loose pages. To record contestants' names.

Captain Nevayna led me through the cavernous space, past the table, and to the throne where I stepped up and sat down, adjusting my dress and robes. Lady Laurel helped me arrange my dress and train before she sat down in the chair beside me. Four castle guard mages in midnight robes gathered around me, magical symbols shifting from purple to gold.

In silence, we waited for the castle bell to ring and the gate to open. Bringing contestants into the warded castle courtyard. Where archers and mages kept watch on the ramparts above, on high alert after the blademaster, the horses, and some members of his delegation were killed.

With the approaching sunset, it would be pitch dark soon.

Bad things happened in the dark. I hoped the truce would change that.

"Lady Laurel?" I called from my throne, feeling self-conscious.

Lady Laurel rose and stood at my right elbow. "Yes, princess?"

"The guards aren't letting just anyone with a sword inside, are they?"

Had we reached that dire point of trying to fulfill the tenets of this prophecy? Letting anyone with a sword that professed interest in the contest inside? They could be the same assassins that killed the blademaster. Butchers and cutthroats. Was this how the people of Badriyah got murdered?

Would killing one of us (me or my sisters) end any chance of fulfilling the prophecy? Or delay it to a point of no return?

Lady Laurel shook her head. "No, princess. Court mages are screening them with magic and—"

A wave of blue magic encircled us, creating a protective enclosure around Lady Laurel and me.

Laurel smiled. "And the guard is protecting you and your family with the most powerful warding spells in Ereth."

The door into the building opened and I tensed as Lady Laurel turned.

Contestants already. Looking scruffy and unkempt.

Granted, they'd had little notice, but the sight of them made me uneasy. My life would be in one of their hands. Over a dozen in the first group. Dusty boots and coarsely-woven fabrics like sack cloth in dull tans and browns and blues. Some were dirty from the fields, trying to coax any meager harvest from the dusty soil and dying plants. Without enough sunlight, nothing would grow in this gathering, misty twilight.

But these men didn't look like farmers or merchants. They looked like opportunists with questionable morals. They wore leather harnesses that sheathed swords at their backs, at their sides, and some had knives and axes in their belts. The sour scent of sweat and stale beer hung in the air. I was so uncomfortable at their presence. None of them looked like heroes. They looked like thieves and criminals. But I had no choice. And I had to keep an open mind, only judging them by their actions. One of them had to be my champion —my bodyguard—and get me safely to Rohesia or we were all dead.

Captain Nevayna stood beside the scribe as men and women lined up in front of the table and gave their names and realm to the nervous scribe at the table. The scribe sat stiff, his body taut and ready to spring into a defensive stance. I saw how little he trusted these people. The group made him as uneasy as it made me. Most of them weren't Erethian.

They were only here for Mother's boon. Nothing more.

I understood that. If I were them, I would have tried to get that boon, too. But without the skills to back it up, they would get everyone in the convoy killed. Including me.

The door slammed open.

A tall, lean man dressed in tight black leather armor that looked like thieves gear stepped inside. He paused, squinting, scanning the room.

Glaring.

Even from the back of the room, he had a forbidding presence. Commanding. And those ice blue eyes were both alluring and terrifying. His thick black hair hung long and wavy past his shoulders. He was younger than the other men. Early to mid-twenties maybe?

The gold hilt of a broadsword gleamed between his shoulder blades as he swaggered into the room, eyes narrowing like he was sizing up the competition. His walk was quiet but arrogant. Challenging. Intimidating.

He took in the room, staring down every part of it. Every person. Until his gaze shot past the scribe and pierced my soul.

It was emotionless. Cold. Dark.

It made me want to pull away as quiet descended on the room. The other contestants turned toward the man, freezing in place. Staring at him with apprehension. Some even looked afraid.

"That's the Butcher of Badriyah," someone whispered.

My blood turned ice cold as he continued to stare at me. Watch me. Record my every move with those ice-blue eyes that bore deep. Right through my heart. Through my soul. And into my head. Like he could hear my every thought. Feel every emotion. Touch every memory and every dream I had ever had.

And crush them all.

I was terrified.

No. This wasn't happening. It couldn't be happening.

With swift strides, he moved past the other contestants to the table.

But in the blink of an eye, he was past the scribe and Captain Nevayna. Inches from my face. Standing on the top rise of my throne. Only the ward's pale blue light stood between us.

He was at least six-foot-two, leanly muscled, strong chin, handsome face, and sculpted nose. Cheeks were taut, jaw line sharp, those ice blue eyes fixed on me, looking through my soul. He smelled of musk and leather, thick black hair framing his oval face, tied in a knot at his crown. His full lips pursed.

He was beautiful. But so very deadly.

Nevayna and the mages were on him in an instant.

His features shifted into a scowl, that ice blue gaze never leaving my face.

"You're already too late," he said, a growl in his voice like worn silk, stroking my skin with every syllable he spoke.

Setting my body alight with fear and intrigue.

"What are you talking about?" Captain Nevayna demanded as she grabbed his right arm.

Two other mages took hold of his left arm.

He stood there unmoving. Unaffected. Not like he was trapped or caged. Like he allowed them to think they had him under control. Restrained. But the slight twitch at the corner of his mouth told me otherwise. He would be out of their grasp—all of them—in a heartbeat. And magic or sword, they couldn't contain this man. This blademaster.

I swallowed a breath.

This Butcher of Badriyah.

My skin crawled, but I couldn't look away from him.

"In the moment it took you and your guard to react...to follow me...I'd have spilled your spoiled little princess's blood all over the cobbles. You were too late to stop it."

Nevayna flashed a gloating smile at the man.

"The magic would have slowed you down."

He cast another scowl at Nevayna. "Wrong again, captain."

His left gloved hand was lightning fast. Grasping hold of the ward.

Shattering it like glass.

In an instant, that sword was out of its sheath and at my throat. And he was right there. Against my body. Holding me like a sack of grain.

The force and the heat that radiated from him wrapped around my head. My skin. Like wool. And I couldn't move. A part of me didn't want to move. To shift my body and break the spell. The contact. The raw, dark connection flowing between us. I meant nothing to this man, but the power and darkness rolled over me in waves—along with attraction—and I couldn't let go. Couldn't react. Couldn't break it.

The entire guard froze, but Captain Nevayna's hand was at his back.

"With one word, I can pierce your heart with a magical burst that will explode it."

With his gaze still fixed on me, the corners of his mouth lifted in the flash of a smug smile.

"Regardless, captain," he said in that silky, deep commanding voice that was stout-beer-dark and bard-smooth, a rasp whispering at the rough edges. "You could never stop the twitch of my hand, laying open her throat right here. Not enough magic to stop her from bleeding out either."

The blade was burning sharp against my throat. My skin. It *was* sharp enough to lay open my throat, like cutting through butter. He was right. The finest mages and sorceresses in Kambria were unable to stop one man from killing a princess. Breaking a prophecy. Destroying the world. All to prove a selfish, arrogant point.

That he was faster, smarter, and better.

The Butcher of Badriyah.

In what seemed like a lifetime, the terrifying man stepped away from me, sheathing his sword. Molding my attraction, my fear into loathing.

Lady Laurel gasped and thrust a handkerchief to my neck.

"Princess, you're bleeding!"

All I could do was stare into his eyes. Searching for some humanity. Some light. Something that made him more than a monster. A butcher.

But I found nothing.

I struggled to lift my hand to my neck, still watching him as the guards relit the ward around Lady Laurel and me.

"I could execute you for harming the princess!" Captain Nevayna said as she and the guard dragged the man backward.

Back behind the table.

But the distance didn't change the strange feel of him. The reality of how vulnerable I was. The presence that filled the room. No, it took over the room.

"Watch him!" Nevayna ordered two mages from the castle guard as she motioned to the scribe who hurried toward her, papers in hand.

Nevayna rushed to the door with the scribe and followed him and two other mages outside to the gate.

The moment the door closed, the man in black leathers had both mages on the ground unconscious.

Drawing his sword, he rushed the other contestants. And drove the point of his sword home, gutting the nearest man to him.

I was horrified. He was killing them without a thought! They were just obstacles to him. Nothing more.

"Stop!" I cried.

With new wards around me, I couldn't cast through them.

I tried to move through the wards, but Lady Laurel held me in place.

Pivoting, the man's blade sliced into a stocky sable-haired man on his right. Sending blood spatter across the floors and onto the stone walls as he freed the blade. And took down the man to his left next.

The remaining contestants rushed him.

Looking unfazed, the man in black leathers lunged at the remaining nine contestants. He was lightning fast. Precise. Deadly.

One by one, they fell like weeds to a scythe.

"Guards! Stop him!" Lady Laurel cried, gathering another ward spell around her and me. "He's killing the other contestants!"

The guards surrounding me were conflicted, but they stayed at their post. At my side while the man fought the other contestants.

Lady Laurel cast another spell, surrounding the blue light with a second ward, the white light glowing.

I could only gape. I should have tried again to cast through the protection wards, but I couldn't look away.

He was the Butcher of Badriyah. Now butchering his competition. And all I could do was stare in horror.

When Captain Nevayna returned to the building, in what seemed like barely a minute later, all twelve of the contestants lay dead on the stone floor. Scattered like bloody autumn leaves around the boots of the man in black leathers.

"By Ereth..."

Nevayna was speechless, staring in disbelief at the bodies. And the blood.

She rushed toward her blood-spattered mages, finding them unconscious.

The man leaned against the wall, hilt of his gold broadsword still clutched in his hand, blade dripping blood onto the floor.

"You...you—butchered them!" Captain Nevayna cried.

The man didn't even look at her.

"Contest rules said to defeat all challengers." He glanced at the bodies and then over at Nevayna. "Defeated. What's next?"

The scribe returned to the building, looking horrified, but he began to shake when he saw all the bodies. Behind him, more of

Nevayna's guard flooded into the room. Rushing the man in black leathers.

"That's him!" shouted the castle scribe. "Oz Tarrant. The Butcher of Badriyah."

Captain Nevayna sighed. "Hope you got more than hearsay to back that up, Jaren?"

The scribe's face darkened. He sighed, the expression on his face falling as he bowed his head.

"No. Just a lot of coincidences I can't prove. And stories about people that claim they saw him in Badriyah that day. But none of them will come forward."

The man called Oz Tarrant looked unaffected. He knew they couldn't do anything. Badriyah was a border town that straddled all three realms. One more dispute in the Hundred Year Sundering. Three years had passed since the night that someone murdered an entire town. And disappeared. Anyone that knew the people of that small village were probably dead now. Like anyone that had witnessed the carnage.

And all the rumors and whispers pointed at this man. Oz Tarrant.

Who had just murdered every competitor in the room. In this contest.

Tarrant leaned against the wall and sheathed his sword, a smug expression on his face. Those ice blue eyes piercing.

"Then unless you have any more competitors, that royal boon— and this job—are mine."

He nodded menacingly at Captain Nevayna.

"According to the contest rules," he added.

Captain Nevayna glanced over at me, looking conflicted.

"No, Mr. Tarrant," she said, matching his dangerous tone. "No more competitors. After they saw you, they fled. And the rules state that in order to receive Her Majesty's boon, Princess Annarissa has to arrive safely at Mirstone Castle to marry a Siridean prince."

"When do we leave for Rohesia?" he asked as his gaze drifted to me.

I looked away.

"As soon as you gear up and get aboard that ironwood carriage with the princess. She is not to leave your sight, Mr. Tarrant for the entire journey. Is that clear? We will go over our very specific rules for the job again in great detail—so there are no questions. I need your verbal commitment to the job. And its rules."

Mother had ordered the carriage reinforced with more ironwood. One of the most trusted cart wrights in Ereth was completing that work as ordered by Mother.

"I am taking the job," said Tarrant in a gruff voice as he stepped over a body, stopping in front of Nevayna. "And I agree to the rules—whatever they are."

"Fine," said Captain Nevayna, escorting this dangerous man outside. "Her Majesty the queen would like an audience to discuss the rules. In great detail."

Lady Laurel and I followed at a distance behind Captain Nevayna as she led Tarrant outside the building. Into the darkness.

Oz Tarrant turned his gaze toward me one last time. Haunting. Chilling. Attractive.

He scared me to death.

I recoiled, stepping behind a wooden barrel at the corner of the building. Lady Laurel stepped protectively in front of me, keeping this dangerous man at a distance. And I was grateful.

He looked me up and down, like he was buying a horse, and followed Captain Nevayna and the unit of four mages away from the building. Toward the steps to the castle entrance.

I didn't look away until he and the guard disappeared inside. When he was gone, my gaze fell to the old wooden barrel. Inside, faces looked up at me.

Gasping, I jerked away from the barrel but then turned back to it. Staring into its depths. At ghostly white faces.

Breath caught in my throat as I reached inside. Touching cold ivory-like surfaces. Porcelain. I exhaled sharply.

They weren't bodies. They were masks.

Stacked in a barrel near the castle gate? Why were there so many?

Were they decorations? For one of Mother's galas that I would never attend. It made me sad and afraid at the same time.

Terror chilled my body and I shuddered at the realization.

I was really leaving the only home I had ever known. To live in a kingdom I had never seen before. Filled with strangers who hated magic and sorceresses. And Oz Tarrant, the Butcher of Badriyah, was the blademaster—the bodyguard escorting me to my fate.

Unless he killed me. And the whole convoy along the way. Like his competitors. Like the village of Badriyah.

4

A SLIVER OF MOON ROSE HIGH IN THE VELVET BLACK NIGHT, STARS FILLING the sky as I left the castle at Skystead for the very last time.

It was time to leave.

I would never see the moon or the stars from these castle windows ever again. Never laugh and sing with all my sisters together again. Or play hide and seek with them among the castle's many hidden passages and secret rooms.

My childhood was over. My dreams had been crushed. I would never marry for love. I would never become Queen of Ereth. That honor would now pass to Aunt Johava's daughter, Idella because the prophecy would truncate Mother's line with four forced marriages.

I didn't want to hold my head high and endure like Lady Laurel. I wanted to cry. To rage. Hop on a horse and flee. My life and its control were lost to me. It was now in the hands of Prince Arence and the Rohesians.

And the Butcher of Badriyah.

Holding back tears, lantern in hand, I watched from the gate as servants I would never see again loaded my three trunks and one valise on top of the carriage. I had changed out of my court gown into riding clothes (there were no Rohesians to impress with the betrothal gown now) and carried a small personal valise. A simple white blouse and long purple A-line skirt. Short black boots over long white stockings. And a lavender silk-lined black cloak. I put my long blond hair up in a braid wrapped across my head. Doing my best to look like a traveler instead of a princess.

Lady Laurel wore a simple green dress over an ivory chemise and short black boots over long black stockings. She wore her mage robes, the color of midnight, over the dress. Hoping to make anyone who dared to open those carriage doors think twice about tangling with a high court Erethian mage.

I kept my personal valise beside me. With the few sentimental items left of my life. Small oval paintings of my sisters and parents. My princess crown. Jewelry that Mother had given me. Letters. And some other small items. Including a locket my father gave me two months before he died on a battlefield near Mirstone Castle.

One of the most talented fire mages in all of Ereth. Felled by a single sword thrust.

I was eight.

A year later, my grandmother, Queen Maelena Thorn died at Ashbourne near Xanthe alongside King Onyx Siridean. Triggering the first truce in a hundred years. And a prophecy that would steal the lives and dreams of my three sisters and me. The price of being born into privilege, I knew. But it didn't make this bitter pill any easier to swallow.

In a whisper of gold light, Lady Laurel was beside me, leading me down the rampart stairs. And through the opened gate. Where I got a short glimpse of the convoy. Three wagons. One massive carriage. Two dozen newly hired swords. Six wispy gold elemental horses now pulled the ironwood carriage, looking like apparitions in the night. Along with three teams of two elemental horses that pulled each of the three wagons.

"I gathered some air and earth mages and we conjured the horses, my lady," said Lady Laurel.

I was grateful. I had no desire to concentrate on casting magic right now—especially to summon elemental horses that would carry me far from Ereth.

I nodded, my eyes stinging with tears.

Lady Laurel gently took the lantern from my hands and handed it to a nearby mage. Taking a deep breath, she and I cast one last look at the castle. She turned back toward the ironwood carriage and threw a grey blanket over my head.

Together, we ran, Lady Laurel leading me to the carriage. Up two steps and through the open doors. Into the luxurious Rohesian carriage. On both sides, gold and glass teardrop-shaped lanterns, flames turned low, perched on the polished dark taupe wood walls padded in plush, dark red fabric. Heavy, pleated damask in a soft red covered the ceiling, fastened in the center by a gold disk engraved with the Siridean royal crest.

In the corner of the ceiling, beneath the driver's perch, was the funnel of a curved gold hailing-horn that allowed the driver to converse with passengers. The carriage floor was carpeted dark red and two long, well-padded plush red seats filled each side of the carriage. Large enough to seat three people on each one. Four ironwood hand rails, wrapped in plush red fabric, had been carved into the walls on each side of the seats.

The lanterns' fragrant oil was soft and savory, reminding me of herbs from Ereth's royal kitchens. Rohesian oil had such a pleasant scent and I liked that it brought back memories of home.

I glanced out the window at the castle while Laurel folded the blanket and laid it in her lap.

Mother stood on the rampart. Stoic. Hands behind her back. Crown glistening. Dress sparkling. Observing in silence. Like the statues in the grand hallway.

The moment Lady Laurel sat down beside me, wooden shields

slid across the carriage windows on both sides. Blocking my last view of the only home I'd ever known. She slid closer to the wall, leaving space between us. And silence.

Regrets? Too late now.

The carriage door creaked open, the elemental horses tossing their manes as hired blademaster Oz Tarrant stepped into the carriage.

I stiffened.

He sat down across from me on the other cushioned red seat, legs splayed as he slouched against the wall, looking pleased with himself as he stared at me. Looking down his nose at me. Like I was no more than an expensive vase he was delivering to Rohesia.

He'd referred to me as a spoiled princess before. And he'd cut the skin on my neck with his broadsword to prove a point to the guard captain. Before he'd killed all the contestants in the room while Captain Nevayna was outside.

I loathed and feared this man. My new bodyguard.

All I wanted to do was get away from him. He looked like he'd just rolled out of a common-house after bedding a faded rose or two. And drank his fill of ale. Distracted. Unshaven. Over-sexed. And hungover.

I shuddered. The Butcher of Badriyah.

I wasn't a person to this man. I was a delivery. A boon to be granted once he handed me off to the barbarians in Rohesia.

I glared at him but he was unfazed. Like he didn't even see me. Or care if I felt anything. The fact that I reviled him almost entertained him. This butcher.

Still staring at me, he thumped the carriage ceiling with his gloved fist three times.

"Mathias!" he shouted into the hailing-horn. "On your way. While we have the cover of an almost dark moon. Alert me to any riders."

I held my breath as the carriage lurched forward. The cushions were thick and absorbed some of the thumps and bumps from the carriage wheels as the driver coaxed the six elemental horses into a slow walk down the hillside. To the level road below. That cut east and west across Kambria. Followed by three elemental horse-drawn wagons.

Tarrant's eyes narrowed and he fixed me with his gaze.

"Now, listen carefully, princess." He said *princess* like I was his biggest annoyance. "You now answer to me, like everyone else on this expedition east. We travel by night and shelter by day until we reach the main roads. We keep to the busiest routes. We stop only when we have to. We eat and sleep when I say. Is that clear?"

I glared at him, saying nothing.

He lunged forward and grabbed my arm. Squeezing until it hurt.

"Is that clear?"

I gritted my teeth against the pain and called up a burst of earth magic.

The shock broke his hold. Only for a moment. It seemed to make him angrier and he grabbed my arm again, holding it tighter.

The carriage began to pick up speed, the elemental horses in a slow trot now. Unusual considering the long journey ahead.

Steady thump of horse hooves joined the creak and rattle of the carriage. Several. Coming up swiftly from behind us.

A chill rushed along my spine. Assassins! Following on horseback.

"If you think you can out-magic my blade, think again, little princess."

The pain was almost unbearable.

"It's Thorn, Mr. Tarrant," I said with slow, painful breaths. "Princess Annarissa Thorn. I am not an object or a child or a scared little princess. I am a woman. An assault sorceress. And your client. Understand that and we'll get through this horrible journey. Is *that* clear?"

"Oz!" Mathias' muffled voice echoed through the horn into the carriage. "Riders coming. A lot of them!"

Tarrant's eyes narrowed, his gaze flicking to the ceiling and then back at me.

The carriage teetered right around a curve, elemental horses breaking into a canter now. Moving faster as the carriage skittered east.

The pain began to dissipate, his grip on my arm loosening.

"Time will tell all, won't it?" he said, his gaze unblinking. "Princess."

"Yes, it will," I said, refusing to rub my arm and show him that he'd hurt me. "Mr. Tarrant."

For only a moment, one corner of his mouth quirked almost into a smile and then vanished.

As the point of a flaming arrow slammed into the wooden screen across the windows to my left.

Thunk, thunk, thunk!

Three more arrows hit, two on the left, one on the right.

"It's an ambush, Oz!" Mathias' voice drifted through the carriage above the din of the wheels against the dirt road.

"Get down!" Tarrant shouted.

He extinguished both lanterns and stretched his arm over me as Lady Laurel slid to the carriage floor.

The carriage thumped and lurched like it was out of control.

In the darkness, elemental horse hooves pounded the ground harder, faster, punctuated by the driver's shouts and snaps of a whip above us.

From both sides of the carriage, the sound of magical equine hooves thumped the ground. The driver was pushing the elemental horses. They could keep that pace much longer than living horses, but magical beings had tempers. If the driver pushed too hard for too long, the elemental horses might get angry and leave them stranded until they could conjure more elemental horses.

"Whatever you do, Mathias—keep moving!" Tarrant shouted.

"Will do, boss!" Mathias shouted from the driver's perch outside. "They can't kill these horses!"

Thunk! Another burning arrow.

With his leather sleeve, Tarrant beat the flames until they sputtered out on the left window block and began to smolder. The right-hand window shield had turned black, fire still tearing across the rough wood covering the windows.

I reached up and flung a burst of earth magic at the fire. Smothering it until it went out. The charred wood cast thick coils of smoke throughout the carriage. Making Lady Laurel cough until she cast a burst of air magic and neutralized the smoke.

"You go tossin' around magic in Rohesia like that, they'll be burning you, two at the stake for witchcraft," Tarrant said with a growl.

The carriage made an abrupt turn left. Rocked forward. And back again.

"Did you know that in Ereth," I said, "sword wielders are considered criminals until proven otherwise. So strange."

He scoffed. "Like I didn't already know that."

I frowned. "You killed a roomful of contestants, Mr. Tarrant! Twelve sword wielders trying to win that boon just like you. What did you expect?"

"Then change your contest rules," he snapped.

"What about Badriyah, Mr. Tarrant?" I demanded. "That entire village was put to the sword. Not fried by mages. Killed at sword point, their bodies left to rot in the streets."

I left the *by you* unsaid.

Something big slammed against the carriage doors, receding sound of a horse nickering and grunting.

Door handles rattled.

Someone had climbed onto the carriage, trying to get inside it now!

"Mathias!" Tarrant shouted, turning toward the doors. "Mathias, one knock if you're okay up there!"

Door handles kept rattling but finally, a timid knock echoed from the ceiling.

Grabbing hold of the handle on the right-side door, Tarrant jerked it open, cocked his fist, and slammed it into a man's masked face. The terrifying ghostly white mask of a contorted face.

The hideous white ceramic mask broke into pieces as the man fell backward, face bloodied, onto the road. His horse had already fled toward the woods.

The man screamed. Trampled as the carriage wheels rolled over him.

Tarrant glanced behind the carriage, frowning, and slammed the door closed. He slid a metal lock bar through the handles.

"Definitely Xanthans," Tarrant muttered, his gaze locked on those doors, hand on the hilt of the long knife in his boot. "A couple dozen on horseback. Question is...who hired them?"

I held onto the hand rail with both hands as the carriage rocked forward and then shuddered, wheels screeching. Lady Laurel stood up, teetering until she managed to climb back into the seat beside me.

"How can you tell?" I asked Tarrant.

"Kambrian Equalizers all wear those white masks when they go on attacks and raids," said Tarrant. "To think that gang started as a peaceful Xanthan artisan pottery guild in Fallsmere."

The Xanthan capital.

"They sure went dark in a hurry," Tarrant continued. "Just like Kambria did. Somewhere between Fallsmere and Snowmelt, they became a deadly gang of assassins and mercs."

"Like you?" I asked.

He shrugged.

"Snowmelt...that's a seaport, isn't it? Magic and sword neutral?"

Tarrant nodded as the carriage lurched again and rumbled down the road. Picking up even more speed. Trying to outrun assassins whose horses would tire long before our elemental horses.

"It's a coastal town where mages and hired swords know how to play nice together." He cast a judgmental, withering glare at me. "If only the major powers like Ereth and Rohesia had learned that, what —a century ago?"

His self-righteous glare indicted me as the sole cause of all the violence ever perpetrated in Kambria by the realm of Ereth. Judging me because I was a princess. A sorceress. A man they called the Butcher of Badriyah judging me. I thought he was Rohesian, but now, I wasn't sure.

"Is Butcher a middle name, Mr. Tarrant?" I asked. "Or a nickname your friends gave you? At Badriyah."

Lady Laurel snorted and covered her mouth.

Tarrant glared at me.

"And do you carry the burden of all of the sword violence in Kambria's history on your shoulders?"

Probably true in his case.

I leaned toward him and lowered my voice to a whisper.

"I'm sure all those people—and villages—calling you a butcher can't be true."

His eyes narrowed and he glowered. Looking down that finely sculpted nose at me.

But the carriage door rocked open about three inches or so. Rattling.

A dark-haired man and a ruddy-haired woman, both wearing white ceramic masks with twisted faces, held onto the side of the carriage, trying to pull open the doors and climb inside.

Stopped by the metal lock bar. Until a sword blade slid it free and it fell to the floor.

They had grabbed hold of the carriage on horseback and climbed aboard it like the first attacker.

Tarrant kicked the man off the carriage and he collided with his fleeing horse. The horse shook him off and trotted toward the trees as the man hit the dusty road hard.

The woman thrust a blade at Tarrant's ribs.

Tarrant feinted left, cocked his fist, and struck the woman in the face.

There wasn't room to draw his broadsword inside the carriage. But he drew the long knife from his right boot.

The woman's awful mask shattered as he kicked her off the carriage into the dust of her fleeing horse.

The wheels thumped twice, rolling over something as the carriage tipped to right.

Whipping right then left, the carriage dove-tailed until the elemental horses eased it out of its oscillations. Straightened its path. Back onto the bumpy dirt road.

Tarrant's hand was against his right side. He smashed his eyes closed a moment, grinding his teeth together.

"Are you all right?" I asked.

He was clearly in pain.

That woman had managed to get a sword thrust past Tarrant's lightning-fast reflexes. With enough force to clear leather and find skin.

Wonderful. We were less than an hour out from Ereth and the man hired to protect me had already been stabbed.

"I'm fine," he said with a growl as he picked up the metal bar. "Bitch just got me with the sword point."

"Let me heal that for you," said Lady Laurel, leaning toward him.

"No!" he shouted, way more forcefully than needed.

Lady Laurel recoiled.

"My apologies," she said with a gasp. "I meant no harm."

"No need for any magic," said Tarrant with a snarl. "It's little more than a scratch."

He despised magic—and apparently anyone casting it. That was clear. But he almost seemed...afraid of it. Why? Had he had run-ins with Erethian sorceresses before? Or some sort of wild magic in Xanthe?

I sighed. Or both?

He replaced the metal bar through the door handles and glared up at the carriage's ceiling, thumping it hard twice.

"Mathias! One knock if everything's good up there."

In a moment or two, one hard thump reverberated against the ceiling as the carriage began to slow down.

"They've retreated," said Mathias through the hailing-horn. "Smart ones didn't push their horses. Dumb ones are trampled and dead on the road.

The elemental steeds slowed to a trot and finally a walk along the road. Even though they were magical with incredible endurance and stamina, they had limits, too. They couldn't run or even canter all the way to Rohesia. Each evening, Lady Laurel and I would have to conjure new elementals out of the ether, letting the others return to their world and recharge.

"Good," Tarrant said with a growl. "Maybe they'll think twice about coming after us again."

"This time," I said with a sigh.

***

THE CARRIAGE PLODDED along for hours under the cover of night, in silence, lanterns snuffed out as Tarrant kept a keen eye—and ear— on the doors. Lady Laurel slept, her face pressed against the opposite wall, legs curled beneath her, her body hugging the wall. Her robes rustled with every bump and turn of the carriage. But the carriage seat was wide enough that both Lady Laurel and I could sit with our legs curled beneath us and still have space between.

Tarrant stretched out in the seat across from me, facing the doors, boots against the wall, broadsword in his lap, fingers clutching that gold hilt. In the faint silvery glow of the crescent moon (Mathias had opened the window shields), Tarrant's thick black hair glimmered, framing his handsome face. Those big, angry ice blue eyes were magic-bright, his lips so full. The gentle slope of his nose gave his face an almost regal silhouette.

This man didn't brawl. He had no scars. He wasn't a common ruffian or criminal. Did he come from privilege? Was that why he seemed to hate royals, magic, and palaces?

Especially princesses?

With my personal valise still beside me, I held in a chuckle as I imagined him in Rohesia's royal red robes and a gold crown of diamonds and rubies nestled against that shiny black hair that hung past his shoulders, the front pulled back and knotted at his crown. Gave his ice blue eyes intensity. Made so much more appealing in the sliver of moonlight.

But every time I felt attracted to his features, the memory of him slaying his competitors at the castle hit me—along with the stories that the servants and mages had whispered. About the Butcher of Badriyah.

Every time, the fear and apprehension pushed me away from admiring his looks.

This man sizzled like a castle hearth fire, his looks refined and almost regal beneath the long hair and unshaven stubble. And those angry, ice blue eyes were hazardous. They could melt away any resolve in favor of poor choices and a night or two in his bed.

But that nickname was sobering. Terrifying.

Especially after I saw him slay contestants. Right in front of me. In the blink of an eye. They had been nothing more than obstacles keeping him from earning that royal boon.

A shiver rushed down my spine as I watched him settle back against the cushioned seat. Apparently, nothing got in Oz Tarrant's way when he wanted something.

For a moment, I wanted him to want me.

I'd never been with a man before. My fate had been decided since I was nine years old, my choice made for me. No matter what I wanted. I had only seen a faded portrait of Prince Arence. Like a weathered painting on the walls of some long-buried temple, his features were vague and blurred. He could have been fifteen or fifty.

Was there any compassion in Prince Arence's eyes? Or the hope of someday loving me? Or would my husband tolerate me at best.

But watching this tall, dark—and dangerous—mercenary in his

tight black leathers, I wanted to touch his long, wild hair. Stare into those fierce ice blue eyes and search for a spark of passion.

Legends said that if an Erethian sorceress kissed her true mate, their love would cast gold sparks dancing around their heads like dreamflies. A sign that their fates were intertwined. That they were fated to marry.

Another bump in the road rocked the carriage back and forth as the elemental steeds lumbered through the cold, dark night. Bringing me back to my senses.

Oz Tarrant was on the wrong side of that beautiful legend. He wasn't Rohesian—that much I knew. Duty demanded that I marry a Rohesian. A Siridean prince. Regardless, with Prince Arence, there would be no love. He was quite outspoken about his disdain of magic and Ereth. He hated both because they had killed his grandfather.

Like Rohesians killed my grandmother.

No, I might survive as his wife, but he would never love me. He would tolerate me at best. He was still a barbarian regardless of his quiet reflectiveness and he relished his time on the battlefields, according to Mother. Calm to a point of apathy. Cold. Calculating.

Nothing like Oz Tarrant who was fiery. Passionate. Controlling. All the emotions that might make bedding him explosive and not mere duty.

But Prince Arence would never love a princess from his enemies. Or a sorceress. Much less a princess sorceress. That was clear from his attitude toward me—and my realm—in his letters to Mother.

Both sides of that coin made me sad. Empty. And hopeless at the thought of the loveless marriage that awaited me in Rohesia. At eighteen.

As the rocking carriage and droning of the wheels lulled me to sleep, I carried those thoughts into my dreams.

"Princess!"

The insistent, anxious half-whisper penetrated the dark haze of a nightmare as I ran through a pitch black Rohesian forest, skeletal trees clawing at me, dry leaves clattering in the wind, assassins clutching knives and swords behind every tree.

"No," I moaned. "The knives. The knives are everywhere!"

Hands shook me hard.

"Princess!"

I opened my eyes.

He was standing over me, his face taut but emotionless. But the moment I gazed into his ice blue eyes, I began to drown.

"What's wrong?" I asked in a raspy whisper.

"Listen carefully," he said.

I glanced to my right. Lady Laurel lay slumped on the floor of the carriage, head against the cushion.

"By Ereth," I said in a breathless gasp. "Lady Laurel."

His hot fingers went to my mouth. Pressing.

"Ssssh," he hissed. "Nod that you understand."

Staring into his eyes, I couldn't breathe for a moment. But I understood. Something bad had happened while I slept.

I nodded slowly.

But the heat from his fingers sizzled across my skin. My mouth. My lips. And I wanted to lose myself in his heat, in the icy depths of his penetrating gaze.

"Carriage wheel broke," he whispered in a sharp voice. "More Xanthan mercs have found us."

Something snicked past the window shields. Again. And again.

Arrows.

I nodded, my stomach twisting into a knot, my heart pounding. But Tarrant was so calm. So unaffected but determined—and dark. He knew what had to be done. It would be gristly work. But it didn't affect him.

Snick...thump!

An arrow slammed into the shield. Another. Another!

"We're pinned down, princess—even the wagons," he said in a silky but gruff voice. "If we don't act, they'll pick all of us by first light."

I frowned. Knowing what he was planning. I felt it. He was going out there alone with a hail of arrows pouring down on them. Alone. To try and take down mercenaries in the dark. Mercenaries that had stopped and surrounded the convoy.

Archers and assassins had trapped the hired swords in the wagons. They couldn't help him.

"Alone? That's suicide," I whispered. "Let Lady Laurel and me help you."

"Lady Laurel hit her head," he said. "She's out cold."

"My magic can help—"

Already, he was shaking his head.

"Sorry, princess," he whispered. "You're staying in the carriage." His glare was fierce—intimidating. "You're not going to play battle mage with trained assassins."

Play battle mage?

I bristled.

He didn't understand. I had trained for battle since I could cast my first magical blow. My realm had been at war for a hundred years. Everyone trained. Everyone fought. It was mandatory. We were all battle mages in Ereth. Others, like me, were assault sorceresses trained to fight with specialized, more powerful magics. And we trained to win. We'd fought expert archers and sword wielders for a century. And we knew war.

I wasn't a helpless royal figurehead with a pretty crown and an empty wave. I was a soldier and I fought with magic not a blade.

Why couldn't he understand that?

"Tarrant, you're wrong!"

"Forget it!" he snapped. "I'm not losing my royal boon because of your inflated royal ego."

I hated this stubborn idiot.

Too filled with prejudice to see that he had a powerful weapon at his fingertips, but he'd rather belittle and malign me for being a royal princess who couldn't possibly be useful in a fight.

"Fine," I said with a growl and shoved him away from me. "Go out there and get killed. I'll tell Mother you were too dead to collect your royal boon. Idiot."

"Arrogant royal bitch," he said, baring his teeth. "I might just open this door and hand you right to them."

I glared at him. By Ereth, I hated this man!

"At least I'd be far away from you," I said. "And the assassins would all be dead."

His ice blue eyes lit with fire and he punched the wall of the carriage as four more arrows slammed into the window shields on both sides.

Drawing his broadsword, he dropped to the carriage floor on his back and stretched his feet toward the doors.

Thunk! Thunk!

More arrows pounded the window shields.

With his right foot, he quietly slid the metal locking bar free and pushed the right-side door open.

Four more arrows slammed into the door.

Taking a deep breath, he oozed out the opening and into the cloying dark.

The moment he disappeared into the darkness, I slammed the door shut and slid the metal locking bar back in place. And turned my attention to Lady Laurel.

But it was too dark to see. And I didn't dare light up anything with my magic. Much less those lanterns.

In the blackness, I pulled Lady Laurel up from the seat and slid my hand along her sleeve, over her shoulder, and up to her forehead. It was wet and sticky. She was bleeding. A lot.

I grabbed the blanket that draped the seat between us and covered her up to keep her warm.

Thump, thump, thump!

More arrows pounded the other side of the carriage.

I wanted out of this wheeled coffin! I wanted to go out there and fight these bastards trying to murder me and end the world.

Reaching down to my skirt, I tore out the hem and held the cloth against Lady Laurel's forehead, trying to stop the bleeding. With my other hand, I felt her hair. It was still dry.

No, the wound was on her forehead not her scalp.

Shouts echoed through the night. Footfalls pounding the ground.

Nervous, elemental horses snorted and grunted nearby, shifting in their magical harnesses. If they felt threatened, they dimmed their golden glow, hiding in darkness, but I doubted these cowards would challenge six magical horses. They also dimmed their gold light to conserve energy.

I kept the cloth pressed against Lady Laurel's forehead as a dozen arrows hit the carriage from all directions.

How long until first light? We had been traveling for hours. And we'd already run from these mercenaries once. Sunrise's frail light had to be close.

Outside, someone cried out in pain and my stomach dropped.

Were the Xanthan mercenaries out there killing everyone in the convoy? Intending to come for Lady Laurel and me last?

Had they already killed Tarrant?

I hoped not. I wanted him to live so I could scream at him about his bigotry toward royals and magic. After I hit these assassins with all the magic I could summon. No, I wanted to show the arrogant and insanely attractive bastard that I was just as good in a fight as he was. Or just that I was damned good enough in a fight. I sighed. And lots of other things, too.

I wanted to go out there and fight. But I couldn't leave Lady Laurel to their mercy.

It seemed like a lifetime before I ran a finger across Lady Laurel's forehead and felt dried blood. The bleeding had finally stopped. I tore the rest of my skirt hem loose and tied it around her head as a bandage. It was all I had. And I waited. For first light.

It was all I could do. For now.

WHEN THE DARK inside the carriage began to lighten enough that I could see my hand in front of my face, I heard Lady Laurel moan and push the blanket off her shoulders. She sat up, groaning.

"Lady Laurel?" I whispered. "Are you all right?"

"My head..." she moaned. "I remember a bump threw me toward the wall. And I was out."

She glanced around the carriage, noticing the silence at last.

"Wait. We've stopped." She grabbed hold of my arm. "Annarissa, why have we stopped? And where's Tarrant?"

I shrugged. "Out there somewhere," I whispered. "We broke a carriage wheel. Mercenaries surrounded us. He made me stay in the carriage while he went out to fight them."

Her eyes widened. "Alone?"

"Alone. Maybe the other hired swords had escaped the wagons and were helping him? I offered to help him fight them with my magic, but he refused. Like I couldn't fight a wet scroll because I was a princess."

Lady Laurel frowned. "Has he not seen a sorceress in action? Especially one trained in assault?"

"Said he didn't want to lose his royal boon. Like I was a trophy he could exchange for a royal prize."

It infuriated me that he saw me as helpless. Useless. Nothing more than an exchange of goods. I wasn't a person to him. I was a transaction.

It made me hate him even more.

"Hope he didn't get himself killed," said Lady Laurel, her hand pressed against her forehead. "Especially when he had magical help right beside him."

"I tried to tell him that, but he refused," I said with a sigh.

With or without Oz Tarrant, I had to get to Rohesia and marry a Siridean prince. But Lady Laurel and I alone? Even with our magic, we stood almost no chance of getting there alive. There were just too many enemies of Ereth that wanted us dead.

Certain factions in Xanthe thought that if Rohesia and Ereth perished, they could survive the curse. Didn't they understand that all of Kambria perished if the prophecy wasn't fulfilled? No one in Ereth believed in the curse until the sun began to dim and their crops began to die. Xanthe wouldn't believe it either until their crops and livestock started dying either. Until then, they would continue to act in everyone's worst interests.

The metal lock bar snapped up and thumped against the carriage floor.

I turned, hands raised, magic glowing blue at my fingertips as the carriage door banged open.

5

As the world outside grew light, Oz Tarrant staggered into the carriage and collapsed onto the cushioned seat across from me.

"Assassins fled after I killed enough of them," he said, exhaustion in his voice.

His blood-splattered face was a weary mask, eyes drooping. He didn't appear injured. Just cut and bruised.

But I had little sympathy for him. He could have had help fighting those mercenaries, but he chose to fight them alone. Like a lone wolf. Maybe the other hired swords helped him? Either way, his expertise with blades made him good enough to get away with it.

"Sleep it off, Tarrant," I said and slid off my seat.

In moments, he was asleep, snoring softly against the side of the carriage. I hoped he got a stiff neck for his roguish—and ignorant—tactics.

I slid out the open doors before he woke up and hauled me back inside. Laurel climbed out beside me as I walked off stiff muscles. I needed to find Mathias the carriage driver. I was starving and needed to ask about getting something to eat.

As the first ashen rays of sunlight tried to warm and light the world but failed, I discovered that the carriage driver, Mathias, and some of the other hired swords had built a small fire. Here, in this clearing surrounded by dying trees, the air was cool. This far from Ereth, the forest still grew thick and dark and wild around the roads. But the blight had already touched it. Soon, most of the leaves would shrivel and turn brown, curling up like dead insects on the dry ground. We called it the Battleworn Forest because it was only a dark and dangerous shadow of the living forest that had been changed by so much war—and the curse. Spirits of soldiers and battles haunted these woods. Making them treacherous to cross.

No warblers sang in the misty treetops. No flame foxes slinked around tree trunks hunting prey. Not even a lace-winged dreamfly darted around the warmth of fallen leaves, bodies glowing amethyst as they signaled to their mates through the mist. The once sweet-scented air smelled dank. Like rotting leaves.

More savage things than bandits and cutthroats prowled these woods. Dark magics. Dark things. Dark shadows. They traveled along the murky paths and hid behind trees. Spirits from of all the killing and death that came from a century of war. And with food so scarce, dark hunters braved the spirits of war, prowling for anything they could eat. Anything.

Getting lost in there was the least of our worries.

The scents of wood smoke and savory root vegetables drifted through the hazy edge of the forest. I recognized the root smell but not the herbs and spices. I wandered closer.

The three wagons and the carriage stood in a circle around the fire. The six elemental carriage steeds and three pairs of elemental wagon horses had faded with first light. Returning to their magical world. Lady Laurel and I would conjure a dozen more after sunset. Fresh and eager to run all night until dawn.

More than a dozen hired swords sat around a bright, crackling meal fire, sharpening swords and bandaging wounds. Behind me, past the tree line, wagons trundled past the camp, traveling east and west along Kambria's main thoroughfare. We had crossed Ereth's border gates into the stretch of no man's land that stood between Ereth and Rohesia. A desolate crossroads where a road cut north toward Xanthe and Covendrie Inlet which separated Xanthe from Ereth and Rohesia. An east-west road ran from Ereth to Rohesia, built long before two the realms went to war against each other.

The wagons that traversed these roads were most likely traders from Dewhaven to the northeast on their way to barter in Skystead or traders from the small haven of Rosebury here at Ereth's eastern border. Some had probably traveled all the way from Xanthe to the north and some were even Rohesian merchants on their way north, avoiding Ereth villages despite the truce. Wagons from all over Kambria traveled this main road. Any attacks by masked assassins in daylight would draw too much attention. Would the Equalizers risk another attack on a major road without the cover of dark?

Like all of the wagon traffic, the hired swords on this convoy had come from each of the three realms. Hired by the Erethian crown (my mother) at a handsome sum. With Tarrant leading them now. Except for someone named Farago he'd mentioned.

Black leather, blond leather, plate armor, and chainmail adorned the assortment of hired blades who sat around the fire talking. Erethian women as tall as Captain Nevayna adorned with the shiniest plate armor I had ever seen sat beside Xanthans in ravaged, faded brown leather. Rohesians in rusted chainmail with silver and black hair. Young Xanthan warriors dressed in tight black leather, long hair tied back with leather cords and close-cropped beards framing their young faces. Erethian soldiers in pristine blond leather adorned with the swirls and symbols of Ereth. And everything in between.

Normally, Erethians proficient with swords (and not magic) left the realm to live in Xanthe where magic and swords were both accepted—and not seen as suspicious. Mother hired a small contingent from Xanthe because she trusted them. It seemed so strange to see them wielding swords instead of magic, but not everyone had magical talents. And even some that did were fascinated by blades (including my sister, Carysana).

The hired swords seemed a little somber and quieter than I had expected as they waited with metal bowls and bent spoons for the roots and grains to heat. They looked tired after that full-on assault by the Kambria Equalizers.

Then I noticed the line of graves just beyond the wagons. More than a dozen that I could see, marked with wooden symbols of Ereth, Xanthe, and Rohesia tied to their swords that had been plunged into the ground at the head of each grave. I wondered how many belonged to our attackers, given a decent burial at least.

And to this convoy.

Mathias, the carriage driver, passed a basket full of crusty bread around the circle and it emptied halfway around. He started another basket of bread around in the other direction, his chainmail tunic clinking.

Fresh supplies from Ereth.

By the time we reached Rohesia, we would be down to flatbread and jerky. With precious little game to hunt as the world continued to darken, the sun fading a little more each day, the hours of daylight had shrunk like the dead of winter.

Without Ereth's protection, the next part of the journey would be even more dangerous. Fighting mercenaries we could see coming was easier than defending a carriage in the wild, foggy forests that strangled roads and blocked passages through the deep valley of the Cimmerian Breach. It was the largest breach that had erupted in Kambria since the curse began and it marked the border between Ereth and Rohesia. Mirstone Castle stood at the eastern edge of the kingdom. And Kambria (the parts that had been explored). Where the sea met towering rocky cliffs and old growth forests. Concealing sink holes and caves where Rohesians mined the first ores to make their blades and daggers and knives.

But the curse had corrupted the forests alongside the crops. Thorny vines tangled tree branches and leeched nourishment from the soil, turning it almost ashen. The valley between Ereth and Rohesia had been hit the hardest. Green leaves had not been seen in this forest for decades. Most of the trees were dead or dying, branches brittle and skeletal. Warblers and rabbits and flame foxes, once plentiful, had disappeared from the area.

And the dreamflies with their glowing bodies and crystalline wings had become sparse—even around forests. In fairy tales, dreamflies were called *fatebringers* because they carried fate's will, foretelling whether lovers were fated to mate. I had never been kissed and had never seen those sparks. But as children, my sisters and I dreamed of seeing them, like in the stories. Now that I was a woman, I knew they were only tales. Storytellers romanticizing the dreamflies' glow that signaled to their mates.

As the mists became pervasive across Kambria, they settled thicker in the lowlands—obscuring the sun and making Battleworn Forest more impenetrable. And more deadly. It was just as easy to get lost forever among those towering skeletal trees and heavy mists— among the battle ghosts—as it was to get waylaid and never seen again.

And the road we traveled led down a steep hill into a valley. Right through Battleworn Forest. And the Cimmerian Breach. It was the only road into Mirstone.

"Princess, are you hungry?"

I turned. Mathias stood behind me, holding two bowls and spoons.

"Mathias, right?" I asked.

He nodded.

He was stocky with light brown hair and a close-cropped beard framing his square jaw. His eyes were moss green, his nose a little too big for his face. He was at least a decade older than me, but he had a kind face despite a two-inch scar on his left cheek, and a bright smile. He smelled like wet grass and ozone from driving the elemental horses all night.

I appreciated his concern about whether I had eaten or not.

Which had not even occurred to Oz Tarrant, the leader of this convoy.

Mathias wore brown leather armor, greaves, and tall leather boots with a chainmail shirt over the cuirass. A short sword in a sheath bobbed against his left hip.

"I am famished, Mathias," I answered. "Thank you for your consideration."

"Since Oz needed to sleep," he said, nodding toward the carriage, "I thought I'd better make sure you're taken care of. You are the reason we're all here."

"I appreciate that, Mathias. Thank you."

"As do I," said Lady Laurel, pushing a lock of brown and silver-dusted hair out of her face.

"And he's the reason we only lost two hired swords back there," said Mathias, nodding toward the carriage. "Best damned swordsman I've ever seen. When we lost Breck Laurant and all the horses at the gate, I thought this trip was doomed, but Oz Tarrant is a thousand times better than Laurant ever was."

So, he fought beside the other hired swords. And according to Mathias, he was as good with a sword as his ego projected.

Mathias leaned toward me, his almost musical tenor voice falling to a whisper.

"Even if they do call him the Butcher of Badriyah. As long as he keeps us alive enough to get paid after reaching Rohesia, I'll follow him there."

I squinted at Mathias. "What do you know about Badriyah?"

I knew little about the village. Or the man that had executed it. But I had heard the stories. So many stories.

Mathias shrugged. "One of those tiny villages on the edge of everything. Stone's throw from Snowmelt, criminal capital of Kambria. Although, can't say I've ever met anyone with family from Badriyah—or anyone that knew someone killed there. Never been there myself. Lots of stories, but no one seems to answer any questions about the place."

"What do you mean?" I asked as Lady Laurel slid the bowl out of my hand and moved toward the meal fire.

They were serving the meal now.

Mathias sighed and slid his hand through his dark bangs, brushing them out of his eyes.

"Just that when someone tells me the story about Badriyah, I always ask questions. Who lived there? What were their family names? Were there merchants or traders in the village? Guilds? But no one seems to know anything about the village. All people know is that everyone who lived there was slaughtered by—" He glanced over his shoulder, toward the carriage, and then back to me. "By Oz Tarrant," he said in a hoarse whisper.

Mathias had a point. Despite the chilling story, I knew nothing about the village of Badriyah.

"All I'm saying," said Mathias, still whispering, "is that maybe somebody should ask Tarrant some questions about that village? And that night. Know what I mean? Won't get a better opportunity at the real story than from the Butcher himself."

I nodded. Maybe he was right? But I had witnessed Tarrant's butchery first hand. Didn't take much effort to believe that he'd murdered an entire village, too.

"That's very true, Mathias," I said. "I'll keep that in mind."

But when I turned to see where Lady Laurel was in the line, the flash of black almost knocked me to the ground. I stumbled backward, my hand raised, ready to cast.

I looked up.

Oz Tarrant boiled with fury in front of me.

He grabbed my arms and shuffled me backward against the nearest wagon. His face was inches from mine. His ice blue eyes were blue flames, his face taut, mouth and eyebrows pressed into angry lines. He smelled like musk and leather and heat.

I pulled in a breath, feeling lightheaded, and stared into his furious glare.

"You left the carriage!" he snarled with an almost feral growl.

I bared my teeth at him.

"I was hungry. And I had to pee."

I jerked my arms out of his grasp and shoved him backward.

"But I have had enough of your controlling and ordering me around! I'm the one throwing my life away so that this world and its three realms survive." I thumped my chest with my hand. "Not you. Me. At least treat me with a breath of respect."

He came at me again, but something in those piercing eyes had shifted. Cooled. He gripped my shoulders with less ferocity.

"You're getting married, not dying, so stop the drama," he said, his sarcasm biting. "These roads are crawling with mercenaries and killers. Equalizers. Hunting you. You. Eager to make sure you never cross Rohesia's border. This isn't an invitation to a ball, princess. This is the end of everything. Starting with you."

Conversations around the fire fell silent. Lady Laurel was beside Mathias now, carrying two bowls of root vegetables and grains, her face tense. All movement around the meal fire stopped as the hired swords stared, spoons motionless above their bowls.

"It's Annarissa!" I shouted as loud as I could, shoving him back from me again.

For a moment, he and I glared at each other, hands on hips, anger burning through him as it shot through me and rippled blue at my fingertips.

"Do you think me so stupid and shallow to think that you're escorting me to some silly dance? I have seen nothing but war since I was born. It took my father. My grandmother. It turned my mother's heart to stone when it made her queen. And it doomed my sisters and me to...to—this!"

He made no move to challenge me. These words had been building up for a lifetime. And he was getting the brunt of them. After all, he was being paid to hear them. Handsomely.

"I've been groomed to fight that war since I could summon my first magic at four, Tarrant."

My eyes began to fill with tears and I was furious at showing him my weakness. I gritted my teeth, vowing not to cry.

"And since I was nine years old, I've been preparing to give up my life to a man that will never love me. That finds me, a sorceress of Ereth...repulsive. All to save Kambria. So don't you dare treat me like some debutante at her first ball. Fairy tales are dead in Kambria."

His expression changed subtlety and I couldn't read it. I could only recognize his anger and his arrogance. But whatever fueled this expression was a new emotion that I'd never seen in him before.

"My first ball, Mr. Tarrant, will be a wake and my virtue will remain intact until the day I die because a Rohesian would rather bed a pig than an Erethian sorceress. Oh, he'll have children. By Rohesian concubine. Never by the likes of an Erethian. I'll be kept in my own room and prison. Far away from the good people of Rohesia. I just turned eighteen! My life is a mere trophy. A means to fulfill a prophecy and I hope it will be a short one. So, damn you, Oz Tarrant —my name is Annarissa Ambren Maelena Thorn! At least have the common decency to call me by it because in Rohesia, they will call me everything but my true name."

Tarrant didn't say a word. He glanced at his boots a moment and then moved gingerly toward me.

He held out his hand, palm up, bowing slightly.

"My lady," he said in a quiet voice, his ice blue gaze staring through my watery hazel eyes—into my soul. "You are not safe out here."

This time, it was a request. Not an order. And not accompanied by a show of force.

For a moment, I was stunned.

This horrible, angry, disagreeable...monster had just bestowed respect and grace upon me instead of overpowering me with force. In front of all the hired swords in his charge. In front of my lady-in-waiting.

Maybe he wasn't a complete monster after all?

But darkness still lurked in this enigmatic hired blademaster. The Butcher of Badriyah.

Nevertheless, he had extended an olive branch to me.

And I was taking it.

With a slight curtsy to match his bow, I put my hand in his.

He kept his hand above my shoulder to keep my head held high and not at a subserviently bowed angle. One I would have to soon adopt in Rohesia.

With all the practice and poise of a prince, he led me across the grass, past the meal fire with his dozen or more hired swords gawking and gaping at me. At him. Including Lady Laurel.

Back to the carriage.

He opened the door with his left hand and his bow deepened as he led me up the two steps. Back inside.

"I'll have your lady-in-waiting bring your meal and bread," he said and nodded at me as I sat down on the red-cushioned seat. "And I will leave the doors open." He paused a moment. "Annarissa."

I couldn't stop the smile from curving across my face. He'd called me by first name.

"Thank you," I said, my voice cracking.

He started away from the carriage but paused and turned back to me.

"And as fond as I am of butcher—or Tarrant—I prefer Oz."

"Oz," I repeated. "Thank you."

He gave me an awkward nod and stepped away from the carriage.

6

Daegal's balls! By the time I turned away from that damned claustrophobic carriage, the entire camp had gone quiet at her outburst. At her expelling eighteen years of truth that had haunted her from childhood.

And I'd been the catalyst. The target.

Over twenty hired swords around me, under my command, took their time getting back to slurping their soup and gnawing on bread like they'd never eaten before. Or seen a man and woman argue before.

But right now, they were absolutely speechless. Staring at me like I'd just murdered everyone in the camp. Starting with that beautiful, brave princess that I had grossly misjudged.

I sighed. Annarissa.

I didn't want to know her name. Or her past. Or anything about the horrible injustice she was being forced into...all to try and save Kambria. I didn't want to see her as anything more than that royal boon I'd earn for completing this job. But just looking at her made my chest burn. And every little thing I learned about her got under my skin. Festered and ached through my soul.

She was grace and humility and heart rolled into the most beautiful woman I had ever seen before. Dammit! I couldn't fall for her. Because I couldn't have her.

And as much I wanted to dismiss it as Erethian hysteria or sorceress drama, I knew better. The Erethian cold indifference to their offspring was legendary. And I knew the Rohesians better than most. Passionate and selfish. I was half Rohesian, according to my Xanthan mother.

I still had dark, ugly memories of the stories she told me about my father's death. And the summer night that she escaped with me in her arms across the border—and the inlet—to Snowmelt. The night had been so cold in Mirstone, she'd said, until attackers set the village fields and the castle on fire.

I was just a baby, so I had no memory of the night my father died protecting the king. But I remembered the first time she told me the story. I was three and it was the first time I'd realized that something was wrong in the world.

My mother's story changed every season over the years, but one kernel of truth remained. My father had been captain of King Daegal's guard. Killed in a skirmish that annihilated the guard detail and his queen. It almost wiped out Daegal and his two sons, too. Along with my mother and me.

Almost wished it had.

Then I wouldn't be on my way to Rohesia to give them the most incredible woman—no, force of nature—that I had ever encountered.

My head was still spinning as I sat down on a rock beside the meal fire, black leather armor creaking, my stomach growling at the savory scent of root vegetables in that rich, spicy Xanthan broth. Damn, I was starving.

I dropped my head into my hands. Who was I kidding? I hurt all over. Aching for her. And the horrible sacrifice that she'd been forced to make. For the good of Kambria.

"Oz," said Farago, a fellow Xanthan swordsman I occasionally ran jobs with in and around Snowmelt.

He robbed wealthy merchants along Kambria's roads when he wasn't trying to help me save the world by fulfilling this damned prophecy.

Questionable life choices but damned good with a sword. A man I could trust to watch my back. Mostly.

But not my coin purse.

He was at the large cast iron pot, ladling root vegetables and grains into bowls for the hired swords. For the survivors of that first bitch of a skirmish just past Ereth's ruined crop fields headed east. Damned Xanthan mercs were tough. And dumber than stumps to believe that this curse wouldn't soon kill their crops, too, and starve them out like the rest of the world. I lived in Xanthe, but I didn't consider myself Xanthan.

Farago's black leather armor looked scuffed and dull, curly brown hair stinking of that flax seed oil he wore. Insisted the ladies loved his wavy dark hair when he used it.

Smelled like week-old seaweed to me.

Farago was a bit shorter than me, thin enough, but he had a bit of an ale paunch after a month or two stuck in Snowmelt, waiting for this job to start. He'd spent them at the pub. Okay, he did appeal to the ladies. He was funny and friendly. Told them what they wanted to hear. He showed off with sword tricks and jokes and they ate it up.

But Farago was good with a sword. And I needed his skill at my back. Someone had been paid handsomely to make sure this convoy didn't arrive at Mirstone. And I needed to figure out who—fast. And unmask their agents who were posing as mercenaries alongside the other hired swords. Without their masks.

Damned Equalizers.

"Another lovely morning without sunlight," Farago mumbled. "Ain't it?"

"Sodding gorgeous," I said with a snarl.

Farago snickered and returned to filling bowls with root vegetables and grains.

But I couldn't get the princess out of my mind. Annarissa Ambren Maelena Thorn. God, what an unstoppable storm of a woman! Sunlit hair. Bright coppery gold eyes like grain ripening in the fields. Slim, shapely body and those full, bow-shaped lips I'd wanted to kiss since she stood up to me at Skystead. Long silky legs. The pert curves of her breasts. My brain had been on fire with the image of her. Brash. Bold. Intelligent. Passionate. And wise for someone just coming of age. At a helluva time.

Regardless, I wanted her like I'd never wanted any woman before. So, what do I get hired to do? Deliver the most vibrant, fearless, and intoxicating woman I had ever encountered to marry that dullard Arence Siridean. Daegal's balls! That fool could never appreciate the beauty and complexity of a woman like Annarissa Thorn. He couldn't see past the fact that she was a sorceress. Besides, that imbecile sacrificed nothing in this arrangement. Didn't have to lift a finger. It was all being delivered right to his feet. Tied up with a big purple Erethian bow.

Annarissa was right about everything she'd said. Arence would lock her away in a pretty cage, so he didn't have to get his hands dirty with magic. He'd produce heirs with a carefully chosen Rohesian highborn and go on with his life. While Annarissa wasted away, alone, unloved, untouched—and forgotten.

Fury burned through me.

I snapped up from the rock and punched the wagon behind me.

Why did my father give up his life to save the likes of the Sirideans? Why?

Someone was at my shoulder. A hand on it.

I turned, ready to lay them out with my fist.

Mathias. Didn't know him well, but he seemed sincere and likable enough. Hired by the Thorns just like Farago and me.

"Everything okay, boss?" he asked, looking concerned.

He had a clear, sharp voice that could carry a tune and the whole choir.

"Fine," I muttered, my head still spinning with Annarissa's heartfelt words that had cut me down to the quick.

I was still spinning with the presence of her. The clear but smoky notes of her alto voice. Her soft linen and rain scent. The painful honesty of every word she spoke. Her pristine, untouched beauty.

It made me hurt all over...because I couldn't have her.

And I wanted her. More than the huge payment for this job. More than the Queen of Ereth's royal boon. More than all the riches of Kambria. I. Wanted. Her.

"Let me know if you need anything," said Mathias. "I'm going to get some sleep now."

I nodded, still facing the wagon, and heard his quiet footsteps pad across the grass. Toward the carriage. But another set of footsteps approached. Softer. Lighter.

Female.

I held my breath.

"Mr. Tarrant?"

My body went slack with disappointment. Lady Laurel, Annarissa's lady-in-waiting. She was an older woman, thin, average height. She had a young look about her though, had a lot of spunk. And she cared deeply about the princess. That made me like her despite the magic she carried.

"Lady Laurel," I said, matter of fact and a little rushed—almost annoyed.

Yeah, I didn't want to talk to her or anybody right now. I needed time to process the horrible fate I was delivering Annarissa to and what would happen if I refused. Helluva quandary that I just couldn't fix. I'd owe these hired swords a fortune, too—more than I could afford. But I was just a selfish enough prick to live in the moment and let this whole world burn to save what was probably the last, best thing left in its dying gasps.

Princess Annarissa Thorn.

"Is it all right if I take root vegetables and bread to the princess now?"

She sounded timid. Frightened. Like I'd bite her head off. An hour ago, I might have done just that.

"Yes, of course," I said, waving her off.

Annarissa's outburst had changed me in ways I could only feel, not explain. Deep down, I was aware of everything she'd said. But in her presence, in her words, it all became so real. Painful. And I couldn't dismiss it or forget it.

Any more than I could dismiss this explosive, aching need for her. One smile and I came apart at the seams. One touch and I could feel the sun on my face again. And I wanted more. I wanted to touch her. Experience her. Love her.

I winced, wanting to punch another wagon.

No. I wanted to save her.

7

BACK INSIDE THE CARRIAGE, I COLLAPSED AGAINST THE SEAT CUSHIONS, MY blond braids askew. I felt drained, my traveling clothes hanging so heavy on me. But I had accomplished something. I had gotten through Oz Tarrant's wall of darkness. I don't know exactly what I said that had poked a hole through that nearly impenetrable barrier of his, but something got through.

And I was grateful.

His expression of respect, offered in front of the entire convoy, meant a great deal to me this morning. He'd made each one of those hired swords recognize that I wasn't just a job or an exchange of coin.

I mattered.

It didn't erase the memory of him slaying all those challengers or butchering a village, but it had smoothed some of those sharp edges. And my fear. It also gave me hope that maybe, just maybe there was more to those stories than I knew.

As I adjusted my skirt and leaned against the wall, my stomach growling, the carriage door opened and Lady Laurel climbed inside. Carrying a wooden tray with two bowls of grains and vegetables, two heels of bread, and two spoons. She set the tray in my lap and picked up her bowl, spoon, and bread.

"You must be starving," she said with a smile and sat down beside me with her bowl.

Nodding, I lunged for the spoon and plunged it into the savory broth and grains. The root vegetables tasted fresh, a rare delicacy in Ereth. But the broth was Xanthan, thick, buttery, and filled with flavorful spices that I had never tasted before. I tore off a piece of bread and dipped it into the broth. Savoring the spices and the warmth. Mother had supplied the convoy with provisions, but they would go fast.

In un-princess-like fashion, I shoveled in my meal and cleaned the bowl with the remaining bread. It warmed my belly and I felt sated. But I needed to stretch my legs. And escape the cramped confines of this box-like carriage. It was the roomiest carriage I had ever traveled in, but after this long, it felt claustrophobic.

Moving to the open doors, I pushed them open until they folded back against the carriage walls and sat down on the floor, letting my legs dangle outside, white stockings showing as I hiked up my skirt and let the cool air wash over me.

In a few minutes, Oz Tarrant sauntered toward the carriage. Making my pulse race.

How would he treat me now that he knew my true fate? Would he continue to treat me with respect or would we soon be back to him sneering when he said the word princess and treating me like a child? Or worse—an object.

He stopped in front of me, his gaze falling to the ground.

Was it a contrite response?

No. It was my white stockings, I realized, as I swung my legs back and forth. Enjoying his attention.

His breath quickened. Pupils dilated.

"I needed to stretch my legs," I said to him.

He nodded slowly, his gaze still on my legs as I swung them back and forth with purpose.

"Oz?" I said, making sure I called him by his first name like he'd asked.

"Huh?"

"Oz?" I repeated louder.

It took another moment and then his gaze shifted upward. To my face. He looked flushed. Sweat beaded across his brow.

"Did you need something?" he asked in a patient and less gruff tone.

I smiled. He hadn't heard a word I said. His mind must be on the next part of the journey. Through Battleworn Forest. Much more dangerous than getting this far.

Or it was still on my stockings?

"Is it safe to have the carriage doors open like this?" I asked.

"For now," he said. "Annarissa."

It was still coming out a little awkward, but he was calling me by my given name and not my station. Treating me like a person.

He turned toward me but froze, an anxious look on his face.

Something silver flashed.

A blade.

A figure in black leather crouched behind him, holding a knife to his back. Wearing one of those hideous porcelain masks, a contorted face that was screaming.

Shadows moved out of the trees toward the carriage. Toward me.

"Move and I gut you like a fish, Tarrant," said a gravelly, angry voice.

The man was several inches shorter than Oz and had two other daggers sheathed around his waist. His black leather blended into the distant, dark forest despite the greyish daylight struggling against the growing mist. It blended into Oz's armor.

But this assassin had called Oz by his name. It was someone Oz knew.

Another man stepped out of the shadows, wearing the white mask of a laughing man. He stepped in front of Oz and grabbed hold of my arms.

"Let's go, princess," he said, his voice deep and dark.

"No," Oz growled. "No!"

Earthen magic roiled inside me and I felt its warmth against my fingertips.

I laid my hands on top of the man's as he yanked me out of the carriage. Past Oz.

Whispering a spell, I cast withering magic on the man.

"I'll kill you for this," Oz growled at the man dragging me away from the carriage. "That's a promise."

The man laughed but stopped pulling me when his hands slipped away from my arms. Confused, he stared down at his fingers.

His arms and hands had shriveled and hardened like the bark of a tree. Rendering them useless.

"What the hell!"

Lady Laurel was at my shoulder, her back to me as she tossed a handful of yellow powder into the face of the man holding a knife at Oz's back.

The man sputtered and coughed, clawing at his burning eyes.

Oz turned, knocking the knife out the assassin's hands. And drew his broadsword.

I grabbed the other man by his black leather tunic and slammed him against the carriage. He crumpled. Falling unconscious into the grass.

Lady Laurel and I turned together as one, calling up air and earth magic. The air sparked gold, a blue glow clinging to the clouds like heat lighting as I rained down lumps of dirt and rock on the assassins, leaving the wagons and hired swords untouched. Fist-sized dirt clods and stones poured into the camp, breaking blades and beating down masked assassins.

Lady Laurel set the wind spinning and it whipped into a tall, glowing white funnel that scattered the masked attackers in all directions. Keeping them busy until Oz and the other hired swords had rounded them up. And put them all to the sword.

I couldn't watch. Death by the blade made me queasy. They would come after us again if he'd spared them.

After it was over, I felt uneasy as I watched Oz and Mathias gather up swords and masks, tossing them into an empty barrel.

I froze.

An empty barrel.

The memory rushed back to me from the castle.

I remembered standing outside the storage room after Oz had killed all twelve of his competitors. When I stepped behind the barrel outside, I'd been startled by seeing faces inside it.

But they hadn't been faces. They were masks!

Maybe Oz Tarrant hadn't cold-bloodedly murdered those competitors after all. They had been assassins. Kambrian Equalizers! And he'd eliminated them to keep them from infiltrating the convoy —or the castle. Killing my sisters and ensuring the prophecy could never be fulfilled. They'd hidden their masks inside that barrel before entering the building.

I whirled around and rushed toward Oz. Grabbing his arms.

"Oz!" I cried.

He was wide-eyed, his gaze intense as he stared at me.

"What is it, Annarissa?" he asked in a quiet voice. "Are you all right?"

I nodded. "Yes, of course. But that whole contest back at the castle!" I couldn't hold back my smile. "It was all pretense on your part, wasn't it?"

He looked confused. "Pretense?" And then he looked worried.

I nodded and motioned toward the barrel.

"You wanted to make everyone believe you were a cold-blooded killer by eliminating all your competition, but you were really protecting my sisters and me. Eliminating assassins. Weren't you?"

He opened his mouth but nothing came out when I slid my hand up his chest, through his silky black hair to his face. Caressing his cheek.

"They weren't contestants at all, were they," I said. "They were

Equalizers. I saw their masks. Hidden in a barrel outside the storage room. And you knew that."

His gaze went right through my heart and burrowed into my soul as my fingers stroked his warm cheek. I wanted to touch his hair. Feel the heat of his skin against mine, letting it surge through my fingers and roil deep in my belly.

Reaching up, he slid my hand away from his face, his breath quickening. He enfolded my hand in his for a moment, squeezing, and then let go. The pupils of his ice blue eyes were as big as saucers and he backed away from me.

"Yes," he said, out of breath. "They were Equalizers. Saw them gathering in the dark beyond your gate when I got there." He sighed. "I need to—secure the carriage."

He whirled around and rushed away from me. Running back toward the carriage.

As he busied himself checking the wheels and undercarriage, an awful thought slid into my head. About the masks I'd seen in the barrel at Skystead.

Oz dispatched those assassins before they had a chance to act. But a bigger question lingered here. Who within the castle had allowed a dozen assassins from a notorious gang like the Kambrian Equalizers through that gate? Letting them hide their identities long enough to compete in the sword contest and infiltrate the procession. And maybe even place one of their own as its leader. There was only one answer.

A traitor in Ereth.

That meant my mother the queen and my sisters could be in as much danger as I was on this journey to Rohesia. With me already a day's ride from the castle.

If assassins gained a foothold inside Skystead and killed my sisters, only my aunt's line remained. Idella and Isadora, my younger cousins. Even if both of them married Siridean princes, the prophecy was still forfeit. And their sacrifices would be meaningless.

How could I protect my sisters from so far away? Much less the prophecy?

Who in Ereth wanted Kambria to perish? Or maybe they just wanted Aunt Johava's daughter on Ereth's throne? Maybe that infiltration was about killing the queen—my mother?

Regardless of the plan, a traitor walked Skystead's halls and ramparts. Somehow, I had to unmask that traitor. But how? When I was so far away now.

And on their list to kill?

8

WHEN THE SETTING SUN DISAPPEARED FROM THE SKY, THE HIRED SWORDS hitched three teams of our newly conjured elemental horses to the wagons. Their gold glow outshined the dying sunlight that was so pale and frail, looking more like a flickering candle than a real sunset, the light quickly swallowed up by dusk as Oz and Mathias harnessed the team of six spirited gold elemental steeds to the carriage.

Rohesians were known for their love of horses and had bred a sleek and fast black and grey merle horse they called intrepids. Like a painter had splattered their coats with black and grey paint. They were tall, stocky, and bold. Spirited with long, silky manes and forelocks, full, luxurious tails, and hooves feathered with long merled grey and black hair. They had strength and endurance. They were fearless in battle and bonded deeply with their chosen rider. These beautiful horses were coveted by all of Kambria. Killing them at the castle gate had been a travesty and still made me sad.

The Sirideans kept the stallions and broodmares in the royal family, only selling geldings to select outsiders. Stallions were too wild for pulling wagons and carriages. The royal family would be horrified to learn a dozen intrepids and their blademaster had been murdered. But I doubted that they would appreciate these sleek, flowing maned elemental horses. They gleamed like sunlight and had the stamina and endurance of a dozen or more horses. Including Rohesia's beloved intrepids.

As the three wagons trudged onto the road behind the carriage, Oz lurched inside and slid the metal lock bar across the doors. He turned up the oil lantern to the tiniest flame he could manage and then slouched into the cushioned seat across from Lady Laurel and me, avoiding my gaze. His tight black leathers looked clean and shiny despite the amount of blood he had already spilled since arriving at Skystead. He'd taken some time to clean up. I longed for a hot bath or even cool river water to bathe in and wash my hair.

He concentrated on his gloves, the doors, the floor. Anywhere but across the carriage. At me. Why?

Was he angry at me? And Lady Laurel? For conjuring the new teams of elemental horses? For using our magic on those assassins? He didn't seem to like magic and right now, he didn't seem too fond of me either.

But Lady Laurel and I had saved him from getting a blade through the heart or lungs! Maybe he was angry or ashamed that he'd been saved by magic? Or women? I sighed. Or both.

I let him stew and avoid my gaze as the well-traveled road's level ground gave the newly repaired carriage wheel a smoother surface. I had seen several spare carriage wheels bolted underneath the carriage train, but the hired swords had been able to repair the broken wheel without a wheelwright's assistance.

This time.

The Battleworn Forest ahead frightened me, but the thought of descending past its eastern slope into the Cimmerian Breach's dark valleys and hollows terrified me.

"Must we travel through the Cimmerian Breach?" I asked him finally. "The Battleworn Forest is dangerous enough without traveling the Breach, too."

Maybe that was his plan? Taking a route to Mirstone so dangerous that assassins couldn't—or wouldn't—follow it.

At last, he looked up at me. In silence for a few uncomfortable moments.

"There is no other way to the castle," he replied in that silky baritone voice that was rich like a deep red wine and had the brightness of a bard. "Blame the idiocy of its royalty for that. In trying to secure their kingdom from invaders—and magic—they locked themselves into dangerous territory even before the sun began to go dark. Only one road in or out. And now...I don't know how they survive in isolation with crops blighted and livestock dying...and game nearly non-existent in the surrounding forests."

His disdain for Rohesia had been clear from the beginning. He had shown no fondness for this eastern kingdom and I wondered why. Because he was Xanthan?

"You don't care much for the Rohesians, do you?"

Those ice blue eyes narrowed and he gripped the seat's armrest tighter, like he was about to rip it off.

"Not at all," he said with a growl as his expression turned surly. "Prince Arence is a selfish prick and his father is a tyrant."

I bit my lip. The man I was betrothed to marry. Selfish or not, I had no choice but to wed him with the world at stake.

"What of the other sons?" I asked, hoping my sisters would fare better with their princes.

Gen had been promised to Orion Siridean. He had been injured in the war, walked with a cane they said. Rumors claimed that he was quiet and reclusive—with quite a temper. Gen was kind and patient, but she was every bit a beautiful but battle-hardened soldier. Maybe they would complement each other? Or would she be ignored like Arence would ignore me? Dante Siridean seemed the most promising. Young, fiery, and handsome, he was a bit of a prankster. And a rebel like my sister, Carysana. Both couples would either fall in love or kill each other, I was certain.

Arianwen, my youngest sister, hadn't even learned about her match yet. There were rumors that Tiryn Siridean, the oldest of King Daegal's sons, wasn't a blood Siridean. That he was the son of the king's second wife, who was still single and almost twice Arianwen's age. Overbearing and controlling according to rumors (like his brothers apparently). Would Arianwen also be trapped in a loveless marriage like me?

I feared for her.

"I don't know much about Arence's brothers," Oz said, his gaze flicking from Lady Laurel to me. "But I hope they aren't like Arence."

Oz pulled off his right glove with his teeth, tossed it onto the cushion, and then pulled the knife from his boot. He fumbled a whetstone out of a leather pouch hanging from his belt, and began sharpening the knife. Like he was eager to avoid my gaze. Or prevent engaging in any meaningful conversation. But I had to bring up the fact that he may have traitors working for him.

Maybe he already knew and didn't care?

"Oz?"

"Annarissa?" he said, glancing up at me through a thick fringe of black lashes that framed those penetrating ice blue eyes.

"There may be traitors employed among these hired swords."

He smiled, but it was almost a condescending response. Like a pat on my head. Like the fact was obvious.

"I have been expecting to find an Equalizer or two among the hired blades," he replied, that whetstone singing along the edge of his knife. "After all, I didn't hire them. Only Farago."

How could I phrase this and get him concerned about the traitor being more than just a member of this Xanthan murder guild? Someone high up in Mother's castle cabinet or staff had allowed that force of Equalizers to infiltrate the grounds. And hide their identities by concealing those masks. A guard or a mage or a servant couldn't have pulled that off. A group of mages or servants perhaps? No, this took planning, coordination, and timing. And keys. No, it had to be someone high up in Mother's court.

"What if I told you it's bigger than that, Oz?"

The whetstone halted and his gaze met mine and held it as his brow furrowed.

"What do you mean bigger?"

"Someone high up in Mother's court is orchestrating it."

I smoothed out the folds of my purple skirt and leaned toward him. Waiting for his response.

He was quiet for several moments.

"What would they gain?" he asked, taking me seriously.

Finally.

"Control of the throne," said Lady Laurel.

Oz frowned, glancing from Lady Laurel to me.

"Explain."

"With her four daughters married off to Rohesians, the queen's heir apparent becomes the queen's nieces," Lady Laurel explained.

"Kill me and kill my sister, Gen, who marries next," I began, fixing him with my gaze. "Then my cousins, Idella and Isadora must take our places. Leaving Aunt Johava as the last of the bloodline that could ascend the throne. Kill Johava and crowning a new monarch becomes a civil war in and of itself."

"It would appear that someone is tired of the Thorn family in power," Lady Laurel added as she settled back against the seat cushions again and gripped the armrest on her right.

"But not someone Xanthan dumb, ignoring the prophecy or the darkening world," I added.

Oz's whetstone was in motion again until the edge of his long knife gleamed.

"But this could be anyone," he said. "And we're a long way from the castle and Ereth." He sheathed the blade back into his boot and put away the whetstone. "Not much we can do to discover their identity out here. Much less stop them."

He was right, of course.

"Consider this," I said, leaning toward him again, letting the volume of my voice fall to almost a whisper so the hailing-horn didn't carry my voice up to the driver.

Oz reached over and pulled a red silk rope on the wall behind him. A privacy panel slid across the hailing horn's opening.

"What if this traitor has engineered much more of this journey than you realize?" I continued, still leaning toward him. "What if there are several Equalizers planted among the hired swords? Or listeners conveying information back to the guild, leaving clues as to which road we are taking. And when. When we will be resting—and vulnerable."

His gaze slid away from my face as he sat back against the seat cushions, a faraway look in his eyes, gaining distance fast.

He hadn't considered the fact that someone didn't just look the other way and let Equalizers infiltrate the hired swords. No, someone hired the Equalizers to make sure that this procession never made it to Rohesia. While making it look like killing me was a political maneuver.

"What if it's a partnership?" Oz offered at last. "With someone in Rohesia? Someone that wants to overturn the Erethian throne. Or usurp it."

It was my turn to be shocked by the possibilities. What if Oz was right? With no one on the throne, Ereth was ripe for takeover. If Rohesia controlled both thrones, and the royal Erethian bloodline was dead, would that render the prophecy irrelevant? Or would it destroy Kambria faster?

Either greed or ignorance would win the day. Regardless, I was a pawn in either game.

"I will watch these hired swords carefully," he said and nodded at me. "But princess—Annarissa—if you see something, tell me. And you, Lady Laurel." His expression darkened. "Your lives may depend on it."

Lady Laurel and I nodded.

"And yours," I added.

With a sobering look, he tugged on the red silk cord and opened the hailing-horn's opening again. He slid his broadsword out of its shoulder sheath and pulled out a larger whetstone. As the stone scritched up and down the blade, metal and stone singsonging, I settled back into the cushions, watching him hone that edge like the finest swordsmith.

As the carriage lumbered along the dirt road, I noticed that the number of wagons we passed, headed in the opposite direction, had begun to diminish. And the occasional whiff of wood smoke rising above the stench of horse dung had faded into the cool, misty scent of damp wood and rain-soaked moss. The creak of wagons and bluster of horses had given way to silence.

Not long after Oz had finished sharpening his broadsword, he turned out the oil lanterns, bathing the carriage in crisp indigo darkness as a sliver of moon clung to the night.

I glanced at Lady Laurel who looked apprehensive.

For a while, I listened to the road, to the rhythmic thump and creak of the carriage wheels until I realized that it had been the only sound around us for some time. The wagon traffic had disappeared, a heavy silence replacing it. We were alone on the road and the world had grown so quiet.

Too quiet.

Until the carriage lurched to a sudden stop.

I felt Oz tense and sit up, hand reaching toward the long knife in his boot.

"Why are we stopping?" he muttered.

He thumped the ceiling with his fist.

"Mathias!" he roared. "Why have we stopped?"

Oz yanked the metal lock bar free from the door handles as Mathias' heavy footfalls trudged down from the driver's perch and thumped against the dirt road. The three pairs of elemental steeds snorted and grunted, fidgeting like they sensed a predator nearby. Something that could harm an elemental.

The carriage doors rocked open and Mathias filled the doorway, lantern in his left hand. The hair on the back of my neck stood up.

The glow of the elemental horses had gone out. They felt threatened by something in Battleworn Forest.

"The road is blocked, Oz," said Mathias, glancing from Oz to me and finally, to Lady Laurel who leaned forward, her back board-straight as she white-knuckled the armrest. "By a huge fallen tree. And we can't go around it. Ground's too soft."

Oz grumbled and started to climb out, but I reached out and grabbed his arm, managing to find the bare skin between his glove and the cuff of his leather sleeve. It was an accident, but I was grateful.

The heat shot through my hand and straight to my belly. His skin was soft and the feel of him was the most comfort I had felt since the first communication from Rohesia arrived, confirming my (forced) betrothal to Prince Arence. I was nine.

I held onto that heat.

To my surprise, Oz let me hold onto him, his gaze falling to my hand and then lifting to my face. With the most curious expression I'd ever seen on his handsome face. Longing? Loneliness? I couldn't tell. It was a moment of vulnerability he'd never shown before.

He shuddered, closing his eyes a moment, exhaling sharply. And then, to my amazement, he laid his bare right hand on top of mine, looking deep into my eyes.

And I couldn't look away.

For a moment, I couldn't breathe, the contact between us so intense.

Finally, I heaved a breath, my heart thundering against my rib cage as I lost myself again in the heat of his fingers, the weight of his hand against mine.

I desperately wanted to touch his body. His face. Feel the press of his fiery lips against mine, feel the strength of his arms around me, holding me tightly against him. I wanted to feel the heat of his bare skin against mine. Find comfort in his arms. Every time I was near him, his proximity, his presence made me forget about everything and everyone around me—and my fate. He smelled like night and warm metal.

I had never felt this way before. I'd had crushes, but I had never felt such aches and such pulls. I'd never felt physically drawn to a man before.

Especially one like Oz Tarrant.

"Be careful," I said, leaning toward him until his face was only a delicious inch or two away from my mouth.

And I wanted to claim that distance that might as well have been fathoms. He was a hired blademaster. He was being paid to guard me and deliver me to Rohesia. Nothing more. Why would he want me? An eighteen-year-old virgin princess from the realm of magic, doomed to marry a Rohesian prince that would lock me away like a priceless—but useless—vase.

"It'll be okay," he whispered. "I promise."

"Whatever's wrong out there might be a stage set for ambush," I whispered. "So, be wary. Even the elementals sense something. Their glow has gone dark."

He pulled in a breath and finally nodded.

Like a shard of ice sliding down my back, his hand slipped away from mine. He slid out of the carriage alongside Mathias and disappeared into the misty darkness, that long knife in his bare fist.

But the intense heat of his touch lingered.

I brought my hand to my face and pressed it against my cheek, closing my eyes as I let myself float away on the warm comfort until it mixed with the hot flush of my skin.

When I glanced up, I realized that Mathias had left the doors cracked.

I dropped down to the floor and slid across on my knees to open the doors wider, peering outside.

Mist hung like apparitions in the night, a strange green phosphorus glow lighting parts of the Battleworn Forest. A massive tree trunk lay across the road, its girth as tall as Mathias, Oz, and now, Farago as they tried to find a way around the massive log. Over it. Around it. Through it.

I heard their quiet, wary voices discussing how to keep the procession moving as I scanned the wild, chirring forest surrounding us. Oz suggested harnessing the elementals and dragging the tree off the road. Lady Laurel and I were willing to summon another team of elemental horses for the task.

Something moved in the corner of my eye. I turned.

Shadows shifted against the strange green glow. Wings fluttered. Like birds taking flight. Or the resonating sound of swords being quietly drawn?

My heart began to race.

Or the scissor-steps of masked assassins slipping from behind one tree to another?

A low growl echoed across the still and silent forest.

I whipped my head around at the rustle of distant brush. Searching for the origin of the sound.

Or the silhouette of those assassins.

Wind rose. Bare branches clattered. Mist shifted. I swallowed a breath. Like a hand had fanned the mist away.

I glanced back over at Oz and the others. Still standing in front of the massive log, still deep in conversation about how to get past it. Not watching the forest and its gathering shadows creeping up on us. Fast.

Gently, I kicked off my boots and slid out of the carriage, letting my stocking feet touch the ground. The soil. Where my magic had been born.

"Princess!" Lady Laurel hissed in a harsh whisper. "Don't you dare go out there. It's too dangerous."

She was an air sorceress. She didn't understand earth magic. Sometimes, before I cast magic, my feet needed to feel the ground.

Like a flower reaching toward the sun, the magic rose in me, quivered through my legs, up my waist, and into my arms as it seeped into my fingers.

Glowing palest blue, the magic bloomed through my entire body. Down into my feet, through my toes, and fanned out across the ground.

Searching.

I closed my eyes, reaching up and out across the ground. Into the mist. Searching the forest for the source of those sounds.

Behind my eyelids, the forest unfolded around me in smoky layers, lit by eerie green light from pockets of gas made by decaying leaves and plants. Sulfur and ozone tanged the air as the blue cast of my magic mixed with the green, softening the unnatural shapes and turning them a rich cyan until they stood out in my mind's eye.

Sword wielders. In white porcelain masks of horrifying faces. Slipping through the mist toward the fallen log. Toward Oz and the others.

My heart dropped into my feet.

More than two dozen. And Oz didn't see them coming. Moving toward him in ambush.

I had to warn him!

9

Mathias turned. Oz a heartbeat later.

Just as a swordsman in black leathers swung down from a tree to the left, knocking Mathias to the dirt road.

Oz and Farago drew their swords, facing off with the assassin standing over Mathias.

But there were too many!

The road turned dark and swollen with assassins in dark leathers, their white porcelain masks hideous against the night and the forest's smoky green glow.

I turned toward the fray as Oz's hired swords leaped down from the wagons and raced past me to defend Oz and the carriage.

The assassins hadn't noticed me yet. They'd been so focused on Oz that they missed their target standing right outside the carriage.

But I wouldn't go quietly. Or easily. I'd fight to my last breath to take them all down.

I barely heard Lady Laurel's desperate shout behind me, trying to get me back in the carriage, but I would not be stopped.

I'd battled squadrons of sword masters. Units of mages.

Shifting into battle focus, I cast a pale curtain of blue light around me, shielding my body, and turned my attention to the assassins.

With my magic, I reached into the dark, marking Oz and the other hired swords with swirls of protective blue light.

In an instant, the tangle of assassins had Oz on the ground, three dozen or more of them swarming over him and the others like hornets. Pinning them to the ground, swords raised.

There were too many.

Oz shouted, a cry of pain behind it.

"Oz!" I called. "No..."

My heart smashed against my breastbone as I lifted my arms into the air and called up an earthly force of raw, shuddering energy. Focusing it on all of the dark shapes swarming Oz and the hired swords outlined in blue light.

Vivid blue symbols crackled like heat lightning across the air as earthen battle magic whispered against my lips.

Like a tidal wave, the force of earth slammed into the overwhelming crush of assassins. Knocking them to the ground.

Dropping to my knees, arms outstretched and fingers splayed, another war spell whispered across my lips.

I called out to the soil beneath us, turning it to quicksand beneath the feet of every dark figure not marked by my shield.

The ground liquefied around me. Becoming a churning lake of mud and sand.

Men and women screamed, scrabbling against unstable ground and roiling air as the quicksand pulled them under. Their voices grew muffled as the ground swallowed them in a miasma of sand and soil and sludge.

And suddenly, the world was quiet again.

I ran toward the massive log, seeing three figures glowing blue on the ground. The other hired swords closed ranks around me, drawing around the injured in a tight circle, swords drawn and pointing outward toward the forest.

"Lady Laurel!" I shouted. "Lady Laurel! Come quick!"

Footsteps ticked against the hard-packed dirt road as I hung over Mathias. He was closest to me. The carriage driver lay clutching his arm. Blood dripped down his leather cuirass, but the chainmail shirt over it had kept him from serious injury.

When Lady Laurel reached me, I pointed at Mathias.

"He needs healing," I said and moved back.

Lady Laurel dropped down beside him and lifted his chainmail shirt.

All elemental mages and sorceresses could heal, even those trained in assault. Like me.

Next, I went to Oz and Farago. Farago was out cold, his curly brown hair wet with blood. He'd been knocked out. Probably needed some magic to seal that gash, but he would be fine. I'd let Lady Laurel heal him next and the others bandage his head.

I dropped down beside Oz.

He was on his side, bloodied long knife lying in the dirt. His bare right hand was still wrapped around the broadsword he'd drawn. Its blade was also bloodied.

Carefully, I slid the broadsword out of his fist. And began unfastening the clasps on his black leather armor. When I lifted it over his head, I found the black linen tunic beneath it soaked in blood. A deep wound just below and to the left of his belly button. Bleeding profusely.

I tore away the stiffening black linen shirt and threw it on the ground. Turning back to Oz's wounds.

Gently, I pressed my hands against his bare muscled chest, so lean and sculpted that it took my breath for a moment. His skin was so soft but so pale against the dark red blood.

The wound was deep.

Calling up healing words, I recited the battle injury spell I'd been taught. With earth magic, new black soil became a plaster in my hands, glowing blue and smelling loamy and rich. The magic-infused mud dripped into the wound, filling punctures, and clogging whatever bled. Slowing and then stopping the flow.

When the bleeding had stopped, I packed the wound with the remaining mud in my hand and tore a wide swath of fabric free from my skirt until it hung just above my knees, showing every inch of my white stockings and short black boots.

I knelt beside him again, motioning for Lady Laurel and together, we lifted Oz into a sitting position. Lady Laurel held him up as I wrapped his torso in my makeshift purple bandage. I wrapped it tight and fused the fabric's ends into the wrap using my magic. Tension drained from my body as I cast a purifying spell on the bandage.

When two of the hired swords hurried over to help, I motioned to Oz.

"Pick him up and carry him to the carriage, please," I said.

Together, they gently lifted him off the road and I led them back to the carriage, both its doors thrown wide open.

They carried Oz up the two steps and placed him on the cushioned seat to the left. As soon as they put him down, I grabbed Lady Laurel's grey blanket and unfolded it, draping it over Oz. I slid off his boots, setting them on the floor beside the seat. And I lit both lanterns.

In the thin gold flicker of lantern light, I examined him more closely. A cut on his chin was caked in blood. And a huge bruise framed his left eye.

Being this close to him was intoxicating. The heat of his skin thrummed through my body as I felt myself falling deeper and deeper into this strange attraction I felt for him.

I smoothed his long, silky black hair out of his face, my fingers tracing the outline of his strong chin, the soft curve of his cheek, and the perfect slope of his nose. His full lips were so kissably warm that I had to fight the urge to brush my mouth against his, wanting to taste it, sip it, guzzle its heat...trace the shape of it with my tongue.

Where were these desires coming from? I had never even kissed a boy before. Much less a man. A man like Oz Tarrant.

He moaned, heaving a breath, his face contorting with pain. He was regaining consciousness.

I wedged myself on the edge of the seat cushion beside him, pressing close to his body, and leaned over him as his eyes opened.

Those ice blue eyes were wide and so intense as his body jolted in a startle. He frowned and his gaze turned toward me, lifting his hand toward my face. So gently, he laid his fingers against my cheek. Stroking. Tracing down to my chin. His touch was white-hot.

A shudder rippled through my belly and I sighed, the sensation so intense. It burned through my cheek and I wanted to drown in it.

"Annarissa?" He said finally in a ragged whisper. "What...what happened?"

I reached over and brushed a lock of black hair off his forehead that had fallen over his right eye.

He closed his eyes a moment, pulling in a deep, unsteady breath.

"You were ambushed, Oz," I said. "Equalizers. They swung out of the trees and poured out of the mist. Overwhelmed you, Mathias, and Farago."

His eyes widened, his mouth gaping, a million questions on his lips.

"Relax," I said, offering him my warmest smile as I leaned into his hand still against my cheek. "Everything is okay now. We didn't lose any hired swords."

He frowned again, that shadow back across his brow.

"But how?" he demanded. "There were dozens—"

"I used my battle magic," I said.

Anger sparked in those haunted, ice blue eyes as he started to object, but I pressed my hand against his luscious mouth, the heat almost scalding.

"No arguments," I said. "I have been training as an assault sorceress since I was a child. And I've fought in dozens of battles."

His anger quickly dissipated, his gaze flicking from my fingers pressed against his mouth to my face. And then I felt his lips purse against my fingers. At first, I thought he was trying to say something, but a shiver shot through my body and sizzled across my skin when I realized that he had kissed my fingers.

His right hand slid up my back and I gasped, the heat of his touch something I'd never felt before. I leaned into his hand as his fingers stroked their way up my waist to my shoulders. His arm wrapped around me, pulling me toward him.

I slid my hand away from his mouth, letting him draw my face to his.

Close enough to brush my lips against his, to taste his heat and his want—and his need.

But the injuries had caught up with him and he slumped against the cushion, out cold.

Like an unwound spool of thread, I collapsed against him, my breaths heaving in time with the rise and fall of his chest.

Cursing his injury and the assassins that had stabbed him.

Disappointed, I sat up and caressed his cheek, his fevered forehead, the side of his face, and his strong chin. I started to rise from the cushion, his arm sliding away from my shoulders, but at the last moment, I turned back to him and brushed my lips across his with a feather touch. Just light enough to feel the shape of those succulent full lips against mine.

A spark of gold light fluttered between us.

It was only a brief flash, like a dreamfly's signal in the darkness to its mate, and then it disappeared.

What in Ereth was that?

Part firefly, part dragonfly, and part magic, dreamflies appeared in an array of pastel shades and legends said that when dreamflies appeared in your dreams, it either meant you were calling out to your future mate...

I exhaled sharply.

Or your future mate had called out to you. And seeing dreamflies along your path three times meant you and your future mate were destined to meet. Soon. And if they fluttered around you and your lover when you kissed and the air sparked gold...you were fated to mate.

I gasped.

But that hadn't been a dreamfly.

Had it been magic? The glow of the elemental horses returning? Or something else I was afraid to contemplate? Something the old legends and fairy tales foretold. Something I could never have—because of the prophecy.

I had just gotten to my feet when Lady Laurel poked her head into the carriage.

"How is Mr. Tarrant?"

Just divine, I wanted to say. Absolutely divine.

"He's resting comfortably," I said. "I applied an earth magic plaster to his wound and got him settled. I expect that he'll sleep for quite a while. His forehead is so warm though. I hope he won't be stricken with a fever."

She nodded but gave me a funny look.

"There is quite a lot of heat there," she said, giving me a sideways glance.

I frowned. Had she seen him touch me? Or me brush my lips across his?

"Yes, there is," I said and motioned out the doors. "Do you need my help healing anyone else?"

She shook her head. "Mathias' arm is sore, but with my magic, it should be fine by morning. Farago will have little more than a headache after I closed the wound on his scalp. The rest have cuts and bruises, that's all."

I glanced back at Oz.

"Oz is going to need a day or so to heal," I said. "He has a deep gut wound, just beneath the navel. Even with my magic, he can't travel far tomorrow."

"I'll inform the others. Shouldn't be an issue." Lady Laurel nodded toward the massive log still blocking the road. "We still have bigger problems."

I smiled. "That can be solved if we combine our magics, Lady Laurel."

"I agree," she said, crossing her arms. "But tell that to a band of hired swords who think the only solution to everything is a sword thrust."

"Until they wake up and find the log cut in half," I said with a wink. "By magic."

A smile lit Lady Laurel's face as she brushed her steely brown hair out of her eyes.

"Let's just do this and let them discover it in the morning. If we have to wait for them to devise a solution to obliterate that log, we'll still be here tomorrow evening. And sitting ducks for more assassins."

I cast one last glance at Oz who slept peacefully and slid out of the carriage beside Lady Laurel. I motioned toward the massive log.

"Lead the way."

Grinning, Lady Laurel moved in front of the carriage, through the smoky darkness, her midnight robes blending into the night and the fog. Together, she and I approached the huge log.

I pressed my shoulder against hers when we stopped in front of the obstacle. I wondered how long it took those assassins to block the road with such a gigantic fallen tree. Without someone seeing and stopping them.

Maybe they hadn't moved it by hand? I'd never considered that they may have some mages in their midst. Perhaps even an Erethian mage? That sent a cool wind blowing across my heart. Someone who could counter my battle magic?

"Do you have an air spell to mask the noise?" I asked, glancing over at her as I faced the cumbersome log.

Air sorceresses had a lot of control over noise and other distractions in the world. Distractions that could alert the assassins to our actions. But I feared they were already among us, so doing this quietly was essential.

Lady Laurel nodded.

"Good," I said as I lifted my hands into the air. "Because I have a battle spell that will shake that log into sawdust."

Lady Laurel glanced over her shoulder at the hired swords still rushing back and forth, trying to check wagons and bandage injuries. And figure out what happened to their boss, Oz who lay injured and unconscious in the carriage.

Most likely, he had appointed one of the hired swords to take charge in the event he was injured. Probably Farago. I'd seen the two of them deep in conversation several times.

I turned away from the log, hands pointed at the carriage. Allowing only the faintest indigo glow, I cast a protective spell on it and made sure to enchant the doorway. If someone tried to enter that carriage while Lady Laurel and I were dealing with this obstacle, I would know it instantly.

I didn't trust all of these hired swords. I barely trusted Oz Tarrant —and I still had a million questions for him. But with my protector unconscious, I needed to protect myself.

And him.

"Are you ready, princess?" Lady Laurel asked as she held one hand out, palm up toward the sky.

"Ready," I said and turned back toward the log.

"I'll support you with my air magic while you call up that battle spell," she whispered.

Nodding, I lifted my hands into the air, fingers splayed, toes flexing against the dirt road. And summoned battle magic.

The ground beneath the log began to rumble, shaking, casting ripples of movement through the forest and along the road.

Alarming the elemental horses.

Their gold light dimmed again as the stomped and tossed their wispy manes, struggling against their harnesses to escape the magical vibrations.

Bark began to peel off the log, falling onto the road like autumn leaves.

Lady Laurel's burst of air magic roiled across the road, sweeping away the gathering bark and sawdust and softening the tremors.

Her magic quieted the elementals' fidgeting and pawing at the ground with their translucent hooves, gold light almost dark.

By the time the wounded had been tended and bowls of cold grains had been distributed (it was too dangerous to build a fire), my magic had shattered the log where it blocked the road.

Lady Laurel summoned more air magic, buffeting the remaining parts of the log until they glowed white in the dark. Her face was a mask of sweat as she gathered fierce winds that rolled the remnants of the log against the sides of the road.

"Princess?" Mathias called to me. "Lady Laurel...I have some vegetables and grains in broth and bread for you. I warmed the bowls over a couple of lanterns."

When the magic dissipated, Lady Laurel staggered. I grabbed her before she dropped to the ground.

"You...removed the log," said Mathias, sounding surprised.

I nodded, not providing any details. He didn't need to know any more than what his eyes told him.

"The log was rotten inside," I said, turning back to the stocky carriage driver. "It didn't take much to move it."

I cast a quick glance at Lady Laurel. She was exhausted, but she understood that I had drastically downplayed the magic. So the assassins wouldn't know the extent and intensity of our abilities. Depending on who had sold me out at Ereth's court, there were only a few Erethians who knew the level of power I carried as a Thorn sorceress.

"Yes," Lady Laurel said, out of breath. "It was rotten to its center. And decaying. The carriage could have almost driven right through it."

She began to waver and I caught her before she collapsed.

"The mist and swamp gases are making me dizzy, princess," she said as she wrapped her arm around my waist.

Even covering her exhaustion. I was so thankful to have her at my side.

"Easy, Lady Laurel," I said in a soft voice. "Let's get you back to the carriage and out of the mist. I doubt the forest decay is helping either. You need to rest and get out of the night."

"And eat," said Mathias, turning away from the road, two metal bowls and a loaf of bread balanced on a rough wooden board.

Eyes half closed and a smile playing across her lips, Lady Laurel nodded and wiped her forehead with the back of her hand.

"Thank you, my lady," she said.

"Eat some grains and rest a while," I said as I walked her toward the carriage.

Mathias followed, careful not to spill the two bowls of root vegetables or roll the loaf of bread off the rough-hewn board.

I helped Lady Laurel into the carriage and she fell onto the cushioned red seat opposite Oz Tarrant, laying her head against the wall.

I turned back to Mathias whose gaze fell to my skirt, the fabric torn away, up above my knees now, showing my white stockings. He set down the board with the bowl inside the carriage.

"What happened to your clothes, my lady?" he asked, concern on his face.

"Bandages," I said and nodded toward Oz who lay on the other seat. "Oz's wound was large and deep, requiring quite a bit of fabric."

"Rohesia does not deserve you, princess," he said, his expression hardening. "You've sacrificed everything for this prophecy. For Kambria. You certainly don't deserve the likes of Arence Siridean."

Another person with nothing good to say about the Siridean prince.

I frowned. "Why do you say that?"

Oz had already offered his views on the Rohesian prince, but this was the first time I'd heard Mathias share an opinion.

"Because those of us that have worked for the Siridean crown have seen him in action. He only cares about himself. King Daegal is a good man. He's got a couple of good sons worthy of the throne—a throne befitting a princess like you. But Arence isn't one of them. Just so you know, most of the other hired swords and me think that if you must marry that swine, he should have to leave Rohesia and marry you in Ereth."

I liked the sound of that. I wanted nothing more than to return home to my own realm.

"Thank you, Mathias," I said, my eyes getting misty. "Please tell the others how much I appreciate—and share—that sentiment."

Mathias nodded toward the other side of the carriage.

"Oz most of all. The closer we get to Rohesia, the angrier and surlier he gets. I am afraid we may have to tie him to one of the wagons when we reach Rohesia. So, he won't assassinate Prince Arence on sight."

I laughed. I could see Oz lunging at the man the moment he saw him.

"We will have to keep a close eye on him, won't we?" I said and Mathias nodded.

"There's no closer eye on anyone than his eyes upon you, my lady. And honestly, between you and me..." He leaned toward me, his voice barely a whisper. "I think this job has become very personal to him."

My heart pounded faster.

Personal? Oh, how I wanted to ask Mathias what that meant, but I couldn't. Oz had some sort of history with Rohesia. That was probably what Mathias meant by personal.

I glanced over at Oz, tossing and turning beneath that grey blanket, his face a mask of sweat. It gave me a splinter of hope to think that maybe I was the reason this job had become personal to Oz Tarrant, but I knew better than make assumptions. Oz had a lot riding on completing this job. A princely sum of coins and a royal boon to collect. He was responsible for all these hired swords and he got difficult jobs done—regardless of how they made him look. Even the other hired swords on this journey said so.

He'd let everyone else, including me, believe he had slaughtered all of his competition to win this job when in reality, he'd been protecting the castle (and me) all along. I even had questions about Badriyah now. And this nickname of his...the butcher.

But I knew I would never hear the answers from him.

His air of darkness and fear was intentional, but I had just begun to know the man beneath that mystique. He was an enigma, for certain. But I was beginning to doubt that he was the cold-blooded killer that he portrayed.

"Let me know if you need anything else, princess," said Mathias. "Or if Oz needs any further tending, but I think he's already in good hands."

"With mine and Lady Laurel's combined healing magics," I said, climbing into the carriage. "He should be ready to travel tomorrow. Could you bring another bowl for Oz? Just the broth? He'll need some nourishment to get back on his feet."

"Right away, princess," said Mathias with a quick nod. "Without him, we have no hope of reaching Rohesia. Or getting through the Cimmerian Breach."

The thought of that dark, dangerous valley made my blood turn to ice. I'd heard so many scary stories about it. Remnants of worlds long gone prowled this Breach and I never dreamed I would ever travel through it. See its ruins. Feel the swirl of trapped ancient magics. Or hear the call of spirits centuries passed and suspended in time. No stories about them or what became of the places they'd left behind existed. They left no written records.

Only shadows and mysteries. Brought back when this deadly Breach cracked open the world and let them tiptoe back in again as spirits.

Would Ereth look like the Breach one day? Our stories lost, only the bones of our world lying on the surface of ashen soil. In a world with a sun that had faded from the sky. Plunging its survivors into hellish darkness, fighting for survival and a way of life no longer possible.

The thought terrified me.

Mathias rushed off to fill a bowl with broth as I moved over to Oz and sat down beside him, the scent of musk and leather and heat intoxicating as I smoothed his black hair off his damp forehead. The earthen magic plaster I had applied needed time to extinguish any infection—and resulting fever. When his eyes opened, I'd get some broth down him—whether he wanted it or not.

By morning, mine and Lady Laurel's magics would have him on his feet again. He would be weak but on the mend. Ready to leave this ambush behind as we traveled through this hell called the Battleworn Forest. And worse—the Cimmerian Breach beyond it.

IO

For hours, while Lady Laurel slept, I sat with Oz, mopping the sweat from his fiery brow and applying another healing earth poultice to the wound in his belly. He tossed and turned, mumbling things I couldn't understand, only the faintest quiver of lantern light beside him. We didn't dare turn it up—or turn on both lanterns.

Too many people out there wanted us dead.

He lifted his arms, as if fending off attackers, and his right hand clutched at the air behind his head. Reaching for his broadsword in its shoulder sheath, I realized. I had propped against the carriage's other wall. Out of his immediate reach.

Heat radiated from his body. He was getting worse.

I feared that sword thrust had pushed an infection deep inside his body where I couldn't reach it.

Regardless, I had to act.

I laid hands on his bare chest, unable to stop myself from marveling at the sculpted curve and rise of muscles so taut and well-defined across his stomach and torso. He was so beautiful with the finest statue's curves and angles.

Closing my eyes, I pulled in a long, deep breath, preparing to cast a lengthy spell.

I held the breath for a moment and then exhaled in a slow, deep pulse as I began whispering the words to the most powerful battlefield healing spell I knew. One that Erethian healers used after a battle to locate the dying and heal the mages and sorceresses fighting to survive.

The incantation sprang to my lips as a misty blue glow of earthen symbols floated above Oz's head. I let the spell fall into a singsong melody, repeating the words over and over.

Healers called it a sorceress' last spell. Because it was our last hope of survival on battlefields far from home. And I sang the words relentlessly, repeatedly, allowing the blue earthen healing light to cascade around him.

At first, the light clung to his skin and scattered across his body, but after a few rounds of the spell, the symbols gathering power, his body began to absorb the light.

I cast the spell until I was hoarse and my throat was bone dry, continuing until he had absorbed every last glowing symbol of magic I had left to give.

Oz Tarrant had to survive.

Without him, we would never reach Rohesia. I had no wish to end up there, much less marry Arence Siridean, but everything would perish if I gave into my own wants and needs. And that decision was no longer mine to make. I represented an unending line of Thorn royalty. Sorceresses. And I had no right to break that chain at the expense of Kambria. No matter what feelings I harbored or dreams I had.

This procession had to reach Rohesia.

The more magic I expended, the more lightheaded I became until, in the dim glow of lantern light guttering above my head, the world began to spin. With only threads of a spell left on my lips, I was falling.

For a while, everything was quiet. Still. Bathed in cool indigo darkness.

Then Lady Laurel's face hovered above me, eyes wide, mouth pursed, moving soundlessly. I couldn't make out what she was saying because of a painful, persistent buzz hammering the inside of my head. And I could only open my eyes to slits.

Around me, things moved like shadows lit from behind in a thick, oozing darkness. People moved in slow, staccato motions. Lady Laurel. Then Pirin, a sandy-haired Xanthe swordswoman I had only seen from a distance. And finally, Mathias, shouting, lifting me up from the floor of the carriage. Into his arms.

And then I felt soft cushions beneath me. The carriage seat.

Lady Laurel cast magic over me, fingers glowing white as Mathias knelt beside her, eyes wide and fearful. Still, the horrible buzzing was all I could hear.

I turned my head, looking between Lady Laurel and Mathias. At Oz Tarrant. Oz was still, eyes closed, the hushed sound of deep, even breaths filling the remaining muffled silence.

"You know you can't ever drain your well of magic, Annarissa," Lady Laurel lectured, her voice quivering as she continued to cast air battle magic on me. "Don't let go now. And don't let the core of your magic completely drain away. Hold onto it, Annarissa, with all your might!" She shivered. "Or you may never wake up again."

Like the Erethian spell sleepers that had turned to stone.

As I child, I always thought that the stone statues in the grand hall and the royal gardens had been sculptures. Until I heard the stories in training sessions about a handful of sorceresses and mages who sacrificed themselves in battle by draining all of their magic and their sunburst gems. They turned to stone, trapped in an infinite sleep when their magical cores completely emptied.

The royal gardens became their tombs after their sacrifices.

I had always been taught to preserve my magical core, just enough magic for one spell. Whenever I walked the grand hallway or strolled through the royal gardens, I always kept a single spell on my lips and said a prayer for the dead and the lost. The spell sleepers. Who gave everything for Ereth.

"Is she going to be all right?" The warm and bright timbre was Mathias' strong voice.

"Hope so," said Lady Laurel, her voice sounding so far away. "She almost emptied all of her magic."

"Well, she completely healed Oz," said Mathias, motioning behind him. "Look."

"No..."

With shaky footsteps, his chest bare and bandaged with part of my purple of skirt, Oz staggered toward me. He dropped to his knees, a fearful look contorting his features.

"Dammit! Annarissa, what did you do?" His voice was weak, a growl still in it, ice blue eyes angry and narrowed, mouth twisted into a grimace.

The heat of his hand pressed against my face and I wanted to lose myself in his concern. In his touch.

"She healed you, Oz," said Mathias who had moved outside the carriage, letting Oz squeeze beside Lady Laurel. "Brought down the Equalizers who ambushed us, too. Then she stayed with you for hours, bandaging your wounds and healing you."

A host of emotions rushed across his anguished face before he tamped them down into a snarl and glare, but the glassy pain in his eyes betrayed him.

Lady Laurel nodded. "Until infection set in and she expended all of her magic, right down to the last breath of it, to save you."

He bit his lip, his pallor still ashen as he swallowed a breath, and shook his head.

"No," he muttered, stroking the hair out of my eyes so tenderly that tears welled in them. "Annarissa...no. Why would you do that? Someone like you? For someone like me?"

It was like slogging through mud to raise my hand, but I reached up and laid it against his, squeezing.

"To save…the good man—here," I said, the words coming out so slowly and painfully as my hand slid down his arm to his chest.

To his heart.

"I know he is there," I said in a slow whisper. "I feel him in everything you do."

Soon, I would uncover all the events that happened in the village of Badriyah and I would know the truth. I would know whether or not he really was the Butcher of Badriyah.

Moisture gathered in his eyes and clung to his long black lashes, an ache that sank into the depths of those ice blue eyes that I could no longer read.

"Annarissa, think of the prophecy," Lady Laurel cried.

She looked shaken. Worried.

"My two cousins…can still fulfill…prophecy."

Oz's expression brightened and his beautiful face was the image I carried into unconsciousness.

I DREAMED of fields of lavender and roses that stretched from Skystead to Rosebury. Turquoise skies were vivid across Ereth and each field of roses was a different color, brilliant in the warm golden sunlight bathing the fields. Fuchsia, blue, purple, and white. Cyan, yellow, red, and orange. The most beautiful and fragrant blooms I had ever witnessed.

Urn after cobalt urn lined both sides of the throne room, each one filled with more roses than I could count. Roses as fragrant as the lavender oil that burned in the braziers beside them. A grand ball filled the room that sparkled with the finest gowns and robes in cloud-soft, jewel-toned silks adorned with gems and crystals that sparkled against the burn of braziers. Princes from all over Kambria danced in their finest polished armor, arm in arm with their lovers as a quintet of stringed instruments thrummed a waltz. Celebrating the prophecy's fulfillment at last and the return of the sun.

As I gazed around the room, I felt sad because not one single Thorn sister danced in her finest gown with a handsome prince on her arm. But staggered around the throne room stood four stone statues. With a name chiseled into the base of each one.

Annarissa, Genevieve, Carysana, and Arianwen.

Sacrificed. To save Kambria.

My shout echoed out of the carriage as I snapped up from the cushions, the nightmare still visceral and bright.

"Easy," said the silky, dark, and rich voice, rumbling, filling the carriage with its warm timbre. "Lie back down. You still need to rest."

Oz Tarrant knelt beside the seat cushion, back in full black leathers, sword sheath between his shoulder blades. His handsome stubbled face had regained some of its color, those ice blue eyes still so mysterious. I wished I could hear the thoughts rushing through his head right now. But those enigmatic eyes gave nothing away.

"How is your wound?" I asked him.

One corner of his mouth lifted into almost a smile for a moment and then fell.

"Quickly becoming a scar, thanks to you. And just how do I thank someone for my life? That assassin's blade spread a sickness through me. It was infected and would have killed me quick if it hadn't been for your magic, Annarissa. My gratitude feels so hollow in response."

The carriage door opened behind him and Lady Laurel climbed inside. It was still light out. Would we be moving on through the Battleworn Forest now?

"I did what was right," I said. "What was needed. Despite what you might think, you deserved to be healed, Oz."

The troubled look in his eyes told me he didn't believe that.

"Regardless of the stories," I said, staring him right in the eyes. "You are not a monster, Oz Tarrant."

He started to object, but I cut him off.

"I know that's what you want everyone to believe. I don't know if it's to keep your enemies afraid or to keep the rest of Kambria at a distance, but I've seen the man in here." I patted the leather armor over his heart. "He is worth saving."

I wasn't prepared for the smile that lit his face with a warm light that I hadn't seen in him before. Ever. By Ereth, he was the most handsome man I had ever seen. For a moment, that smile took my breath away.

"Well, I thank you, Annarissa Thorn. For everything you did. Now, you rest. When the dark is upon us, we're heading through Battleworn Forest."

"Toward the Breach?" I asked with a gasp.

His smile turned hollow and he nodded.

"I know the magic that lives in those ruins is as dangerous as the creatures suspended there," he said, sounding wary but determined. "And the dark. But we'll get through all of it to the border of Rohesia."

Once we reached the Rohesian border, we still had a long journey eastward. To the edge of Kambria. To the sea where Mirstone Castle had been built into the spiny black cliffs that overlooked the deep blue Sapphire Sea with its wild waves, stretches of flat sand, cool salty air, and sea creatures born out of legend. Horses with hooves and fins that rode the waves. Whales and water spirits with magical voices. And seals that shed their coats and walked on two legs.

I had always wanted to see Mirstone, but not like this. Betrothed to a man who would never love me.

When I looked up, Oz was staring at me with a tenderness in his eyes that I wanted to reciprocate. And a longing that I shared. I wanted to touch him. To risk it all and tell him everything I felt. I sighed. To love him.

But I felt the distance between us growing at the mention of Rohesia's border. He and I both knew that no matter how we felt, one thing had to happen at Mirstone. I had to marry a Siridean prince. That was set in stone.

And staring into Oz's eyes now made me deeply question my

duty, fear it for the first time since I was nine and learned that my husband had already been chosen for me.

Lady Laurel cleared her throat and Oz turned toward her.

She was trembling, holding a folded burlap sack against her chest.

"Mr. Tarrant, we have a problem," she said, her expression darkening.

He glanced at me and then back at Lady Laurel.

"Explain, Lady Laurel," he said, eyes narrowing, brow furrowing.

She thrust the burlap sack at him.

Still looking confused, he stared down at the sack and then back at Lady Laurel. Sighing, he opened it and slid something out.

I gasped, recoiling when I saw the white porcelain mask with its evil, twisted expression. An Equalizer's mask.

Oz glared at the mask. "Where did you find this?"

Lady Laurel looked indignant as she crossed her arms, cheeks flushing.

"The sack was hidden beneath the supplies from Ereth—in the last wagon." She pulled in a nervous breath. "I found it by accident as I was searching for the remainder of root vegetables left from Ereth's supply cache." She gripped Oz's forearm. "Mr. Tarrant, there is at least one assassin hiding among us. One Equalizer."

Oz glanced over at me and then back at Lady Laurel.

"Either the Cimmerian Breach will coax them out." He gritted his teeth, balling his right hand into a fist. "Or the blade of my sword will."

From the fire and fury churning in his face, he meant that.

He glanced over at me again.

"Rest now, Annarissa," he said in a clipped voice as he pushed past Lady Laurel to the carriage doors and shoved the right-side door open. "In an hour, we move out. Just after sunset."

My stomach twisted into knots as he exited the carriage. The next leg of the journey would be more dangerous than the last. The one after that, the most dangerous of all—unless I counted being delivered into my enemy's hands. Ereth and Rohesia had been a war for a century. And the only things keeping the truce in place were dying crops and fading sunlight. The assassins were running out of time. But the world changed at Rohesia's border. The rules changed and so did the consequences.

And maybe by then, we would discover who hired these well-trained professional killers. And why.

Before they succeeded.

II

OUTSIDE THE CARRIAGE, THE SOUND OF WAGONS MOVING INTO A LINE creaked through the mist. The golden glow of three pairs of elemental horses illuminated the edges of the window shields and around the carriage doors. In front of the carriage, harnesses thumped as the six elemental steeds whinnied and dragged their hooves, fighting the push deeper into Battleworn Forest. The sound of their hooves tapped fearfully against the hard-packed dirt, echoing in the stillness, smell of tilled soil and rotting leaves pungent. The elementals probably sensed the shadow creatures that lurked ahead in the fog and green phosphorus glow.

If the elementals got too upset, they would go dark. And eventually retreat back into the ether. Leaving the carriage stranded until the danger had passed. And Lady Laurel and I could conjure more elementals.

Footsteps were heavy around the carriage and along the road as Oz's hired crew checked the elemental's harnesses and leads, the condition of wagon—and the newly repaired carriage wheel. Soon, wagons creaked, boots thumping against wood as the hired swords climbed back aboard the wagons.

"Get ready to move out!" Mathias shouted, his voice distant. "And make sure those elemental horses don't get too stressed. If one fades back into the void in this forest, a wagon gets stranded. And you die. Understand?"

Mathias was somewhere behind the carriage.

Heavy footfalls stopped in front of the carriage doors, loud voices carrying above the din of noise. Probably wagons shifting around loads and people. There were still one or two seriously injured hired swords who needed another day of rest.

"Did you hear me, Oz?" said an insistent but muffled voice outside. "Elementals or humans, I guarantee you some of them will bolt when we hit the Breach. The forces in there are too dark. The magic is too strong."

That was Farago's worried voice. And he was right. Even magical horses got spooked. And this job didn't paid well enough to die for it.

"They knew there was only one way into Rohesia when they accepted this job," Oz said with a growl. "There's no way around the Breach. Everyone knows that—even a dumb Xanthan like me."

Farago's sigh was heavy. "I know, but some of them act like it's the first they've heard of a Breach. And they're Rohesian. They're saying they'll refuse to cross it when the time comes."

"When did this...mutiny get proposed?" Oz demanded with a snarl.

"It reached a fever pitch while you were injured. They thought since I was in charge, I'd just change our route." Farago chuckled. "Or conjure a new one, I think. Possibly with wings. Fools. Did they think a job that paid this much coin would be easy? Or safe?"

A few moments of silence hung in the air as the creak of wagon wheels echoed in the cool green darkness.

"If they want to quit, they'd better do it here," said Oz, his voice sharp. "If we get any deeper into the Battleworn Forest, it'll be too late. Trying to leave the convoy would be suicide."

"Agreed, Oz," said Farago.

"For those staying, tell them to sharpen their blades and keep their heads down. And dammit, tell them to stay in the wagons and keep moving because something dark and wraithlike will take their scalps in this forest. If the Battleworn wraiths don't get them, the spirits of the Breach will devour them whole. Anyone who stops moving—or gets caught out there alone—dies. Period."

Farago's laughter echoed. "I'm not telling them a thing about wraiths and spirits, Oz, or it'll be just you, me, and maybe Mathias delivering a princess to Rohesia. For lots and lots of sweet, sweet coin though."

A pause.

"They're paying us a fortune to save our world—not for delivery work. And you know it, Farago."

Another pause.

"Cheer up. We're just delivering a princess. It's not like she'll be missed. I hear there are more sisters and some cousins if needed."

"Listen up, Farago," Oz growled, his voice dark and threatening. "You don't know shit about her. She's so much more than some stupid royal figurehead. She's smart and kind and fearless. And she's a kick-ass sorceress trained in assault magic. She saved our asses when those assassins attacked and you know it. She made sure those bastards didn't touch us."

"I'd like to touch her." Farago said in a laughing, leering voice that made my skin crawl.

I'd seen Farago staring at me before. And it gave me an unsettled feeling each time, like he'd been watching me since I left Ereth. Undressing me with his eyes.

A commotion echoed outside until something slammed against the carriage. Hard.

"Oz, stop! Oz!"

"Touch her and die," Oz's voice was cold and feral. "That's the only warning you get, Farago."

"Oz...you and me have known each other a while, haven't we?"

A pause.

"A year or two."

"I've helped you with so many jobs—including Badriyah. You siding with a royal wench over me?"

The sound of a fist hitting something soft echoed.

"Shut your mouth, Farago," Oz ordered through gritted teeth. "I won't tell you again. Leave the princess out of this. She's not a trophy. She's one of the reasons that Kambria is still worth saving."

"All right, I take it back," said Farago, sounding like the wind had been knocked out of him. "She's not a royal wench. There, you happy?"

"Be very careful, Farago," said Oz, the threat in his tone and his words clear. "Now, go get that last wagon lined up. We leave as soon as these elementals are secured to the wagons."

Footsteps pounded away from the carriage, behind us, moving back toward the wagons. Quieter steps moved past the carriage. Toward the six elemental horses drawing the carriage.

Apparently, not everyone appreciated my magic or my healing. Or royalty of any kind. Not that I could blame them. The difference in quality of life was staggering. And so were its privileges—until the prophecy. But even then, most of the population saw my sacrifice as a mere inconvenience, not realizing the lonely, barren life I would lead in Rohesia. And I couldn't blame them for feeling that way. I would still have access to fine foods and luxuries that the rest of Kambria had never experienced.

From the beginning, it felt like Farago was either leering at me or seeing me as just another crate in the wagons. Like Oz had. I'd always felt something dark behind Farago's eyes, too, behind his charming smile. Maybe it was his chosen profession? Or maybe it was something darker? Either way, to him, I was still little more than something to trade for coin. Or a woman he thought he had the right to have his way with—royal or not. If he tried to violate me, I would introduce him to my assault magic.

"What was that about?" Lady Laurel remarked, an indignant but worried look on her face.

I shrugged and sat up in the seat.

"Not sure," I replied. "But I plan to keep an eye on Farago."

Lady Laurel nodded. "And so will I. He's more of a beast than I realized. I wonder if that assassin's mask I found belongs to him."

Maybe she was right? I didn't want to find myself alone with this man. Even if he wasn't one of the assassins, he was still dangerous. But I wouldn't hesitate to slam him with my battle magic if he tried to touch me, but Oz's response unsettled me. Oz threatened to kill him. I didn't want drive a wedge between Oz and his hired swords, but a part of me warmed all over to hear him stand up for me like that. And I was grateful.

The carriage lurched forward about a foot and stopped. Wheels creaked as they rolled a little forward again, elementals grunting, not wanting to move ahead. The team of six snorted and pawed at the dry ground. They sounded nervous. Skittish.

Once more the carriage lurched and then halted again.

Finally, Mathias' heavy footfalls thumped up onto the driver's perch on top of the carriage as one of the doors opened. Oz thundered inside and dropped onto the opposite cushion.

"You're looking much healthier, Annarissa," he said. "I hope that means you're feeling better."

I was. The well of my magic was refilling, slower than I liked, but filling just the same. But I also felt heartened by how Oz had ordered his right-hand swordsman to keep his distance from me or risk death. And I hoped that lasted until we reached Mirstone Castle.

I smiled. "I am, thank you. And thank you for looking out for me."

His gaze slipped to the floor and he nodded. Finally, his gaze shifted to the ceiling and he thumped it with his fist. Twice.

"Sun's down. Let's get moving, Mathias!"

"You got it, boss!"

Mathias' muffled voice faded beneath the snap of leather reins as he coaxed the elementals forward with some clicking noises and another snap of the reins.

The carriage rolled forward and shimmied into motion, wheels scraping past the remains of the log that still littered the road. The carriage made it through as the elementals settled into step and found their stride, taking us deeper into the Battleworn Forest.

Behind us, each wagon scraped against the tree trunk's remains, their teams of elementals neighing and stomping their hooves, not wanting to squeeze through that opening. But wagon wheels creaked forward, the wagons lumbering onward behind the carriage.

When I looked up, Oz was studying me. A thoughtful expression touched his face, almost playful.

"What?" I asked finally.

"I must have been a little delirious when you were tending me," he said, rubbing his hand against his forehead.

I frowned. "You were, but why do you mention it?"

His gaze moved around the carriage but returned to my face.

"Because I am a little foggy on everything that happened, I wonder if you could answer a question for me?" he began.

"Of course," I said with a nod.

Lady Laurel pretended to read a book that she took from the small valise at her feet, but her gaze kept flicking up from her book to me and then to Oz.

I reached down and felt my own personal valise still where I had left it when I climbed aboard the carriage in Ereth. It sat untouched and unopened against my feet.

He leaned across the carriage toward me, his darkly handsome face so serious.

"I would swear that I saw a dreamfly in this carriage."

My eyes widened and I stared at him, a million thoughts rushing through my head.

Had he been awake when I brushed my lips against his? When the gold light of my magic had sparked? Like a dreamfly. What could I say?

I inhaled sharply, twisting the fabric of my torn purple skirt in one hand as I struggled to explain what happened.

"A dreamfly?" I repeated, stalling.

He nodded, those ice blue eyes brightening. "Yes, a dreamfly."

"The carriage door had been open for some time," I said finally, my gaze moving toward the doors. "There were some dreamflies flitting around us outside, so most likely, one flew into the carriage."

I felt the first blush warm my cheeks.

It wasn't an outright lie, but I was misleading him. I had no idea what that gold spark had been and I wondered whether it had come from a dreamfly or my magic somehow.

But I wasn't sure. I didn't believe in those childhood fairy tales.

His gaze lingered on me, the corners of his mouth quirking upward and then falling again.

"Did you see it?" he asked.

"What? The dreamfly?"

He looked amused now.

"Yes, Annarissa. The dreamfly."

He could tell I was stalling and misdirecting him. Was he trying to get me to admit that I had almost kissed him.

Almost.

"I confess," I said finally with a sigh, watching his expression intensify, the anticipation burning in his eyes. "I saw a gold spark, but I never saw the dreamfly. If that's what it was. Probably remnants of my earth magic."

At that, he nodded, the lightness leaving his expression. Plausible. To a blademaster that didn't use magic. He sat back against the cushions and adjusted his gloves. Back to his gruff, dark self.

I was relieved that explanation had quieted his curiosity. But I still couldn't help wondering if he had seen (or felt) me brush my lips against his. And why there had been a magical spark between us.

Once Oz settled back in his seat, looking lost in thought, Lady Laurel settled into her book, but I was restless. Worried about getting through Battleworn Forest—and unmasking the assassin hiding among us. So many stories, but I was more worried about assassins than the forest spirits.

Supposedly, a great battle late in the Hundred-Year Sundering had been fought in these haunted, poisoned woods. The Battle of ShadowGlen Forest had been one of its the bloodiest battles. Hundreds of dead on both sides. Sorceresses and sword masters fell in droves along with mages and hired blades that day.

King Onyx lost two of his four sons in that battle and Daegal, next in line, became the heir apparent for Rohesia's throne. When Onyx died later at the front, along with Daegal's last brother, Daegal became king. His dead brothers' children could only become king if Daegal's bloodline was wiped out. But those children were still spares for the prophecy. I had heard little about these cousins to the Siridean throne. Just that they were spares to fulfill the prophecy should Daegal lose any of his sons. If the rumors about Tiryn Siridean were true, then Arianwen would be betrothed to one of them.

"Are there really trapped, murderous spirits of the war dead inhabiting this glen?" Lady Laurel asked, snapping her book closed.

She had directed her question to Oz.

He reached over and slid the wooden shield away from the window to Laurel's right. And then the one to my left.

In the misty grey of the darkening forest, glowing with pockets of green phosphorescence, ghosts moved in the night. Armored sword wielders fought robed ghosts clutching ghostly fireballs as other strange lights danced along the ashen ground. They appeared all around us as colored lights shot through the mist, sound of metal clashing against metal. Swords flashed in the growing darkness.

The carriage passed through ghost after ghost on the road, even spooking the elementals as they began to trot, fighting the reins. A dank, sulfury smell hung in the air like an old root cellar filled with old animal hides and dead birds.

"I've been told that the secret of surviving Battleworn Forest," said Oz, gripping the edge of the window's wooden shield. "Is not to stop. For anything. The spirits will chase us. Try to attack us as they relive the battles all over again. But if we keep moving, they can't harm us."

It seemed like a simple, straightforward approach.

"I told each wagon and Mathias to keep going no matter what," said Oz, his gaze divided between the ghosts and Lady Laurel. "We break a wheel, we drag the damned along the road and keep going. Reins get tangled, we keep going. Harness gets busted, we keep going."

I studied him for a moment.

"What happens if we stop?"

His face got a little pale.

"Wraiths would overwhelm us," he said. "Overpower us fast. Drain our magic and our blood. Trap us here as one of them, fighting this battle for eternity."

The thought of that was chilling.

Oz thumped the ceiling with his fist.

"Faster, Mathias!" he shouted. "Drive those elementals hard until we're past the pond!"

"The pond?" I said, glancing out the window as spirits and trees and mist whipped past the windows.

Oz nodded. "When you see the pond on the left, we'll be close to the end of Battleworn Forest. And close to the curve in the east-west road. The road will begin to shift north as it heads into the valley. And the Breach. Once we pass Rohesia's border, the road slopes sharply north. Through the mountain pass headed southeast into Mirstone."

"So, we're still several days out from Rohesia?" Lady Laurel replied.

Oz nodded.

A disembodied face appeared in the carriage window, startling me.

I gasped and pulled back.

With a moan, the spirit stepped through the window. Into the carriage.

With dead eyes and ruined plate armor, it turned toward me, ghost sword raised.

Oz lunged off the seat cushion, long knife in hand, and plunged it into the ghostly figure's chest.

The spirit shattered in a burst of mist and dissipated.

"Knife blade is made of iron," said Oz, gripping it as he knelt in front of me, almost against my legs. "Had it made just for Battleworn Forest."

"Thank you," I said, still shaking.

His gaze fell to the remains of my purple skirt. With its short, frilly purple petticoat showing underneath now. And my white stockings.

I admit, I enjoyed his gaze on my bare stockings. He had admired my legs before.

"I used the remaining length of my skirt to bandage your sword wound," I said, running my hands across my silky white stockings as I straightened the petticoat.

His attention made me feel warm all over.

"I'm sorry you had to ruin your skirt to bandage my wounds," he said, sounding distracted, his gaze still on my stockings.

I flexed my feet, pointing my toes, and his pupils widened, his breaths deepening. My short black boots sat beside my valise.

"It's fine, Oz," I replied. "I will change into fresh clothes as soon as we make camp again."

His eyes narrowed. He didn't seem to appreciate my skirt lengthening.

He shuffled back to his seat and slid the long knife into his boot sheath.

"Do these wooden shields stop the ghosts?" Lady Laurel asked.

Oz shook his head. "No, the shields are to block conventional attacks. Sword thrust or a hail of arrows. Not ghosts or spirits. I need the shields open right now. To see the wraiths coming. We're going to deal with a few like that one before we're free of the forest, so be on guard."

THE JOURNEY through the dark Battleworn Forest felt like it went on forever with endless stretches of mist, infinite numbers of barren, skeletal trees sliding past the window, and the number of ghosts multiplying as the carriage trundled onward. Out of the forest and toward the valley. And the Cimmerian Breach.

With the passing of every season, as the world got darker, more places like these haunted woods rose out of the devastation. Abandoned villages became havens for cutthroats and robbers. Battlefields raised specters of the dead, dooming them to fight for eternity. And places where great violence happened—like Badriyah—became repositories for shadowy magical resonance with the darkest spirits drawn to these places because of the carnage. And wraiths that had entered the world through the deaths and growing darkness—like so many other creatures that had invaded Kambria—created breaches between the magical realms and the physical world. Like the Cimmerian Breach.

There were worse horrors than hired assassins and their traitorous benefactors. Magical and spirit abysses collected in the hollows of violence and war, creating dangerous buildups of energy and wild spells that became unpredictable. The worst of these kinds of voids was a Breach with the Cimmerian Breach being the deadliest so far. I had no idea what lurked on the other side of the border either. In Rohesia.

Oz seemed to grasp the danger, but the hired swords he'd been thrown in with seemed ignorant of what lay on the very roads they had traveled to reach Ereth for this job.

Another ghost in tattered misty purple mage robes burst through the doors, fireballs clutched in each hand.

Oz thrust the long knife forward and the mage dissipated into smoke.

The carriage picked up speed, careening along the road. Into the first serpentine curve. The elementals were up to the run, but if they feared for their existence, they would vanish.

The sharp angle threw me into Lady Laurel who put her hand up against the carriage wall, keeping us from slamming against it. Oz had both arms out, palms up as he braced himself between the walls.

The carriage lurched out of the curve and I slid back to my side of the seat. I grabbed the hand rail to keep me there.

As the conveyance rumbled over bumps in the road, a ghostly battle raged around us. The sickly green glow illuminated the spirits against the dark tree trunks and thickening mist. Dozens and dozens of swords wielders fought ghostly mages and sorceresses. An army of spirits battled through the woods and smoky green haze.

"What keeps these spirits fighting like this?" Lady Laurel asked, looking horrified as she glanced out the windows.

Oz sighed. "Wraiths. They entered Kambria through the pockets of growing dark and rage and magic and created a breach. Then enslaved this battlefield. And all its restless spirits."

That made my heart ache. This was a later battle in the Hundred-Year Sundering, but there was no telling how long these poor souls had been fighting this same battle. Over and over. While a wraith gathered strength and power from their clashes. And unless someone slayed the wraith and closed the breach, the fighting would go on forever. And ever.

"Can't we help them?" I asked, turning toward Oz. "At least slay the wraith and close the breach to free them?"

Oz shook his head. "Unfortunately, my lady, if we stop, the captive spirits would consume us. The wraith is too powerful with all these spirits at its command and control."

"If we had a silver sword, I could cast a mirror spell to reveal its heart," I said. "And we could slay it. Release these souls."

He nodded toward the window. "Nothing would give me greater pleasure, my lady. But to get to the wraith, we would need an army of hired swords with a unit of assault sorceresses protecting us."

I bowed my head. Feeling awful for these poor trapped souls.

"Once the prophecy is fulfilled, perhaps the return of the sunlight will weaken the wraiths' breaches. Force them to return to where they came from."

"I hope you're right," I said.

Two armored ghosts leaped into the carriage, ending the conversation.

Oz was on his feet, driving that long knife forward until the first one exploded in a fine white mist.

The second ghost thrust a sword into Oz's chest.

He dropped the long knife, his body flailing against the wraith's power flooding through this ghost.

I lunged for the knife as Oz's body began to shake, his pallor fading.

Lifting the knife, I shoved it into the ghost's side. It shattered into a shower of gold light.

Oz dropped to his knees, panting, trying to gather his breath.

That's when I saw how deadly these ghosts were to living and breathing people.

Gently, I laid the knife's grip in his hand as I knelt in front of him and held his fingers around the knife. It took him a moment to realize it was there and grasp it.

"Oz, are you all right?"

He nodded as the color returned to his face.

"This...is why we can't stop to help them, Annarissa. Without—magical shielding, they'd absorb all of our life forces."

The heat of his hand washed over me and I stared into his eyes, into the crisp blue depths of his gaze that hadn't left my face since I returned the knife. I saw the desire burning in his eyes and I hoped that he felt my own flame churning. I wanted him. I needed him. And I wanted to get past the unseen mask he wore, the walls he'd put around his heart, keeping everyone out.

"Look out!" Lady Laurel cried.

A ghost in decayed mage's robes slipped through the window behind me.

Gritting his teeth, Oz rose on his knees and thrust the iron knife blade into the ghost's chest. It exploded around us in a burst of white light.

Turning, Oz held out his hand to me. I put my hand in his fever-hot hand and got to my knees.

He eased me backward to the seat cushion and I returned to my seat, my gaze still locked with his as I tried to slip into the depths of those eyes. But just when I felt that he and I had connected on some level, he turned away, moving back to his seat. He slid the knife into his boot and leaned his head against the wall. Watching both windows for any sign of movement.

For ghosts. Or the wraith controlling these restless spirits.

After a few minutes, he leaned forward, glancing out the windows, but a grimace soon touched his face. He pounded the carriage ceiling with his fist twice.

"Mathias!" he shouted. "How far to the pond?"

"I can see it in the distance!" Mathias shouted. "Elementals are still running hard and strong."

"Is Mathias okay up there?" I asked.

"He's got two hired swords beside him," said Oz. "And we're almost to the pond."

On hearing that, Oz settled back in his seat again, but his muscles were corded, his expression dark, mouth pressed into a taut line as his hand hovered near his boot where that iron-bladed long knife rested in its sheath.

"With the pond almost behind us," he said, his gaze moving from me to Lady Laurel. "We'll be out of the forest in no time. We can make camp and rest up for the journey through the Breach's dark valley."

A journey that would make this one look like child's play.

I dreaded the Breach. The magical creatures inside could tempt you away from your life and lead you to your death. They could be anything from wraiths to sirens to old gods. Inside these trapped magics, footpaths and caves became labyrinthian mazes where you get lost forever.

And the magics inside were unpredictable. The forces inside could stop your heart and take your soul. Enslave you. Or turn you into a monster. And the ruins held traps, secrets, and illusions left by people who disappeared from Kambria long ago. I had heard that the entire Cimmerian Breach was bathed in thick, heavy darkness that required lanterns to traverse. And somehow, we had to get past all of that to the other side.

Soon, when Rohesia and Ereth got their seaports operational again, damaged during attacks, a faster route to each realm would return, one that eliminated these lengthy overland journeys. And their dangers. Xanthan ships still traveled to Rohesia and Ereth to trade, but their goods were too expensive for most villagers.

By the time the carriage passed the pond, Oz had used his long knife on four more deadly ghosts that had stepped into the carriage.

I had never learned any spells to fight ghosts or wraiths, so my magic—like Lady Laurel's—was no help to Oz. He had to keep a sharp lookout and dispatch the apparitions as soon as they arrived. Or they would drain our life forces in moments.

By the time the forest began to lighten around us, the number of ghosts diminishing, Oz had shattered five more.

The mist began to recede, the green phosphorescence dissipating as the sun cast first light across the fragile greyness that clung to the chill and receding night as the road evened out.

And like a burst of fire, the carriage emerged out of Battleworn Forest and onto the road that began to gently shift northward as we moved toward the valley. Toward Rohesia. Through the Cimmerian Breach.

The grey sky had a rosy blush to it as the sun's delicate rays reached across the night and tried to warm the world. The light seemed tired, worn out, and faded, but the sun still rose every morning. Still cast its light across the fields of crops. Giving me hope that we would fulfill the prophecy and bring back the sun's rich, vibrant light and bright hues that we had taken for granted.

"We're out!" Oz cried, collapsing against the seat cushion as the elementals slowed to a walk.

Oz's brow was sweaty, long black hair falling against his

shoulders. Much of his hair had been pulled into a knot at his crown with a black leather cord. The beard shadow that covered his jaw and chin made his eyes look so intense and the dark stubble around his mouth framed those full lips. His muscular, sculpted body made him look more like a work of art than a butchering brute. His black leather armor hugged his lean body, its lines and curves making me want to explore underneath that black leather.

Now, we could make camp and I could escape the cloying confines of this carriage for a while. And maybe get to know Oz Tarrant better? Without an argument.

MATHIAS DROVE the carriage along the road toward the north. Where the Cimmerian Breach caused the road to dip sharply down toward a cold, dark valley. The road narrowed at the bottom of the hill and snaked through the Breach's ancient ruins filled with unknown entities and creatures. I had never wanted to enter the Cimmerian Breach, but to the courageous and adventurous, it held treasures and magical gifts only found in this valley.

If they lived long enough to receive them.

It seemed like forever until Mathias thumped the top of the ceiling.

"Boss, found a wooded area just off the road," he said, his voice tinny as it traveled through the hailing-horn. "It's a safe distance from the Breach. Good place to circle the wagons and rest."

"Proceed, Mathias," Oz shouted into the horn.

Mathias snapped the reins, yelling commands to the elementals, but they had a tendency to do what they wanted and instead of obeying the driver. They plodded along at their own pace no matter how much Mathias shouted and prodded them.

The carriage passed a wagon or two along the road. I wondered where the wagons had come from and whether or not they had braved the Breach on the way to wherever they were headed. Had they turned around to avoid it. Most of the people in the wagons looked ill-prepared to battle whatever lurked in the Breach. Most likely they had come from some nearby village, heading away from the Battleworn Forest and the Breach.

We passed three more wagons before the carriage turned right, the ground rough and the trees almost bare until I felt grass beneath the wheels.

After a bumpy few feet, the sun shaded by tall trees with a handful of amber and gold leaves still on their branches, the carriage stopped. Mathias thumped across the top of the carriage and down to the ground. He opened the carriage door.

"All three wagons accounted for, Oz. We'll release the elementals and build a meal fire to heat the last of our cooked grains and vegetables. We have enough supplies for one more large pot of broth and grains that should last us three days if we're careful. And enough bread to get us to Rohesia, thanks to Queen Ambren."

Mother loved her bread. And Ereth bakers made some of the best yeasty bread in Kambria. Merchants traveled for days to purchase our bread—even the Xanthans crossed the inlet and docked at Skystead's port to barter goods for bread. Mother knew how much I loved Erethian bread, too, so she sent enough to cover most of the journey. I had learned how to bake bread as a child, so I would have to bake my own bread once I reached Rohesia.

"That's good news, Mathias," said Oz with a nod. "Take care of it. Make sure all the hired swords eat first. You, too. Farago and I will eat after they eat."

Mathias smiled. "You got it, boss. I'll put everyone to work securing the camp while I get the meal fire going. I'll eat when you eat."

"Lady Laurel and I will eat last as well," I said.

Oz and Mathias stared at me a moment.

"But princess—"

"The hired swords come first," I said, cutting him off.

"Thanks, Mathias," said Oz who turned to me. "And thank you, princess—Annarissa."

Mathias gave Oz a sharp nod and headed away from the carriage.

I stretched my legs and reached for my boots, slipping my stocking feet back into them.

"I am going to stretch my legs," I said and stood up, valise on my shoulder.

Made from rugged Xanthan wool and dyed royal purple, the valise was lined in silk and carried all the little things I still cared about.

Oz snapped to his feet as Lady Laurel stretched and rose from the seat, valise in hand.

"Princess, you really shouldn't go out there unescorted," he said and glanced at Lady Laurel. "Will your lady-in-waiting be accompanying you?"

Worry burned in his eyes.

"I won't leave the wagon circle, Oz, you have my word."

I saw him fighting back the urge to order me to obey, but he bit his lip and swallowed the commanding tone.

"Annarissa," he said, a forced calm in his voice. "As long as you stay in the circle and don't wander off behind wagons or into the forest alone, I..."

He stopped abruptly. Was he about to say that he would allow it? Was he about to make demands or order me around like a child?

I stared at him a moment, my brows furrowing, waiting for him to shout an order at me.

"You what, Oz?" I asked finally when he didn't speak.

He sighed. "I won't...worry. But please—stay in the circle. I don't know the character of these hired swords. Some of them may wish you ill. Some may want to sully you because of your beauty. And one of them is an assassin."

I liked his use of the word worry. I liked that he was worried. And that he thought I was beautiful. It warmed my heart to hear him say that to me.

Regardless, it was a fair request. With an assassin out there that no one had yet unmasked, it was dangerous to leave camp and the sight of the people protecting me. Lots of Kambrian factions wanted me dead. They didn't want the prophecy fulfilled, believing that Ereth would gain an unfair advantage. And they didn't want Rohesia, the kingdom of swords, to be tainted by magic. Others didn't want Ereth, the kingdom of magic, to be tainted by swords. I was an assault sorceress, but I could still get ambushed.

I stepped toward him and laid my hand on his forearm, squeezing, enjoying the warmth of his skin against my fingers.

"I appreciate your concern, Oz. I will stay in the circle and walk only around the camp."

His gaze fell to my stockings. And moved back to my face.

"Would you like me to have Mathias bring down one of your trunks? So you can change clothes?"

I squeezed his forearm again. "Thank you for your kindness. That would be wonderful. After he's eaten, I'll change clothes."

He nodded and laid his hand on top of mine. The heat of his hand enveloped me and I wanted to bath in it. Bath in his eyes and the heat of his body.

"If any of those mercenaries tries to touch you," he said, an edge in his silky warm voice, "use your battle magic. Or shout for me. I'll kill them."

That worried me. I had already heard him threaten Farago if he dared touch me.

"I will call for you if I'm in danger, Oz, thank you," I said.

He nodded and opened the carriage door for me. A gentleman lived somewhere inside him, along with the poise and manners of someone familiar with courtly circles.

Reluctantly, I let go of his arm and headed outside.

12

Daegal's balls! She insisted on going out there alone. With all of those wolves. Hired swords. Mercenaries I didn't hire and never got a chance to investigate—much less approve. They came from all over Kambria and all of them had different motivations. But one goal: coin. And lots of it. Regardless, I was stuck with them. Forced to trust them to watch my back.

And hers.

Made me anxious as hell.

Farago walked past the carriage, a smirk on his face as I climbed out into the almost chilly air. He always looked like he was up to something. And usually, he was. He carried a small load of tinder in his left arm and rested his hand on the sheath at his right hip, black leather armor a little worn and faded around the edges and seams. He handed Mathias the tinder who laid it in the fire pit and stacked a bundle of kindling on top, building a meal fire in the center of the makeshift camp.

At the edge of the fire pit, the others unloaded supplies for the short stop. The camp looked dark, almost felt colder after Lady Laurel released the elemental horses back into wherever they came from—I didn't understand magic. The air smelled gritty and cool, quickly warming with the fragrant scent of wood smoke from Mathias' crackling meal fire. A hint of the broth's savory Xanthan spices hung on the breeze. Peppery. Brackish. Tomatoey. A bit of nutty garlic. A hint of camphor. It tasted like home.

My heart pounded with a rush of heat when I saw Annarissa strolling along the edge of the camp in front of the wagons and woods, Lady Laurel beside her. Their clothes looked dusty and creased, battleworn, especially the length of Annarissa's skirt. To think a princess of her stature had torn up that expensive skirt for me. But I worried about the leering eyes upon her. And whether one of them was stupid enough to act on it. If they dared touch her, they'd get my blade through their gut.

The trees along the road to Rohesia were young and spindly, grey trunks hard to make out against grey skies and misty rain that blanketed the hilly terrain. But rain and clouds obscured the horizon, allowing the three wagons and ironwood carriage to blend into the background. From everything but Equalizers. I knew them well. I had killed enough of them—and they were ruthless.

They never took prisoners. Only trophies which meant body parts.

Annarissa didn't know about the massacre they had planned at Skystead. They had already managed to get past the castle gate and were on the grounds when I got there. If I hadn't killed them, all twelve in the guise of that competition, they'd have hidden away in the royal chambers and slit the throats of her sisters and mother the queen before Annarissa even boarded that carriage. And that death squad of Equalizers I encountered on the castle road would have hunted her down and eliminated her. Along with the rest of the convoy and all hope of fulfilling the prophecy.

Of course, killing them all made me look like a monster. But I hadn't cared what people thought of me for a long time. Besides, scared people left me alone. It was better this way—even if she hated me. The thought of that made me wince though.

Still, one of the Equalizers had infiltrated this crew and left his or her mask for us to find. Taunting us. Letting us know we weren't safe. Part of their terror tactics.

Letting me, the convoy leader know that she wasn't safe. And that thought continued to ache through me.

I had doubled the watch. With rogues that knew how to walk in the shadows. I could only hope that they remained loyal to Ereth and me. And Princess Annarissa. Like Mathias Vorton and for the most part, Farago Daleon.

Farago had worked other jobs with me before—including Badriyah. We had been paid a king's ransom for that job. It was ugly work and had soured my desire to continue slaving away for the guild—any guild. It was the job that made me walk away from that life. Seek new opportunities—like escorting a beautiful princess to an empty, vacuous life in Rohesia.

It made me sick.

But Farago stayed with the guild, at least for a while until it even became too much for him and he walked away. I had reasonable trust in the man, but he had a cruel streak in him (that I first witnessed at Badriyah). He loved to control people. And he wanted to take Annarissa's virtue with a meaningless roll in the hay. Thought it gave him some kind of power. I made it clear to the rogue that he'd never touch her with me in charge of this convoy. Hope the message got through his thick, selfish skull.

He was a reminder of all the things I once did for coin—and it was a long list. No job had been too small or too bloody.

I'd been on my own in Snowmelt since I was eleven when my mother took up with a worthless thief who hated having me around. Damn my father for dying! I'd already been knocked around by the other men she'd been with, but her new beau demanded she choose: me or him. So, she chose him. After that, I raised myself in the streets of Snowmelt, a busy Xanthan seaport. Where I learned to swindle people out of coins, lift coin purses, and steal food from the markets. And use a sword.

Until I had enough skills to join a guild.

I had just turned fifteen when she finally left the brutal bastard. She located me on Snowmelt's streets, begging me to come home (she needed my coin). Like hell I would. When she found work as a seamstress, I stopped hearing from her. Just as well. I knew nothing about her or my father's family, just that he'd been Rohesian. And captain of the king's guard. Killed in an ambush that nearly wiped out the royal family.

After that, I moved from guild to guild, training and honing my sword skills, gathering experience and respect until I got into the largest and top thieves guild in Xanthe. In Snowmelt, guild was code for gang. I'd been born in Rohesia, but growing up in Snowmelt was hard. Not a place to raise a child. And I'd raised myself. My mother lost all interest in me when she realized she couldn't manipulate me into bringing her coin. She'd never shown me much love or affection anyway, reserving that for the men she brought home.

I hadn't spoken to her in a decade. Not since I was fifteen.

Annarissa walked around the camp's circumference in slow, measured steps, those shapely legs and white stockings so enticing. I wanted to run my hands up and down the length of her legs and slowly peel down those silky stockings. Slide my hands beneath that frilly purple petticoat that peaked out from underneath her torn purple skirt. And make love to her. Hold her in my arms for a lifetime.

And save her from Prince Arence, that selfish prick she was fated to marry.

Farago walked away from the meal fire as the others carried the big iron pot over to the roaring flames, but it paled against Annarissa's golden beauty. His gait had purpose as he crossed his arms and—

I bristled.

And walked toward Annarissa.

All around her, hired swords watched her every movement as they worked or rested. She didn't seem to notice. And she wasn't afraid. She had no idea how beautiful she was or how bright her beacon burned among this crew of misfits who kept to the shadows. And had never been around royalty before, much less this close to a young woman of Annarissa Thorn's caliber. A woman who cared about everyone, regardless of their station. Something that had already surprised and stunned this crew whose loyalty to her was growing.

Like mine.

The guild taught me everything about royalty, but most of these hired blades were independents. Many of them wanted to do the job they signed up for and save the world. Some were good people, but a few—like Farago—only wanted what he could take. For sport. Like the princess' virtue. Something I would never do. He seemed to think it was okay to steal anything he wanted. He'd left the guild behind, but the guild hadn't left him. Not yet anyway.

I stepped away from the carriage, clinging to the forest's morning shadows as I followed Farago at a distance when his path crossed Lady Laurel's and Annarissa's path. I moved close enough to hear what Farago had to say to this beautiful, innocent princess. Close enough to be at his throat with my blade in a heartbeat if he touched her.

"Good morning, princess," said Farago, bowing until his sword hilt scraped the ground. "How are you faring?"

She turned, a smile setting her porcelain face alight, those blushed bow-shaped lips so enticing as she greeted him. Her eyes were like summer along Xanthe's coast when the sunset turned the horizon citron gold and fiery orange against dusky amethyst clouds. Where the sun still warmed the coast and melted the mountain snowpack every spring.

"A little stiff and a little claustrophobic," she said with a smile that burned right through my heart. "But well, thank you. How are you, Farago?"

She called him by name. That would endear her to the self-centered mercenary who believed that every woman with breath and a pulse desired him. Including this alluring young princess that had caught Farago's interest.

And if he touched her, it would be the death of him.

He knew that she was hands off. And I would cut his off if he tried anything untoward with her. Besides, he only wanted to bed her and brag that he had bedded a princess. To feed his overblown ego, the braggart. I warned him not to touch her.

"I am well, too, thank you," said Farago, still bent in that deep, exaggerated bow like he had probably imagined courtiers bowed to royalty.

Lady Laurel looked unimpressed.

Farago had never been this close to royalty before. He'd told me that enough times since the first time he saw Annarissa.

"Princess," he said, straightening. "What happened to your skirt?" He smiled. "Not that I mind this lovely new look with those fancy and attractive stockings."

I wanted to tear him apart for leering at her stockings. Her legs.

Annarissa responded by shifting the still-long sides of her skirt forward and covered her legs. She didn't like him looking at them apparently.

"Oz's wound was serious, requiring immediate care," she said. "So, I used the fabric of my skirt as bandages. As soon as my legs have stopped cramping, I will put on a more suitable skirt."

Lady Laurel stepped forward, shielding Annarissa. Making me smile.

"Mr. Tarrant has arranged for our trunks to be temporarily unloaded, allowing the princess to change clothes." She glanced back at Annarissa. "We should probably see if that has been done. Come, my lady, and we'll get a more suitable wardrobe for you."

"Please excuse us, Farago," said Annarissa, walking closer to her lady-in-waiting.

Still covering her legs from Farago's overly attentive gaze.

She had reacted differently when I asked about her skirt,

stretching out and rubbing her legs. Had she been inviting me to look or did she just feel comfortable in my presence?

I still had hazy memories of her leaning over me, so close that her face almost touched mine. And the world sparked gold. Had it been a dreamfly? Or had she cast more magic on me? I sighed. Or was it something else? The spark of something between us that I wanted desperately?

I glared at Farago as he watched her walk away, a hungry expression on his face, in his eyes. I wanted to slit his throat for looking at her like that. But the princess' lady-in-waiting had controlled the situation. I was grateful that a woman of her experience was with Annarissa. Getting her away from people like Farago.

Before I killed him.

Bowing, Farago turned and moved back to the meal fire.

I hurried around the camp in the other direction. To make sure that Annarissa had no trouble getting to her things. Or didn't receive unwanted attention from anyone else who dared to leer at those white stockings.

13

It hadn't felt good—not like a bonfire on a cold night when Oz admired my legs. Both times, I wanted more of his attention. I wanted to feel the heat of his hands against my bare legs, his fingers rolling the silky stockings down my calves, and off my toes. I wanted to feel him stroking my body, the weight of him against my bare skin. I wanted to feel his touch as a woman, not as a virgin princess likely to stay that way until I died. Prince Arence would never touch an Erethian sorceress. Besides, the thought of his hands—like Farago's —against my skin made me shudder.

The last thing I wanted was to lose my virginity to a man as bigoted and selfish as Prince Arence. Much less bear a brood of his heirs like a brood mare in constant heat.

But I wanted Oz Tarrant in ways I didn't even understand. My body understood. And it ached for his touch.

I was grateful for Lady Laurel's acuity in sensing my discomfort and spiriting me away from that mercenary. Back to the safety of the carriage. And for the first time since this journey began, I was grateful for its protection.

When we got back to the carriage, the doors were still open. In front of it sat one of my brown leather traveling trunks. I smiled. And Oz Tarrant carrying the second one off the carriage's top rack. He set it down beside the first one in the grass and turned to climb back up to retrieve the third one. But I grasped his arm.

His breath quickened as he turned toward me, those blue eyes burning in the grey haze of mid-morning. His long black hair looked so shiny against the wash of lantern light coming from inside the carriage. I wanted to run my fingers through it. Undo the knot of hair at his crown and let it cascade against my cheeks. He smelled like soap and leather and musk and I wanted to press my face against his chest and breathe in his scent.

"Something wrong, princess? I mean, Annarissa?"

I shook my head, rubbing his arm, feeling the flex and tense of those sleek, sculpted muscles. Wanting to run my hands across his body and explore the length of it.

"Did I get the wrong trunk?" he asked, those ice blue eyes like a frozen mountain stream.

But the heat of his body was like the summer swelter gathering within the castle walls as the Festival of Lights burned across the night sky and bonfires roasted meat and root vegetables brushed with oil and garlic.

"No," I said, my smile widening. "These two are more than enough. I'll find something more than suitable in one of them. Thank you."

To my surprise, a full-on smile lit his face. There was no darkness behind it. No hesitation. No mask, I realized. He had let his guard down enough that he finally felt comfortable sharing a smile with me.

"I must say, I will miss that purple petticoat and those white stockings, but I also understand about maintaining propriety."

I didn't want to take my hand away from his arm, so I kept gently stroking it.

"As much as I regret having to change clothes," I said and nodded toward the meal fire. "I realize that out there, the world is different."

His eyes brightened, that smile lingering longer than I had ever seen it. Until finally, he lowered his gaze to the ground and nodded.

"When you've chosen a garment, let me know and I will put up the window shields and stand guard at the door until you've changed."

He was being as protective as Lady Laurel. Perhaps even more so. And I found his protectiveness intoxicating. It made my pulse race and my breath quicken. I patted his arm and let go.

"You are too kind, Oz. I thank you for your assistance. And your protection."

He looked down at me, the burn in his eyes sizzling through me. And I wanted to share that heat with him.

"I am honored, Annarissa," he said in a quiet voice and stepped away from the carriage. "I'll leave you to sort through your clothing in private."

He was no more than five feet away as he turned his back to me, giving me all the privacy he could while still watching over me. And by Ereth, I found that so attractive. Him so attractive.

With a key that Lady Laurel kept in her coin purse, I knelt in the grass, unlocked both trunks, and opened the lids. I had more clothes than a woman needed in her lifetime, so I had only packed my favorites and the ones I would need for official functions. The rest I gave to my sisters. Inside one of the trunks was every single skirt, blouse, and dress that I loved, many in the royal purple of Ereth. I had other colors, too.

And I knew exactly the skirt and blouse I wanted. A sheer gold blouse and a pale blue skirt that matched Oz Tarrant's eyes. With matching petticoat and pale gold stockings that I would have to figure out how to uncover once we were back inside the carriage. Only for his eyes.

I gathered the items from both trunks while Lady Laurel

retrieved two more blankets from the second trunk. She laid them inside the carriage as I stacked the clothing together and closed both trunks. Locking them. I handed the key back to Lady Laurel and she returned it to her coin purse that hung on a thin gold chain belt around the waist of her long lacy-sleeved lavender gown.

"Oz?" I called.

He whirled back around, his eyes still bright with a lighthearted expression.

"That was fast, m'lady," he said.

I nodded and handed my clothes to Lady Laurel who carried them inside the carriage. It creaked and shifted as she got comfortable on the seat cushions to the right.

"Are you ready for me to return the trunks to the overhead rack?" he asked.

"Yes, thank you for carrying them down."

"Of course," he said and hefted the first one onto his shoulder.

So polite now as we both tiptoed around the churn of heat that I knew both of us felt.

He climbed up to the top of the carriage and I watched him strap the trunk back onto the carriage's storage rack. Turning, he hurried back down the steps, his lean body so agile, black leather tight and creaking. And it lit a fire deep in my belly as he hefted the second trunk off the ground and hurried back up the steps, strapping the second trunk between the other two. He took the steps two at a time and landed with a thump on the hard ground.

"Ready to change clothes?" he asked.

I nodded and climbed into the carriage. He followed me inside, putting the first wooden shield in place on the windows beside Lady Laurel. He slid the other shield in place on the windows beside me.

"Knock on the door when you're done, my lady," he said and closed the doors tightly.

As I slipped my feet out of my short black boots, I heard the creak of leather and imagined that he had turned away from the carriage again, to guard me, and give me privacy.

With Lady Laurel's help, I unfastened my torn purple skirt and let it fall to the floor. I rolled the white stockings off my legs and then my purple petticoat. And discarded the matching purple blouse. Then I slipped the silky ice blue petticoat up my legs and around my waist, tying the ribbons. I pulled on the sheer gold blouse and buttoned it. Lady Laurel helped me into the skirt, fastening its hooks and buttons for me. When she was finished, I sat down and rolled the sheer gold stockings up my legs and secured the tops with their tiny gold bows.

Quickly, I slid my skirt up over my knees, pretending to adjust my stockings and put on my boots.

Reaching over to the carriage door, I knocked on it.

"All finished," I called out to Oz.

He opened the doors and froze, his gaze locked onto my sheer gold stockings as I kept pretending to straighten them.

I looked up at him, but he was still staring at my legs, giving me that warm feeling from his attention.

I think I had rendered him speechless.

I reached over and picked up my boots and slowly put them on as his breath heaved in his chest. He pulled in a long, deep breath.

"Princess, I..." Oz Tarrant was stammering.

I felt the glow of his attraction wash over me like a warm hearth fire.

"Annarissa," I corrected him.

Finally, his gaze lifted from my legs, but a sadness touched his face now. Like he had suddenly realized that his attention was inappropriate. Something I couldn't stand to see in him. I admired his devil may care attitude and his self-assurance in every action he took. Before today, the stockings had been lighthearted fun between us and I loved the flirty attention from him. But now, he seemed almost...ashamed.

Then I realized that he had been watching Farago. And disapproving.

"Forgive me, Annarissa," he said finally, taking a step backward. "I apologize for staring. I meant no insult or threat, I—"

I rose from the cushions and moved to his side, a hand against his arm.

"Oz," I said. "You did nothing wrong."

"But I—"

I smiled. "You politely admired my stockings. Unlike Farago who saw them as an invitation to more."

His gaze turned faraway for a moment and finally, he nodded.

I squeezed his arm. "You have done nothing but protect me since we met, Oz Tarrant. And I don't mind you looking."

Lady Laurel pressed her hand to her mouth, to hide her chuckle. Yes, it was very forward of me (Oz's attitude was rubbing off on me). But I didn't care. I didn't want to lose his attention. The flirts we had exchanged. They had been the best moments of this terrible journey.

His eyes widened and he could barely hide his surprise.

He laid his hand on mine as I kept gripping his arm and squeezed. The contact with his hand was like a hot stone underneath the blankets in winter. It gave me shivers and I wanted to entwine his fingers with mine. And kiss him. But I slid my hand away and sat back down on the cushions.

"You are too kind, my lady," he said, backing out of the carriage doors, a blush on his cheeks. "Please excuse me. I must check on the hired swords and confirm the route for the next part of our journey with Mathias. I'll have him bring a meal to you both as soon as it's ready. Get some sleep if you can. We'll leave at sunset once you've conjured more elemental horses."

Before I could reply, he disappeared out the door and into the gloom. I couldn't help chuckling. I had managed to make fierce, terrifying Oz Tarrant blush.

As soon as he left the carriage, Lady Laurel whirled around, grinning.

"Annarissa Ambren Maelena Thorn," she scolded. "You have feelings for that man."

Now, it was my turn to blush.

I never had a choice about anything in my entire life. And that included being betrothed to Arence Siridean. My meals were planned for me. My clothes chosen. My ambitions and my magic had even been planned without my being allowed to choose an elemental magic. It had chosen me.

Oz Tarrant was the first man I ever had feelings for and choosing his attention had been my very first choice. One I hadn't made lightly. Knowing he was the Butcher of Badriyah and that he'd exterminated twelve sword wielders vying to deliver me to Rohesia still frightened me a little. Gave me concern. But he'd already proven a good gamble. Those dead swords for hire had been Equalizers and he'd prevented a massacre at the castle by killing them. No, Oz Tarrant had kept me safe at every turn so far.

Granted, we almost killed each other in the beginning, but the moment we connected had turned up the heat even higher. And the attraction. He felt it and I felt it.

And I would carry the memory of him with me for the rest of my days in Rohesia. By Ereth, my duty made me so sad. Because I could never love him as my mate. Even if those fairy tales were true.

"Admit it—my lady," Lady Laurel chided me playfully. "You care about that dark-souled tyrant."

I shook my head as she slid closer to me and gripped my hands.

"Beneath that crafted veneer of fear and darkness is a soul of pure light, Lady Laurel," I said, squeezing her hands. "I feel it!"

"The only thing beating in that man's chest is a dark heart. Annarissa! He murdered the entire village of Badriyah! All those swords for hire—his competition!"

"No!" I cried. "Those competitors were all Equalizers and you know it. I saw the masks, Lady Laurel!"

She gave me a scornful look. "What about Badriyah?"

"I don't know yet," I said. "But I intend to find out."

"He's been a controlling tyrant since you got into this carriage. Treating you like a child at best, a crate for delivery at worst."

I motioned toward the carriage doors. "You just saw him apologize and graciously handle a difficult situation. He blushed, Lady Laurel!"

At last, a smile touched her face. "He did blush. I acknowledge that he's had some sort of change of heart, but Annarissa, can you really trust this man? This—this butcher for hire?"

"Don't call him that!" I shouted.

"You really do have feelings for him, don't you?" she said in a quiet voice.

I nodded, my eyes beginning to sting.

"I've never felt this way about anyone before. Ever. And every time I'm near him, I feel the heat and the attraction. I'm drawn to him in ways I don't understand yet, but his touch is like the once-summer sun. When I look into his eyes, I melt and all I can think about is touching him. I can't stand it when he's out of my sight and all I want to do is protect him from harm." I sighed, staring down at my boots. "And I don't want to leave him."

Lady Laurel sat back against the cushions, a faraway look on her face.

"Oh, my...you're in love with Oz Tarrant. Your mother would lock you in the tower until you were thirty to keep you from this dark and dangerous mercenary."

Lady Laurel had no idea that comment made Oz even more appealing. I had never been in love before and I had no idea what it even felt like—but everything I felt for Oz Tarrant was deep and fiery. And it grew stronger when he was away from me. It was everything I thought love might feel like, too.

Except that I could never have him.

I turned to her and nodded.

"Oh, my dear, Annarissa," she said, hugging me tightly. "Of all people to fall for and you pick a Xanthan scoundrel who murdered an entire village."

Somehow, I had to uncover the truth about Badriyah and show her Oz Tarrant's true character.

The knock on the carriage door startled me.

"Enter," I answered.

The carriage doors swung open and Mathias greeted us, a smile on his fleshy face.

"Good afternoon, Lady Laurel and Princess Annarissa," said Mathias with a warm grin as he handed Lady Laurel a wooden tray with bread and two bowls of warm grains, the savory spices reminding me of the wild onions we used to pick in Ereth for roasting alongside the root vegetables.

"Thank you for bringing the meal to us," said Lady Laurel.

"You're very welcome." He waved his meaty hand toward the bowls. "The grains are hot and the bread is warm. Enjoy it."

"We shall," said Lady Laurel. "Thank you."

"It's only a couple of hours until sunset," said Mathias as he crossed his arms against his worn brown leather armor. "As soon as the sun retreats, we'll set out toward the valley. And the Cimmerian Breach."

"Thanks for the update, Mathias," I said with a nod.

"Better replenish that magic in a hurry, princess," said Mathias. "You'll need it in the Breach. I hear it's the most dangerous place in Kambria. And so dark that you can't see your hand in front of your face."

If he was trying to rattle us, it was working.

He backed out of the carriage, one hand on the open doors, pausing.

"But I'm told the dark is the least of our worries. No matter what lurks in there, we'll protect you both. Fear not."

With a quick bow, he closed the doors and disappeared into the grey afternoon mist.

And I wondered who would protect our protectors.

Lady Laurel picked up the tray and I took one of the bowls of grains and broth. And one of the spoons tucked behind the small loaf of bread.

"We'll need more battle magic," I said and dipped a spoonful of hot broth out of the bowl, blowing on it.

"I hope that place doesn't scare off the elemental horses," said Lady Laurel. "It would also be the perfect place for the assassin among us to strike. Or bring down another ambush."

She was right. The Breach was the perfect place for another ambush.

14

After the vegetables and grains in broth and some bread, I fell asleep against the carriage wall, dreaming of summer and the Festival of Lights. Ereth's indigo sky burned with stars as the magical glowing strands of purple, red, cyan, and blue danced across the sky in electric patterns and trails. The scents of smoked meat and roasted root vegetables dusted with sea salt and spices was mouthwatering against the fragrant lavender oil burning in the braziers as I twirled around the throne room in a sparkling lavender dress and faced a row of princes from across Kambria. The courtship dance was about to begin.

The royal quintet musicians played, an ocarina's notes flitting above the lute's accompaniment as a vielle and gittern strummed beneath it, the timbrel's thump and jingle keeping the rhythm lively.

Tonight, I would choose one of these princes to be my mate.

But I turned away from them when I saw the man with long hair the color of night, dressed in pristine black leather armor. His ice blue eyes burned through me as Mother appeared to my left. My sisters Gen, Carys, and Ari gathered around her in their finest Erethian silk gowns in powder blue, red, and palest lavender.

"You have been gifted with a chance to choose your prince tonight, Annarissa," said Mother, her amethyst and gold crown bright against the dancing lights.

She wore a royal purple gown, her neck and arms dripping with gold jewelry wrapping around amethyst gems. She held out her arms, motioning to the row of princes before me.

I shook my head. I wanted none of them. Instead, I turned around. Toward the tall, roguishly handsome man in tight black leather armor.

"I choose him, Mother," I announced as the entire court heaved a collective gasp and stared at me in shock.

"Your Majesty," one of the courtiers gasped. "He's the Butcher of Badriyah!"

The entire court and the princes looked horrified.

"You must choose another," Mother ordered, turning me back toward the princes dressed in royal blue and red uniforms, gold crowns shining on their heads.

They looked bored. Disinterested, their eyes empty of emotion. They all turned away from me, studying my sisters like I was not even in front of them.

"No!" I shouted and grabbed hold of the roguish man's hands.

The Butcher of Badriyah's hands.

"I choose him. You gave me a choice, remember?"

Mother shook her head. "Between princes, Annarissa." She pointed at the man in black leather. "He is not a prince. He's a criminal. Choose again."

"No," I said with a snarl. "I won't. I won't!"

I turned back toward him as he leaned down to me, his mouth covering mine in a hot, anxious kiss.

Gold light erupted around us, sparking like the dancing lights in the sky as the entire court cried out and backed away from us.

I awoke to Lady Laurel shaking my shoulder, the dream fading.

I was back in the ironwood carriage as it rolled along the main road toward Rohesia. And the Cimmerian Breach. Only a tiny flame burned in the lantern beside Oz Tarrant, giving the carriage a warm sliver of light to keep it from being bathed in the new moon's darkness.

His gaze was calm and steady. Fixed on me as he weathered the carriage's rocky ride along the road.

"We're headed toward the Breach," I said with a gasp, sitting up and glancing around the carriage.

I shifted an aqua-colored blanket off me, one that Lady Laurel had probably draped over me while I slept, and sat up straighter.

"We're getting close, too," said Oz, sitting cross-legged on the cushion, right elbow propped on his knee. "It'll be a long, twisty ride through all those ruins that stretch for miles. Just hope we can avoid the most dangerous rogue and magical elements in there. Or bandits waiting to waylay travelers headed to Rohesia."

"Or worse," said Lady Laurel as she set her book in her lap, a green blanket draped around her shoulders.

Oz nodded. "Yes, there are much worse things lurking in the Breach than bandits and rogue mages."

He looked tired. And worried. He had already shielded the windows. The wooden window shields had been burned and badly battered since we left Ereth. They were blackened and pocked with holes from being bombarded with flaming arrows. I wondered how much more they could take.

"I plan to open the shields when we enter the Breach," said Oz. "We need to anything approaching the carriage out there."

He glanced above him where Mathias sat in the driver's perch on top of the carriage, driving the six elementals that Lady Laurel and I had conjured at the camp. And six more for the three wagons. This time, I had increased the amount of earth magic within the elemental steeds, giving them extra courage and endurance. Traits they would need inside the Breach. We couldn't have them getting spooked and fleeing back to the ether. This time, they had to be fearless. Aggressive. Brazen.

"Lady Laurel and I conjured more aggressive elementals this

time," I said. "Their glow is darker. More copper than gold. They can be more difficult to control, but they won't bolt like the average elemental if threatened. These elementals thrive on danger."

"Like me," Oz said with a smirk and motioned toward the carriage's ceiling. "Mathias knows that we don't stop in the Breach —not for anything." Oz returned his attention to Lady Laurel and then me. "Back at the camp, while you were both sleeping, we took some spare armor and covered the outside of the carriage with it. Reinforced the outside of the window shields with it, too."

I shuddered at the thought of our elemental horses bolting, leaving us stranded inside that place. No one knew much about the long stretch of ruins in the dark valley of the Cimmerian Breach. Most people who saw those ruins didn't live to tell the tale. Courtiers in Mother's court once mentioned that some of the ruins were controlled by a race of stealthy spirit warriors who used shadows and surprise to defeat their enemies. They captured travelers and sacrificed them to twisted faced gods whose stone likenesses lined the rim of a small amphitheater that overlooked a blood-stained altar.

Beyond the stealth warriors' encampment was a haven of square wood and mud buildings with a large mead hall in the center of the settlement where its people once gathered. They had been hunters and very territorial. Now, they hunted trespassers for sport. Led by a wraith-lord of dark magic that could freeze prey in place like statues. Or control them. Make them do its bidding.

And the last set of ruins was a collection of towering stone temples with graceful white capitals and statues that came to life. Where the first inhabitants of Kambria first settled and discovered the first gods who had been the first mages and sorceresses. These first gods ruled over those without magic. And they were worshipped until their people honed the first blades. Before that, anyone who did not worship these first gods and pay them tribute paid a fatal price. Through a challenge of wills. Or magical trial.

"Oz, what exactly do you know about the Breach?" I asked.

He shook his head. "Only that we need to stay clear of any ruins and keep moving no matter what pursues us. There are a hundred ways to die in there."

In my studies, I had learned about the three old races that had built the ruins, each a forerunner of Ereth, Xanthe, and Rohesia. But I knew little about the magics and spirits that had taken control of them in the Breach.

"We may face the spirits of three old races who control these abandoned places in the Breach," I said. "No one knows their names, only how they kill."

Oz frowned. "How they kill?" he asked, glancing at Lady Laurel and then back to me.

"The first set of ruins is controlled by spirits of ancient Rohesian stealth warriors," I said. "They capture trespassers and sacrifice them on an altar to their gods. By draining the sacrifice's blood, they offer the body to their gods."

"Okay, that's a lot worse than I had heard," said Oz, looking uneasy now. "What comes after these spirit warriors?"

"Dark Erethian spirit hunters control the next set of ruins. They hunt travelers for sport. And consume them with dark magic. And the last set of ruins is haunted by ruined temples and magical creatures thought to be old Xanthan gods that use magic and weapons to challenge interlopers to rigged contests."

Oz was quiet for several long moments, staring at his hands. Finally, he looked up, his face pale and his voice quiet.

"We keep to the road," he said. "No matter what."

I couldn't agree more. Or face trials of magic, blade, and spirits of gods. If we were fast, maybe we could avoid all three and reach the Rohesian border?

"Agreed, Mr. Tarrant," said Lady Laurel, her features taut with trepidation.

"Call me Oz, Lady Laurel," he said, casting a sideways glance at her.

"All right, Oz," she said with a nod.

The carriage shook and bounced for a while, blinded by the reinforced shields over the windows. I couldn't see the metal on the other side, but the armor would make it harder for any archer's arrows to burn anything.

At night, the valley that led into the Cimmerian Breach was the darkest place in Kambria. Day or night.

The elemental horses had fallen into a hurried, anxious rhythm, the wagons behind us keeping close, their elemental teams keeping pace. Staying close.

Mathias thumped the carriage ceiling with his fist.

"Coming up on the road into the Breach, boss," Mathias shouted into the hailing-horn.

My stomach did a somersault, imagining all the dangers inside.

Oz looked a little pale, his eyes haunted.

We were about to enter the Breach. No wonder most Rohesians never left their kingdom, waiting instead for their war-ravaged seaports to be rebuilt—like Ereth. Risking a trip through the Breach wasn't worth it. Unless the kingdom had somehow negotiated some sort of protection agreement between Rohesia and these Breach creatures. I doubted they could be reasoned with, but there were stranger things in Kambria.

"Oz?" I said, fixing him with my gaze. "Do you suppose that the Rohesians made a deal with the creatures inside? To allow them safe passage somehow?"

Oz laid his hand against his chin, rubbing it as he considered my question.

"It's always possible," he said. "Probably unlikely though. I wondered how the late Blademaster Laurant planned to get you safely through the Breach, but we'll never know because he's dead. He was the only Rohesian aboard that convoy. The Rohesian royals couldn't be bothered to come to Ereth and escort you back there themselves."

He had a point. They hadn't even sent a contingent to lead the carriage back to Mirstone. They'd hired one instead and sent this carriage, leaving all the arrangements up to Ereth and my mother, including hiring swords for the blademaster to protect me and the carriage all the way back to Rohesia.

Or maybe they had planned the event like this on purpose? If the procession perished inside the Breach, then Prince Arence wouldn't have to marry an Erethian sorceress. Maybe this was Arence's way of getting rid of me and dipping into Aunt Johava's bloodline? Forcing his duty onto one of his cousins?

"Maybe Prince Arence had planned it this way all along, Oz," I replied.

This made him sit up straighter, his eyes wide and angry at the thought. But I couldn't help wonder if something else was going on. Something darker and more insidious.

I had no proof, so I kept the rest of those thoughts to myself. But Lady Laurel looked disturbed and Oz looked deep in thought as he seemed to ponder these possibilities.

Abruptly, the carriage halted.

Looking alarmed, Oz snapped out of his seat and yanked the shields away from both windows. With broadsword drawn, he gazed out into the dark night. There was no moon overhead.

After a minute or two, when the carriage didn't move, Oz rapped on the ceiling.

"Mathias! What's happening?" he shouted into the hailing-horn.

Footsteps thundered down the carriage ladder and stopped at the carriage doors. Mathias thrust them open and climbed inside. He plopped down beside Oz.

"Boss," he began. "We're at the valley entrance to the Breach."

"Why haven't we started into it?"

"I know we discussed the battle plan earlier," Mathias began, his voice bright and tactful, but I heard the hesitation in his tone.

He was afraid to tell Oz something.

"Then why aren't we enacting it?" Oz asked.

"Some of the crew are having second thoughts."

Oz's brow furrowed, fury flickering in his eyes, mouth pressed into an angry line.

"About getting paid? They planning to quit right here?" Oz demanded. "They do know that it's a helluva long walk home. Back through Battleworn Forest."

"The wagon you ordered to go in first objects," said Mathias. "They want to go last."

Oz bristled. "Farago is playing games, I see. I wanted the princess' carriage second in line, protected front and back. If we lose the princess, this trip's over."

"Farago thinks that he's in a better position to attack from the flank."

"And he's one of the best swordsmen in this crew. I need him close enough to defend Annarissa if it comes to that." Oz leaned back in the seat, arms crossed. "Tell Farago no deal. I need him in a position to defend Annarissa. And that's final. If he doesn't like it, tell him to come back here and discuss it." Oz's eyes narrowed. "With swords. To the death."

Mathias looked scared now.

"I'll tell him, boss. We'll hold position while I inform him."

Oz turned his gaze away from Mathias, looking distracted. Looking livid.

Mathias scurried out of the carriage and into the night.

Oz sheathed his broadsword and adjusted the long knife in his boot as he waited for Farago to show up at the door of the carriage.

Finally, a quick knock echoed and Mathias entered the carriage again.

"Boss," Mathias began, looking a little less stressed, his stocky presence and musical voice filling the carriage. "Farago understands what you want from him now. He'll drive the first wagon into the Breach, but he plans to fall back on foot to the wagon behind you and stay very close to the carriage."

Oz looked satisfied. "We went over this. But I'll allow it. As long as he's protecting the carriage. And Annarissa. We done here, Mathias?"

"I'll let him know," said Mathias.

"Tell him to drive that carriage as fast as it can safely run until we're out of the Breach," said Oz, a growl in his voice. "Watch the wheels and don't over-stress the elementals. Just get the convoy through this hellscape in one piece."

Nodding, Mathias hurried out of the carriage and slammed the doors. His heavy footfalls traveled up the carriage ladder to the driver's perch. We waited a few moments. With a pop of the reins, Mathias called out to the elementals and clicked his tongue. With a jolt, the carriage lurched forward.

Into the Breach.

The carriage picked up speed rapidly until it careened into the first serpentine turn. Nearly toppling onto its side.

"Mathias!" Oz shouted into the hailing-horn. "What the devil is happening out there! You're running too fast!"

The carriage swerved right and then turned abruptly left. Into another tight turn.

And another.

Lady Laurel and I braced ourselves against the carriage walls and held onto the hand rail to keep in our seats.

The elementals were in an unrestrained gallop, the carriage skimming along the road, wheels barely hugging the dirt. Until the horrible sound of wood cracking apart reverberated on my side of the coach.

"We broke a wheel!" Oz shouted.

The back of the carriage dropped to the road and skidded along it as everything turned sharply left, the carriage tilting on two wheels.

It righted itself, dragging the back left side, and began fishtailing.

Oz leaped out of his seat and threw himself in front of me as the carriage tipped onto its side. Against the road.

He threw his arms around me and rolled against the wall,

shielding me with his body as the carriage slid at least a hundred feet in the dark and slammed into something hard and immovable.

As silence and darkness engulfed us.

15

Not a sound echoed through the dark, dusty coach. Nothing stirred.

I opened my eyes in the pitch-black stillness, head throbbing, and tried to make out the position of the carriage. Where we landed—and how?

As I struggled against the heavy layer of dust covering everything, I tried to locate Lady Laurel and Oz in the silent blackness of the still carriage.

It was too dark.

Where was Mathias? The three other wagons?

My heart began to race, fear chilling my body. Had Oz and Laurel perished in the crash? What had happened to Farago and Mathias? And the other hired swords?

Was I alone in here?

As feeling returned to my body, I felt Oz's arms still around me, his body pressed against mine. He'd put himself between the carriage wall and me, to keep me from slamming into the ground. Or being thrown out a broken window.

I reached up, brushing away dust and glass from his hair and face, my fingers traveling across his cheek. Wet with blood. I couldn't see his beautiful face, but I felt the warm stickiness clinging to his right cheek and dripping down his neck.

"Oz?" I whispered against his ear. "Oz, answer me."

He was out cold.

I pressed two fingers against his neck, feeling for his heart's rhythm (something I learned from the healers in Ereth). It felt a little slow and uneven, but the rhythm was there. That meant he was still alive.

Wrapping my arms around him, I hugged Oz tightly against me. He felt so warm and safe. I didn't want to slide out of his embrace, but I had to know if Lady Laurel survived.

Finally, I shimmied out of Oz's iron grasp and reached out to my right, searching for Lady Laurel. But she wasn't next to me.

Reluctantly, I crawled across the dusty carriage. And felt my way to the other side. Until I felt fabric.

Lady Laurel's dress.

I slid my hand around until I found her face. Bloodied.

My fingers slid down her neck and found the rhythm of her heart. Still beating.

One of the windows on the up side of the carriage slid open and a black leather glove reached inside. These windows hadn't shattered in the crash. A lantern's thin light illuminated the inside of the carriage.

"Princess?" a voice called. "Princess, you in there?"

That was Farago's voice.

"Farago!" I called out in a weak voice. "I'm here."

"Thank the sky, princess!" Farago called. "We need to get you out of there. Take hold of my hands and I'll pull you out. Can't get to the doors yet."

His other hand reached into the carriage for me.

I grabbed for his hands and he firmly but gently eased me out through the window. Into darkness. Onto cold grass.

The wagon behind the carriage was on its side, too, its team of elemental horses anxious and glowing copper, tossing their heads. They were still hitched to the overturned wagon, but they looked defiant and feisty. Mathias worked on separating them from the wagon. Unharnessed from the carriage, the team of six elemental horses snorted and pawed at the ground, gleaming a bright copper. A look of fury burned in their wild eyes, daring anything to mess with them.

I looked left. Farago's wagon was unharmed and so was the last wagon.

Footsteps whispered through the spindly trees surrounding both sides of the empty road, making me uneasy in the heavy darkness that had swallowed up everything except the glowing elemental horses and the feeble light of a few lanterns surrounding us.

Farago knelt beside me, pressing his finger to his mouth as his gaze shifted around the darkness, hand on the hilt of his sword. Watching for movement.

Bandits? Assassins? Or worse?

"Oz and your handmaiden okay?" Farago whispered.

"Unconscious," I replied in a whisper. "We need to get them out and make sure they're okay."

Brush crackled off to the right.

Another twig snapped.

Surrounded by dense forest and old growth trees, the Breach's leaden darkness let no light into its interior. A dusty haze hung through the Breach and clung to the grass, the air smelling musty and dirty. Like an old cellar. No, worse. Like we had opened a sealed tomb a century or two old.

We hadn't expected an attack so soon, but in this thick darkness, there had been no way to avoid one.

Fear was icy against my fingertips. Was it men or spirits? I hoped it was only assassins. Those, I could handle.

"Farago," I whispered against his ear. "We need to get Laurel and Oz out of that carriage. Now."

Dry leaves rustled. An ominous warble trilled as the wind died.

He started to argue with me, but I cut him off.

"Now, Farago."

He cursed under his breath but finally nodded.

Together, we crept back ten feet to the overturned carriage. I heard movement inside.

Farago leaned down through the open carriage window.

"Oz?" he called in a sharp whisper.

"Lady Laurel?" I whispered beside him.

A gloved hand shot up out of the window, grabbing hold of the ledge.

Oz!

"Farago, take her," said Oz with a grunt as he lifted Lady Laurel through the window.

Farago set down his lantern and took Lady Laurel from Oz's grasp, lifting her out. He carried her over to the first wagon and laid her down in it as Oz climbed out of the carriage. He dropped down on his haunches beside me, a gash on his forehead trailing blood.

I slid a blue lace handkerchief out of my skirt pocket and dabbed it against the bleeding cut. I couldn't risk healing light right now. It could draw wraiths like sharks to blood.

He tried to pull away, but I held it firmly against his forehead. To stop the bleeding.

"You saved me from a lot of pain in that crash, Oz Tarrant," I whispered against his ear. "Thank you."

"Always," he said and allowed me to hold my handkerchief against the wound until it stopped bleeding.

Farago returned, dropping down beside Oz, the two of them barely illuminated in the dim lantern light.

"Oz, thank the stars you made it," Farago whispered.

"We lose anyone?" Oz asked.

"No," said Farago.

"We know what happened yet?"

Farago shook his head, those nut brown curls softening his features. "Not yet."

Twigs snapped all around us. Footsteps whispered across the foliage.

"What about the elementals?" Oz asked, his gaze darting around the line of trees and brush on both sides of the narrow road. "They okay?"

Farago shrugged and glanced around. He hadn't had time to assess anything.

"I see twelve coppery glows," he replied. "None of them fled."

Oz trilled three notes in a soft bird call that echoed through the silence. I'd heard those notes before. The signal to draw swords and fight.

If only we knew who—or what—we were fighting.

Farago drew his sword, crouching as his gaze swept the darkness.

For any sign of movement.

I called up my earth magic. And scanned the surrounding woods.

In the wake of my magic, the cyan forms of eight elemental horses were bright as they gathered together into a single magical force, ready to attack. Two teams of elementals were still attached to Farago's wagon, nickering and snorting. Ready to bust some heads. All twelve were ready to fight.

To my left, the carriage glowed cyan, lying on its left side. At least one wheel was busted. I sighed.

I turned, scanning the other two wagons. They turned a pale cyan through my magic. The second wagon was upright and undamaged, the third one was on its side, wooden frame splintered. Both axles were intact though and all four wheels unharmed. It could still travel.

In the way of my earth magic, each hired sword turned cyan, including Farago, Oz, and Lady Laurel.

But where was Mathias? Had he hidden in the brush after rescuing the horses, shielding himself from the growing sounds of footsteps around us? My magic should have found him.

Unless something in the Breach had gotten him.

"Farago," I whispered. "The elemental horses are all accounted for and all the hired swords. But I can't find Mathias."

Someone cried out.

Oz turned.

The scream came from the last wagon. A grunt and a thump.

Two hired swords fell beside the first wagon.

Stealth magic! By assassins or spirit warriors?

Oz whistled two notes. One by one, the hired swords rushed forward, encircling us, swords raised. I smiled. Including Lady Laurel who stood beside me now, a little unsteady. A hired sword beside her. She had called up a pale white ward around us, but we were no longer two dozen strong though.

Four maybe five were dead or missing.

Farago moved to Oz's right side.

"Ready to rip these fools apart?" Lady Laurel asked me through gritted teeth.

I grinned. "More than ready."

Lifting her hand into the air, Laurel summoned the wind.

It buffeted the trees and area around us. Anywhere someone could hide and ambush us. Trying to shake them out of their blinds.

"Close ranks," Oz said in a quiet voice and whistled two notes.

He and the hired swords pulled into a tighter circle around Lady Laurel and me, facing outward toward the menacing haze and dark surrounding us. Farago's lantern, on the ground at his feet, was the only light around us besides the faint white ward.

But abruptly, coppery light washed over us as the eight elemental horses encircled us, facing outward in protective, aggressive stances.

"Protect our charges!" Oz ordered as swords hissed out of sheaths and pointed into the darkness.

I scanned the tree line on both sides of the road, sensing a growing presence.

The hideous white porcelain masks were barely visible in the darkness, contorted expressions disturbing.

They weren't ancient stealth spirits looking for sacrifices or old gods. They were common assassins. Equalizers.

"Repel these monsters," Oz commanded as the assassins stepped out from behind brush and trees and moved toward the road, advancing on us.

They became shadows, barely visible in the faint light. Moving toward us from all sides.

I dropped to my hands and knees and dug my fingers into the dusty grass and ground, calling to the earth to hollow out a trench around us and the elemental horses.

The elemental horses reared up, hooves in motion and rushed at the shadows. Carrying away most of the light until a faint white glimmer kept us from complete darkness.

"Tighten the circle!" Oz shouted.

Dozens of shadows rushed at us from all sides. Equalizers!

Swords flashed. Shouts and whispers filled the silence and darkness as another force of Kambrian Equalizers rushed the convoy.

I lifted my hands, fingertips rippling blue, a spell on my lips.

Until I felt a blade against my chest. I froze.

"Time to die, princess!" said the muffled voice behind the mask as a figure materialized out of the darkness.

I recoiled as the sword rose toward my neck, trying to finish my spell.

But a blade pierced the assassin from behind. Right through the gut.

As the assassin dropped, Farago appeared out of the dark, black leather armor splattered with blood.

"Farago!" I said with a gasp. "Thank you!"

He grinned and crouched in front of me, bloodied sword raised.

"Finish your magic summons, princess," he said in a quiet voice.

Calling the words to my lips, I whispered the magic into the night. As the last syllables hissed into the dark, the soil collapsed around us, creating an island around us and a ten-foot drop.

In the dark, the assassins wouldn't see the drop. The soil hadn't made a sound when the magic had compressed it into a trench.

Someone shouted, the sound swallowed up by the drop. Followed by another. And another.

One by one, half of the assassin's forces disappeared into the trench.

I waved my hand through the air, commanding the soil to rise.

The muffled shouts abruptly fell silent, strangled by the rising dirt that buried them ten feet below ground.

Lady Laurel called up whorls of wind that spun with incredible force and tore through the remaining forces. Assassins flew into the air, thrown hundreds of feet in all directions.

When only a handful of Equalizers remained, Oz gave the command.

"Rush them!" he shouted, charging the masked assassins, sword raised.

Farago and the other hired swords followed him into battle. The elemental horses joined in the fight. Scattering the assassins and killing most of them before calm descended on the dark, bloody road.

In a few minutes, Oz, Farago, and the others returned with bloodied swords. Most of them were hurt, cut and bleeding from the fight. Thanks to Oz and Farago, I'd escaped without a scratch. But Lady Laurel had suffered several injuries. And I wondered if Oz had wounds beneath that tight-fitting black armor that hugged his leanly muscled body like a hot, sexy glove. That I wanted to slowly peel off and explore beneath.

"All right, let's get this carriage and that wagon upright," Oz called out as he approached the felled carriage.

Farago moved beside him along with a dozen of the hired swords. Together, they struggled against the heavy ironwood conveyance to get it upright. The elemental horses pushed their muzzles against the carriage, pushing until the carriage rose and sat upright again. The damaged wheel had broken in half and lay in pieces on the ground as the back of the carriage sat at an angle on its wooden axle.

The rest of the crew gathered up one of my traveling trunks and two valises that had slid free of the carriage's storage rack. They stacked my things beside the carriage as the three wagons circled it for protection. One of the wagon's back boards had broken apart, splintering along its outer edge, but the structure was still sound.

I glanced underneath the carriage. The four spare wheels bolted beneath the carriage looked unharmed and the elementals still looked unfazed, so it wouldn't take long to get the carriage moving again. But the people were a different story. Wounds and injuries had to be treated and the dead loaded into the wagons. We would bury them outside the Breach.

A hand pressed against my arm. I jumped, turning around. Oz!

"Are you all right, my lady?" he asked.

I nodded. "Farago saved my life."

A dark look I couldn't read touched his face.

"When?" he snapped.

"From an assassin as I was trying to cast some battle magic."

As if on cue, Farago moved toward me, casting a quick glance at Oz and then he turned on a big smile as he faced me.

"That was a close one, princess," he said with an arrogant smirk.

Then I realized he was gloating, taunting Oz with the fact that he had saved my life, not Oz. But Oz saved my life inside the carriage.

Regardless, I was grateful to Farago and owed him a warm thanks for what he did.

I reached out and squeezed Farago's arm.

"Farago, you saved my life—like Oz saved it inside the carriage. I am grateful to you for challenging that assassin. If you hadn't run him through with your sword, he would have plunged his through my chest."

"Let's get you over to one of the wagons to rest, princess," said Farago, still grinning at Oz as he led me past the carriage, toward the last wagon. "Lady Laurel is already resting back there. Under guard by the hired swords."

The last wagon had the most room in back as the crew began to shift around loads and supplies to accommodate the broken wagon's back board.

"Switch out this wagon wheel," Oz ordered. "Fast!" He glared at Farago as I walked beside him toward the last wagon. Oz didn't like this one bit. "And I want five swords guarding that wagon! You hear me, Farago?"

"I hear you," said Farago, those brown curls damp around his face, blood-spattered black leather armor dusty.

After climbing into the bed of the last wagon, I laid down on a pallet beside Lady Laurel, my head still aching. I felt a knot on my forehead that throbbed. Beside me, Lady Laurel's breaths were deep and even. I shifted onto my side as Farago climbed into the wagon, sword drawn, and kept watch. I could barely make out four other hired swords stationed around the wagon as my eyes began to close.

For a while, I slept heavily, no dreams just darkness until I felt someone beside me, pulling me out of the depths of sleep.

When I awoke, I found Farago hanging over me, watching me sleep. Lady Laurel was gone and I was alone with Farago. Where were the other hired swords guarding the wagon?

Unnerved, I sat up, staring at Farago.

"How did you sleep, princess?" he asked, the stubble along his narrow jaw darkening into a short beard.

His brown eyes were warm, bright as he reached out and brushed back the wisps of blond hair that had escaped my braids. I did my best to endure the movement, the touch, not wanting him to come any closer. I barely knew this man and I didn't want him to touch me like that.

"Fitfully," I said finally, pulling back.

His smile fled. "So sorry to hear that," he said. "They're still trying to fix the carriage, so you have time to rest."

I drew my legs up against my chest and stared at him with an uneasy gaze.

"You are so beautiful," said Farago in a quiet voice, reaching his glove toward my face again. "Much too beautiful for Arence Siridean."

I pulled back from his touch.

"I should go find Lady Laurel," I said and started to rise from the pallet.

But Farago slid closer, his arm slipping around my shoulders, drawing me closer.

"No," I snapped.

But he ignored me.

"You owe me at least a kiss for saving your life," he said, pressing his body against mine as his mouth covered mine. He smelled sour. Sweaty.

His beard scratched my face, his mouth tasting bitter. Like stale bread.

I tried to shove him off me as I pressed my lips together, but he held me tighter, his mouth all over mine, his body pushing me against the back board as I struggled.

Finally, I pushed him off me. Hard. Tearing my blouse.

I called up some battle magic that roiled blue at my fingertips. My blouse hung off my left shoulder, my lavender corset showing underneath.

His eyes got wide as I scrambled over the side of the wagon, still holding onto the piece of my torn gold blouse, my chin and mouth burning from his rough beard stubble against them.

"Princess, I'm sorry," he said. "I just...wanted to kiss you, I..."

I broke into a run from the wagon, back toward the carriage as my eyes stung with tears. Longing for Oz's presence. His protection. That was the worst kiss I had never imagined.

My first kiss. Stolen by a grubby mercenary who thought he could take liberties because he'd saved my life. I felt grimy and cold as I ran past the pairs of coppery bright elementals. Toward the carriage.

The new wheel was already in place and I was so grateful as I threw open the carriage doors and leaped inside.

Tears threaded down my cheeks as I held onto my torn blouse and huddled against the wall, shaking. Wanting to bathe away the feeling of grime and violation from my skin. Feeling foolish.

I was an assault sorceress and I'd let that mercenary assault me.

The carriage door opened and I froze, fear an icy bloom through my body. I expected Farago to be standing there. I lifted my left hand, cursing myself for not throwing magic at him in the wagon. But I had been too frightened and shocked.

"Annarissa?"

Tears rushed down my face. I was so relieved to see Oz.

He looked frightened as he dropped down beside me. "My lady, what's the matter?"

I couldn't hold it in. The sob broke free and I threw myself into his arms.

He wrapped me in his embrace and held me tight.

"You're shaking," he whispered. "What's the matter?"

But I couldn't talk. I couldn't call up the words as I cried in his arms, wanting only to feel his warmth and protection right then. To erase Farago's stench and roughness. The feel of his dry, sour lips against mine.

Oz's hand went to my hair, stroking gently as he whispered against my ear that everything was all right.

It seemed like an eternity before my shaking stopped. Only then did he hold me out at arm's length, his gaze searching for answers.

A fire began to burn in his eyes, his hand gently touching my reddened face where Farago's beard had scratched my chin and around my mouth. But fury welled like hellfires when he saw me clutching the edges of my torn blouse against my chest.

His voice was cold rage. "Who did this?"

I didn't want to tell him. He would go berserk when I told him.

My face contorted again and I shook my head, not wanting to tell him.

"Annarissa," he said, his angry voice so clear and silky, the timbre of it trembling through me as he pointed at my blouse. "Who did this?"

I pulled in a breath. "Farago."

His face darkened, the fire molten in his eyes, teeth gritted as he snapped up from the carriage floor.

"Farago?" He roared, hands smashing into fists. "Did he feckin' touch you?"

By Ereth, I didn't want to tell him that Farago had forced a kiss on me, hard enough to abrade my mouth with his beard.

Oz dropped down in front of me again, his fury barely controlled.

"Did he feckin' touch you?" Oz demanded.

I bit my lip, bowing my head. Finally, I nodded.

He had a wild look in his eyes, his rage barely in check as he gently held my shoulders, hands shaking with rage.

"Are you all right?"

I nodded as his fingers brushed across the abrasions around my mouth.

But he wasn't.

He snapped up from the carriage floor and shot out the doors.

"Oz, no!" I shouted, getting to my feet.

I rushed out of the carriage after him.

He ran straight toward the last wagon. Right at Farago who leaned against it.

"I'll kill you, Farago!" he raged and leaped at Farago, his fist slamming into the mercenary's mouth.

"Oz, no!" Farago shouted, trying to get away from him. "I'm sorry! I'm sorry!"

Oz landed punch after punch, the two of them rolling underneath the wagon. Farago tried to fight back, but Oz was an automaton, bloodying Farago's face again and again.

Farago rolled out of Oz's choke hold and tried to outrun him, but Oz tackled him in the grass, still swinging at his face.

"My lady, what happened?"

I turned.

Mathias stood behind me, his leather armor dusty beneath his chainmail shirt.

"It's a long story," I said with a sigh. "Can you please stop Oz before he kills Farago?"

Mathias pointed as two of the hired swords, a tall Erethian woman named Pirin with sandy hair and a lanky, older Rohesian with thinning dark hair, grabbed hold of Oz, trying to pull him off.

But Oz lunged at Farago again.

"Bastard! You're an Equalizer! You're one of them!"

"Oz, no!" Farago shouted, holding up his arms to protect his face. "It wasn't me, I swear!"

"You planned this whole ambush, didn't you?"

Oz swung, catching Farago in the head. When he stumbled, Oz leaped at him again and they hit the ground hard.

"My lady, let's repair your blouse," said Mathias, his hand gently brushing against my upper back. "There isn't time to risk changing it, but I have needle and thread with me. And maybe a spare shirt. Lady Laurel's in the first wagon resting and asked me to repair it enough for you to travel."

She did? That didn't sound like my lady-in-waiting.

"We need to get moving," I said. "I'll worry about my blouse later. When we're safe."

"But my lady, a few quick stitches will hold the rip in place until we're free of the Breach. I assure you, I'm good with needle and thread. I apprenticed to a Rohesian tailor for three years."

Maybe if I stitched up my torn blouse, Oz wouldn't try to kill Farago again? I had never seen him so defensive. And protective.

The two other mercenaries struggled to get between Oz and Farago.

"All right, Mathias," I said. "Let's fix the tear and get moving again."

He motioned me toward him and I followed him to the first wagon. I leaned over the side, but Lady Laurel wasn't back there resting. She must be in the second wagon.

"Right this way, princess," said Mathias, his voice bright as he led to the edge of the tree line where a leather rucksack sat on top of a crate.

From here, I could only hear the fight raging at the last wagon as Mathias gathered a small pouch from the rucksack and turned toward me.

"My lady, may I stitch the tear with you still wearing the blouse?" he asked, sliding a spool of gold thread out of the pouch. "I promise to be quick."

A needle protruded from the tightly wound spool. He pulled the needle free as he unwound a long measure of gold thread.

"Of course," I said.

He set the rucksack on the ground. "Sit on the crate, my lady. I apologize that it isn't a suitable chair."

"No apology needed," I said. "I appreciate your kindness."

I climbed onto the crate and he approached my left shoulder. After threading the needle quickly, he opened the small leather pouch and put the needle inside it.

"Let me just check the tear, princess," he said. "To make sure I have enough thread to the job. It's such a delicate blouse."

It was sheer and the fabric was fragile. But right now, all I cared about was it staying together long enough to ease Oz's fury.

Mathias set the pouch on the crate beside me and gently took hold of both edges of the torn blouse.

"Yes, shouldn't take much thread at all with a few well-placed stitches."

He reached into the pouch and pulled out the needle and thread. He tied a knot at the end of the doubled thread, the needle looking almost shiny.

"Now, look straight ahead and I'll put a dozen or so stitches in to keep it together."

I nodded, focusing my gaze on the massive black tree trunks ahead in the haze. The tree limbs were bare and dried, curled up coppery leaves littered the ground around the trees' gnarled roots that looked like arthritic hands.

Mathias put the first stitch in place, the needle and thread whispering across the delicate fabric as he worked his way up my shoulder. He was almost to my collarbone when a sharp poke pierced my skin.

I jumped, gasping.

"Blast it! Please forgive me, my lady! I am so sorry." His voice was a bard's lament. "I slipped with the needle. Forgive me. I'm not used to sewing clothes when someone's still wearing them."

I wanted to rub the sting off my skin but I held back the urge, wanting him to hurry and finish.

"It's all right, Mathias," I said. "Please, just finish."

"Of course, princess," he said and I felt the needle in motion again and tried not to flinch, afraid he would poke me with that too sharp needle again. "A few more stitches and the tear will be back together again."

He put in a dozen or more stitches and then tied off the thread. Reaching into the rucksack beside him, he pulled out a small blade and cut the thread.

"There, my lady!" he cried in a jovial tone. "Boss won't even notice that tear now."

"Thank you so much, Mathias," I said and rose from the crate.

I turned around, back toward the carriage, rubbing the spot on my shoulder where the needle had pricked my skin until the burning pain disappeared. But already, I felt lightheaded. Dizzy.

Suddenly, I felt cold as the world began to rise.

I grabbed hold of the crate to steady myself.

That's when Mathias grabbed my arm.

"Forgive me, princess," said Mathias, leading me away from the crate.

Toward the dark, dense woods ahead.

Slowly, through the strange clammy haze, I realized that he meant me great harm.

I tried to fight. To struggle, but I was quickly losing control of my arms and legs as a bitter taste clung to my lips.

Mathias glanced at me and slid a white porcelain mask out of his rucksack. He put it over his face and grabbed my arm as I collapsed against him.

"It will all be over soon, princess," he said as he picked me up in his arms and carried me toward the trees. "I promise. Now, we wait for Tarrant to show up. But he will be too late to save you."

As the pain snaked through my body, the last remnants of light fading, I knew it hadn't been some sort of sedative or dwale that Mathias had given me.

It was poison.

I tried to scream. To fight. To summon my magic, but the darkness was too heavy, pressing against my eyes until I lost consciousness.

16

I SLAMMED MY FIST INTO FARAGO'S BRUISED AND BLOODIED FACE AGAIN AND again, rage a firestorm through me. It was a torrent of flame that I couldn't shut off. Couldn't shut down.

Every time I thought about Farago putting his dirty hands on Annarissa, kissing her while she tried to fight off his attentions, my fury exploded. The memory of the abrasions reddening her flawless moon-pale skin made me murderous.

Daegal's balls! She'd been too scared to even summon her magic.

But the torn blouse—I wanted to kill him with my bare hands!

With a wild howl, I landed two more punches to his smug face. Splattering blood across his black leather armor and all over the wagon behind him.

To defile a princess like Annarissa Thorn was unforgivable. She'd probably never even had her first kiss and this bastard stole it from her like he had a right to take it. Because he saved her life.

Nobody had a right to take something like that. Not from Annarissa. Not from anyone.

"Oz, please—" Farago groaned, stumbling backward, trying to get away from me. "I'm sorry. I'm sorry!"

I bared my teeth as I grabbed him in a headlock. And squeezed. Hard. Wanting to pop out his eyes. He was only sorry he got caught.

"I told you I'd kill you if you ever touched her!" I smashed my arm tighter around his neck. "I warned you, Farago. I warned you!"

"Oz, stop!" Pirin, a tall sandy-haired Erethian swordswoman tried to free Farago from my hold. "You've hit him enough. I think he's gotten the message loud and clear."

"I said I'd kill this asshead if he touched her!" I shouted as Norval, an older Rohesian swordsman grabbed my arms and drew my attention for a moment.

I looked away.

"Boss—stop." Norval's voice drew my gaze back to him.

"Please don't kill him. We need him."

"You made your point," said Norval. "He knows how big an idiot he was. Don't think he'll touch her again, but boss, we still need him."

At last, Pirin and Norval's words got through my enraged brain and I eased the pressure around Farago's neck. Letting him go. But I wanted to pound his smug face and put my blade through his heart.

Gasping, Farago stumbled backward, wheezing for breath, and Pirin stepped between us, arms out, trying to keep us separated.

"It's over now," said Norval, standing in front of Farago as he grabbed hold of the wagon to steady himself, breaths coming in gulps.

I pointed a finger at Farago. "You're the one that set us up, aren't you, Farago? Thought I could trust you, but the mask we found in the wagon..." I glared at him, feeling my rage ignite again. "You're an Equalizer! Admit it. You led us into this ambush."

And he'd forced himself on Annarissa. I wanted to pound him into paste.

Farago, chest heaving, eye swelling, held up his hands.

"Oz, I swear to you...I made a mistake. My judgment was bad when I kissed the princess. I'm sorry." His voice was weak and raspy. "I didn't mean to hurt her. But I swear to you, I didn't put that mask in the wagon. It's not mine. I am not one of those bastard Equalizers. I would never betray you like that. Or the princess. Or my fellow hired swords."

He leaned against the wagon, still sucking in air.

"If we don't get the princess safely to Rohesia to marry Prince Arence," he continued. "Then our world will perish. I get that. I'm not trying to kill all of us."

I wasn't sure if I believed him or not. Farago wasn't the most honest person I'd ever met. And he'd lied to my face before. But I don't think he'd lie about the mask. About being an Equalizer. But the suspicion was out there now, in the heads of people he had to rely on to stay alive.

They watched him with uncertainty now. Now, he'd have to prove to them—and me—that he could be trusted. A big uphill climb now that we were stranded inside the Breach. And he'd assaulted Annarissa.

"Ask anyone!" Farago said, motioning toward Pirin. "I wasn't the one that loaded the supplies, Oz. Mathias was in charge of supplies. Some Erethian paid him to load all of it back at Skystead. I saw him carrying several burlap sacks of food and some crates, too." He sighed. "And pocket a hefty coin purse."

Mathias?

I squinted, glancing around the camp for the stocky, easy-going mercenary that had become the carriage driver and camp cook.

Was congenial, laidback Mathias the assassin?

Acting all helpful and pleasant. Pretending to take care of all the cooking and caring for the crew. And the princess—Annarissa. Cooking meals. Making sure her needs had been met. Seeing to all her and her lady-in-waiting's needs. All the while, had he been hiding that hideous mask among the supplies? Taunting us with its presence. Waiting for the right moment to strike. And ambush the whole procession. Like just now.

I gritted my teeth, glancing around at the group of hired swords that had gathered to watch the fight.

"Where's Mathias?" I demanded. "I haven't seen him since we defeated the Equalizers. Since he untangled the elementals' reins from the downed wagon."

The hired swords began searching for Mathias, but one of them moved beside me and stopped. Coen, a Xanthan like me. He was average height, long dark hair, stocky build. Almost as good with a sword as Farago. And Pirin.

"Just saw him," said Coen, pointing over his shoulder.

I frowned. "Where?"

"He was with the princess. They were walking toward the forest."

"What?" I cried, a rush of panic washing over me. "With the princess? Walking toward the forest in here—in the Breach?"

Coen nodded. "He was sewing up her blouse and then he led her toward the woods. She was leaning on him."

I grabbed hold of Coen's shoulders and shook him.

"Coen! Where? Quickly! She's in danger...show me!"

Farago was right. Mathias was the assassin!

Later, I owed Farago an apology. My not killing him was enough of an apology. But right now, I had to find Mathias. Before he killed Annarissa. That's what he'd come here to do and I had to find her. Save her from the Equalizers!

Whirling around, I ran alongside Coen as he led me past the carriage on the left, past the first wagon on the right. To a crate that sat an uncomfortable distance away from the wagon. A crate that had been placed there on purpose.

"She was sitting right here, Oz," said Coen as I walked around the crate, looking for clues, for anything that told me where Mathias had taken her.

My heart smashed flat, my chest aching as I fought down a wave of panic. I had to find her quickly.

The other hired swords began scouring the area, trying to find her.

Finally, Coen pointed toward some tall, barren trees, their

gnarled roots covered in dry leaves. The trunks were almost black and almost as wide as the wagons.

Where had Mathias taken her? I couldn't call for her. And I had no magic to find her.

"What's happened?"

Lady Laurel's voice shook me out of my panic. I turned.

"Lady Laurel!" I cried, gripping her shoulders. "Annarissa is missing."

"What?"

Her face turned white as she held up her hand and closed her eyes. Her fingers began to glow white as a mist descended in front of her, stretching outward toward the forest like an icy vapor. It engulfed the trees ahead, spreading through the night and the dusty haze as it highlighted even the slightest movement behind the trees.

Lady Laurel stared into the white mist for several moments, silent and stiff. Finally, she pointed to her right.

"There!" she cried. "I see them just ahead in a forest clearing."

I broke into a heated run through the white mist, the other hired swords and Lady Laurel rushing behind me. She quickly caught up to me, following some magic I couldn't see. We wound our way through the dense trees until we stumbled into a small clearing.

Where Mathias, wearing one of those fiendish masks over his face, leaned over Annarissa who lay motionless in the grass. When he saw us, his hand slid to the sheath around his portly waist.

As we got close, Mathias whirled around, sword in hand. That gruesome white mask covering his face.

He grinned. "You're already too late. In a few minutes, she'll be gone and you can't save her."

I rushed at him, sword raised.

His blade slammed against mine and I forced him backward.

He came at me.

I side-stepped him, my sword missing the mark as Lady Laurel ran to Annarissa, falling down beside her.

Mathias lunged at me, almost plunging his blade into my chest.

I blocked the blow, pivoted, and slammed my sword into his gut. Running him through with it.

He crumpled, dropping to his knees as the sword fell out of his hand. He collapsed face first into the grass. The mask broke in half and fell away from his face.

I ran to Annarissa, falling on my knees beside Lady Laurel.

Annarissa's skin was white, her golden hazel eyes frozen and staring straight ahead. Then I saw the red mark on her shoulder.

"He nicked her with something. Magic? A tainted blade?" I said as I gathered her in my arms and cradled her against me.

Then I saw the rucksack beside her in the dusty grass. I grabbed it, emptying it out beside me. A small grey cloth pouch fell out, a glass vial rolling into the grass when it tilted onto its side.

I motioned at Lady Laurel. "Open it!" I cried.

She grabbed the vial and removed the cork, sniffing the pink liquid. Shaking her head, she held the vial out toward me. I sniffed the contents. Tart fruity scent, had a pungent trace of vinegar to it.

I knew that smell. It was a poison. The juice from a galatas fruit!

And the only use for galatas fruit, unless you were a Xanthan snow bear immune to the toxins, was to poison someone. It acted fast. Annarissa didn't have much time. We had to neutralize it or she would die a painful death.

"Lady Laurel, that's poison!"

She picked up the vial, casting her magic at it.

"It's from a Xanthan galatas fruit," I said. "Deadly poison."

Galatas looked ripe and juicy like a bright pink apple, harmless, delicious, but they were lethal to people and killed quickly. They only grew at the base of Kirval's Shards, the mountains overlooking Snowmelt. Someone slipped me a bite of one once and I almost died, but I remember the healer gave me a draught of some clear liquid that neutralized it. Something that smelled alkaline and tasted of brine.

I shook the rucksack but it was empty. Again, I checked inside the pouch.

Then I saw the tiny vial wedged inside it.

Clear liquid! That was the antidote!

I reached into the pouch and pulled out the small vial. Yanking the cork free.

"Wait!" Lady Laurel leaned toward me, sniffing the liquid. "We must be sure it's the antidote or it could kill her."

I frowned and handed her the vial.

"I am familiar with galatas poisoning," she said, dipping her finger into the clear liquid. "The antidote is concentrated mineral water from a mountain spring and lots of salt from the seas. And the tart juice of the eliander plant known to absorb this particular poison."

She cast some magic on the bottle and her hand. White crystals appeared in the bottle and on her finger.

"Sea salt," she said. "The liquid is still clear, indicating pure water." Then tiny white bell-shaped flowers appeared inside the bottle. "Yes!" she cried, handing it back to me. "Those are eliander blooms. This is the correct antidote."

When Lady Laurel handed me the vial, the magic disappeared and it turned clear again.

I pressed the vial to Annarissa's lips. They were turning blue.

"Hurry!" Lady Laurel cried, kneeling beside Annarissa.

Tilting Annarissa's head back, I tipped the vial into her beautiful mouth, still red from Farago's forced kiss. The clear liquid spilled into her mouth and ran down her throat.

I held her tight against my body, doing my best to keep her chilled skin warm as I rose from the ground. And ran with her. Back toward the wagons. Toward the carriage, the one place I could keep her warm and safe while this antidote neutralized the poison.

Hired swords took up positions in front, behind me, and around me, swords raised as they watched for more assassins. Or spirits of ancient warriors. I didn't know if they were real or just stories, but if they attacked us now, Annarissa would die. Hell, we would all die.

When I got to the carriage, Farago's lantern was still lit, leaning against the newly replaced back carriage wheel. Lady Laurel hurried in front of me and threw open the carriage doors.

I ducked through the opening and dropped down on the seat cushion, still cradling the princess. Lady Laurel picked up the aqua-colored blanket and draped it across Annarissa, drawing the soft blanket up to her chin. In the struggles with Farago and Mathias, her braids had loosened. Now, her long, summer-gold locks hung in soft waves around her face and shoulders.

I pulled in a breath.

She was more beautiful than I had ever dared to imagine and I wanted to love her for the rest of my days. I wanted to turn this carriage around and huddle with her in a little cottage by the sea until all the light in Kambria went out and the world stopped turning. Showing her love and affection, giving her a little happiness even if it couldn't last. If the world had to end, at least it would end with her in my arms.

But I knew deep inside that she was too good a person to pursue her own happiness at the expense of the entire world. She would do her duty—no matter how much it hurt. She would marry this selfish asshead Rohesian prince and endure a life of loneliness, trapped in a bargain she had no say in, a life she never wanted.

And I had the horrible task of giving her over to this prince who would never love her.

Lady Laurel sat down on the floor of the carriage and leaned her head against the wall as she and I held a vigil over the princess. Hoping that the antidote was enough. That it had been given in enough time to save her.

17

For a long time, I struggled against the twilight, against this half-sleep that permeated my body and kept my head in a strange sort of hazy dream-like state. It kept me from sleeping and waking. Every movement hurt and made my stomach sicker.

Just before I lost consciousness, I realized what Mathias had done. But I couldn't do anything to save myself. Now, the bumps and shakes of the carriage were the only thing that felt real.

And Oz beside me.

As the convoy moved onward through the Breach's perpetual night, my stomach roiled and my body ached, a fever burning through me like I had been set on fire. I couldn't stop groaning and shifting, trying to get comfortable.

Despite the flames burning deep and the pains and sickness in my stomach, I felt Oz's constant presence. He cradled me against him, soothing my fiery forehead with a cold compress. Easing my nausea with drops of peppermint oil against my tongue.

I wanted to fall into the heat of his arms and stay there forever. His concern radiated, his persistent care so comforting. I kept my face pressed against his chest, breathing in his musk and leather scent, losing myself in the thrum of his heart against mine and the steady rise and fall of his chest.

And I couldn't have loved Oz Tarrant more than I did in these moments that I never wanted to end. I could have stayed in them with him for a lifetime and felt fulfilled. Feeling like I had lived and loved. It brought tears to my eyes, knowing that when I awoke from this dream state, it would all go back to the distance and stolen glances, infrequent touches, and accidental connections that I had lived for since this journey began. As soon as the convoy reached Mirstone, I would never see him again. And that hurt deep into my soul.

But one thing I knew for certain—I loved Oz Tarrant. With all my heart.

I would give up everything to stay with him—except my duty. I wouldn't serve my own selfish desires to sacrifice Kambria and love him. When my fever broke and I regained consciousness, the fear and heaviness of my duty would return. And so would the pain of losing him all over again.

Because of my duty—this horrible prophecy—I could never have him.

Battles erupted in the thick darkness surrounding the carriage, forcing it to stop or change course while I slumbered. While I dreamed. I felt hired swords dying around me. To ensure that I reached Rohesia and fulfilled my role in the prophecy. One by one, they made the ultimate sacrifices—much greater than mine—to save our world. And I would make certain that Ereth and Rohesia remembered their names—and what they gave to get me to Mirstone.

As the carriage pressed deeper into the Breach, Oz felt so far away from me. Fighting for my life. Only to hand me over to another man at Mirstone. I felt his pain and his anger. And the helplessness that drove him into blind rages as he defeated bandits and assassins who dared to attack the convoy.

As I slipped in and out of more dreams of Ereth's royal court, of masked balls and jeweled gowns, of harvest feasts and intricate dances with crown princes, I felt Oz at my side again, stroking my hair. Holding me close.

I pressed my fevered skin against him, chills shaking my entire body as I fought against the poison to dance with a tall, dark prince with long black hair and eyes like glass. In Skystead's throne room. Bathed in the warm glow of lavender-scented braziers, the ocarina's clear, melancholy notes resonated above the strum of the gittern. Timbrel's jangle was sharp above the carefully choreographed court dance.

Until the bumps and shudders of the carriage began to lull me out of the twilight, out of the heat, and the dreams. Until I opened my dry eyes and stared up into Oz's tired, worried, but handsome face.

I reached up and laid my hand against his cheek, caressing.

"You're...still here with me," I said, smiling as his warm skin soothed the pervasive chill clinging to my body from when Mathias had pricked me with a poisoned sewing needle.

"Annarissa!" Oz cried, his face lighting up, a smile playing across those full, luscious lips.

I ran my fingers across them and he closed his eyes a moment, his lips pursing against my fingers in a gentle kiss.

"Princess Annarissa!" Lady Laurel cried, sitting up as the carriage rocked and shimmied. "The antidote worked!"

I frowned, staring up at Oz. I didn't remember anything about an antidote.

He cradled me against him, an aqua-colored blanket across my body as Lady Laurel leaned over him and laid the back of her hand against my forehead.

"Oz, it's cool," said Laurel, smiling as they both exchanged a relieved glance. "Her fever has finally broken."

She called him Oz. Had they become friends while I slipped in and out of the twilight?

"Thank the heavens," said Oz, a heavy sigh shuddering through his chest.

"Princess, you gave us quite a scare," said Lady Laurel. "We thought you would never wake up again. We tried everything, but nothing worked."

"We even gave you a second dose of the antidote we found in Mathias' things," said Oz.

His silky, warm voice rumbled through his chest and I lost myself in the sound and timbre, how each word vibrated across my skin, and trembled through my body. I didn't want to move. Didn't want his arm to slide away from me. He brushed the hair out of my eyes. Waves of hair. My braids had come undone.

I felt a sigh flutter through my heart every time I looked at him. Every time I felt his touch. A man I could never love as my mate.

"How long have I been asleep?" I asked in a raspy whisper.

He stroked my hair and I lost myself in his rhythmic touch again. Wanting his mouth against mine. His body against my bare skin.

"Days," said Oz, glancing across me to Lady Laurel.

"We battled those spirit hunters who tried to use us as sport," said Lady Laurel. "Until Oz put down their leader. After that, they turned tail and ran back to the ruins of their mead hall."

Oz shrugged and looked away. "Did what needed to be done."

"You saved the whole convoy, Oz," said Lady Laurel. "Don't be modest."

Modest?

I lifted my head and studied his face. Oz Tarrant had never been a braggart, but Lady Laurel called him arrogant and egotistical—especially about his sword skills. But I had never seen him in that way. He knew that he'd killed those swords for hire back at Ereth to stop a massacre, but he said nothing. Let all of us think he was a...I sighed...a butcher.

"I'm being paid like a king to lead this procession," he said, shaking his head. "It was my job to control the situation. And in this case, it meant putting down the leader of those crazy spirit hunters."

I smiled, rubbing his arm. "Or eliminating a bunch of assassins before they could infiltrate the Erethian court."

Lady Laurel's eyes widened and finally, she nodded toward him.

"Yes, Annarissa. I believe you now after I saw Oz protect all of us through this dark valley. And our journey from Ereth, too. You're a good man, Oz Tarrant."

She saw it! At last, she saw what I saw in him.

He bowed his head and thanked Lady Laurel in a quiet voice.

"So, that means we're approaching the northern end of the valley?" I asked.

He nodded and I realized that I needed to sit up. But I hated to lose his touch.

"Once we get past those old temples and escape the first gods who supposedly inhabit them, we'll almost be at the border," said Oz.

The border of Rohesia.

Suddenly, I felt cold. From that border, we were probably two day's journey from Mirstone. I wanted to cry. And rage at the thought of losing him forever.

By Ereth, it hurt!

I rose unsteadily from the seat cushion that he and I had probably shared for days.

"Here, let me help you, princess," said Lady Laurel, draping the blanket around my shoulders as she helped me weather the shaking carriage, back over to the other seat.

I stared longingly at Oz who felt like an ocean away from me now. His gaze locked onto me and for a long time, I felt the heat—and desire—burning in him.

For me.

I tried to stay awake. I tried to ask all sorts of questions about where we were and how we would avoid the first gods and the ruined temples, but I couldn't keep my eyes open. I faded into a deep sleep again.

Until someone shook my arm. With an urgency that frightened me.

My eyes snapped open.

Oz knelt in front of me, hands in the air as he protected me from something in the doorway of the carriage. Lady Laurel huddled beside me, playing the part of a helpless and harmless prisoner, hiding her mage training and battle magic.

"Take them from the carriage!" a commanding female voice ordered. "Now!"

"I told you she's ill!" Oz shouted. "She was poisoned and she's no threat to your magic."

"Out of the carriage!" the crisp, clear voice demanded.

The intruders wore linen robes in muted blues and greens and they carried weapons that glowed with magic along their golden surfaces. Spears. Swords. Bows. Men with short brown hair and close-cropped beards and women with thick sable locks knotted into braids and ponytails.

The point of a sharp, glowing spear pressed against Oz's throat as two of these beings grabbed him by the arms and pulled him through the carriage's open doors. A woman with shoulder-length sable hair and kohl smudging her eyelids stepped into the carriage, pointing a nocked arrow at Lady Laurel and me. The arrow's golden head shimmered with a purplish glow.

"Out of the carriage," she said again, her tone flat as she motioned us up from the seat cushions with her bow.

When we didn't obey, her deep brown eyes narrowed and she moved toward us. She grabbed Lady Laurel's arm and jerked her to her feet.

She reached toward me, but I shoved her backward.

"I need no incentive and you will keep your hands off me."

I glared at the woman as I got to my feet, my earth magic roiling at my fingertips.

I expected her to come at me or try to shoot me with that arrow, but the hint of a smile brightened her face. Surprising me.

"Backbone," she said, nodding. "At last."

The woman held out her hand and motioned toward the doors. Inviting me out of the carriage.

I moved toward the open doors, my head held high as I descended the two steps. Out into the Breach's darkness.

All around the convoy, ruins of white marble temples rose on hillsides and into the valley's depths. Tall capitals flanked the myriad structures with statues mounted on top. The once-bright paints had faded from the stone. They must have been brilliant to behold in full color and pristine marble that hadn't weathered centuries of neglect and decay.

The strange group of warriors—or were they gods—rounded up all of the hired swords, little more than a dozen strong now. The warrior gods and goddesses carried magic-infused weapons that shimmered orange in the darkness. It was the only light around us. The elemental horses' coppery glow had gone dark, but they hadn't bolted back to the ether.

Not yet anyway.

These strange warriors held Oz in front of them, a sword to his throat as these arrogant gods in pale linen robes surrounded us. Pointing magically infused weapons at us.

"So, you wish to pass through our lands," said a tall, shapely goddess bearing a gold crown on her head, thick sable hair cut blunt above her shoulders. "You could have done us the courtesy of requesting passage, but you decided to barge through them uninvited instead."

Her eyes were the color of emeralds, so bright against the kohl surrounding her eyes. She wore a pale green linen robe edged in gold that shimmered against the light of their torches. The scent of burning sage mixed with tallow and smoke.

The guttering of torches was the only sound I heard in the twilight.

"And how would we have petitioned your agreement?" I asked,

my eyes narrowing at this condescending priestess who was obviously toying with us.

Oz didn't even glance in my direction, but he frowned. I felt him trying to focus all their attention onto himself. Away from me.

Oz looked through this priestess with almost a bored stare. "We were on our way to the Rohesian court at Mirstone when one of us took gravely ill. We have to reach Mirstone quickly—to find a healer. We travel a public road. Do you plan to stop us from continuing toward Mirstone?"

There was that strength that I admired in him. Not only had he stretched the truth, but he disputed their claim on the road through the Breach. It was the main road into Rohesia. The only road. Owned by no one. Certainly not first gods lost to time and history and only returned to Kambria through this magical breach.

With a leering smile, this queen or priestess to these first gods walked around him, studying him. Sizing him up.

"You speak for all of your people?" she asked, still pacing around him, a glowing short sword in her belt.

"I do," he fired back.

"I like your fire," she said to him, reaching out, and running her fingers through his long black hair. "And your appearance."

I bristled.

"I like yours, too," said Oz.

I could tell he was playing along, but I still didn't like watching her devour him with her eyes. And touching him.

"What do you offer us for this safe passage?" she asked, stepping around him again, staring at his tight black leather armor with a leering smile.

The chance to continue existing, I wanted to shout at her.

This goddess was demanding tribute and we had nothing to give. No treasures. No coin. We carried nothing of value.

Oz was silent for a few moments.

"What do you want for safe passage?" he asked, turning the question back on her.

She sauntered in front of him, holding out her arms toward the temples and buildings surrounding the road that led to Rohesia's border.

"As you can see," she said, turning in a circle, arms still outstretched. "We have riches beyond your imagination. We have power and we have numbers. What could a pathetic flesh and bone Rohesian offer a goddess?" She got in Oz's face. "I could destroy you with a flick of my finger."

I stepped away from Lady Laurel and approached this arrogant shrew. I had had enough.

"Then why haven't you?" I demanded.

Oz's expression darkened.

"What did you say?"

She turned toward me, looking surprised that I would address her like that.

I stopped a foot away in front of her.

"I said, why haven't you? What possible enjoyment could a goddess get from swatting dreamflies?"

She looked down her nose at me. "You know your place, Erethian."

"A shame you don't know yours—spirit," I said.

"How dare you!" The goddess rushed at me.

I spun earth magic around me, preparing for her attack, but she stopped inches from me. Looking...surprised? Wary?

"In case you don't see it, you and your people are no longer corporeal," I said.

The first god's robes hid the faded appearance of her skin—and the sallow forms of her followers. First gods or not, they were all spirits. Giving the impression that they were more powerful than they were. Spirits tied to a location were weakened by its draw. Drained over time. As a sorceress, I could sense her power. It was faded and weak like the others. She wanted to kill us, but she couldn't.

She wasn't strong enough. And in this form, neither was her magic.

But she and the others could still harm us. Because of that, we had to bargain with her in a way that kept us on equal footing. I remembered something about these people delighting in challenges and contests. So, we had to pique their interest while showing them we were a bigger threat. Not an easy task.

These first gods and goddesses had magic, but again, it was a faded remnant of what had once been the most powerful forces in Kambria. Long before the three realms emerged.

"That makes no difference, little Erethian," she said, glaring at me. "Spirit or flesh, I can end every one of you."

I smiled. "More talk."

Lifting my hands in the air, I rained down rocks and dirt clods on her and her entourage until they cowered beneath glowing shields.

"What...are you?" the priestess finally demanded.

"An earth sorceress with full physical powers," I replied.

Lady Laurel whipped up a whorl of air that knocked a bunch of the priestess' court to the ground.

"And I'm a mage of the air," she said. "Tread lightly."

"Because we aren't the only sorceresses and mages among us," I added.

The priestess gave Oz a sideways glance and returned her attention to Lady Laurel and me.

"How to resolve this?" she said, sauntering around Oz again with an amused look on her face.

"A contest...right," said Oz in a flat tone. "Like you hadn't already had that word on your lips since you saw us on the road."

"Ah, yes," she said with a smile, crossing her arms against her green linen robes, gold edges glittering in the torchlight. "A contest. It is the only enjoyment we have left. Please. Indulge us. If you win, you go free with our protection."

"If we lose?" I demanded, hands on my hips.

She cast a hungry gaze at Oz.

"Then we take slaves."

"No," I snapped. "Out of the question."

She threw a taunting smile at me.

"Scared, little Erethian?"

She wanted Oz and I wanted to break her arms.

"Just wary of how the first gods like to cheat," I said.

"We accept," said Oz. "If the contest is acceptable."

I glared at him. "Only if it is acceptable," I added.

The priestess looked down her nose at me again.

"Solve a riddle, give a tribute, or defeat my champions in combat. Your choice. Discuss it and give me answer." She nodded toward Oz and me. "Quickly. Before my patience runs out."

Oz had a dark expression on his face as he grabbed my arm and led me toward the carriage. Lady Laurel rushed after him.

"What do you think you were doing?" he demanded of me. "You have no idea what you're dealing with here."

I glared at him. "And you do?"

He crossed his arms and looked away from me.

"Lady Laurel and I studied these gods while training in battle magic. They were selfish and self-centered in life. As spirits, they are worse. But the difference is that in spirit, their powers are vastly diminished."

"Annarissa's right," said Lady Laurel, nodding toward the priestess who paced back and forth in front of her squad of spear carriers—out of earshot. "Their magic is no match for our elemental magic."

"So, we engage them in combat?" Oz replied, an eyebrow raising.

She'd given us three choices. Some sort of riddle. Combat. Or tribute.

"Princess, you're still too weak for combat," Oz replied, anger tightening his features. "And you know it."

As much as I bristled as his comment, he was right. I needed time to regain my strength. So, combat wasn't the best choice. And we had nothing to offer this first goddess as tribute. No artifacts. No jewelry. No coin. Did Oz want to risk escaping the Breach on solving this first goddess' riddle? Riddles were designed to trick and confuse people—especially when they came from a self-centered spirit goddess trying to win a contest.

"Well, what do we choose?" Oz demanded. "Sounds like all three choices are bad. Designed to trick us at every turn."

I nodded. "I agree. I would prefer to offer her tribute, but I think she would scoff at anything we had to offer. It's not like I am carrying any sort of bride price or dowry. Not even a trousseau with anything of value."

"What about our magic?" Lady Laurel replied. "What if we took an old sword, polished it to finery, sharpened it to perfection, and infused it with magic? She seems bloodthirsty enough to appreciate enchanted weapons."

An enchantment would wear off, but this priestess didn't know that. Based on what I knew about these first gods, the appearance of the tribute was more important than the tribute itself. If it was shiny and sparkly enough, would she be satisfied with it? This goddess was too shrewd to be duped by a shiny, glowing blade though. And she was deliberately trying to fool us into believing her forces were small, trying to goad us into choosing combat. It was too much to risk and we had no right to gamble with Kambria's future.

That meant we had to risk everything on solving a riddle or puzzle. And this goddess thought she was much too clever and more intelligent than the likes of mere mortals. Even though hundreds of years had passed since the last of these first gods' bodies had lost their substance and become spirit. Gods and goddesses were immortal, but their spirits faded along with their power and influence. And this goddess was in extreme denial.

No, our only hope was to outwit her and solve her riddle. But I was terrified that we would guess wrong and she would take Oz as her slave.

"Oz," I said, gripping his hand. "This goddess is trying to trick us into choosing combat. She has a huge force of warriors and gods—and magic—just waiting for us to choose combat."

His brow furrowed as a heavy sigh escaped his lips.

"I confess, I've been worried about that since she offered it as a choice."

I fixed Lady Laurel with my gaze. "And trying to offer her the tribute of an enchanted weapon is a waste of time. They already carry enchanted weapons. Unless we have something valuable or unique, we're wasting our time."

Lady Laurel frowned. "Then you want to risk us being trapped in here forever on solving some riddle?"

It seemed like the only possible choice. And if we got it right, there would be no question that we had won her contest. If we got it right. Besides, it played to her ego and arrogance. She thought herself smarter than us. I just hoped we could figure out the riddle. It was a dangerous gamble, but the other two options weren't options at all. They were tricks.

And this goddess knew it.

I squeezed Oz's hand. "Oz, what do you think?"

Oz motioned the hired swords over to the carriage. A dozen and a half or so. They hurried over with worried glances at the first gods clustered around their priestess, those glowing weapons so intimidating.

"All right, crew," said Oz in a raspy whisper. "We have three choices."

Farago was cut and bruised, dried blood on his face, left eye swollen almost shut. He nodded toward the first gods.

"They're just waiting for us to call combat and tear us apart, aren't they?" said Farago, his gaze intense.

Pirin looked uneasy, her hand on her sword hilt. "There's too many of them," she said. "I don't care how many we can see. I guarantee there are dozens more that we can't see. That choice is suicide."

"I agree, boss," said Norval who looked so small beside Pirin's six-foot-tall height. "It's a trap and a good way to die."

Oz nodded. "Or be enslaved for eternity. I agree."

Farago rested his gloved hand on his hip as he surveyed the crew. "Unless someone has a golden statue on hand, we don't have anything to offer a goddess. Do we?"

I shook my head. "I have nothing that would interest a goddess and if we tried to enchant a weapon, she would show no interest in such an ordinary tribute."

The rest of the group, including Lady Laurel, nodded.

Pirin looked frightened now as Farago gave her a worried glance.

"Then we have one choice," said Pirin, her hand resting on the hilt of her sword that hung at her hip. "A riddle."

Farago whistled and ran his fingers through his curly brown hair. "That's risky. Who knows what she'll trot out for that option? What if the answer is something none of us has ever heard of?"

"Then I become her slave and the rest of you high-tail it for the Rohesian border," said Oz, black leather armor creaking.

"No way," I snapped.

"It's what she wants," he fired back at me.

That thought terrified me and I wanted to rush at this goddess and slay her right now. And take that possibility completely off the table. She was trying to maneuver us into a corner and force us to give up Oz in exchange for safe passage.

That wasn't happening. I wouldn't agree to that. Ever.

"Either we all get out or none of us gets out," I said, crossing my arms against my chest. "We're going to challenge her into giving us a riddle and by Ereth, we will solve it."

The corners of Oz's lips lifted into a smirk for a moment.

"But princess," he said. "If I surrender to her, the danger disappears. Pirin can assume command of the convoy and—"

I grabbed him by the leather armor, shaking him.

"I will not sacrifice you, Oz Tarrant. Do you hear me? I will not hand you over to a first god for the rest of your days."

His eyes narrowed as he stared into my eyes a moment.

"But it's okay to hand you over to a selfish prick of a prince for the rest of your days?"

I bowed my head, my hands slipping away from his leather armor. No, it wasn't okay. And if I had any way to save Kambria without marrying Arence Siridean, I would take it.

"Because the world's prophecy demands it," I said, trying to keep the pain out of my voice. "But make no mistake, Oz Tarrant, it is not okay."

He seemed to approve of my response even though neither of us could change it.

Oz turned back to the hired swords. "Are we agreed then?" he asked in a quiet voice. "We all have to agree. Do we choose this riddle?"

The group fell silent for a few moments, looking pensive and worried, but one by one, they agreed. When the crew said yes, he turned back to Lady Laurel and me.

"Lady Laurel?" he said.

"Yes," she said. "A riddle."

I nodded. "A riddle is the only choice we have if we want to survive."

"Agreed, Annarissa," he said and nodded toward the impatient group of first gods, their forms looking as faded as the paint on the statues above the capitals. "Let's tell them our decision and get this over with."

I followed closely beside Oz as he swaggered over to the priestess. Her warriors moved in close, looking hungry as they gripped their weapons tighter in their fists.

"Well, what have you decided?" asked the priestess, glancing from Oz to me.

Oz folded his arms against his chest. "We choose the contest by riddle."

Her warriors immediately looked disappointed as they glanced from the priestess to us, a thirst for blood burning in their bright sapphire blue and emerald green eyes. Even the priestess' gaze changed as she cast apologetic glances at her army. She already knew we had nothing to offer a goddess.

"Very well," said the priestess with a sigh, motioning toward the closest white marble temple that perched on a hillside overlooking the road. "In one of your hours, we will return to this spot and deliver our riddle. You will have half that time to solve it."

Half? Why did she get to make all the rules?

"Why do we not get an hour?" I demanded.

The priestess' emerald eyes narrowed. "Because you are trespassing on our lands, so we make the rules, not you."

Another way these contests were designed to trick and let the first gods win by ridiculous exceptions. I was livid.

Half of one hour. Which could turn into an eternity. I just hoped we solved this riddle quickly and escaped the Breach.

18

I never liked riddles. They were Mother's favorite thing to share with her court and I wished that I'd paid more attention to them. Maybe they would have helped the convoy answer this riddle we were being forced to answer by a priestess of the first gods. If we got it wrong, she would enslave Oz. I wanted to stab her right through the heart with every ounce of battle magic I possessed.

Part of me wanted to shove Oz into the carriage and order the entire crew to bolt north out of the Breach and not stop until we hit the Rohesian border. But with three wagons and a carriage, we were much too slow—even with a dozen elemental steeds. These first gods—these spirits—would overtake us quickly. Or rain down enough magic arrows to kill most of us. And if they didn't kill us in pursuit, they would kill us after they caught us. Slowly and painfully.

The only way past this contest was through it.

No, we had to face the priestess' riddle with all our wits about us. And solve it.

Oz paced around the carriage, nearly kicking over Farago's lantern several times, so pensive that I wasn't sure he heard any of the crew's objections. Or proposals on how to escape the Breach—

and these first gods. Oz's steps were brisk, his strides long, arms against his chest as he swaggered around the dark landscape. He was so distant that he might as well have been back in Xanthe.

I had so many questions for him and I feared we were running out of time to answer any of them. I wanted to carry as complete a picture of him as I could with me to Rohesia. So, I would never forget a single detail of the man I loved but could never have.

There hadn't been time. And he was so far away right now that it frightened me. Would he keep slipping farther and farther away from me until we parted as strangers at Mirstone? I sighed. Maybe that was best in the long term, but my heart refused to allow it.

Finally, Farago moved behind him and laid a hand against Oz's shoulder. Startling him out of his thoughts.

Oz whirled around, reaching over his shoulder for the hilt of his broadsword.

Farago's hard brown eyes widened as he shrank back, hands over his cut and bruised face.

"Boss," said Farago in a quiet but fearful voice. "Time's almost up."

Oz's brows pressed into a hard line over his ice blue eyes as his gaze shot to the hourglass perched on the driver's seat of the closest wagon. Like he hadn't realized how much time had already passed.

The sand had all but run out of the glass. The first gods would return soon—with a riddle.

As leader of this expedition, Oz controlled what happened next. How we dealt with whatever these old gods had dreamed up for us to solve. He was too smart for the priestess' games. Too calculating. Even with her tall, sultry spirit circling him like prey to bed. No, he'd already been sizing up this alluring dark goddess in his head for the best move to set her off guard.

I had learned much about Oz Tarrant on this journey and now, I knew him well enough to know that his first move always set his opponents off guard. Off their center. It gave him a true picture of them, one only found in this first moment of combat—until he had them by the throat. No, his first move staggered his enemies in a way that gave him the advantage. And he didn't need much. He was an expert swordsman who knew just when to strike—and where.

But I also saw that in many ways, he was out of his element. This goddess wasn't corporeal. She was spirit. Magical. So, he was trying to figure out how a swordsman struck that same blow against a deity. A specter. With magic and blade.

"Thanks, Farago," said Oz finally in a quiet voice as he gazed around as if trying to reorient himself to these first gods—and where we had stopped.

He whirled around and rushed toward me, hands against my shoulders, the heat of his touch sinking through my blouse in warming layers.

I pulled in a breath and stared into those ice blue eyes, so wide and intense right now.

"Annarissa," he said as Lady Laurel moved closer. "Your battle magic. Is it strong enough to defeat this goddess?" His gaze shifted sideways to Lady Laurel. "Or your combined magics?"

I started to reply, but Lady Laurel cut me off, her voice almost a whisper.

"Judging by the style of those old robes," said Lady Laurel. "I would place these first gods at three centuries before the Hundred-Year Sundering."

Oz frowned. "And why is that important?"

She cast a quick glance at me and then returned her attention to Oz.

"They lived over four hundred years ago and have languished as spirits in this Breach since the curse upon Kambrian caused the fracture." she said. "Throughout that time, this magical abyss has leeched power from their magic. Absorbing it into the dark and the soil and the fog. Granted, they are strong, but their magic is now diluted and corrupted. Weakened, Oz."

"Lady Laurel is correct," I said, barging into the conversation. "I don't know if we could defeat a horde of spirit gods casting old magic, but the priestess...I could take her with my battle magic. So could Lady Laurel."

A smile brightened Oz's face and the tension left.

"Excellent," he said in a quiet voice and motioned toward the towering but faded temples on the hills surrounding us. "We don't have to defeat all of them. Just the priestess."

"Why is that?" I asked, frowning.

He leaned toward me, whispering a brilliant plan in my ear. One that would require a little stalling and Lady Laurel working quickly behind the scenes.

He squeezed my shoulders and I breathed in his musk and leather scent as he turned toward the crew while I leaned against Lady Laurel's ear and explained what she needed to do.

"It will be my pleasure, princess," said Lady Laurel with a wry smile as she motioned Farago to her side.

Confused, Farago complied, casting an uneasy glance at Oz as he moved behind the tall and darkly handsome mercenary to stand beside Lady Laurel who had moved to the back of the carriage.

I smiled. Out of sight of the first gods.

"All right, not much time, but all of you, gather around Lady Laurel," Oz ordered his crew in a quiet voice. "She needs to work quickly. So cooperate and maybe we'll live to hoist an ale at a Mirstone pub."

The hired swords rushed toward the back of the carriage as Oz turned to me and gripped my hand, squeezing.

"Are you ready to solve an ancient riddle, Annarissa?" he asked. "Or bury a goddess with your magic—if it comes to that?"

With my thumb, I caressed his strong, squared fingers.

"If solving a riddle keeps you from being her slave and gets us out of their clutches—yes," I said. "But I would much prefer slamming her hard with all my magic."

He nodded, the hint of a smile lifting the corners of his mouth.

"As much pleasure as that would bring me to watch you in action, we need to save that contingency."

I frowned, confused by his statement. A contingency? Why?

"Why do you say that?"

His smile became a smirk. "Because I expect her to cheat—even if we get the riddle's answer right. And when she does, you can demolish her."

I expected her to cheat, too. She kept devouring Oz with her eyes and I saw the hunger in her every movement. She wanted to bed him. Own him. No, she wanted to consume him. Maybe that's what these first gods did? Challenged travelers to rigged contests and then devoured them one by one to bolster their waning magic?

As long as we were ready with a trick or two up our sleeves, then we could out-cheat them at their own treachery.

He glanced past me, toward the marble temples dotting the hillside, the tension returning to his face.

"They're coming," he said and let go of my hand.

I turned around, watching the first gods file out of the closest temple, torches guttering around them as they approached us with their archers and spear carriers, weapons glowing in the fog. Their gold-trimmed linen robes, in colors of the sea, looked a little threadbare in the glow of their weapons, the light brighter than it had been earlier. But their complexions looked a little more washed out than they had an hour ago. I squinted. Like they had thrown all their power and magic into that unearthly glow. Thinking it might frighten us?

Or intimidate us.

The priestess stepped up to Oz and reached out, running her hand across his chest. Underneath his black leather cuirass.

Oz took a step back, out of her reach, but the goddess seemed to enjoy the fact that she'd have to pursue him.

And I enjoyed the fact that I would unleash an earthquake beneath her feet to shatter her spirit form into pieces that would take another hundred years to locate. And a hundred more to put her back together again.

"Well, mortals, we have your riddle ready," she said, hands on her hips as her gaze moved up and down Oz's body, and then over to me, across the empty wagons, and around the landscape at the trees surrounding us.

"And we're ready to solve it," said Oz, hands behind his back as I moved closer to him.

The priestess' smug expression didn't change, those emerald green eyes twinkling like we had just stepped into her trap.

"All right," she said, glancing back at her large entourage—more than fifty first gods and goddesses in tattered old linen robes, gripping their glowing weapons close to their bodies. "Attendant, bring me the riddles."

A black-haired young man stepped out from the back of her entourage, dressed in a simple tan robe frayed at his knees. He held a glowing spear against his shoulder as he hurried toward the priestess with a small reed basket jammed full of scrolls in his left hand. He bowed, spear tilted against his right shoulder, and held out the basket to her.

The priestess stared at the young man for a moment and then nodded him toward Oz and me.

He straightened up and shuffled past her, stopping in front of us. His expression was empty as he held out the basket containing at least a dozen rolled up scrolls that stood end on end in the basket.

"Choose wisely," said the goddess in a sardonic tone. "Once you have read the riddle, you will have thirty minutes to answer it."

Oz looked at me and then nodded toward the basket. He wanted me to pick the scroll.

Nodding, I reached toward the scrolls. Using my magic, I scanned them until the words on each one turned cyan. I couldn't read the actual words, but I looked for one that wasn't too long or two short, trying to avoid anything confusing or too vague, a riddle that might be impossible to solve.

Holding my breath, I slid a scroll out of the basket that seemed to be a reasonable length and handed it to Oz. His face showed no emotion as he unrolled it and read the words. A shadow touched his forehead, eyebrows pressing slightly downward.

He didn't like what he was reading.

Now, I was scared. Had I made a bad choice?

I hoped we wouldn't have to try and fight our way out of the Breach, but I was prepared to use every last breath of my magic to help us escape.

He handed the scroll to me.

"Read it aloud, please," said the goddess in that condescending tone of hers.

Like I was one of her servants.

I glanced at Oz and took a deep breath. And read the riddle out loud.

"I have no head and a tail I lack," I began, glancing at Oz who didn't look happy. "But oft have arms and legs and back. I inhabit the temple, the tavern, and cot. 'Tis a pauper's abode where I am not. If a queen is present, I tell you no fable, I still should be placed at the head of the table. What am I?"

"You have half an hour," the goddess snapped and turned away, following her entourage back toward the closest temple with six capitals lining its steep marble steps. From the top of the capitals, six pocked-faced statues gazed out into the Breach with faded and ambivalent expressions.

Clutching the scroll, I followed Oz behind the carriage where Lady Laurel paced alone.

"Where are the hired swords?" I asked.

"Waiting in the wagon beds and the carriage," said Lady Laurel, clutching the hourglass, sand already sifting into the bottom. "I hope this works."

So did I.

She saw the scroll in my hands.

"The riddle!" she cried and I handed it to her.

She unrolled the old, stiff parchment and read the words.

"I have no head and a tail I lack?" The color left her cheeks. "By Ereth, we have to solve this?"

I nodded and the three of us huddled together, staring at the parchment as Lady Laurel set the hourglass on a flat part of the curve around the carriage's back wheel.

"It's a thing with arms and legs and a back?" Oz replied, his face scrunching in confusion.

"But no head or tail," said Lady Laurel.

"But it inhabits the temple, the tavern, and cot," I said, adding another line from the riddle.

But all I was doing was confusing myself and them.

"What is a cot?" Oz asked.

"A small bed...isn't it?" I replied.

Lady Laurel frowned, staring at the words, and finally, she shook her head. "No, I don't think so," she replied. "Not in this context."

"Why do you say that?" I asked.

"Because the first two words are places," Oz added. "A temple and a tavern. So, is cot also a place?"

Now, Lady Laurel was nodding. "Yes, it has to be. I think it's referring to a small house."

"A small house?" I had never heard that word used in that way before. "Where are you getting that from, Lady Laurel?"

"Grandmother Wilvie always used that word when she moved from Skystead to the village of Rosebury. Said she missed her cot by the sea." A wistful smile touched Lady Laurel's lips. "Until now, I always thought she meant her bed by the sea, but it suddenly dawns on me that she meant her little cottage. Cot is short for cottage."

"Okay," I said, glancing from the hourglass to the scroll. "So, it's a house."

"And it's not in a pauper's abode," Oz read aloud. "So, that means whatever this thing is, it cost more than a few coins."

I nodded. "I agree. It's not a living thing. It's inanimate—costs a few coins."

Oz didn't look convinced. "Are you sure?" he asked. "Doesn't have a head or tail. But it still has arms and legs."

"Paupers don't have it," I replied. "Meaning it must be an expensive thing."

Finally, he nodded. "Okay. So, not a servant or slave. Or something living."

"But...if a queen is present, it still belongs at the head of a table," said Lady Laurel, reading to herself.

She was deep in thought and Oz began to pace, hand against his chin, as he pondered the line that Lady Laurel had just read.

Belongs at the head of a table. What did that mean?

I remembered when I was nine and Mother held an important dinner at the castle. For the heads of state from Xanthe, Ereth, and Rohesia. As the new queen, she took one look at the sadly unimpressive—and rather rustic—royal table with its bench seating and decided it would never do. This meeting was too important to have her guests seated on uncomfortable, hard benches. So, she hired Skystead's best carpenter to fashion a grand polished wooden table to befit a royal gathering. Ornate, cushioned dining chairs with upholstered armrests, all of it in rich velvet royal purple. She wanted her guests to take all the time needed—in comfort–to discuss how to fulfill the prophecy.

Those twelve chairs cost three times as much as the table where Mother sat at the head. In her chair.

It was a chair!

"Oz! Lady Laurel!" I cried, grinning as I ran to Oz and gripped his arm. "It's a chair."

I watched them read the riddle, the realization settling.

Lady Laurel grinned. "That's it, princess!"

"A princess—the perfect person to solve that riddle," said Oz. "Well done, Annarissa."

He picked me up and twirled me around in his arms. When he set me down, all I could do was stare into his eyes, my head spinning. Wanting only to be back in his arms again.

His gaze lingered, hungry, locked on mine until Lady Laurel's voice broke the spell.

"The sand is about to run out," she said in a quiet voice, her gaze shifting from Oz to me.

For a moment or two, he watched me and then his attention moved to the hourglass. We stood at the back of the carriage, staring at the unrolled scroll as the last of the time slipped away.

For a couple of minutes or so, we huddled together in the fog and the dark and the silence. Until the rattle of shields and spears clanked in the distance.

The goddess and her entourage were headed this way.

"Lady Laurel," Oz said in a wary voice. "Is everyone ready?"

"Ready and waiting," she said and leaned against the carriage after picking up the hourglass.

All twelve elemental horses were still harnessed to the wagons and carriage, but they had extinguished all their coppery elemental light. I hoped they wouldn't panic.

Oz's gaze hovered on the priestess as she moved toward him, looking smug. Like she'd already won.

"When you hear me say something about offering tribute, mobilize the crew behind me, Lady Laurel," said Oz, picking up the scroll.

"I'll pass the word," she said and rushed around the carriage, opening its doors and whispering to the hired swords waiting inside.

Oz nodded at me and took hold of my hand as we approached the goddess.

Lady Laurel ran behind us, headed toward the nearest wagon to pass along Oz's signal to the rest of the hired swords.

"My time passes quickly," said the goddess, looking Oz up and down until she saw him holding my hand. "But yours is up."

Her gaze encompassed me fully this time, sizing me up. She had discounted me before, seeing me as insignificant. But him choosing to hold my hand in front of her was a sign she hadn't missed. She now saw me as a rival. A threat. And I had her threat roiling at my fingertips, ready to unleash a massive burst of earth magic right in her smug goddess face.

"It was more than enough time," I replied, staring at this priestess who thought she could take whatever pleased her.

Not this trip.

Smiling, she turned away, trying to show that she wasn't afraid of me, but her overconfidence made her overlook my assault sorceress power. She chose to ignore a dangerous enemy who had a lot more magic than her faded powers. Time did fly, but she had lost track of it by four hundred years or more. And she would soon regret that when she tried to ambush us and take what she wanted.

I had had enough ambushes to last a lifetime by now. And she was just a bump under my carriage wheel right now.

She focused her hungry, leering attention on Oz.

"Read the riddle aloud please," she said, motioning at him.

Oz cleared his throat and held up the scroll.

"I have no head and a tail I lack," he began, his silky voice bard-bright and stout-beer dark. "But oft have arms and legs and back." He glanced at me and smiled. "'I inhabit the temple, the tavern, and cot. 'Tis a pauper's abode where I am not." His gaze shifted back to the priestess who still looked smug. "If a queen is present, I tell you no fable. I still should be placed at the head of the table." Once more, he looked at me. "What am I?"

The priestess looked pleased. "Well, what's the answer?"

"I am a chair," I said, forcing her to look at me again.

Her expression darkened as she glared at me.

"What did you say?"

"I am a chair," I repeated, almost shouting it at her.

Her face looked pinched with anger now and I felt tension radiate from her. Rising. She knew that was the correct answer.

Oz tugged on my hand, drawing me closer.

"We'll be on our way now," he said in a challenging tone. "Priestess."

Her hands moved to her hips as Oz turned with me toward the carriage.

"Not so fast," said the goddess, her tone darkening.

Oz turned back around, his grip on my hand tightening. He'd been expecting her to fight.

"Problem with that answer?" he said, his voice deep and sharp.

"Not at all," she said in a flippant tone.

As her entourage began to move. Toward us.

"You just took too long to answer it," she said.

"We answered it in the time you allotted us." Oz glared at her.

Chuckling, she shook her head slowly as the spear carriers began to advance on us, archers dropping to one knee, nocking arrows.

"Afraid not, mortals," she said, looking pleased with herself. "Looks like you belong to us now." She grinned at Oz. "Especially you."

"What?" Oz replied. "You expect us to offer you tribute now?"

The goddess' emerald green eyes narrowed. "Take them."

Oz put his body in front of me as the spear carriers raised their weapons.

But the spear carriers suddenly stopped in mid-stride, mouths falling open. The archers held their ground, but fear froze their hands at their sides. Far from their bows.

Even the goddess' face had gone pale.

As more than a dozen hired swords stepped out of the mist, their swords and armor glowing with eerie white light. Air magic. Cast on all the armor and weapons by Lady Laurel. She'd expended most of her magic doing it.

To make this goddess think that our entire convoy had magic. As well as enchanted weapons and armor. To these first gods, this convoy looked impenetrable.

And now, it was my turn.

I lifted my hands in the air and made the ground in front of the goddess glow a soft blue. As it began to shake.

Oz chuckled and crossed his arms as I stepped out from behind him.

"Did we neglect to tell you that in addition to being sword masters, we are all mages and sorceresses?" he asked as the entire crew lined up behind him, weapons raised. "Spellswords. And all of our magic is at full power. Sure you want to try us?"

The elemental horses chose that moment to reappear, their coppery gleam intensifying the magic glow surround the entire party.

"Oh, please," I said, calling up a ball of molten earth that burned blue and white in my hand. "Do try us. So I can disintegrate you with my battle magic."

"What say you, priestess?" Oz asked, watching the defeated expression spring to the spirit goddess' angry face.

With a heavy sigh, she lifted her hand in the air.

"All of you, stand down," she said, sounding defeated.

"Farago," Oz called, his gaze still on the goddess. "Get the wagons in line and headed northeast toward Rohesia. Lady Laurel, prepare to drive the carriage."

He waited, his hand still clamped tightly around mine as he waited for the first wagon to line up in the road.

Lady Laurel drove the carriage behind it. It was five feet behind Oz and me. The elemental horses fidgeted, snorting and grunting as they obeyed Lady Laurel's commands.

Pirin and Norval drove the last two wagons behind the carriage. All of the elemental horses looked fierce but wary in the wash of copper light as they pawed at the road, elemental hooves gouging deep into the dirt.

The tension was thick as the entire crew waited for Oz's signal, nervous uncertainty hovering in the air.

"Now, we must take our leave, priestess," said Oz, backing away from the goddess as I led him by the hand around the carriage.

He waited at the back wheel, keeping the goddess in sight until I opened the carriage doors and climbed inside.

He hesitated a moment and then climbed inside behind me. After closing the doors, he thumped the carriage roof.

"Let's roll, Lady Laurel," he said into the hailing-horn.

"Move!" Lady Laurel called out and snapped the reins hard, coaxing the elemental horses into motion.

The carriage rocked backward and the lurched forward, the elemental horses' coppery glow brightening as they began to trot. Lady Laurel drove them into a canter behind Farago's wagon. The other two wagons creaked forward, elemental horses glowing bright copper, hooves thumping the road as we left the temple ruins behind us.

And the first gods standing slack-jawed in the road.

Only when we were a safe distance away did the cheering erupt from the wagons. And from Lady Laurel who sat in the carriage's driver seat.

"We did it!" I cried as I shot across the carriage interior.

Into Oz Tarrant's arms.

He held me tightly and then let go.

"You were incredible, Annarissa," he said, a dreamy look in those beautiful ice blue eyes.

"No, you were so calm and intimidating!" I cried, laughing as I hugged him again. "She was afraid to cross you!"

He reached out and ran his fingers through one of my braids that had lost its clasp and unwound into wispy blond waves around my face.

I moved closer, hands sliding up his neck. To his cheek.

He cupped my face in his hands and let them wander down my neck, through my hair to my shoulders, tracing the sewn-up tear across my blouse.

I let go of his face and reached up to my blouse, unfastening buttons, sliding it off my shoulders.

He pulled in a breath, eyes widening as he stroked my bare shoulders.

I pressed my body against him, hands sliding underneath his black leather armor. To his bare chest.

His heart raced against mine, the heat in my belly roiling as I slid my hands away from his chest. Reaching up, I unbuttoned the rest of the buttons on my blouse. Letting it fall off my shoulders. Revealing the lavender corset underneath.

"You are the most beautiful woman I have ever wanted," he whispered against my ear.

His lips slid across my jaw to my neck, his hot mouth pressing kisses down my neck and along my collarbone. Sliding along the cleft between my breasts.

Gasping, I leaned into him, his breath so hot against my skin, quickening as his hands traveled down my waist.

I pushed my skirt up over my knees. To my thighs. Revealing my sheer gold stockings.

His breath caught, hands moving to my calves, sliding up them. Stroking up my thighs. To the tops of my stockings.

I spread my legs and his hands slid between them, caressing my inner thighs, running his hands down them. Up them. And across my thin silk underpants. I gasped. No one had ever touched me there before. Or anywhere. But I wanted Oz Tarrant to touch and kiss every part of my body.

Stretching out my legs for him, I laid them across his lap. He rolled down my stockings one by one, in soft strokes, and ran his hot hands up and down my legs as his kisses burned against the tops of my breasts.

Arching my back, I reached behind me and slowly unhooked my corset.

His breath raced in time with his heart as I slid forward. Straddling him. When the corset was undone, I ran my hands across his leather armor. Unfastening the clasps of his cuirass.

When all the clasps were undone, I pushed it off his shoulders. Along with his broadsword sheath. And laid my face against his bare chest, pressing kisses down the length of his torso as he pushed my corset aside. And cupped my breasts in his hot hands.

He lifted my face from his chest and leaned into me, wrapping his arms around my bare chest. Pulling me close. His hot mouth pressed against my hardening nipples, kissing and suckling as his hands slid underneath my skirt. Pushing it and my petticoat away from my bare legs. I felt his hardness straining against his tight leather pants. And I wanted it inside me.

I gasped when his fingers slid between my legs again, into my silk underpants, pushing them away from my sex. With gentle strokes, his fingers pressed between my legs in charged, shuddering circles until I was wet and aching for him. I pushed my pelvis against his fingers, moaning at his touch, his mouth still against my breasts, his tongue encircling my nipples until I was feverish for more. Feverish for his naked body on top of mine and his hardness inside me. I rocked my hips against him, grinding against his hand.

"Make love to me," I whispered in his ear and wrapped my arms around his neck, pressing his face against my breasts, my body shuddering as he slipped a finger inside me.

He lifted his face from my breasts as I moaned at his finger's slow rhythm inside me.

"Are you sure, Annarissa?"

Already, I was nodding.

I nibbled his ear and brushed my lips against his neck. Virgin or not, Prince Arence would never touch me, much less make love to me. The question of my virginity had never even come up in discussions with the Rohesian crown. Because it made no difference to them. I would never birth their heirs or have a wedding night with my new husband. No, he wouldn't risk an Erethian having his child.

But I wanted Oz Tarrant like I'd never wanted a man before.

"I want you inside me."

His member strained against his leather trousers as I reached down and unbuttoned them.

He slid off the seat, snaking off the trousers until he was naked.

Quickly, I unbuttoned my skirt, dropping it to the floor as the carriage rumbled down the road, headed out of the Breach. Toward Rohesia's border.

My petticoat and underpants joined my skirt as Oz lifted me into his arms and laid me on the carriage seat beneath him. Then he kicked the lock bar across the carriage doors and pressed his body against mine. Rolling on top of me.

His hands explored my breasts, the curve of my hips, the length of my thighs. Parting them as my body shuddered beneath him.

I spread my legs as he pressed his pelvis against mine and guided his member gently against my wet entrance. And slowly, with the push of his hips, he entered me.

It hurt a little, but he was gentle and patient, pressing lightly as I arched my back against him, feeling his hardness push deep and slowly move inside me. The measured, steady rhythm burned through me, making my body quiver and pulsate in ways I'd never felt before.

Pulling in a heated breath, I wrapped my arms around his back, drawing his hips closer, relaxing my body against his as the rush of heat and the strokes of his erection vibrated through my belly, building in exquisite sensations. Growing faster and intense as his rhythm quickened, his strokes becoming thrusts, each one inciting a hot wave of pleasure through my entire body.

Gasping, I moved my hips with him as every stroke built on the last, fast and frantic until his movements exploded through me in a shuddering burst of heat and need and pleasure until my chest heaved and my body rocked with his thrusts like a bucking horse. I pulled him tighter against me, losing myself against his fiery skin and thrusts until he moaned, moving still faster and more frenetic until I felt him peak.

His thrusts began to slow. Becoming strokes that finally stilled until he collapsed against me, his member still inside me. I just held him, reveling in the press of his hot body against my bare, wet skin, the feel of his member still inside me, the heat and ecstasy still throbbing through my sweat-slicked body.

Smiling, he lifted his face from my breasts and at last, his mouth found mine, his tongue pressing deep. Devouring my mouth with his, his mouth so hot against my lips, his tongue against mine as his lips worked fiery, tingling magic against my mouth.

At first, the gold light confused me.

Until I realized that his mouth pressing against mine in a burning kiss had sparked a strange glow. Something I had never seen before. Were the fairy tales real? It was just like the spark of gold light that had flashed when I brushed my lips against his mouth earlier.

What did it mean? Were the old legends true? About fate? And true love?

How was that possible?

It had to be my earth magic. After all, this was my first time kissing or making love to a man. But he wasn't a prince. He was a mercenary from Xanthe.

Oz lifted his head, staring at me in confusion.

"Annarissa, what is this gold light?" he asked.

I shook my head. "I don't know. I'm fated to marry Arence Siridean."

A sad look touched his face as he slid off me. He sat down and gathered me in his arms, cradling me against him.

"Don't remind me," he said with a sigh. "To save Kambria."

I snuggled against his heated skin and kissed his lips again. Another spark of gold light filled the carriage and dissipated.

He grabbed one of the blankets and wrapped it around us. Together, we laid naked in each other's arms and held each other as the carriage bumped and lurched along the road. Out of the Breach.

Toward the Rohesian border.

It was the last place that either of us wanted to go. But Oz and I both knew there was no choice. Regardless of who fate had chosen as my mate, if I didn't marry a Siridean prince, the prophecy went unfulfilled, causing the already dim sunlight to fade further. Killing more crops. Starving more people. Until Ereth became a wasteland alongside Rohesia. Leaving only Xanthe to slowly starve and freeze to death.

Until all of Kambria perished.

I already knew that when I kissed the man I was fated to marry, there would be no sparks. Not like kissing Oz. And neither of us wanted to cause the death of our world.

19

It took more than two hours to reach the last dark stretches of the Cimmerian Breach and then leave it behind. Even with the sun's washed-out light, the air smelled clean and crisp, the scent of cool rain clinging to everything as the world grew a little lighter beyond the valley.

The surrounding forests that stretched along both sides of the sparsely traveled northern road almost gleamed with fragile sunlight, reminding me of autumn in Ereth. But only in books and paintings. The sun had been faded and pale in the sky my entire life and I had only seen the bright, warm rays in paintings. That kind of sunlight hadn't touched Ereth or Rohesia for more than two decades.

Nevertheless, I was grateful for this clear gold light that had a warm orange cast and lit the leaves and branches with gentle tongues of flame. Even the pale green grass sparkled briefly with fresh-fallen rain that clung to the tender blades and puddled along the road.

After we emerged from the Breach, into the daylight as the carriage rushed onward, Oz laid me down on the seat and we made love again.

"There's a small lake just ahead," he said, stroking my hair and kissing my lips in another spark of gold light as he held me, only a blanket covering our naked bodies. "Near the border. Farago knows we will camp there for a few hours. Long enough to bathe and eat." He stretched and sat up, his eyes looking tired. "And sleep. Until nightfall and then we cross Rohesia's border."

I leaned up and kissed him in another burst of golden light.

"Then I had better get dressed," I said and bent to gather my clothing off the floor of the carriage.

He looked sad as I began to dress.

"I want to bathe and sleep," I said and leaned against his bare chest as he pulled on his leather pants. "With you beside me."

He pulled me into his arms, those icy blue eyes thawing into a smile as he held me one more time and I lost myself in his touch again as I ran my hands across his chest, caressing his smooth skin. Wanting only to stay with him.

But when the carriage began to slow, he let me go to finish dressing. By the time the carriage had lurched to a stop, I was back on my side of the carriage, Oz on his side, watching me with a longing gaze that made me want to launch myself across the carriage. And back into his arms. Wanting him to make love to me again.

The carriage doors creaked open and Lady Laurel stepped inside, exhausted but smiling as she sat down beside me, rubbing her arms and shoulders.

"Driving a carriage and a team of elemental horses is difficult work," she said with a groan. "My arms will still hurt this time next year."

But after glancing at me and then Oz, her expression changed. Into a wary look as she watched Oz a moment. And then me.

Her eyes narrowed, studying me. My clothing was all in its proper place, but a blush burned against my hot cheeks and some of my hair's braids had come undone.

"Princess, your hair," she said and cast a dark look at Oz who met her gaze without a blink.

I reached up, feeling my braids that had come unplaited around my face. "My braids have come undone," I said, feigning surprise. "The carriage's movements must have shaken them loose. It was a rough ride out of the Breach."

Oz covered his mouth with his hand and I could see him smiling beneath that black leather glove.

"Well, we will braid them again," said Lady Laurel. "After a meal and some rest."

"And a bath," I said and nodded toward Oz. "Oz says there is a small lake where we can bathe when we stop."

"It's still quite warm this time of year, despite the fading sun," said Oz. "Last chance until we reach Mirstone. But to be fair, their bath houses are incredible, Lady Laurel. After we arrive, you and Annarissa can enjoy Rohesia's private hot springs after such a long, arduous journey. Or so I'm told."

I smiled, imagining Oz and me making love in a mountain hot spring with stars filling the night sky, moon rising overhead.

"Do you travel to Mirstone often, Oz?" I asked.

It was a dim hope, but I ached for the chance to still love him. After I reached Mirstone Castle and the prince locked me away in favor of his Rohesian concubine. I would find a way to sneak out. Find him in the village. And love him like my heart ached to do now.

Oz exhaled sharply, his longing gaze enveloping me again.

"Rarely, my lady," he said with a sigh. "It is a long journey from Xanthe, even when the seaports are operational. Not as long as Ereth, but unless I have business in Rohesia, I won't be returning to the kingdom any time soon. And the crown is not fond of me despite my father's sacrifice."

His words stung. He was trying to make me understand that loving him would be impossible after he delivered me to Mirstone. That all we had was here. Now.

My head understood, but my heart screamed and raged at his words.

"Your father's sacrifice?" Lady Laurel asked, squinting at Oz.

He nodded, staring down at his hands.

"My father was Rohesian. Captain of the Siridean family guard. Died saving the king's life and his two young sons—according to my mother anyway. Who was a pickpocket and master of tall tales."

Lady Laurel looked shocked. "Your father was captain of the Siridean guard? But aren't you Xanthan?"

Oz nodded again. "Half. I was just a baby. I don't remember any of it. My mother, a Xanthan, hates the Rohesians for sacrificing my father that night. She left Mirstone that very night and never returned." He looked up, his gaze fiery as he stared at me. "Not sure that's the complete truth because according to the Rohesian border guards, they would still love to get hold of her for crimes against the crown."

Lady Laurel's mouth gaped. "Crimes against the crown?"

He shrugged. "She refuses to tell me what she did or what really happened to my father that night," Oz said, shaking his head, a frown furrowing his brow. "Mother liked to carry off things that didn't belong to her. Like royal jewels." He sighed. "And other people's husbands. Taught me everything she knew about pickpocketing when I was five. Before she chose her latest lover over her son and turned me out into Snowmelt's streets to fend for myself."

My heart ached at his story. It was first time he'd ever shared something so deeply personal with me before.

"Oz," I said, my eyes stinging. "I'm so sorry."

He shrugged again, brushing it off.

"Mother probably tried to steal Daegal's royal jewels while he was still wearing them. While battling assassins. She's certainly made a name for herself in Xanthe for similar activities. No wonder the Tarrant name is mud in Rohesia. My father died protecting the king and his heirs. His name should have been revered, not sullied by her stealing things that didn't belong to her. She never learns. Or cares."

Silence descended in the carriage, my protector and my lady-in-waiting both deep in thought.

"Lady Laurel," I said, turning to her. "Will you assist me with bathing in the lake?"

"Certainly, my lady," said Lady Laurel with the bow of her head.

"My lady, would you like me to bring down one of your trunks?" Oz asked as he rose from the seat.

"Would you mind, Oz? I would prefer to change into more suitable clothes before we reach the border."

"It would be my pleasure," he said and ducked out of the carriage.

And I felt cold in his absence. And so sad. Moments that would expand into forever once we reached Mirstone Castle.

"You can use this blanket to dry off with," said Lady Laurel, picking up the grey blanket beside her as she motioned me toward the doors.

Nodding, I got to my feet and exited the carriage. Around me, the woods fanned out toward a pristine lake with the clearest waters I had ever seen. Hundreds of tall, mature trees with ruddy trunks surrounded the small, round lake, wrapping it in a layer of privacy from the road that I hadn't expected. Dried brown leaves still clung to the branches, clattering like the rush of waves when the wind brushed through the tree limbs. They also covered the ground, crunching and rustling as the hired swords made camp. The smell of dried leaves was crisp in the cool air, warmed with wood smoke, and herbs from the meal fire. Peppery. Garlicky. Tomatoey. It smelled delicious.

To my left, the fire crackled beneath a large iron pot as the hired swords gathered the remaining fresh root vegetables and containers of Xanthan spices from the wagon. Pirin and Norval oversaw the huge pot, working together to construct a savory meal from the last of our fresh supplies from Ereth. Loaves of golden brown Erethian bread warmed on stones beside the fire. Once the broth and grains and these bread loaves were gone, we would be reduced to hard flat bread and jerky. Mother even sent along some jars of butter and a wheel of Skystead cheddar to make swallowing the dry foodstuffs easier.

With the grey blanket draped over my arm, I hurried past the wagons gathered in a circle around the meal fire. The elemental horses had all returned to their realm. Lady Laurel followed, carrying a small satchel on her shoulder.

To my right, Farago sharpened blades and helped mend armor. The scent of warm metal, sweat, and leather hung in the air as I walked down a gently sloping bank into the trees. To the edge of the small lake, its rippling clear waters eddying against smooth dark stones. Steam clung to its warm surface, floating like spirits above the mirror-calm surface, the sky overcast as it began to weep a fine mist against my face. I slipped behind a large tree as Lady Laurel helped me disrobe, holding up the blanket to keep anyone from peering at me.

I hated to wash away Oz's touch or his musk and leather scent that still clung to my face and skin, the memory of him making love to me still vibrated against my body as I peeled off my petticoat and stockings and piled them on top of my torn blouse, corset, and skirt. I had already slipped off my black boots and set them on a large, flat rock. Lady Laurel removed all of the gold clasps from my braids and brushed my pale blond hair until it glistened.

"Here, princess," she said, handing me a sliver of soap scented with lavender oil.

Crouching, I waded into the water, Lady Laurel still holding up the blanket as I submerged my body beneath the warm, soothing lake waters. Under the pale light that had broken through heavy swaths of grey clouds, I scrubbed my hair with lavender soap and rinsed it away by plunging under the water. Wishing Oz was beside me. Wanting to feel his body against mine in this warm lake water. Aching for his caress.

But it was only Lady Laurel and me at the lake's edge as I scrubbed my body with the gritty soap and rinsed the suds away. I wanted to let my body float along the surface, feeling the cool air and warm water caress my skin, but there was no time. And I had no desire to put my bare body on display to the hired swords. Especially Farago.

With my long blond hair dripping down my back, I stepped out of the water, onto some rocks behind the trees, shivering as Lady Laurel wrapped me in the blanket. She applied some fragrant oil to my hair that smelled like warm cotton and rosewater, working it through with a comb. I rubbed my skin dry with the blanket and with rigorous movements, Lady Laurel helped me dry my hair until it stopped dripping.

I applied oil to my skin until the tightness left and it felt soft. The warm lake water and the heady scented oil energized me and I quickly slid my feet back into my boots. Draped in the grey blanket, I hurried alongside Lady Laurel back to the carriage.

In front of the doors sat one of my trunks.

I glanced around until I caught sight of Oz leaning against a tree near the meal fire. His long black hair was wet around his shoulders. Had he bathed in the lake while I bathed? The thought of him being near me in that water gave me chills.

He wore a pristine set of black leather armor, cut a little differently than the armor he'd worn before. His broadsword perched between his muscled shoulders, the hilt of a long knife peeking out of taller black boots. He had changed into fresh armor. After bathing in the lake, I wish I could have caught another glimpse of his tall, leanly muscled naked body.

His gaze smoldered as he watched me from across the camp. Standing there draped in a wet blanket, naked beneath it, my shoulders bare, and my damp blond hair curling into waves around my shoulders.

I grinned, fighting an urge to blow him a kiss. Or run across the camp and throw myself into his arms.

But he kept his distance despite that sad look in his ice blue eyes.

And then I knew. I would never hold him in my arms again. And he would never make love to me again. Those moments were gone—now that we were almost at Rohesia's border.

My heart smashed against my rib cage and I wondered if he loved me. Had he ever loved me or was a roll in the hay all part of the job?

Fighting back the sting of tears, I rushed inside the carriage.

"Hand me something to wear," I said to Lady Laurel from inside carriage, trying to keep the pain out of my voice—and failing. "I don't care what you choose."

"But princess," Lady Laurel called to me. "Don't you want to pick out your own ensemble."

"It no longer matters," I said, trying to keep my voice from cracking. "It's not like Prince Arence has feelings for me. Or ever plans to bed me after we're wed. I could arrive naked and draped in this wet blanket and it wouldn't matter to him."

While Lady Laurel pulled out something for me to wear from my trunk, I pressed my face against the wall and cried hot tears. Wanting a man I could never have. Who probably didn't even love me.

20

As twilight settled like an old blanket across the camp and along the lake, Lady Laurel carried two bowls of hot broth into the carriage where I sat huddled against the wall beside the broken windows. Dressed in a long red Rohesian court gown with a low neckline that made the tops of my breasts peek out with the help of a tight, lacy corset. The sheer red trumpet sleeves dripped like mist from the silky, almost sheer red fabric, the dress hugging my waist with a matching belt that hung down in front.

The entire dress dripped silky fabric and showed hints of bare skin. At the shoulders, sides, and hips. It had been made using one of my own dresses for size, but its style revealed more of the body than Erethian gowns. The skirt had a straighter cut and it had a sheer red train that floated like fog behind it—by sewing mastery rather than magic. Red was Rohesia's court color, so Lady Laurel asked me to wear the court dress sent for me to wear. Along with shimmery gold slippers I would have never worn in Ereth. Impractical. And they flaunted the crown's wealth at a time when so many families didn't have enough food on their tables.

All of this for the Rohesian court and my soon-to-be husband, a man that would never even look upon me with more than a passing glance. No matter what I wore. But wearing the gown would get us past the border guards without issues.

I smiled at the fresh pair of stockings (white this time) I had donned, the memory of Oz's hot, strong hands rolling them off my legs. The memory of his touch lingered and as much as I cherished those moments, they made me sad. He had returned to his militant, detached bodyguard persona, his distance painful. But deep down, I understood. His job was almost complete. No matter how he felt about me, my destiny was set in stone. So, why prolong the pain—if he felt any at my absence.

My hair was still damp and the hair around my face had been braided back into a series of small braids, secured with gold clasps. Drying slowly—as long as the wind didn't blow through the carriage's broken windows and turn them into tangled straw.

I carried my Erethian amethyst and gold crown in the valise beside me, but Lady Laurel put the Rohesian crown, simpler and less ornate, on my head. It looked like one of Ereth's simple gold traveling crowns, dotted with five small, oval rubies. If anyone stopped us along the road to Mirstone Castle, my Rohesian appearance might save our lives.

Or get us waylaid and robbed.

Lady Laurel draped another grey blanket across me, covering the dress, and set a plate in my lap.

"Broth and grains are nice and hot, princess," she said and sat down beside me, a plate for herself in her other hand. "Alas, the vegetables and bread are gone."

I picked up the spoon and dipped it into the bowl. Lifting it to my mouth, I sipped the warm liquid. I had no appetite and almost pushed the bowl aside. But I knew she would keep at me until I ate. So, I ladled the savory broth into the spoon and drank it. To keep the peace.

"Princess, what's the matter?" she asked finally, setting down her spoon on the plate as I leaned my head against the wall.

"I despise the thought of going to Mirstone," I said with a sigh. "I know it's my duty, but the thought of living among strangers who despise me for the rest of my days makes me hurt all over."

"I know how hard this must be for you to leave behind everything you hold dear, my princess." She bowed her head. "I, too, share your fate as your lady-in-waiting, but at least I was given a choice. And I volunteered."

I turned toward her, shocked by her admission. "You… volunteered?"

Lady Laurel nodded.

"Why would you volunteer for this banishment?" I asked, my eyes stinging with tears.

"Because I couldn't bear the thoughts of that little baby I nursed and the child I cared for like my own daughter growing into a beautiful young woman alone. In the company of our enemies. I asked to become your lady-in-waiting, knowing I would make this trip beside you. So, you would have someone who cares for you at your side."

My eyes brimmed with tears.

"Lady Laurel," I said as the tears threaded down my cheeks. "Your sacrifice humbles me."

"And your courage gives me hope for Kambria, princess," said Lady Laurel, taking hold of my hand and squeezing it.

I didn't feel courageous, especially the closer we got to Rohesia. And Prince Arence.

She studied me for a few moments.

"He bedded you, didn't he?" she asked.

Gasping, my gaze shot to her face, my cheeks flaming now.

"How did you know?" I cried.

"It burns in your eyes, princess," she said with a smile. "And on your cheeks."

"If I am honest, I bedded him," I replied and Lady Laurel's mouth fell open. "But it was definitely mutual between us, Lady Laurel. It was my only chance to be loved and I wanted the memory of his love to comfort me during the emptiness ahead. Besides, Rohesia didn't care about a purity test."

"What?" Lady Laurel cried, aghast. "No purity test? But why?"

Because Prince Arence never planned to touch me. Ever.

"A month or two ago, I heard two officials from Mother's court talking about the prince and how he already had a woman he loved. He'd insisted that he would never consummate our marriage. That it was in name only, to satisfy this prophecy. Nothing more."

"So, he sacrifices nothing," Lady Laurel said, an edge in her voice. "Returns to his current life while you give up everything to live in an enemy's court. Alone. Without love. Without family. Without support." She shook her head. "This is wrong, princess."

I nodded.

"Do you love him?" she asked, nodding toward the carriage doors.

I pulled in a breath, my face contorting as I nodded again. "With all my heart. All I want is to be with him."

She moved the bowl and plate out of the way and put her arms around me. Holding me tight in a motherly embrace that I had never felt from my mother.

"I'm so sorry, princess. But you know he's a rogue. He's probably bed and fled half the women in Xanthe."

I shook my head, pulling away from her. "No, you're wrong, Lady Laurel," I said. "Oz Tarrant isn't like that. I know it," I said. "I feel it."

"And worse, princess...he's the Butcher of Badriyah," she insisted. "And apparently, he's wanted for thievery and worse in Rohesia. Along with his own mother. The rot doesn't fall far from the tree."

"That's not true!" I snapped, crossing my arms. "I don't know any of these details and neither do you. He was a baby at the time. Your baseless speculations aren't fair to Oz. Lady Laurel...please—I love him."

"But once he delivers you and me to Mirstone, you'll never see him again, my princess. You know that. He said as much. And in little more than two days, you must be prepared to tell him goodbye."

Two days. That moment was only a breath away and I hurt all over at the thought of it. Her words were daggers to my soul.

"And that is the reason for my bitter mood, Lady Laurel."

I pushed away the wooden plate and turned back toward the window, watching the hired swords pack up the camp site as I refused the rest of the grains and broth.

"I'll save this for you," Lady Laurel said in a quiet voice as she opened the carriage doors. "Better get some sleep. We'll be headed for the border in a few hours."

Lady Laurel hurried out of the carriage as I pressed my tear-streaked face against the wall and closed my eyes.

I dreamed that the carriage thundered down an endless road while old gods pursued it. The conveyance trundled and shook, elemental horses galloping like demons pursued them. Shaking me hard as I struggled to remain in my seat.

When I awoke, the carriage was in motion.

Lady Laurel sat beside me.

But my heart fell when I gazed across the carriage and saw the empty seat.

"Where's Oz?" I asked in a raspy voice as I turned to Lady Laurel.

She pointed toward the ceiling. "He graciously agreed to drive the carriage and allow my body to recover from my time in that awful seat."

I bit my lip, trying to force back the sting of tears filling my eyes. He wanted nothing to do with me now that he had bedded me. Lady Laurel was right—and I felt sick inside. A prince and a mercenary and neither of them wanted me.

Maybe it was best that I was making this sacrifice? Because fate had a cruel sense of humor and would have probably left me an old spinster in Ereth anyway. But at least I would have been in familiar surroundings. Spending more time with my sisters, for a little while anyway.

"How long have I been asleep?" I asked, the carriage shuddering along the rough road, a road I had never traveled before.

The blackened and pocked wooden shields (reinforced outside with old plate armor) had been placed across the broken windows, to keep the chilly wind out—or the possibility of another attack from the Kambrian Equalizers. Traces of savory herbs and my lavender soap hung in the air. The red seat cushions seemed so dull against my vivid red Rohesian court gown.

"More than five hours, princess," said Lady Laurel. "We've been on the road for three hours and we're almost to the border." She smiled. "And I think we have finally left the assassins behind."

I didn't think so, but I kept quiet. Not with Rohesia so close and two days left to murder me.

For a half hour, the hurried jaunt along this rough, twisty road nearly shook all of my braids loose again. I held onto the hand rail while Lady Laurel tried to read her book, but the bumps and turns made it almost impossible.

Until finally, the carriage abruptly careened to a stop.

My heart beat into my throat, a chill dancing along my spine. My hands began to shake.

We were here. At the border of Rohesia. In two days' time, we would be at Mirstone Castle. And I would never see Oz Tarrant again.

I swallowed the painful breath and gazed at Lady Laurel who looked relieved.

"We've finally reached the border!" she cried, slapping her book closed. "This horrid ordeal is almost at an end."

For me, it was just beginning, but I kept that thought to myself.

"Will the Sirideans send soldiers to at least lead us to the castle? Or must we do that ourselves, too?"

"I honestly don't know, princess," said Lady Laurel as she tried to look out the windows through the sides of the wooden shields. "Those details died with Blademaster Laurant."

But the wooden shields were flush against the window frames, covering any holes made by assassins—or accident.

The heavy thump of footsteps crossed the top of the carriage and pounded down the ladder.

Oz. My heart skipped a beat. Climbing down.

In a few moments, muffled voices echoed outside the carriage.

What would the Rohesians say about our elemental horses? They'd be either terrified or furious. But after their intrepids were murdered alongside their blademaster, we had little choice.

Oz's clear strong voice responded. Loudly. Insisting something was unnecessary.

More muffled words. Followed by Oz declining. Forcefully.

A scuffle erupted. Sound of punches thrown. Lots of movement.

Until finally, footsteps approached the carriage.

Lady Laurel cast a fearful look at me.

I felt it, too.

Something was wrong. Even Oz had felt it and denied something to whoever waited for us at the border.

Was it another ambush?

I wasn't about to just sit here and find out.

Reaching inside for my magic, I closed my eyes and lifted my right hand in front of me, palm up. Calling up earth magic. As it encircled my fingertips with blue smoke, I pictured a shower of dirt clods and rocks and called the spell to my lips.

Slowly, I recited it, giving it an activation word of *assassin* and let the spell's energy roil in the air in front of me, around me. All the energies were in place, ready for me to speak a single casting word that would rain magic down on anyone who dared to open that door and try to harm Lady Laurel and me.

The blue glow lit the entire carriage as Lady Laurel's air magic lightened the hue with its white mist as she, too waited to level some painful air magic at anyone who meant us harm.

"Trap, Annarissa!" Oz shouted from somewhere beyond the carriage doors, until the sound of a fist slammed into his gut— silencing him.

The carriage doors snapped open.

Standing in their wake were five men dressed in the red and blue uniforms of the Rohesian army. I'd recognize that uniform anywhere. My mother continued fighting the hundred-year war against the Rohesians, one started by her grandmother. Under her own mother—Queen Maelena Thorn, the fighting had intensified. So, I had seen these uniforms my entire life.

The stone-faced men stood at attention until a man with a short beard and brown hair well past his uniform collar stepped in front of the four guardsmen. He had gold braids across his red and white jacket's shoulders that ended with the thick gold-fringed pads of a Rohesian officer.

But the hair.

Soldiers in Ereth and Rohesia were required to tie back any hair past their collars. Or crop it close. Always above the collar.

"Princess Annarissa Thorn," said the tall, scarecrow-thin man in the red and white Rohesian officer's uniform. "At last. We have waited more than a week for your arrival at Rohesia's border."

Except for the hair, they looked official, uniforms correct. Officer's uniform with the right flourishes and the right colors. Officers wore red and white. Foot soldiers wore uniforms in red and blue with white trousers.

Not a sound emanated from the hired swords. Or Oz. Everything felt deathly—and unnaturally—quiet.

I needed to step out of this carriage so I had maneuvering room. And could battle this trap—and these assassins. I had plenty of magic at hand to ruin their day. So did Lady Laurel.

I rose from my seat and moved toward the carriage doors.

"Annarissa," Lady Laurel hissed in a sharp whisper. "Don't. You heard Oz."

But I couldn't cast magic confined inside this carriage. And I wanted to look these mercenaries in the eyes and defeat them.

I climbed out of the carriage, down the two steps, and into the cool darkness. My elegant, sleek red Rohesian gown sparkled against the torches two of these soldiers carried.

The road was blocked by a wooden barrier and gate across it. But ahead, in the distance, I could barely make out a tall stone wall that stretched along Rohesia's border to the north and south. Barely illuminated by the thinnest crescent moon waxing in the clear night sky.

It was too dark and too distant to make out what stood between those stone walls.

As I glanced at the wooden gate and the tents on either side of the road, I knew it was a trap.

Rohesia's border wasn't some makeshift wooden gate thrust across a road and surrounded by tents. Where was the guard post? And the lanterns on poles that they carried when they met travelers at the tall iron gate that stretched between the stone walls built around the entirety of Rohesia.

These soldiers were home. At their own border, a post that had been established more than a hundred years ago. They would never have a makeshift wooden gate, sleep in tents, and carry torches. There would be tall iron gates and stone walls preventing anyone from entering Rohesia without permission because this border had been closed for a hundred years. And the current delicate truce was temporary at best.

This *border* was fake. The real one was probably just up ahead in the dark. And these soldiers were probably Xanthan Equalizers. Without their masks.

Intending to kill the entire party and blame it on someone else. Like Oz Tarrant and the hired swords.

"We are switching carriages, m'lady. A plain carriage just beyond the gates, Princess Thorn," said the officer with an overly fake smile as he bowed and held out his hand. "Sent by King Daegal himself."

He intended to lead me somewhere remote. And kill me.

"We must hurry, princess," said the fake officer. "Out here in the open, you are a target."

Lady Laurel exited the carriage behind me.

There was no sign of Oz or the other hired swords.

I glanced behind us. The three wagons had no drivers. I shuddered. Or passengers in the back. The elemental horses gleamed with coppery light in the darkness. They snorted and pawed at the ground, looking agitated. Angry.

I looked at the soldiers carefully again. They hadn't batted an eye at the magical horses pulling their carriage. In a realm that despised and outlawed magic.

But Rohesians would have known that they were facing a battle mage and an assault sorceress with full battle magic. They would be treating us warily, knowing the magic we carried.

That we were about to rain down on these assassins.

My gaze shot to the two tents on either side of the road. Were they holding Oz and the other hired swords inside? Or more assassins?

I felt a little insulted that they thought three assassins could overpower an assault sorceress and a battle mage. But because I had emptied my magical core, my well of magic took a little longer to fill. I needed a bit more time to cast at full power.

"Where is this carriage again?" I asked, glancing around, feeding their ridiculous assumption that I was helpless. "It must be one used only by the royal family," I demanded, crossing my arms against my chest, hiding the blue glow of my fingertips as my magic churned. But I needed another moment or two to gather all my magic. "I am a princess. I refuse to travel in the likes of one of these wagons."

The officer smiled. "Unfortunately, it is rather austere, Your Highness. If you insist, we will be forced to continue using this reinforced ironwood carriage," he said, patting the side of our carriage. "The one we sent to Skystead."

So...they knew that the Rohesian crown sent this carriage to Ereth. The only way they could have known those details was—again, from someone high up in Mother's court. Only a handful of people knew this carriage had been reinforced with Erethian ironwood. And that an Erethian craftsman did the work. Ordered by Mother and handled by two Erethian court officials.

I had a bad feeling about this—Erethian traitor. There were only two people in Mother's court who knew–and one name rose to the top.

Now, I just needed to prove it.

I gazed at the officer. "I never mentioned that the carriage was reinforced with ironwood," I said.

The officer chuckled nervously as he moved closer to me.

"Well, His Majesty assured us the carriage was safe when he mentioned the ironwood reinforcement."

I smiled and let my arms fall to my sides, feeling the magic thrum through my fingertips. Almost ready…

"Isn't that fascinating," I said, flexing my fingers. "Because Rohesia didn't reinforce the carriage. Ereth did. And only three people not present knew that."

The smile slid off the officer's face as tent flaps rustled.

"Assassins!" I shouted as more than two dozen assassins in black armor poured out of the tents.

Right into a hail of dirt clods and rocks as I lifted my hands and activated my spell.

Lady Laurel called up deadly whirling columns of air that whipped right through the horde of assassins descending on us.

I whispered another spell, turning the ground in front of me into quicksand. Catching the bulk of the forces in the cloying, claggy mix of water and sand that pulled the surprised assassins into the soupy ground and closed it up around them.

Still, more assassins rushed toward us.

But Oz and the hired swords tore out of the other tent and engaged them.

The officer rushed me, a razor-sharp dagger in each fist. Aimed at my heart. How very foolish.

I slammed him backward with a boulder than hit him broadside. Knocking him and four other soldiers several feet off the road.

Raising my hands to the sky, I whispered another spell that

rained down exploding rocks that pounded the imposters with stones until they fled from the road and ran toward the forest.

Oz's broadsword was in deadly motion, Pirin and Norval at his right, Farago at his left shoulder. Farago used stealth and daggers, cutting down assassins with their backs turned. Oz plowed right through the two dozen assassins as he moved toward me.

When he finally reached the carriage, he stood his ground at my left shoulder. Lady Laurel was beside me on my right.

As another wave of assassins flanked us. Led by the officer that had retreated.

He reached for me, a blade in one hand.

Oz turned. "Touch her and die!" he shouted at the officer, stepping in front of me to engage him.

He and the officer assassin faced off, the officer brandishing a long sword. He was fast and he was good, but Oz took him apart with speed, footwork, and precise blows that staggered the assassin twice. The third time, Oz's blade went right through the man's chest, laying him out on the road. The man bled out in minutes.

One more time, I called up a shower of dirt clods and rocks, Lady Laurel summoning a burst of wind that leveled the assassins. My magic kept them down, struggling to rise from the dirt road.

Oz and his hired swords ran each assassin through until only the dead in Rohesian uniforms paved the road.

And it was over.

"Annarissa!" Oz shouted and rushed toward me.

He had a cut lip and a black eye as he threw his arms around me and held me tightly against his sweaty, blood-spattered black armor. His chest heaved and he fought to catch his breath. His warm musk and leather scent washed over me and I wrapped my arms around him. So happy to see him. Thrilled that he'd held me in front of the entire procession.

"I was so scared they'd killed you," I said against his ear. "I'm so relieved you're safe."

I felt his mouth stretch into a grin against my neck. He pressed his face against mine, his mouth sliding over my lips in a scintillating and body-slamming kiss that made me weak in the knees. I kissed him back with a hard, urgent kiss as gold sparks danced around us like a cloud of dreamflies flitting around our heads.

I didn't want to let him go. I wanted to hold him forever. And fate taunted me with its gold sparks and soft gold glow that hovered around our heads for a moment or two.

"Princess!" Lady Laurel cried, grabbing hold of my arm as Oz let me go.

He joined the other hired swords to secure the road, the carriage, and the wagons. They had to clear these bodies fast. In case more assassins followed behind them. We needed to erase as much evidence as we could and get moving fast. For Mirstone Castle.

"Do you know what that was?" Lady Laurel's voice was shrill and excited.

"Fate in its infinite cruelty," I replied.

"Yes," said Lady Laurel, her voice falling to a whisper. "I mean no. That was fate all right. Showing you the man fated to be your mate."

I glared at her. I had heard all the fables. All the legends. All the fairy tales. Growing up, my naïve princess heart had craved that romance. Of seeing those gold sparks after kissing the man I loved. But all of those stories missed a very important point. A prophecy older than Queen Maelena. One that had taken all these romantic notions and set them on fire. Denying me the magic of my heart's desire in exchange for the cold steel of duty.

All the magic in the world couldn't change the fact that fated or not, my mate was a cold-hearted enemy prince who would marry me and lock me away alone for the rest of my days. While my heart shattered into pieces that could never be put back together. Pining for a love I could never have.

"Apparently, fate hadn't heard of this damned prophecy or seen the devastation plaguing Kambria. Destruction only fixable by my marrying the enemy. A man I don't love. One who will never love me."

I turned away from her and tripped over the officer's body that slumped in the middle of the border road.

Stumbling, I fell into the dust beside the dead man.

"Princess!" Lady Laurel cried, rushing toward me.

In the dirt, something gold and shiny glinted. Covered by a thick sheen of dust. Dropped by this assassin.

I plucked the object out of the road, brushing away the dirt.

A purple and gold signet pin shaped like a spiral. In its center gleamed a sunburst gem, its color shifting from gold to amethyst. Glowing with magic.

An Erethian captain's pin.

Cold chills shuddered through me.

The gold and amethyst sunburst gem was the rarest form of these gems, adorning only royal crowns and the uniforms of the highest officials in Mother's court. Including this spiral insignia that designated one rank: captain of the guard. And only one person in the realm carried it.

Captain Nevayna Otirys. Traitor to Ereth.

Most likely, Nevayna had sent orders sealed with this pin to indicate they had come directly from her.

Apparently, she had been behind every attempt to kill me since I left Skystead. The presence of this pin—here and now—proved that.

Mother didn't even know that her most trusted soldier and protector was trying to kill her daughter and stop the prophecy from being fulfilled. With Nevayna involved, Mother's entire army could be behind this plot—without her knowing it. That meant battling a lot more swords, assassins, and magic to reach Mirstone Castle.

Maybe all at once?

With two days left until we reached the castle, we had a fight on our hands.

<h1 style="text-align:center">21</h1>

OZ DROVE THE CARRIAGE ALONG THE ROAD UNTIL THE STONE WALLS OF Rohesia's border post loomed ahead in the night. Tall iron gates blocked the only entry through that long, rambling stone wall that surrounded the kingdom. The forbidding metal gates cast long, fluid shadows in the dark as lantern light flickered behind it. A stone and iron guard post stretched across the top of the gates between two small, octagonal towers manned with archers. A hint of wood smoke hung in the crisp night air, dull murmur of voices echoed above the creak and rumble of the carriage.

In the perpetual twilight and so close to the Cimmerian Breach, the temporary border blended into the darkness. These walls and gates were far enough away that they disappeared into the landscape, making it easy to setup a temporary border ahead of it—especially for anyone who had never traveled to Rohesia by carriage before. Had never seen these gates and walls before.

Along the thick stone walls, punctuated with more of those octagonal towers, additional clusters of archers held position as Rohesian sentries in red and blue uniforms patrolled the narrow rampart that stretched along the wall in both directions. At this distance, they never even saw the temporary roadblock in the darkness. Only torches along the road. Four cannons perched in roundabouts on top of the rampart. Angled toward the road. Two small squat stone buildings crouched on either side of the road just beyond that grim, dark gate. The air was tinged with sulfur and hot tallow from torches and lanterns as the cool wind swirled the scent of dead leaves and ash along the road.

The Rohesian border. Armed to the teeth.

Like I had expected to find it—not a couple of tents and a handful of guards. Was I really at the border of Ereth's most bitter—and dangerous—enemy?

I still clutched the Erethian spiral pin in my hand that belonged to Captain Nevayna Otirys. Part of me wanted to tell Lady Laurel and Oz about the pin, but I had no idea who might be listening. So, for now, I kept it quiet. And the pin hidden. After all, I had no way of knowing who else Nevayna had bought off.

Could I trust anyone now that I knew Nevayna was in league with the Equalizers?

She brought assassins inside the castle gates and hid their masks in that barrel outside the castle armory. She arranged for them to gain access to the grounds in the first place. It had to be her.

I feared for my sisters. And I wished I could be back in the castle at Skystead protecting them. Hopefully, Nevayna's attention was still focused on me.

I sighed. I couldn't even warn them.

Quickly, I stuck the pin under a silky fold in my red dress where it wouldn't been seen as my stomach began to churn. I had never been this close to so many Rohesian soldiers without a battlefield beneath my feet.

Biting my lip, I tamped down my fear, waiting for the soldiers to surround us. And hopefully, send us through that gate on our way. Quickly.

Unless the truce had deteriorated since I'd been en route to Rohesia.

I flexed my fingers, feeling the tingle of my magic replenishing, an assault spell on my lips, as I prepared to call up my magic again with a single word—if needed.

Already, the carriage slowed to nearly a stop, elemental horses' light going dark as they sensed the fear and hatred of magic. They went quiet too, not even a nicker as voices flowed around the carriage, moving alongside the convoy. Until finally, the carriage halted in the road.

The soldiers' voices carried, moving on both sides. Stopping us to search our convoy. Inspecting our supplies.

In a few minutes, the doors to the carriage creaked open and a tall officer in a red and white uniform stood on the top step, his dark hair tied back at his nape.

Above his collar.

"My lady, Princess Thorn," he said, bowing in a sharp, practiced manner, and stepped into the carriage as a relieved sigh escaped his lips. "At last."

Nodding, I remained seated and so did Lady Laurel.

"It is an honor to receive you at this border post," he continued and I did my best to appear relaxed and confident. "Your Rohesian court gown is—stunning. A gift from King Daegal as I recall."

"Yes, it was a lovely surprise," I said.

I had no idea. I had not even seen this dress until Lady Laurel insisted I wear it today.

"What are these...creatures?" The officer cried, looking horrified as he stared at the team of six elemental horses fidgeting in front of the carriage.

"Elemental horses," I replied.

"What happened to the intrepids sent along with the carriage?" asked the officer. "And the wagons. A dozen of our finest horses."

"Unfortunately, assassins ambushed the carriage in Ereth," I said. "Blademaster Laurant and all twelve intrepids perished in the assault."

The officer's eyes widened and he cast an uneasy glance at a soldier beside him.

"All of them, m'lady?"

"All of them," I said. "We had no choice but to conjure elemental steeds to replace them. No horse in Kambria can match the intrepids' endurance and stamina. Much less be capable of hauling such a massive carriage at this distance. So we made do with our magic."

He nodded, studying all of the elemental horses harnessed to the carriage and the wagons behind us.

"Incredible," he said with a hiss and returned his attention to me. "I admire your creativity and fortitude, m'lady." He smiled. "And I would wager that our realm's princesses will rejoice at your wedding to Prince Arence."

"Why is that?" I asked, not sure why he would mention it.

"They will be relieved that you are no longer eligible to court the other available princes at the next ball. With your beauty, you would have quite the entourage of princes vying for your hand. As I said, Rohesia is honored by your presence, princess. I'm Captain Brevard by the way."

"Thank you, captain," I said. "You are very kind."

He was good-looking, well-mannered, and soft spoken. Treating me with respect, something I hadn't expected in Rohesia. I had expected to be dragged out of the carriage and brought before the Rohesians in shackles—especially after arriving with a team of elemental horses. Maybe the kingdom—and the Sirideans—were not the monsters that rumors claimed?

I smiled. Like Oz Tarrant.

"The honor is mine, Captain Brevard," I said with a deep nod. "Thank you for receiving us at such a late hour, but we had to travel at night because of the myriad dangers threatening this convoy—as I'm certain you've been well-briefed throughout my journey from Ereth. I hope my new life in Rohesia will be fulfilling—and that all its eligible maidens find their own princes to love."

He nodded. "I will convey your words to the court immediately, my lady," he said. "They will be much appreciated. And we understand the additional caution your convoy has taken by traveling at night. We have had a large influx of wagons and travelers attempting to enter the kingdom. And we've already put several Equalizers to the sword."

But I worried about how many had already slipped past this post. These assassins were very skilled at their jobs. And persistent. And now that I knew Nevayna Otirys was in league with them, I worried that they knew everything about our defense tactics and our planned route to Mirstone.

"As have we," I replied. "We dispatched a large contingent just south of here, trying to fake a border post."

Brevard frowned and gave me a sharp nod.

"Your convoy leader indicated as much and warned us about the graves. Mr. Farago gave us detailed location information, so we will take care of the bodies and destroy that fake post. I have also sent couriers north ahead of you, to hopefully help secure your route to Mirstone. I regret that we do not have enough soldiers to escort you all the way to the castle."

A dark-haired foot soldier leaned into the carriage and whispered something in Captain Brevard's ear. Brevard turned and nodded at the dark-haired soldier and the soldier slipped back out to the road.

"Forgive the interruption," said Brevard as he returned his attention to me. "Princess, the truce has freed up many units, but the Equalizers have been causing havoc at the castle and surrounding villages. Requiring us to station those units elsewhere. And we fear our presence alongside your convoy would draw unwanted attention and increased numbers of assassins, so perhaps it's for the best that I have no units available to escort you to Mirstone. We have loaded fresh supplies onto your wagons, so at least you will dine on something more palatable than hard bread and jerky the rest of the way."

I didn't think them wise to gamble the fate of the world on this tiny convoy reaching Mirstone without an escort, but maybe Brevard was right. Perhaps the official attention would put us in greater harm? Regardless, we were still on our own.

"We will unfortunately discover that answer on the way to Mirstone," I answered. "Thank you for the supplies, captain. We are most grateful."

He bowed and started out of the carriage but stopped and glanced up at me.

"Your Highness, let me be frank. Mr. Farago is a known associate of hired sword, Oz Tarrant and..."

I frowned, giving him my best confused expression.

"Who did you say, captain?"

"Tarrant," he repeated. "Oz Tarrant. Tarrant is wanted by the Rohesian crown—by the king himself. And his mother, Tressa Tarrant is wanted for high crimes against the crown in a longstanding warrant. If Mr. Farago comes into contact with either Oz or Tressa Tarrant, would you please alert the first soldier or post you encounter?"

What had Oz done in Rohesia?

And his mother—wanted for high crimes against the crown. That did not bode well. That meant either murder or high thievery— at least it did in Ereth. Had she truly stolen a crown jewel or royal heirloom? Gold from the royal treasury? I had seen such proclamations issued in Ereth before and those high crimes were either an expensive theft or a murder.

"My word, he and his mother sound quite dangerous," I said, shaking my head. "I will be sure to watch Mr. Farago's acquaintances closely."

"King Daegal promises a tidy sum of coin for any information leading to their capture," said Captain Brevard. "As I said, it is a longstanding crime, but the reward still stands."

A longstanding crime? I wondered how long Oz had been wanted by the Rohesian crown. He mentioned that he was wanted here in his vague and sketchy way and yet, he had still taken this job. And Rohesia was still actively looking for him. Why would he risk capture? Maybe my mother was paying enough to keep Oz far away from Rohesia? Or maybe he was counting on Mother's royal boon to clear him of all charges?

I would ask him, but I doubted if he would tell me about any of it. He kept his personal life locked away—even from me.

"Good to know, captain. Thank you. We'll watch for any new associates visiting Farago. Please excuse my abrupt departure, but we need to be on our way. There is a lot of road between us and Mirstone."

"Safe journey, princess," said the captain. "I look forward to attending the royal wedding. Arence will be the first prince to marry, so the event will be quite the celebration."

As opposed to it feeling like a wake for me. My last moments of freedom before being chained to a royal residence for life while Arence lived as he pleased. Charming.

"Thank you, captain," I called to him as he backed out of the carriage and closed the doors.

In a few minutes, I heard footsteps climb up the carriage ladder to the driver's seat. They weren't Oz's forceful, determined footfalls. They were lighter. Slower. A little timid. Someone who had never driven a team of horses—or a carriage—sat in the driver's perch.

"Let's move out!" shouted a woman's alto voice.

Pirin. She had assumed control of the carriage, snapping the reins, and coaxing the six spirited elementals into a steady walk as the carriage creaked forward. I wondered where Oz had hidden from the Rohesian soldiers as the carriage lumbered forward on the hard-packed dirt road, turning sharply north as the road sloped upward. Away from the border's iron gates.

I had a vague memory of seeing a map of Rohesia. The main road from the border had a series of serpentine curves that wound up into a hilly expanse of forest until it cut across snow-capped mountains and curved down through hilly grasslands. Down to the sea where Mirstone Castle overlooked rocky cliffs and sandy flats that wrapped around the ocean's wild—almost magical—shoreline.

The air smelled cooler and a little sharp with the scent of pine trees and a hint of mountain snow.

"What was that about?" Lady Laurel replied, staring at me in shock. "His mother is wanted for high crimes against the crown? And he's also wanted by the crown?"

I turned toward her, feeling a mix of anger and surprise. But I wouldn't tolerate her calling him a criminal. We didn't know the full story yet and I would not condemn him until I knew everything.

"Lady Laurel," I said, giving her a hard look. "Before they negotiated a truce at Ashbourne, my sisters, my mother, and I were all wanted by the Rohesian crown for crimes against the crown. It means nothing until it does. Let it go until we know the truth."

My point quieted her outrage.

"You're right, princess," she said, bowing her head. "Forgive me. I worry about your safety and happiness. And he frightens me sometimes."

For quite a while, he frightened me, too. Until I saw behind his mask. The one he kept there to frighten people into keeping their distance. In a way, I understood his distaste for people. It sounded like the world always wanted to see the worst in him, so he let them. It gave him a fearsome reputation and kept most people away. For someone running from something that happened in Rohesia, it was perfect.

But now, Oz Tarrant might be forced to face those charges—and whatever had happened here with his mother.

"I have seen the man behind the mask, Lady Laurel. His loyalty is unquestionable. And his love is deep. So, I will continue to see the best in Oz Tarrant until I have reason not to see it. And I will not entertain any speculation or rumors."

"Of course, princess," she replied and settled back against the seat. "I will keep silent on the subject for now."

So, Lady Laurel and I sat in uneasy silence for a long time as the carriage pressed on through the darkness. I wondered where Oz was. I fell asleep against the carriage wall, waking up to find that it had halted. Lady Laurel stretched beside me and sat up in the seat.

"We've stopped," I said and struggled to sit up beside her. "I wonder where we are?"

From the feeble lantern light inside the carriage, I could tell it was still dark outside. We dared only light one lantern, fearing assassins would find us. The one lantern's wick was as short as it could be made and still be able to light it. The reinforced window shields were ready to slide over the windows, should another attack arise.

Pirin's light footsteps crossed the top of the carriage and tapped down the ladder. She paused at the carriage doors and then gingerly knocked before opening a door.

"Princess Annarissa," she said in a quiet voice. "We're making camp."

I stared at her in confusion. We were only a few hours beyond Rohesia's border. Why would we make camp in the dark?

"Why now?" I asked, casting an apprehensive gaze at Lady Laurel who also looked concerned. "It's still dark enough to keep moving."

"We're almost to the mountain pass," said Pirin, sounding apologetic. "Oz felt it was too dark to travel the pass. We will wait until it's light enough to traverse it. And then make camp in the hills below until it's dark again."

I smiled when she said Oz's name. Relieved that he hadn't left the procession—and me—when the Rohesian soldiers started inquiring about him.

"I trust our leader found a suitable hiding place from the Rohesian guards," I said.

Pirin chuckled. "Inside one of your trunks, princess. He apologizes for any wrinkles."

I couldn't help but laugh, imagining him pressed against all of my gowns, petticoats, and stockings, hiding from the soldiers.

"Tell him he's forgiven," I said. "If he comes and apologizes in person."

Pirin raised an eyebrow.

"I'll tell him," said Pirin with a nod as she slipped out of the carriage.

"Annarissa Thorn," Lady Laurel scolded me. "That was shameless."

"When have you known me to ever show shame, Lady Laurel?" I asked with a wry smile.

She shook her head, smiling. "Never. One of your best qualities—and I confess that grudgingly."

"I won't hide my feelings for him," I said, crossing my arms. "And I won't let anyone shame me for it either."

Even the villagers in Skystead knew that Prince Arence loved another. And that he intended to stay with her, despite his fate to marry an Erethian sorceress. Why should I be the good servant and live an empty life over a *sacred* vow that meant nothing to Prince Arence when I had a brief chance at some happiness?

Oz and I had about two days left together. My heart ached. Two days until he and I were separated forever. And I would love him as deeply and as much as I could in that time and carry the memories into this loveless marriage, fulfilling my part of the prophecy. And I wouldn't let anyone steal that one source of joy from me.

Even Lady Laurel.

22

I never dreamed there would be an order for my arrest waiting at the Rohesian border post. And after a score of years, a standing order to arrest my mother for high crimes against the crown.

What in blazes did she do the night my father died?

I was only a baby. Had no memory of what happened that night in Mirstone. I only knew what my mother told me—which was not much. Only vague details about my father's death that night. That he'd been a hero, saving his king and their two young sons. As captain of the guard, he'd protected one of Daegal's infant sons with his body that night. Mother said my father still had one of the babies clutched in his arms when she found him dead—beside the queen. Only steps from King Daegal and his other infant son.

Was any of that even true? I had no idea. Mother tossed out lies like she emptied the morning chamber pot, splattering the streets and anyone in her way.

Mother claimed she'd placed the baby prince that Father had saved in the king's arms and fled with me from the Equalizers that had ambushed the castle. Not stopping until she and I got to Xanthe.

She was Xanthan and always said she would never go back to Rohesia even though we had a cottage there. A life. She said the memories of Father's death were too painful. That's why she left. Ran.

But now I knew otherwise. It was never about those difficult memories. It was about the royal warrant—and price on her head.

What in blazes had she done?

I loved my mother once, even though she'd been a thief and a liar my whole life. I don't know if she even felt love. She used people up and tossed them into the streets. And she probably brought me along to make her living when I was old enough to lie and steal for her.

What she had stolen from the Rohesian crown that night? The queen died in that attack. Had she taken jewels from the dead queen? Her crown?

Mother was an expert pickpocket and experienced thief. Taught me everything I know about the art of the con—her biggest one on me when she abandoned me at eleven. She could lift the heaviest coin purse without giving herself away. I'd watched her do it dozens of times. She could con a beggar's last coin out of his shaking hands. Taught me how to pickpocket when I was five. How to pick locks at seven. And how to make up stories and steal from the marketplace at nine. It was how we survived and that included Snowmelt. Until she met a new lover and moved in with him. Getting us off the streets while I was little at any rate.

But at eleven, I quickly became a problem to her new lover. Bastard beat her and me at every turn. When I fought back, he threatened to leave her if she didn't get rid of her bastard. So, she turned me out into Snowmelt's streets with all my skills. She despised the man but craved his Xanthan soldier's pension more than being a mother.

We hadn't spoken in over a decade. She lived in the Xanthan capital of Fallsmere to the north. Probably went through a dozen more suitors until she finally conned someone quasi-respectable (with a bigger pension) into marriage.

Whatever she'd stolen that night must have been too visible to sell. Too hot. Requiring her to hold onto it for a long time. Still, it made no sense. Especially after all this time. Even now, she was probably still waiting for it to cool down, so she could fence it. Regardless, the Rohesian crown obviously still wanted it back—and someone to pay for the crime. And that wasn't going to be me.

While the soldiers talked to Annarissa and her lady-in-waiting, I scaled the back of the carriage to the roof and picked the lock on one of her trunks. I climbed inside and closed the lid, covering the mechanism with my glove to keep it from locking me inside. The trunk was open just enough for me to observe the soldiers below.

I huddled in the dark among her soft lavender and rain scent, holding one of her gold stockings and remembering when I had slowly slid it off her silky, shapely moon-pale legs. Pushing up her skirt and parting those luscious thighs until I had her beautiful naked body beneath me. Making love to her at last.

Daegal's balls! I wanted more than a roll in a carriage. I wanted more than bedding her. I wanted to marry her. I wanted to love her for a lifetime.

Damned prophecy.

Below, more soldiers gathered around the carriage, their voices rising.

I froze, pressing my face against something soft and silky that smelled like lavender and rain. I sighed. Like Annarissa. Like my body after I'd held her in my arms.

I groaned. It was her purple petticoat.

One of the soldiers stood at the carriage, going on and on about my being wanted by the crown, about Farago being one of my...what was it that he said...my known associates. The soldier talked politely around the princess, tiptoeing around the story because he was referring to Badriyah. And it was obvious that he had no idea about that place. He'd just heard the stories like everyone else.

Yes, Farago had been with me at Badriyah. He and I murdered the entire village. It was true. But Captain Brevard was a Rohesian and like most of Kambria, his opinion of me was as colored as Ereth's about that night. They could think what they liked. I didn't care. It had been a Xanthan matter. A guild problem. And the guilds had all paid us handsomely to do that job.

But the job had backfired on them. And turned me into the most reviled and feared criminal in Kambria.

If Annarissa asked me directly about that night, I'd tell her the truth. I'd tell her everything.

I didn't think Brevard would ever shut his Rohesian gob. This damned trunk was making me claustrophobic, but while the good captain talked to Annarissa, his soldiers were busy scouring every wagon for a sign of me. Seemed odd. I hadn't worked with Farago since I left the guild. The Rohesians would have known that if they were keeping track of my whereabouts and activities like they claimed. Like working with Farago. Why did they expect? To find me leading this convoy right into Rohesia? The Erethians hired me—and at the last minute after Equalizers killed the blademaster Rohesia sent. Laurant something or other. Hired by King Daegal himself.

Someone at Ereth had been communicating with the Equalizers this entire time. And with Rohesia. Someone higher up than an axeman like Mathias.

Anger burned my gut. It was true. Someone sold out Princess Annarissa. One of her own people. Had to be—even she suspected it. How else had the news that I was leading this procession gotten to the Rohesian border ahead of me. Knowing that I was wanted in the kingdom. Of course, with a price on my head, that kind of news traveled fast.

Daegal's balls, I wanted out of this trunk! But not until we were safely past the guard post.

It seemed like an eternity until I heard the carriage doors close and footsteps on the carriage ladder. Someone climbed onto the roof and slid into the driver's seat. A quiet, smoky voice called for the elemental horses to move out.

Reins jangled and snapped until the carriage lurched forward.

The jerky movements continued, the horses not even at a lumbering trot yet.

An eternity later, the carriage picked up speed as the elementals at last found their rhythm. Whoever drove the carriage finally coaxed the convoy into a steady canter and the carriage shot down the road that turned sharply right and wound around a hill, up toward the snowcapped peaks to the north and slightly west. When the road began a sharper incline, the carriage slowed, elemental horses walking at a careful, measured pace now.

I knew this road well. A gentle but winding amble to the pass. The road through the pass was steep. Narrow. Treacherous. Icy because of the faded sunlight.

Either we traversed the pass before it got dark or camped at the base of the mountains until it was light enough to travel the road across. And on the way down, the turns were sharp, sudden, and deadly. Attempting that descent with a carriage and three wagons in the dark was suicide.

So, we'd have to see how much light remained when we got to the base of those mountains. The thought of running into an Equalizer ambush in that pass terrified me. No, to keep the princess safe, we had to cross the pass in the daylight.

But I still expected another ambush. And soon.

Equalizers were running out of time to stop us from fulfilling part of the prophecy. Why didn't Annarissa have four sisters or cousins of age? I wanted her more than anything in this world. And that prick Arence didn't deserve her. Dammit! Why'd she have some destiny, somewhere I couldn't follow? I'd duel that bastard. I'd pay any price they demanded to stay with her.

But they'd probably throw me in Aracar and I'd never see her again (nobody escaped from that hellhole mountain prison.) Why couldn't there be a way around this damned duty she was forced to fulfill and still save Kambria? A duty that forced me to give her up to a man who would never love her. Damn, it hurt!

As the carriage lurched along the road, I lifted the trunk lid and peered over at the driver's perch.

Pirin, a hired sword from Skystead, drove the carriage. Her sandy-colored hair blew in the wind as she gripped the reins, her gaze focused on the road ahead. It was still pitch black around us. Too dark to even see the snow-capped mountains rising around the road as it sloped upward toward the pass.

Even at a leisurely pace, we'd reach the pass in the dark. Farago knew to make camp if we got to the base of the mountains too late.

Farago drove the wagon in front of the carriage, leading the convoy north toward Mirstone. I could see his tangle of brown curls from here as he slouched in the driver's seat. I glanced over my shoulder at the other two wagons. Still lumbering along behind the carriage.

Carefully, I climbed out of the trunk and crawled across the top of the carriage to the driver's perch. Pirin had closed the hailing-horn. I plopped down on Pirin's left. Startling her.

"Oz!" she cried, her face going as pale as the crescent moon rising over my shoulder to the right. "You scared me."

"Sorry," I said. "Soldiers give any of you trouble?"

She shook her head, smiling. "Just you. Enjoy the ride? In one of the princess' trunks?"

I bowed my head, chuckling. "Smelled incredibly nice in there. Hope I didn't wrinkle all of her beautiful clothes too much."

Pirin laughed. "Don't think she minded. As long as you're safe."

The thought of her caring anything about someone like me made my heart ache. I hoped I meant more to her than that. Much, much more. Daegal's balls, I'd fallen hard for this innocent but battle-trained sorceress. And as much as I wanted to, I couldn't tell her. Couldn't complicate something that was already the hardest challenge of her life. I wouldn't add to her pain. But, damn did I love this beautiful, fearless princess. And I wanted to spend the rest of my days with her. If it weren't for that damned prophecy...

"It'll still be dark when we hit the pass, Pirin," I said. "We'll make camp at the base and cross at first light. Once we're down, we'll camp until it gets dark enough to travel safely again."

She nodded, looking tired. She needed a break from the reins.

I pointed to the lantern that oscillated on a pole to her right. The wick was turned all the way down. The smell of tallow was warm, only a touch of sulfur in the cool night air.

"Signal Farago and the other wagons to stop with the lantern when we get close to the base of the mountains," I said and eased the reins out of her hands. "Now, sit back and rest your body."

"Thanks, Oz," she mumbled and settled back against the padded seat as I snapped the reins and coaxed the elementals into a slow trot out of the next curve. We could afford a little speed on this side of the pass.

Farago's wagon led the way, the coppery glow of the elemental horses making the wagon visible in the darkness. He'd maintained the on-point position in case of attack. The other two wagons moved close behind the carriage in tight formation. Without my telling him. Good man, Farago. Almost glad I didn't kill him.

The elemental horses had a faint torch-like glow in the dark, just enough to see the road. They had dimmed their otherworldly light since we hit Battleworn Forest, sensing the need not to draw unnecessary attention to the convoy. At the border gate, they'd gone almost dark, but their light had brightened a little since we'd left it behind.

Three more turns until we reached the mountain road that led over the pass. With the curse of dimmed sunlight, Rohesia and Ereth both had grown cooler. The mountain passes were icy all year instead of during winter. And slippery. So, we had to cross it in daylight.

According to Farago and the Rohesians in the convoy, a thick stand of trees off to the right concealed a hidden clearing beside a small stream. Just before the pass road. It was the perfect place to bed down and rest until first light...or to walk into an Equalizer ambush.

Tonight, I'd rather walk into a hundred ambushes than do what I had to do.

My chest ached at the thought. Tonight, I had to tell the woman I loved goodbye. Tomorrow night, the convoy would camp one last time at the edge of the village of Mirstone. But by then, I had to disappear or be arrested by Rohesian soldiers.

Maybe it was best for her this way? I had already caused her enough pain by loving her. And now, I had to give her up to another man—that prick, Arence. I wished against fate I could stand with her and help her through this awful marriage, but they would arrest me on sight. Even if they didn't throw me into Aracar, once she married Arence, they'd never let me near her again.

Already, I felt like a monster, but I had to tell her that we could never be together. Tonight. Because, it was the last time I could hold her in my arms and love her even if I couldn't tell her what she meant to me.

THE CLIMB through the hills went faster than I wanted it to as I coaxed the elementals and the carriage to follow Farago's wagon through the copse of skeletal trees and rusty brown evergreens to the right. Behind me, the other two wagons struggled up the incline and followed not far behind as I brought the elementals to a gentle stop in the clearing.

When the last two wagons stopped, the twelve elemental horses stomped and whinnied and in a shower of coppery sparks, they faded into the darkness. Leaving.

I descended the ladder and hurried over to the wagon where Farago and Norval started unloading the supplies we'd gotten at the border post.

"Norval," I said and pointed at the hard ground. "Grab a shovel and dig that fire pit real deep so our meal fire can't be seen from the road."

He nodded and rushed over to the bed of the wagon, retrieving a worn, rusty shovel.

"I'll help him," said Farago, nodding at Norval.

"Thanks," I said in a quiet voice and bowed my head. "Thanks for having my back, Farago. I couldn't have gotten her this far without you."

He had a strange look on his face.

"You can count on me, boss," he replied. "And I'm sorry about kissing her. It was wrong. I know that now."

He poked my shoulder with his fist.

"I mean it," he said. "I can see what she means to you and I see how she looks at you."

The thought of seeing that sultry burn in her beautiful golden hazel eyes made me ache all over and I couldn't control the pain that contorted my face.

"Listen, Farago," I said in almost a whisper as the last two wagons circled the carriage and the crew began to bed down the horses for a rest. "This is the last night I'll be in the camp."

His eyes bugged out. "What?"

I stepped closer to him and lowered my voice to a whisper.

"Once we cross the pass, the next place to camp is right at the edge of Mirstone. Which will be crawling with soldiers. Eager to arrest me. It's as far as I can go on this journey."

I bowed my head, feeling like I was abandoning Annarissa when it was the last thing I wanted to do. I wanted to storm those castle gates and fight every last Rohesian for her. But every time I ached to follow my heart, my damned head reminded me of the prophecy. Her duty. And how my selfishness would destroy the world.

Even I couldn't be so cruel.

"Oz…" Farago shook his head. "She's gonna break when you leave. You know that, don't you?"

His words burned right through my chest. But I shook my head. In time, she'd get over me. She had to.

"She's a Thorn, Farago. With all that assault sorceress strength behind her. She'll have forgotten all about me in a year."

Farago sighed and bowed his head. "You're wrong, Oz."

I crossed my arms against my chest.

"What can I do?" I glanced toward the north. "If I stay, I get arrested. Aracar arrested."

His face turned pale. "Damn...Aracar?"

"I'm not just wanted, Farago. I'm wanted by the crown." I paced around him. "If I took Annarissa and we ran and managed to elude those guards, we would doom Kambria to a slow death by loving each other. I know her. She could never agree to that." I bowed my head, black hair sliding away from my shoulders. "And neither could I."

"Damn," said Farago finally.

"After tonight, I'll meet up with all of you again in Ereth to collect our pay."

Farago forced a smile on his face, but he looked worried.

"Holdin' you to that, boss." He stared at me a moment. "When you gonna tell her?"

I shoved my hands into my pockets and watched the camp preparations ramp into high gear as Annarissa and Lady Laurel climbed out of the carriage, walking toward the meal fire that Norval had just lit.

"After the meal," I said, staring off into the dark trees.

He nodded and patted me on the back as he moved toward the meal fire.

<hr>

IN AN HOUR, when the waxing crescent was high overhead, Norval and Farago had finished cooking some sort of meat over the fire. It had a tangy scent to it with a hint of garlic and onions as they filled plates with the meat and fresh bread. A large jug of Rohesian red wine sat away from the fire and Pirin filled cups, passing them around the circle as everyone ate.

My stomach was too nervous to eat, but I grabbed a glass of wine and guzzled it, hoping to find enough false courage to protect my beautiful sorceress from what came next. I never dreamed I would fall in love with the princess I'd been hired to protect.

Now, I had to make her forget me.

I paced near one of the wagons, watching her gaze search the camp for me, her radiant face lit by the meal fire, those blushing full bow lips almost pouting as she sipped her wine. Her eyes were like embers and all I wanted to do was hold her. Love her.

Finally, Pirin walked toward me. She grabbed my arm.

"Boss! The princess has been looking for you everywhere."

I chewed by bottom lip, hating myself already. Before I broke her heart, I owed her some truth. About me.

"Tell her I'll come find her shortly," I said.

Pirin's gaze narrowed and she stared at me a moment. "You're avoiding her. Why?"

I sighed. "Trust me, Pirin, it's for her own good. No matter what happens, know that I'm still protecting her, okay?"

She frowned, looking confused.

"Okay," she said. "I don't understand but okay."

I ducked behind the wagon, watching Pirin saunter across the clearing and drop down beside Annarissa. Worry immediately shadowed the princess' stunningly beautiful face. She looked around the clearing again and finally nodded. And I felt like a monster again.

About to break her heart.

So, I waited, trying to gather my thoughts as I slammed another glass of wine and tried to collect enough courage to deliver this painful blow to the most amazing woman I had ever met. I hated myself.

After most of the crew had wandered off to the wagons to sleep, I approached the meal fire.

When she saw me, her face lit up like a summer afternoon when the sun baked the seashore and everything turned bright green against a crisp, Xanthan blue sky. Lady Laurel had already returned to the carriage, leaving me to escort Annarissa behind the first wagon that Farago had kept empty of anyone bedding down for the night. Giving my princess and me a modicum of privacy. The other two wagons were parked across the camp, behind the meal fire. Beside the carriage.

"Oz!" Annarissa cried, grinning as she reached out and stroked my hand.

Daegal's balls, I wanted to crawl into a hole and die.

"Annarissa," I said, trying to keep my voice steady. "At last."

She reached out and ran her fingers through my hair. I leaned into her touch, but my heart ached at every warm brush of her fingers. I put my hand in hers.

"I missed you," she whispered, setting down her wine glass and moving closer to me.

"I missed you, too," I said and tugged on her hand, leading her away from the fire's light and toward the darkness behind the wagon.

When we got into the cool blackness behind the wagon, I slid down beside her as she sat down on the ground. Her arms slipped around my neck. And she kissed me with an urgency that shuddered through me, those damn gold sparks like dreamflies in the night. I wanted her so badly. I wanted to make love to her, but it wasn't fair to her. And she wouldn't want me near her after I told her goodbye.

But my body reacted to her touch. My kisses were frantic, my hands gliding down her arms, fingers slipping underneath her blouse. She unfastened my armor, letting it slide to the ground as she ran her hands across my bare chest.

And I was falling again.

She pressed me back against the ground and laid beside me, the silky red folds of her dress sliding up her thighs.

"Make love to me," she whispered against my ear, nibbling my earlobe.

And I was lost in her touch, in her embrace. In her heat. And already hard.

I unfastened my pants and slid them off my hips. Naked, I rolled on top of her and pressed my body against her, parting her silky thighs. She wasn't wearing those soft silken underpants. My fingers stroked her sex and she arched her back with every touch, her hips moving upward as she pressed against my hand. She unfastened her dress, letting it slide off her shoulders and off her body. Revealing her pert, firm breasts.

Sliding forward, I moved my hips, guiding my erection until I entered her gently. She wrapped her legs around me, pulling me closer as I moved inside her, thrusting against her shapely body.

She gasped, hips rocking against mine, her breath hot against my neck, my movements deep and intense as I explored her bare breasts with my mouth and hands. Her hips moved in frantic shudders as she arched her back, moving with me until her body trembled. Her skin was fiery as she moaned against my neck.

Pulling in a heated breath, she pressed against my hips as I kept thrusting faster, frantic until I felt her give in to the sensations, legs squeezing against mine. She held me in her arms, pushing her hips against my erection until the first rush of climax pulsed through me. I pumped faster with heated thrusts inside her until I felt release and the rush of sensations begin to subside.

I lay panting against her, still inside her as I held her so close I could feel her heart pounding against my sweat-slicked chest.

After what felt like an eternity, and the last time I would ever love her, I rolled off and pulled on my pants. She slid her dress back on, fastened it, and adjusted her skirt. When she was done, she lay back in my arms and I kissed her, ignoring fate's gold light that taunted us with its sparks. Her duty meant I had to give her up to another man. And I hated it.

"I love you, Annarissa Thorn," I said.

Dammit! I wasn't going to tell her that, but the words just slipped out. I meant them, but I didn't want to hurt her any more than I had to.

She grinned, a glow clinging to her alluring oval face as she nuzzled my neck with her mouth and pressed soft kisses against my collarbone, down my neck.

"I love you, too, Oz Tarrant."

My voice caught in my throat and I held my breath, trying to gather the courage to do the right thing. For her. Because I was already lost.

"And I..." I sighed and sat up, pulling in another breath as my mouth went dry. "I want you to know that right now, no matter what happens from here...I—"

She pulled away from me, turning her head to stare at me a moment, her fingers caressing my cheek.

"That sounds like you're trying to tell me something, Oz," she said in a quiet, wary voice.

She was right. And here it comes. The truth. The pain. The goodbye I didn't want to say.

"Annarissa..."

God, I was stalling, trying so hard not to tell her goodbye but knowing I had to say it.

"You know I'm wanted by the Rohesian crown, right?"

She nodded, those gold eyes so intense and unblinking as she studied my face. Like she was memorizing it.

"Were you going to tell me about that?" she asked.

I shook my head. "Wish I could, but I don't exactly know why myself. It has something to do with my mother's crimes. I was a baby, but for some reason, they think I'm her accessory. Or that I can lead them to her."

"What did she do in Rohesia, Oz?" Annarissa asked, frowning.

I shrugged. "She's always claimed that she didn't take anything, but my mother is as good a liar as she is a pickpocket and thief."

Annarissa wanted more than that from me. It burned in her intense expression. And I'd tell her everything I knew. Which wasn't much.

"What happened to your father?" she asked.

I wrapped her in my arms.

"My father was Rohesian. My mother was Xanthan. Father was captain of the guard for King Daegal."

Her eyes widened. "He was guarding the king?"

"With his life," I said with a nod and pressed kisses down the side of her face. "According to my mother, there was an attempt on the king's life one evening. My father saved the king and his sons. But the queen died in the attack and my father died saving one of their infant sons. And his own family. I was just a baby, so I only know what my mother told me. She left Rohesia with me that very night to escape the bad memories—or so she said. And she returned to Xanthe. Probably stole the queen's crown right off her body."

"So, he saved the king's life and his sons?" she asked, looking impressed.

"That's what my mother claimed. One of them was Prince Arence, I'm told."

Annarissa had a funny look on her face, like she wished he hadn't, but she didn't say anything.

"And you have no idea what your mother stole that night?"

I shook my head. "Not a clue, princess."

She slid closer to me. "Maybe they do want you to draw out your mother."

I couldn't help it. I broke out laughing.

"Wrong bait. Maybe if they dangled my father's pension in front of her, they'd capture her. That's all she's after these days. She abandoned me in Snowmelt's streets when I was eleven so she could live with a man and his pension. Haven't seen her since."

"Oz, that's awful," she whispered, running her long fingers through my hair.

Her touch was all heat and comfort and I ached to wrap her in my arms.

I shrugged. It hurt for a long time, but I learned to bury it and channel anything that had survived into mercenary work. Like Badriyah.

"I haven't thought about that for a long time," I said, kissing her lips in a spark of gold light. "But there's something else on my mind."

"What?" she whispered.

I turned her face toward me. "Badriyah."

Her eyes widened and she stared at me with so much innocence and trust that it leveled me for a moment. I had to concentrate and pull in a few breaths before I could explain it to her. She had a right to know the truth.

She took my hand in hers and squeezed it tight.

"Did you really murder a whole village?"

I stared at her as I pulled in a quick breath. And spilled the story.

"Yes," I said. "And Farago was there with me."

Her gaze fell and she looked so disappointed.

"See, the second biggest thieves guild in Snowmelt hired me to travel south to Xanthe's border. Where the Kambrian Equalizers had usurped an entire village. They ran off the villagers who lived there. Killed anyone who fought back. And used it to launch attacks on Snowmelt and Fallsmere—and the rest of Xanthe."

"Wait," she cried. "That village was mostly Equalizers?"

"No," I said and she began to fret. "The village was all Equalizers. All the world's best professional assassins. In one village they'd assassinated. Stole it from the people that used to call it home. So, Farago and I went into the town in the dead of night and executed every last Equalizer to avoid deadly attacks on Snowmelt and Fallsmere—Xanthe's capital."

For a moment or two, she stared at me, as if still processing everything I had just told her and then finally, a smile lit her face.

"You're not a butcher. Nobody knew that town had been taken over by Equalizers, did they?"

I shook my head. "No one but a couple of Xanthan thieves guilds."

"That's why everyone else calls you the Butcher of Badriyah," she cried, her hands sliding up to my face. "Because they thought you had murdered all the people from the original village."

I nodded and she threw her arms around me, holding me tight.

"You're not a butcher at all, Oz! I knew it!"

I shook my head and she kissed me hard on the lips. In an instant, I melted at her touch. And I hated myself for what came next.

"Why didn't you tell me the truth before now?"

Stroking her hair, I pulled in a breath as I began to shake all over.

"Because I needed you to know the truth about me, Annarissa. And part of that truth is..." I sucked in a breath, my stony heart beginning to crack apart.

"Is what, Oz?"

"Is telling you the truth about what uh...what happens next."

Her brow furrowed, pain creeping into those golden hazel eyes, but she didn't speak.

"Once first light arrives, we're going over that pass and traveling until we reach the grasslands at the edge of the village of Mirstone. Where the Rohesian royal family resides in a castle at the east end of the village. Mirstone will be teeming with soldiers, awaiting your arrival. So, see—tonight is when I..."

The words stuck in my throat that got so tight I could barely speak.

"When I have to say—uh, goodbye to you."

Her big hazel eyes got watery, her mouth quivering.

"Goodbye? Why?"

I was shaking so hard I could barely talk.

"I can't love you anymore, Annarissa."

Those words tore through my heart like a Rohesian arrow as the tears threaded down her cheeks. And I felt like an ogre for making her cry.

"We could take one of the elemental horses and head south," I said as she pulled away from me, shaking her head. "To the port of Summerreach. I know it's still being repaired, but maybe we could find a way aboard a ship from there."

"No...Oz, please."

"We could keep riding until we ended up in the westernmost part of Ereth or we could head to Xanthe to the northernmost village. And ignore the prophecy, loving each other until the sun went completely dark and every person in Kambria starved to death." My voice cracked and I couldn't stop it. "But we both know that neither of us is a person who could ignore our duty and let the world perish so we could love each other for a short while."

Daegal's balls, I hated myself for saying all of that to her, but it was the reality. It was the prophecy. And our duty. And we couldn't change any of it, no matter how desperately we wanted to.

For a long while, we sat apart in the cold darkness as the crescent moon faded into the lightening horizon and I could hear her still sniffling. I could almost feel the hot tears rushing down her soft, dewy cheeks.

It was the first time in my life that I truly felt like a monster. And damn did it hurt!

Finally, she rose to her feet.

"Then—I guess this is goodbye."

Her quiet voice was icy, tear-strained. Numb. And I felt the same way. But I couldn't do a damned thing to fix it. I would get her and her lady-in-waiting safely to the edge of the village of Mirstone and fade into the shadows to avoid being arrested. And she would never have to see me again.

"Goodbye, princess," I said in a weak voice, trying to keep every last quiver of emotion out of my tone. "I wish you all the best in Rohesia."

But I failed miserably.

She turned away and ran across the clearing as first light stretched its pallid fingers through the trees, traces of wood smoke clinging to the crisp air from the dying meal fire.

I hoped she could find some happiness in Rohesia. Soon enough, she would either hate me or forget me.

It was all I wanted now that I knew it was impossible for us to be together and still fulfill the prophecy.

23

His words were hot coals against my heart and I could still hear the echo of his voice in my ears. Telling me goodbye as the sky began to lighten.

That after tonight, I would never see him again. I would never feel the warm weight of his lean body against mine. Or the velvety rumble of his voice whispering my name against my earlobe.

I couldn't hold in the flood of tears burning down my cheeks and overflowing my stinging eyes. And I couldn't go back to the carriage, enduring a million questions from Lady Laurel right now. I couldn't talk about this. I couldn't say the words, that he'd just said goodbye to me.

In the back of my head, duty and reason had always nagged at me with their tiny little voices tearing through the happiest moments of my life. With him. I knew in my head that we could never be together. He knew it, too, but for a little while, we both chose to believe in fairy tales. We both chose love even when we knew it couldn't last. Knew that it was impossible to be together because of the prophecy. And not those gold sparks or my magic or his all-consuming love could change that.

It was over.

And my heart was broken into shards around me. Into pieces so small that I could never put them back together again. Not back the way they were.

That time and place—and love—didn't exist anymore. All that was left was a stretch of road over the mountains to the village of Mirstone and the castle where it all would have ended anyway. But because there was a warrant for his arrest, he couldn't even walk me to the castle door for one last kiss.

And I couldn't stand the pain of losing him and marrying a man who would never love me. It was too much to ask of one person. Even a privileged princess like me.

I hid behind the trees skirting the wagons and cried my eyes out until I couldn't cry anymore. When I had no more tears left, I wiped my dry, raspy eyes with my handkerchief and crept along the edge of the camp. Back to the carriage.

Quickly, I climbed inside and hid my face against the wall.

"Princess? Where have you been?" Lady Laurel cried and I winced, not wanting to talk to her.

Or anyone.

"Thinking," I said, doing my best to steady my voice. "Now, I'm tired."

I closed my eyes, the pain of his words piercing my heart all over again. But all I wanted to do was run right back to him and throw my arms around him. I knew what he was doing. What he always did. He took the blame for it, to make it easier for me to bear.

Regardless, all I wanted was him. But that could never happen. It was over now. By nightfall, he would disappear and I would never see him again. Trapped here in Rohesia for my lifetime.

I pretended to sleep, making sure I didn't have to talk to my lady-in-waiting—much less tell her it was over between Oz and me. I couldn't even say the words out loud to myself. How could I voice them to Lady Laurel?

I couldn't.

I must have dozed off because when I opened my eyes again, the carriage was in motion, jerking and shuddering in a way I had never felt before. Somehow, Lady Laurel had managed to conjure the elemental horses alone.

"What's happening?" I asked.

Something didn't feel right.

Lady Laurel frowned as her book slid off her lap and fell to the carriage floor. She was dressed in a dark blue gown with trumpet sleeves and a heart-shaped bodice, skirt grazing the tops of her short black boots braced against the carriage wall. I still wore the red Rohesian court dress I had on yesterday.

I bit my lip. Back when I foolishly thought Oz and I could still love each other a little while longer.

"I'm not sure," said Lady Laurel. "It's like the carriage is struggling over something."

The carriage slowed and lurched forward and I grabbed the wall to keep from pitching into the floor beside Lady Laurel's book. The back end of the carriage lifted and it took all my strength to stay in the seat. The window shields were across the windows, so I couldn't see out.

Outside, the elemental horses nickered, sounding almost panicked. Their elemental hooves scrabbled against rock, like they were trying to gain purchase. The carriage wheels slid sideways and then stopped.

Like the driver had thrown on the wheel brake.

"Stay exactly where you are inside the carriage! Don't move."

I winced at Oz's clear, strong voice echoing through the hailing-horn. He was in the driver's perch. His beautiful voice was bard-smooth and stout-beer dark and the sound of it went right through my heart.

Finally, the carriage leveled out.

"Don't move until I tell you it's safe!" he called out.

Lady Laurel knocked on the ceiling to tell him that we'd heard his orders.

Again, the carriage rose and shifted, wheels shuddering and sliding until everything dropped about a foot underneath the carriage.

I gasped, smashing my eyes closed as I grabbed for the hand rail.

Everything halted.

The fear was icy, trembling through my body as I imagined the carriage toppling over the side of the mountain. Or dangling over a deep precipice where we would never be found again.

The elemental horses shrieked, stamping their hooves until their cries softened as everything turned silent.

And still.

In a moment or two, the carriage began to move again.

Slow, careful starts until the wheels began to turn and the ground evened out. One more shift and the ground finally felt level beneath the carriage. Like it was back on the road to Mirstone. The wheels creaked and then whispered to a stop.

"Okay, we're clear," Oz called out above us. "It's safe to move around again."

Lady Laurel reached up and knocked on the ceiling to acknowledge his all-clear signal.

"Let's go, elementals! Move out!" he shouted.

The carriage began to roll normally now, bouncing and thumping along what felt like a level road again.

"That was terrifying," said Lady Laurel as she retrieved her book from the floor.

"Thought we were going off the mountain," I said, grateful that the windows had been covered with the wooden shields.

She nodded and opened her book.

But the carriage slammed on its brakes again and stopped abruptly.

"What now?" Lady Laurel cried, eyes narrowing as she glanced around the carriage and reached up to the hand rail again.

"All right, mercenaries!" a familiar voice shouted from somewhere nearby. "That's far enough."

"What's that about?" Lady Laurel replied.

She snapped up from the seat cushion and shoved open one of the carriage doors.

Immediately, her face turned pale, her gaze flitting around the carriage.

"Oh, no."

I frowned. "What's the matter?"

"We're—we're surrounded."

Her voice had a finality to it that made my skin crawl.

I rose from my seat and opened the other carriage door, climbing out onto snowy grey rock and a road that began a gentle downward slope. Down to the hilly, pale grasslands in the distance.

But an army stood between us and those warmer grasslands. Assassins. Standing in silence, blocking the road down from the mountains. Wearing those twisted, hideous white masks and sleek black leather armor.

I turned around in a circle, pressing my folded arms against my chest to retain some heat. The edge of the mountain pass was still chilly.

Behind us and the three wagons stood at least another dozen or so assassins. Same black armor. Same contorted white porcelain masks.

But where had that familiar voice originated from? Who was it?

Oz climbed down the carriage ladder and I wanted to wrap him my arms. But he moved out of reach, assessing the huge force in front of us. And the sizable one on our flank.

"Not sure what you think you've won here," Oz called out, his voice echoing against the rocks, the snow and ice patches along the road sharpening it as it rose in layers around us.

"The end to war," said that still-familiar voice.

"By starting one yourself?" Oz shouted.

"When the prophecy fails to be fulfilled, Kambria will seek new solutions," said the voice, echoing from somewhere in front of the carriage. "Besides, Xanthe alone will survive to start our world anew."

This person was incredibly arrogant and ignorant. Impressive to be both of those things at the same time.

I moved in front of the carriage, staring down all the masked assassins surrounding us. Their hands hovered near their swords, ready to draw them and attack on the signal of whoever pontificated behind them.

"Show yourself, coward!" I shouted and studied the sea of masks.

Waiting for this pompous idiot to step forward.

Silence.

"You do know that the sun fades from Xanthe's skies, too," I announced. "When Ereth and Rohesia go dark and can no longer grow crops or feed themselves, Xanthe will be the last kingdom all right. And they will watch as their crops begin to fade and die. Just like we did. But then, there will be nothing Xanthe can do to stop it. Because there will be no one left to fulfill the prophecy."

"You're lying, princess," said the voice, so familiar. "Xanthe will survive this century of war and the deaths of Rohesia and Ereth."

I couldn't help myself. I burst out laughing.

"Look around you. You refuse to see the same signs we saw in Ereth. In Rohesia. That makes you a zealot and an idiot. And wrong. A triple threat."

Oz chuckled behind me.

Finally, someone moved in the army of motionless, masked assassins. A tall woman with dark brown hair dressed in sleek black armor and a mask that covered most of her face except her mouth. But I knew her without her even removing it. She'd discarded the uniform I remembered her in—when she was captain of the Erethian guard.

Nevayna Otirys.

"Captain Nevayna," I said and propped my hands on my hips. "I've been waiting for you."

Nevayna grimaced as she stared at me from the front line of her Equalizers now.

"Oh, yes," I continued. "I've known for a while that you were an Equalizer, but I just realized yesterday that you were commanding them, too."

"Clever, princess," she said with the hint of a smile as she removed her mask. "Too bad no one will ever learn that. A shame the carriage careened off the side of the mountain, carrying you and Lady Laurel with it."

Nevayna had been chosen for her post as captain of the guard because of her battle prowess. Not her magical talent. Hers was average at best. Ordinary. Barely strong enough to become a battle mage. She was no match for an assault sorceress, but she made up for her shortcomings with sheer numbers.

I reached down and felt for the spiral pin she'd dropped in the dust, the one I had pinned to the soft inner fold of this red Rohesian court dress.

"It was a good plan, Nevayna," I said as I unfastened the pin and gripped it in my right hand. "And it almost worked."

Nevayna laughed, some of her assassins joining her in her smug merriment.

"Annarissa, what are you doing?" Oz whispered to me.

"She's my problem, Oz," I whispered back to him. "And I have a plan. But I need to stall her while I cast."

He nodded.

"Yeah, it almost worked!" Oz shouted at her as he swaggered across the rocky ground, moving behind me to stand at my left shoulder.

Lady Laurel moved closer until she stood at my right shoulder.

"You have a plan?" Lady Laurel whispered.

I smiled. "Stall her."

"What do you mean almost, princess? Mercenary?" Nevayna demanded. "It's a breath away from happening."

Oz laughed. "Not quite. See, you and your trained monkeys have to get through my crew and me first."

This time, Nevayna laughed.

"This tiny little group? We'll crush the lot of you."

"Lady Laurel," I whispered, not looking at her. "I need you to throw every last ounce of your air magic behind us at those assassins on our flank."

"Gladly," she snapped, glaring at Nevayna. "Just tell me when."

I smiled. "Oh, you'll know when."

The corners of Laurel's mouth lifted into a smirk. "Think I'm going to enjoy this."

"Yeah, this tiny little group," Oz called out. "That has kicked Equalizer ass from Ereth to Rohesia this whole trip."

I gripped the spiral pin with its inset sunburst gem in my fist. The gem was rare because it gathered remnant magic from the battlefields and the sorceress who wore it, creating a well of magic. A backup in case a sorceress exhausted her magic on the battlefield and needed more to turn the tide of the battle. Its amethyst and gold color made this one even rarer. And its power to absorb remnant magic even stronger.

Assault sorceresses and battle mages knew that at the end of the battle, they needed to release all that magic from the gem. Otherwise, the gem would gather it exponentially until it became impossible to release. Because when a simple reversal spell tried to release it, the gem would explode into a torrent of pent-up magic and return to its sorceress. A blast that could destroy an entire battlefield. And all the armies upon it.

I smiled as the first words of the reversal spell touched my lips.

But again, Mother had hired Nevayna to be captain of the guard because of her battle prowess, not her magical expertise.

And I had never felt so grateful to deal with a magical idiot in my entire life. I would have to thank Mother for this gift.

Later.

"Equalizers, on my mark," said Nevayna, her voice ringing out across the still mountain pass as she drew her sword and lifted it high into the air, the blue shimmer of magic in her outstretched hand. "Prepare to storm the carriage."

As the last words of the spell slid off my lips into the air, I held out my hand, exposing the pin with its sunburst gem. It began to hum and shake as the reversal spell completed in a swirl of blue light that settled onto the gem.

And sparked.

Quickly, I cast a magical funnel in front of my hand that began to glow blue.

"Take them!" Nevayna shouted.

Her army of assassins clambered up the rocky path toward us as Nevayna followed behind them, sword raised.

But the pass began to rumble and shake.

In a burst of brilliant purple light, the totality of magic that had built up in this sunburst gem since it had been given to Nevayna Otirys. Years ago. Exploded.

I tossed out a blue ward of earth magic that covered the wagons, people, the carriage, and the elemental horses. Shielding us.

As the massive buildup of magic released from the gem.

The magic shot through the funnel and arced across the mountain pass. Slamming into the huge force of assassins charging toward us.

With a fiery purple burst that cascaded in waves down the mountain, the combination of elemental magics rolled over Nevayna and her army.

Disintegrating them as it tried to return the magic to Nevayna.

Lady Laurel turned, tossing every shimmery white glow of air magic she possessed into a huge writhing cone of wind and air that swept down the other side of the pass. Taking Nevayna's flanking force of Equalizers with it. Off the mountainside. They plummeted into the snow and rolled hundreds of feet down the mountain. Disappearing.

It was over.

Grinning, I held out the pin with its blackened gem as Lady Laurel hugged me and pointed at it. Oz was still beside me, smiling.

"How did you know?" Lady Laurel asked.

"I found the pin on the road where we were ambushed near the Rohesian border. That's when I realized Nevayna had been leading these attacks. And the Equalizers. But when I felt the deep resonance and saw the glow in the sunburst gem, I realized that she had forgotten about the well of magic inside it. So, I did a simple reversal spell to release all of it back to her."

Lady Laurel shook her head. "I don't understand."

I laughed. "All those years of trapped magic, upon release, returns to the owner of the gem. That well of magic belonged to Nevayna. Who wasn't a very good mage. Everyone in the castle knows she couldn't even summon a strong warding spell. And she never bothered to clear the magic from the gem. It was always lit–always full."

Lady Laurel burst out laughing.

The gem had been the key to Nevayna's defeat and she never realized it.

"Annarissa, that was amazing," said Oz.

I thanked him.

He kept his distance and I ached to go to him. But I knew we both had a duty to perform. One separating us forever. And it hurt so much. Especially when he turned away and climbed back onto the carriage. Into the driver's perch.

"All right, crew!" he shouted, grabbing hold of the reins. "Let's move out."

With a heavy heart, I climbed back inside the carriage behind Lady Laurel. With another shout from Oz, the carriage lurched forward and the convoy started down the last bit of mountain pass. Onto the road to Mirstone. Where we would arrive by nightfall.

I winced. Where Oz Tarrant would leave me forever.

24

The air began to warm as we left the mountain pass behind. With the wooden window shields removed, Lady Laurel and I watched the mountains recede into faded, sickly green hills and yellowed grass that grew southwest of Mirstone.

The crisp, dry chill of the mountain air laden with occasional flakes of snow and ice crystals grew warmer as the grey sky began to turn a watercolor blue and the grey and white rocks and snow became muted green grass with hills striated yellow and green. Until the wilds turned into rectangular, plowed plots of faded brown earth where handfuls of delicate plants pushed up through the mounded soil to find the fragile, pale sunlight. Just like the crop fields in Ereth.

By the time that the sun set and night soaked up the last rays of dusk, our convoy reached the edge of the village of Mirstone. By tomorrow afternoon, we would be at the castle gates, being received by the Rohesian king, King Daegal and his royal guard.

And Prince Arence.

In a stand of mostly bare trees framed by darkening hills, the carriage lurched to a stop, the wagons circling around it.

For the last time, I heard Oz's heavy footsteps climb down the carriage ladder and thump against the ground.

I felt him pause outside the carriage doors, as if he wanted to open them. But the door handles didn't even rattle.

My eyes welled with tears, wanting desperately to go to him. To tell him that I loved him and that maybe together, we could find a way to love each other and still fulfill the prophecy.

But I felt his hopelessness from inside the carriage. It matched my own.

I heard him sigh and walk away.

And that was it. The man I loved was out of my life forever.

I hung my head and pressed it against the carriage wall as darkness filled the space, lanterns still unlit. And in the dark, I cried silent tears. Hiding my face so Lady Laurel couldn't see my heart breaking into pieces right there in the carriage.

I felt her hand on my shoulder.

"Princess, you should eat," she said finally. "The meal fire is burning bright and I can smell the hot, marinated meat from here."

I didn't react. Didn't move as I kept my face against the wall.

Thinking I was asleep, she climbed out of the carriage. Only then did I weep bitterly. I didn't want to leave its confines. I knew when I stepped out into the camp that my protector, my lover would be gone.

When the scent of roasting meat filtered through the carriage's broken windows, my stomach betrayed me. I hadn't eaten since last night and I was famished. Forcing me out of the carriage.

I walked around the darkest edge of the camp, the village lights in the distance, burning bright across the fields, and then I shuffled toward the meal fire where Norval and Pirin put food onto the plates of hungry hired swords. Less than a dozen now. I stared at every face, studied every black-haired mercenary. Every tall, lean hired sword.

But none of them was Oz Tarrant.

I got in line behind the hired swords and waited my turn. When I got to the spit where the meat roasted, Pirin set a steamy piece of marinaded meat on the plate and a heel of bread for me.

"He's gone, isn't he?" I asked as I paused beside her.

She bowed her head a moment and then fixed me with her gaze.

"Yes, he's gone, Your Highness," she said. "He headed out on foot toward the village as soon as we got here."

She saw my face and winced. Like she could hear my unasked question of where he'd gone.

"He was headed north to the port of Summerreach. To book passage on a schooner back to Xanthe. To Snowmelt."

It was real. He was gone. And I was alone again. Like I would be for the rest of my days.

Nodding, I bit my lip to keep my eyes from welling with tears and turned away with my plate. To find a place where I could eat in private—and cry in the Rohesian darkness. Where I would remain even after marrying Prince Arence.

25

When morning rose pale and sickly over the western edge of the village of Mirstone, thatched rooftops and stone houses casting short, flat shadows across the nearly barren fields, I resigned myself to my fate. The air was warm, scent of woodsmoke and manure strong on the wind as I climbed into the carriage for the very last time.

With Lady Laurel's help, I dressed in the other dress that the Rohesian crown had sent. Another red dress with a black bodice in a damask rose print and silky A-line skirt. A sheer, deep red overskirt covered the delicate fabric embroidered with red swords. The royal house's symbol was a sword. Ereth's was a rose. So, both were represented in this dress. It had the same sheer trumpet sleeves that encircled the elbows and dripped down my forearms and hands. Separate pieces from the dress and its strapless corset bodice.

"You look beautiful, my lady," said Lady Laurel, spreading out the skirt and overskirt in the carriage seat as the conveyance jaunted along the winding road through the village.

Headed toward a tall hill where the dark, forbidding Mirstone

Castle stood, casting a thick, heavy shadow across the village below it.

"But I've never seen you look so sad," she said, her eyes watery as she watched me slouch against the carriage wall. "Sadder than when your mother told you that you had been betrothed to Prince Arence Siridean."

I just couldn't bring the words to my lips. Talking about Oz hurt worse today than it had yesterday and my dry eyes couldn't summon any more tears. If I spoke about him, they would start to leak again and then I could never turn them off. When I reached Mirstone Castle, I intended to hold my head high and face my fate with a stony heart and dry eyes. I would never let them know how much I had to give up to save Kambria. But my heart darkened at the thought of Prince Arence, knowing that he would sacrifice nothing to save the world. And Rohesia would worship him for his sacrifice.

It made me sick.

All I had left was my resolve, my magic, and my memories of loving Oz Tarrant. It would be enough when I faced them.

"I will do my duty, Lady Laurel," I snapped, feeling my anger bubbling up. "But I will not smile about it and I will not lay praise on a man who forced me to give up everything while he gives up nothing to save the world. And I will not be happy about it."

She left me alone after that, once the carriage trundled over cobblestone streets, entering Mirstone village proper.

The people of Mirstone lined both sides of the narrow streets as we passed stone buildings on either side. Bakery. Seamstress. Tailor. Pub. Healer, wheelwright, and blacksmith on the other side. A dry goods shop and an apothecary, their symbols painted on brightly colored signs that hung in front of red doors. Even a dress shop graced the village.

But the villagers surprised me. Even though they gasped and gawked at the elemental horses pulling the carriage and wagons, they still cheered for me, throwing flower petals along the street in my path. Flowers grown at great cost no doubt. And never had I felt so honored and touched that my sacrifice would help these people survive. They wore simple linen clothing in muted blues, greens, purples, and browns, women in kerchiefs and men in leather aprons. Men wore their hair around their shoulders, some loose and some tied back with leather cords. All of them seemed happy to see me.

I feared they would shout obscenities at me and throw rotten fruit. Curse me for being Erethian. Enraged at my magic on display as elemental horses pulled me to the castle gates. Maybe Arence would never love me, but maybe his people would? That gave me hope and brightened my mood.

By the time the convoy stopped at the gates of Mirstone Castle, I had managed a small smile, calling it up from the strength of these wonderful villagers who came out to cheer my arrival.

"That's the strength of the princess I know," said Lady Laurel as she returned my smile.

I turned toward her as royal guards dressed in red and blue coats and white trousers, tall black boots shiny and polished, rushed toward the carriage and placed wooden steps in front of the doors.

"I smile for them," I said as the villagers' cheers became a bright roar around me. "And know that no matter what happens here, I will love Oz Tarrant until the day I die."

She nodded, her smile fading, but the carriage doors opened and a line of soldiers stood on either side of the carriage. A line of red, blue, and white stretched all the way to the gates. Where the king of Rohesia stood tall in full red and white regalia, black boots gleaming, and golden crown on his head. He had black hair dusted grey at the temples and along his hairline, light blue eyes, and a charming smile. His queen stood beside him in another ornate crown of diamonds and rubies, her long-sleeved red gown sparkling with crystals as it swept into a straight skirt and a train that tumbled several feet behind her. She had silky black hair and soft brown eyes.

But standing in front of them was a tall, dark-haired prince in a sparkling red coat adorned with gold flourishes and two rows of shiny gold buttons. He wore white trousers with a red stripe up the side. And a gold crown on his head.

He looked stoic. Distant. Complacent.

My mood darkened. Because as I stepped out of the carriage and walked along the red and gold carpet toward him, rose petals fluttering around me, villagers cheering, I realized that he looked unaffected. Almost bored. Annoyed at having to deal with any of this. Like he was counting the moments until he could return to his routine and chosen life.

While I had been forced to give up everything.

It sparked anger in me. Rage that I had never known until I looked upon Prince Arence's face in person.

Fortunately for him, the king walked past him to greet me.

"Princess Annarissa Thorn," he said in a booming, commanding voice that shot across the cheering crowd and silenced it as they waited eagerly for him to speak.

"Your Majesty, King Daegal," I said and I curtsied with my best court manners, just as Mother had taught me.

And then the king surprised me. He bowed to me. Deep and humble.

"You have sacrificed everything to give your hand in marriage to my son, Prince Arence. And princess, I am humbled by your great gift to Kambria."

I cast a scornful look at Prince Arence who remained silent and at a distance. Completely uninterested.

The king saw my dark look and instead of frowning, he smiled.

"There is also great strength and courage within you, Princess Annarissa, firstborn of Queen Ambren who has proven to be an intelligent and strong advocate for peace instead of continuing a senseless war where there are no winners. And I am committed to making Rohesia worthy of your sacrifice."

"Thank you, Your Majesty," I said and turned to look back at the convoy of hired swords who had gotten me here alive—all thanks to Oz Tarrant.

My heart smashed against my chest and I swallowed a breath, fighting back the sting in my eyes as Lady Laurel walked out of the carriage toward me.

The king held out his hand to me and for a moment, I was stunned. Treating me as his equal, he bade me to walk alongside him. In a place of honor. And right then, I realized that like Oz Tarrant, there had been a lot of lies told about this man. Time would tell, but he seemed sincere. Humble. Committed to saving Kambria not to further Rohesia's interests for selfish, short-term gains. Unlike his unconcerned son, Prince Arence who couldn't be bothered to meet me eye to eye. Instead, he almost looked down on me from the gate, from a distance, expecting me to meet him on the high ground.

But before I went any farther, I needed to speak for my convoy. For the men and women who got me here.

"Your Majesty, I must ask that Rohesia provide these men and women who risked their lives getting me here with warm, comfortable lodgings, some hearty meals, and fresh supplies so that they can rest and eat well before undertaking that long journey back to Ereth and Xanthe. And they'll need transportation."

The expression on the king's face brightened. He motioned for a well-dressed dark-haired young woman in a sapphire blue gown who stepped out of the group of courtiers behind Prince Arence. She rushed down the red carpet and curtsied to the king.

"Yes, Your Majesty," she said.

"Please take all of these brave swordsmen and women to the Dragonshead and fill the inn, paid for by the crown. Make sure the innkeeper includes all meals and beverages. Three nights should get them all well-rested. In the meantime, prepare one of my flag ships at the port of Summerreach. To carry these heroes back to Ereth and Xanthe."

"Right away, Your Majesty."

The young woman grabbed hold of her skirt and lifted it as she ran down the red and gold carpet toward the wagons.

"Thank you, Your Majesty," I said and curtsied.

"Thank you for taking care of these people who have also sacrificed a lot," he said and bowed his head. "I've been informed about Blademaster Laurant and the dozen intrepids that perished getting you here. Now then, princess, are you ready to meet your betrothed?"

I nodded. As if I had a choice.

The king swept his arm toward the castle gate and I frowned. Where Prince Arence stood motionless. Still waiting for me to come to him.

And that wasn't right.

I started toward the gate, but his attitude infuriated me. We were equals. I was a sorceress of Ereth and I would not be subservient to this stuck up Rohesian prince. Who should be much more like his father the king.

When Arence made no move to step down off his high horse, I stopped and stared at him. His brow furrowed, but he just stared at me. Like he was confused as to why I hadn't already prostrated myself before him.

That would be a cold day in Rohesia.

"Prince Arence," I said, projecting my voice to make sure he heard me. Clearly. "I have traveled more than a week from Ereth to Rohesia along bumpy roads infested with assassins and ambushes at every turn. I have battled dozens of Equalizers, traversed dangerous breaches, endured many hardships, and lost much to get here. I had to leave the only home I've ever known, leave all my family behind, and everything familiar to marry you and save the world according to prophecy. I am not some bride price. I am your equal. And the least you could do is step down from your own comfort and meet your intended halfway."

The silence was deadly and stifling as the Rohesian court stared with wide eyes at me. Prince Arence had an astonished look on his face. But I would not let them treat me like some lesser realm trying to marry up and increase their stature. Ereth and Rohesia were equals. And I would have him know that.

The queen looked flabbergasted at my gall. The soldiers looked stunned. The villagers gaped at me in stunned silence.

When I finally turned around to motion Lady Laurel to me, I looked toward the king. To my surprise, he was smiling.

As I turned toward the crowd, the villagers began to cheer me. I curtsied to them. As monarchs, these people were the reason for that authority and power, something Mother never let anyone in her court—or her family—forget.

The king moved beside me on my left as Lady Laurel took hold of my right arm. She, too was smiling.

The king motioned at Prince Arence.

"You heard the lady, Arence," said the king. "She has given up everything to try and fulfill the prophecy. The least you could do is meet her halfway to the castle gate."

It wasn't an unreasonable request. And quite frankly, I yearned to fling a sky full of dirt clods at him. The thought of marrying this puffed up, self-important prince was nauseating. And there was no such practice as dissolving the marriage. What would happen to prophecy if I walked away?

But I already knew the answer. Mother told me that separating from my intended would negate the prophecy.

Arence nodded finally, his gaze traveling across the red and gold carpet to the queen. That's when I realized she was not the queen. The way he looked at her was as a lover. She was not his mother. She was the woman he loved and he had placed her in the procession like the queen as a show of arrogance. To assure me that there would be no love in this marriage. Ever.

"Your Majesty," I said and nodded toward the dark-haired, brown-eyed woman in the crown. "I would love meet your wife, the queen."

His face grew pale and he glanced down at his feet.

"My wife the queen died many years ago," he said with a sigh.

"And you never remarried?" I asked.

He nodded. "I did remarry. Like my fair Elise, Selara bore my children. I loved them both very much. But I lost both of them long ago."

His admission stunned me to tears. It was so sad to think that his children were grown and all to be married soon. Yet he was alone. No, he was lonely. I saw it shining in his eyes.

"Your Majesty, I am so very sorry. Losing two wives must have broken your heart forever."

He nodded. "Maybe someday I will court again?"

Prince Arence stepped away from the gate and made grudging steps toward me. Like every step was killing him. I wanted to roll my eyes but didn't.

King Daegal looked at me with sad eyes, but when he saw the tears in my eyes, his own gaze grew watery.

"Your empathy touches me deeply, princess," he said in a quiet voice. "I wish that circumstances were different." His gaze traveled to the woman wearing a queen's crown. "You see, my son loves another."

I bowed my head. "As do I."

His hand lifted to my cheek and he gently caressed it. "The court demands Rohesian born heirs. She comes from a highborn family and grew up with Arence. They fell in love and she is miserable because she will never marry him, only bear his children."

"I understand her pain. I must stay in a loveless marriage for the rest of my days to save Kambria."

The king sighed, shaking his head. "I understand your bitterness, princess. You have given up everything and you gain nothing. He gives up nothing and gets to be with the one he loves—mostly. That makes you courageous and him selfish. I wish you could be with the one you love, but know that I, as a father and your king, realize everything at play here. And I will do my best to protect you from Rohesian politics."

"And I am grateful you are the king of Rohesia. My mother was right about you."

He gave me a surprised look as his hand left my face. "Ambren said that?"

I nodded. "She said that you were the reason she was entrusting her four daughters to Rohesia's four sons."

He smiled and then turned as Arence's shadow rushed along the red and gold carpet ahead of him. Until he stopped and gave me a look that was a thinly veiled glare. He had walked exactly halfway to me. And he damned well expected me to walk the rest of the way to him. Even though I'd gone through hell and back to even get here. Spoiled child. I hated that I had to marry this man.

I turned, head held high again, and walked every one of those steps, my unblinking gaze on his face. Showing him that he could do his worst and I would stand my ground. But I would accept none of it. I was a sorceress of Ereth—not his servant.

The king escorted Lady Laurel to my side and stepped between his son and me, holding out his hand as he faced the cheering crowd of villagers.

"Mirstone and Rohesia," he announced in a booming voice. "I present to you, Princess Annarissa Ambren Maelena Thorn, firstborn of Ereth and Prince Arence Ocenae Siridean, firstborn of Rohesia. Fulfilling the first part of the Prophecy of Magics and Blades as they wed tomorrow. In the royal garden at the royal hour. And you are all invited to the reception afterward on the grounds. To celebrate Kambria's first hope."

As the crowd cheered, the king's words sank into my swirling brain as my heart began to race.

Tomorrow. I was getting married tomorrow. To the one of the most selfish and self-centered men I had ever encountered.

It was the worst feeling in the world.

26

IN A LONG, NARROW CHAMBER THAT OVERLOOKED THE GARDEN, I STARED OUT the tall floor-to-ceiling window at the wedding preparations happening below. The garden was massive. Divided into sections that had once burgeoned with hundreds of blooming flowers in fuchsia, cyan, purple, and blue. Trumpets and bells and blossoms— even tiny delicate blooms the size of my fingernails.

Once adorned with thick wiry box hedges in the brightest green, cut and shaped into animals and shapes, the edging had been replaced by short stone walls and sculptures of flame foxes, warblers, and intrepids. The footpaths had been perfumed with all those flower scents and dotted with a few bouquets. Once framed by rich turquoise skies and fleecy clouds, the sky was a pastel blue with thin wisps of clouds. The fading sun had killed most of the flowers and ornamental plants that had once made this garden magnificent.

Like Ereth, stone statues and benches divided with stone walls and fountains had replaced the gardens. Stepping stones and paths wound their way through the space with its short, yellowed grass, all of them meeting in the center at a grand gazebo that was two stories tall with a polished copper roof. The posts and arches of the stone gazebo were adorned with patina-green metal vines. Lanterns hung on poles around it, gleaming like dreamflies. A hint of sage mixed with warm tallow and wood smoke, the flower essences growing stronger.

Red rose petals had been strewn across a white fabric runner that led from the grey stone castle with its five towers and tall ramparts that wrapped around the garden to the gazebo steps. On both sides of the white fabric, white dining room chairs with oblong backs and red cushions lined up in dozens of rows. They must have gotten roses brought in by a schooner from Xanthe, the only place where flowers still grew. Those rose petals that the villagers had thrown for me when I arrived must have cost the king a small fortune to provide. My affection for King Daegal grew.

But not for his horrible son.

Arence's sister and three brothers stood tall and stoic to the right of the altar. Tiryn with short cropped brown hair and an emotionless stare was shorter than the other two brothers, dressed in a royal blue and red coat, white trousers, and black boots. He looked a little unkempt. Beside him stood Orion, his royal blue and gold flourished jacket was pristine, white trousers pressed and sharp, black boots spotless. He stood ramrod straight and looked pensive, intense, brooding—like he didn't want to be here. My sister, Gen's betrothed. He was strikingly handsome with tousled, deep brown hair and light storm-grey eyes.

Slouching beside Orion stood Dante, the tallest of the brothers. He was lanky and lean, his hair a light sandy blond, eyes a clear glassy blue. He had a mischievous smirk on his handsome face, royal blue jacket unbuttoned at the collar and his hands shoved into the pockets of his white trousers. Like he was about to pull a prank on someone. He was betrothed to my sister, Carysana.

And beside Dante stood a sable-haired young woman with a big smile and wide glass-blue eyes that matched her ice blue gown. She leaned against Dante's sleeve and sighed, looking anxious to get this ceremony over. I wouldn't meet Arence's siblings until after the vows. But I hoped against hope that they were better people than Arence.

I wondered where Oz was right now. My heart ached for his company. For his touch. And I hoped that when my sisters had to walk down this runner to that gazebo, their princes loved them. But I was terrified for them now after meeting Arence. Were all the Siridean men like this? But King Daegal wasn't. Maybe his other sons weren't either?

"Annarissa, you need to get dressed in your wedding gown," said Lady Laurel as she stood across from the window, beside my Rohesian wedding gown draped across its dress form that stood in front of an empty hearth.

A close-fitting white dress covered in pearls and crystals, with what looked like off-the-shoulder straps beaded with more crystals, pearls, and sheer fabric. Layers of diaphanous fabric draped the skirt and fanned into an ethereal train. It was beautiful. But I didn't want to be beautiful for that selfish spoiled prince.

I swiveled around on the window seat, turning away from the window. And the dress form.

The dressing room walls were a soft cream color, a chair rail separating an ice blue hue that covered the ceiling, making the room feel cool and light. But the color reminded me of Oz's beautiful, sexy blue eyes and I was sad all over again.

To my right was a four-poster bed, painted cream and ice blue, with a red and gold spread stacked with small silk pillows in cream, ice blue, and red.

Scenic paintings from around Rohesia hung on the walls between sconces with fresh candles. The gold frames were complex with lattices and scrollwork and they gave the room a stuffy feeling. Except for the scent of dried rose petals and peony blooms that softened the stale air. The room looked like a museum instead of living quarters. To the right of the fireplace were two tall, deep wardrobes that stood against the wall. They had been painted in that same cream and ice blue. A third matching wardrobe stood to the left of the bed.

Between the hearth and the window was a small sitting area with two red sofas and a small, round marble-topped table. Against the wall on the other side of the huge picture window was a cream and ice blue desk with a padded ice blue chair. For writing my letters to Ereth, the only way I could go home now.

"Annarissa!" Lady Laurel called as I turned away from the window, still in my royal purple dressing gown and white stockings. "Did you hear me?"

Sighing, I rose from the window seat with its soft cream-colored cushions and moved over to examine the dress that I had tried to ignore since I entered this room.

I moved over to the gown as Lady Laurel turned up the four lanterns that stood on stands surrounding the dress.

This close, I realized that the dress wasn't white. It was cream colored. And it looked nothing like what I saw from the window. At least it wasn't another red dress. I didn't care much for the color red. Only in small doses. Not that I even cared about the color because the man I was marrying had already established his lover as queen of Rohesia. Sending me and Rohesia the message that he considered me to be no part of this court.

Of course, his father the king wouldn't tolerate whatever Arence was planning. Especially since I had established in front of the court and the villagers that I was his equal. No, he wouldn't be able to shove me away into some tower prison and forget me until someone found my bleached bones rotting in the fading sun and swirling dust motes.

I liked the gown's crystals and pearls, but on closer inspection, the off-the-shoulder straps had puffy long sleeves attached to them. They weren't sheer long sleeves either. The dress looked so old-fashioned along with its gathered wide skirt that made it look almost matronly. It ignored the waist completely and refused to acknowledge that princesses had hips and cleavage and bodies that weren't shaped like church bells. And that just maybe I wanted to show off my assets a little instead of bury them.

If I was marrying a man I loved, this dress would have been returned to the seamstress for alterations. LOTS of alterations.

The more I stared at the gown, the more I thought that maybe Arence's lover had picked out the dress to make me look awful when I married the man she loved. Like I even wanted to marry this man? I'd rather hit him with every last drop of my magic and start back home to Ereth through the Breach. Alone. But I had no choice. To save Kambria, I had to marry him. As insufferable and insulting as he was.

And my heart still ached for Oz Tarrant.

"It's hideous," I said. "But I couldn't care less about what I look like in it. It's not like the man I love will be waiting for me at the altar."

Lady Laurel reached out and pulled me into a hug. "Princess, my heart breaks for you," she said finally. "I despise Prince Arence and I know how you feel about Oz Tarrant. It's all over your face and has been since he left the convoy."

I bit my lip and tried to stifle a sob. But I couldn't. I loved him so much and only wanted to be with him. But he couldn't even be my lover like Arence with his because Oz was wanted in Rohesia. I refused to have him rotting away in a Rohesian prison for daring to be with me here.

"If I could change the prophecy, I'd do it in a heartbeat," said Lady Laurel, letting me go as she turned back to the wedding dress. "But Kambria's running out of time and the wedding is in an hour, princess. We have to get you into this...this dress and get your hair ready. The king said that he has a bouquet of flowers for you to carry. Came all the way on a boat from Fallsmere."

I frowned. "I don't know why Oz called the king a prick and said bad things about him. He's the only person here I admire and respect. I'd rather rain down rocks and dirt clods on Arence than marry him."

Lady Laurel laughed and began unfastening the back of the wedding dress. All the way down. It looked like there were two dozen more buttons down the back of the dress. Beside the dress sat a gaudy pair of gold slippers. Not my style but again, I no longer cared. I was playing a part now. One I despised, but at least I was saving Kambria.

When Lady Laurel had the dress completely undone, she removed it from the dress form and held it out for me to step into it.

I shucked off my dressing gown that pooled on the cream-colored tile floor painted with fountains and flowers. Shrubs and urns. Warblers and flame foxes. Down to only white stockings, I shuffled across the cold tiles and stepped into the dress. I held out my arms as Lady Laurel shimmied the dress's balloon-like waist over my hips and wrestled with those old-looking sleeves to get them up onto my shoulders.

"It's hideous, Lady Laurel," I said with a moan, trying not to cry as she pulled up this hundred-year-old monstrosity and began to button me in it like pounding nails into a coffin.

But somehow, that sensation felt fitting.

I wondered if the hired swords, like Pirin and Norval, would be at the reception. At least Captain Nevayna and all her assassins had been eliminated. And with the whole kingdom of Rohesia surrounding this wedding, I doubted that any of those Equalizers could get near the garden. Or the gazebo.

But an uneasy feeling roiled in my belly as Lady Laurel arranged the skirt and adjusted the stuffy wedding dress sleeves.

Somehow, the Equalizers had turned Mother's captain of the guard to their agenda. Would it be any harder to get someone in Rohesia on board to assassinate me before the wedding? Prince Arence for one. And his angry concubine that should have been standing at the altar in this dress, marrying her perfect man. Her gaze on me had been dagger-sharp and I'd never seen anyone project so much hatred.

Of course, it made no sense. With the fate of Kambria at stake, she was blaming me for marrying her man. When I detested him.

But there were always people out there with tongues so smooth that they could easily convince bitter and angry people to do things that went against their best interests. Because passion and hatred were the two most powerful emotions in the world. Convincing people to end the world when all they really wanted was a life with the one they loved.

When the dress had been reasonably styled, Lady Laurel set down the gaudy gold shoes and I stepped into them. They were comfortable at least. The court seamstresses and tailors had all my sizes, so at least I wouldn't be wearing ill-fitting shoes.

Lady Laurel grabbed a brush and a comb and began brushing out my hair. I had already removed the gold clasps for my braids. When she had my hair smooth against my back and shoulders, she began to section off locks that she braided into small tight accent braids. She clipped the little gold clasps at the ends and stepped back from me.

"You make that dress look beautiful, Annarissa," she said and I couldn't help but laugh.

"Thank you," I said as she reached out and hugged me. "For everything. I couldn't get through this without you."

"I'm with you no matter what, Annarissa," she said, her voice getting tight. "You're the daughter I never had and I'm so grateful that I get to be with you on your wedding day and throughout your life. Something your mother had to sacrifice."

I sighed. Wishing my mother was here. Right now, I needed her strength and poise. I was ready to bust some heads. Already tired of Arence and his sour-faced mistress.

"Oh, I can't stand it any longer," said Lady Laurel, groaning.

She reached out with both hands and gripped the dress sleeves. In a white burst of magic, she transformed the sleeves into delicate, sheer trumpet sleeves edged with pearls and crystals.

"Lady Laurel!" I cried, smiling.

They were perfect.

"And that hideous skirt has to go, too," she said. "A little more air magic should do the trick."

Lady Laurel grabbed hold of the heavy, bulky skirt and whispered another spell, turning the skirt into a lithe, form-fitting skirt draped in diaphanous layers of sheer fabric that fanned out into a sheer train behind it. Almost like a mermaid's tail.

She flung a handful of air at the skirt and bodice, scattering pearls and crystals until the dress sparkled. The bodice changed into a heart-shape with a sheer drape of fabric that looked like straps that had slipped off my shoulders. She even turned the gold slippers to silver.

This gown was breathtaking! And the slippers had tiny heels.

"Lady Laurel...thank you."

"You're welcome," she said and adjusted the trumpet sleeves of her royal purple Erethian court dress adorned with crystals and hugging her lithe body. "At least that jerk-of-a-prince will see you shine out there."

I hugged her and she held me tight.

Shortly before four o'clock, the royal hour, a detail of guards in pressed red and blue uniforms, white trousers with sharp seams, black boots, and gold buttons mirror-bright, arrived at the chamber door and escorted Lady Laurel and me down the stairs. Out the back of the castle. Onto the garden path to wait at the end of the white fabric runner that led to the altar beneath the gazebo. Where the king waited to marry his oldest son to a sorceress of Ereth.

I wondered how much the surrounding courtiers had already gossiped about that. And me. And my attitude. Yes, I would stand up to Prince Arence every time he tried to put himself above me.

The gazebo had been draped in swaths of red fabric around the dome. Underneath, the altar where the king stood had been wrapped in ice blue fabric with a long, cream-colored cushion on the stone floor where we would kneel and exchange rings. And kiss to seal the vows.

The thought of kissing Prince Arence made me recoil.

I glanced around the garden, at the surrounding grounds where long tables had been draped in red and ice blue silks and set with fluted glasses of golden bubbly wine, ripe yellow pears, crisp red apples, and delicate iced pastries. Beyond the tables was an iron gate in the stone wall where droves of people waited. Villagers. Through the gate and holes in the wall surrounding the castle, villagers peered into the garden to watch the wedding.

At that moment, all I could think about was turning around and running as hard and as fast as I could until I got to Summerreach. Where I could stow away on a schooner bound for anywhere but Rohesia.

And Prince Arence.

Guards in red and white uniforms had been posted all along the castle walls and along the back of the castle itself. They wore a sword on either hip, ready to engage anyone breaching the peace. Details of guards had been stationed at the tables along the white runner, and around the gazebo.

Did the king expect trouble? Or was he trying to show any lingering assassins that it was foolhardy to even attempt to stop this wedding?

I had no idea. But it made me uneasy.

The young woman in the blue gown from yesterday who had arranged stays at the inn for the hired swords rushed up to me. She wore a red dress today, her brown hair swept into a loose knot at the back of her head. With a quick curtsy, she handed me a huge bouquet of pink and purple flowers.

I couldn't help but smile. The bouquet was awash in pale pink roses, the symbol of Ereth, in full double blooms mixed with fragile lavender blossoms that made me tear up because they were everywhere in Ereth. And their scent reminded me of home. Interspersed through the bouquet were bright purple lilies with a sweet musky scent that made me bite my lip and fight the tears collecting in my eyes.

They reminded me of Oz and his leather and musk scent and I wanted to cry my eyes out all over again. He was probably at sea by now. On a boat headed for Snowmelt's port.

When Lady Laurel leaned over and smelled the lavender, her eyes got teary.

"The lavender," she said as her voice cracked. "It reminds me of Skystead."

To my left, soldiers led four musicians dressed in cream and blue linen shirts and dark trousers behind the gazebo where four chairs had been placed. They carried a harp, a vielle, an ocarina, and a timbrel. A fifth musician hurried in behind them carrying a chair and an old, greying citole.

"Princess," said the young woman, the king's courtier who had brought my beautiful bouquet. "We'll be starting momentarily."

My stomach did somersaults and all I wanted to do was run toward that gate and escape a lifetime with this horrible, selfish prince. But my duty to Kambria kept me rooted to the spot in my magically redesigned wedding gown and silver slippers.

"Your gown," the courtier cried, bright-eyed, mouth open. "It's... breathtaking."

"Thank you," I said and nodded at Lady Laurel. "My lady-in-waiting made a few...changes."

The musicians began to tune up their instruments, notes and harmonies floating in the charged air.

My stomach dropped when Prince Arence appeared on the opposite side of the gazebo, flanked by four guards in pristine red and white uniforms, buttons glistening against the afternoon grey skies. This detail was comprised of all officers.

Soon after, dozens of courtiers flooded into the garden wearing their finest gowns and clothes, but only in the prescribed colors of red, ice blue, and cream. They took their seats on both sides of the white runner where apparently, Arence and I would walk from different directions and meet at the gazebo. Where King Daegal waited to officiate the wedding.

I gazed around at the sea of strange faces, unfamiliar styles, and foreign manners, feeling so far away from anything familiar. I gripped Lady Laurel's hand so tight I thought I might cut off her circulation.

The musicians began to play in unison. The harp began, casting out a delicate melody that floated above the noise and flurry of activity and tangles of people moving around me. In moments, the ocarina's haunting notes danced a harmony above the harp, the vielle a soft but aching lament that swept over the garden and rendered it silent as the romantic music lilted above the din of the crowd. Until the gittern's crisp notes joined the aching harmonies and brought tears to my eyes.

It was the most beautiful song I had ever heard and it wrapped around my heart and held me hostage in its refrains as I willingly gave myself over to it.

"It's time, princess," said the king's courtier as she took my hand from Lady Laurel who was already in tears.

And together, the courtier and I walked with slow, measured steps toward the gazebo.

Two notes later, Prince Arence and a male courtier in an ice blue tunic and white trousers started toward the gazebo with those same measured steps.

But somehow the timbrel's gentle taps interrupted the song for me. Like a bard taking a breath in the wrong places. Every beat felt off with the measured steps the courtier took, that I had to mimic. And still, every beat made me uneasy.

Off to my left, movement slipped past the chairs. A flash of black. I turned my head.

Late afternoon shadows.

Still, the timbrel's beat tripped me up as I made my way to the gazebo. When I got close enough to see Prince Arence's face, his red officer's uniform pressed and buttons mirror-bright, he looked frustrated.

"Sina," said Prince Arence in a quiet but annoyed voice to the female courtier beside me. "Send that timbrel player away immediately. That cadence is all wrong for the music. And a wedding."

"I couldn't agree more," I said and he nodded at me.

The courtier called Sina left me as Prince Arence and I met at the steps of the gazebo. She walked around behind it and interrupted the intense timbrel player, pulling the dark-haired young man out of the chair. She motioned him toward the gates. Looking angry, the young man gripped the timbrel in his left hand and walked around the gazebo.

He moved past Prince Arence and me as we turned toward the altar. And King Daegal who stood behind it, smiling and holding out his arms. Waiting for us to kneel before him.

At least that part was similar to Erethian weddings.

Prince Arence nodded toward me and extended his hand, motioning for me to go first.

To my left, another shadow shifted as I started up the gazebo stairs.

And suddenly, the timbrel player was behind me. The hollow twitter of bells jangled as the timbrel fell out of his hand, a knife sliding out from beneath the instrument.

The man grabbed my hair and jerked my head back.

"Annarissa!"

The knife blade sank into my back as someone slammed into the assassin, knocking him and the knife away from me.

Guards swarmed the downed assassin as the music halted, people shouting and running through the garden in a panic.

Arms gathered me up and cradled me. When I looked up, I was staring into Oz Tarrant's watery ice blue eyes.

"Annarissa," he moaned. "No..."

I felt the pain and the heat and the stickiness seeping across the back of my wedding dress, but the feel of Oz's arms around me made up for the pain and the fear.

"You came back for me," I said, my voice sounding so weak as he held me close.

Lady Laurel was beside me, ripping open the buttons to get at the wound. Her air magic was white hot against my skin, her healer's instincts taking over as Oz held his hand tight against the wound. The heat of his hands washed over me like warm sand and I wanted to lose myself in his touch. Forever.

"Hang on, princess," he said with a moan. "You're going to be okay."

A Rohesian healer knelt beside Lady Laurel, a steel-haired stocky man with strong hands and a square face. His brown eyes were anxious, but he was controlled and professional as he pressed a thick cloth to the wound.

"Hold that as tight as you can," the healer said to Oz who nodded and pressed hard.

And then King Daegal was in front of me, his frightened gaze moving from me to Oz.

"Can you save her, Frey?" he asked and his gaze moved to Lady Laurel. "Lady Laurel?"

"We're doing everything we can, sire," said the healer called Frey.

Then the king's scrutinizing gaze shifted to Oz. "Who are you?"

"The man I love," I answered him.

One of the guards stopped beside the king, her eyes wide as she pointed at Oz, sword drawn.

"Sire, that's Oz Tarrant!"

"Oz Tarrant? Detain him immediately!"

27

Daegal's voice carried across the garden, bringing a flurry of guards in my face. Dammit!

Gritting my teeth, I reached for my broadsword hilt, but the bastards were too fast. They surrounded me, swords drawn. And me looking stupid holding onto the hilt of my sheathed sword as I held Annarissa in my arms.

Lady Laurel pressed the bandage harder against the knife wound in Annarissa's back and held it tight.

One of the guards grabbed my arm, but I jerked away from him. Two more were on me, forcing Annarissa out of my arms and my arms behind by back. Another guard held me around the waist, hold so tight it was cutting off my air. I struggled against the hold but couldn't break. Dammit!

"No," Annarissa cried in a weak voice, her voice weak and I was terrified as it disappeared into the chaos and the shouting and orders flying across the garden. "Let him be!"

They tried to pull me away from her again, but Annarissa locked her arm in mine and pulled me against her beautiful face. She wrapped her arms around my neck, refusing to let go.

Daegal's balls, I loved this woman!

"Stop," she moaned. "Don't take him."

"Princess, hold still," said Lady Laurel, the white glow of her air magic spilling onto the front of Annarissa's dress, illuminating the crystals for a moment.

Annarissa lifted her face to mine, smashing her mouth against my lips and I kissed her back with every ounce of strength I had. Only wanting to hold her in my arms for a lifetime.

Gold sparks flew as we kissed, the guards still trying to pull us apart.

"Wait! Stop!" Daegal demanded. "Guards, step down. Now!"

The guards immediately stepped back as the king dropped down beside me, a desperate look in his blue eyes and a hand gripping my arm.

"That light..." Daegal cried.

"Ask her," I snapped, shrugging. "It's earth magic or something."

But already Daegal was shaking his head.

"No, that light—that spark is fate. It's the last line of a very long story. And the reason I've had a warrant out for your arrest for over twenty years, Oz Tarrant."

I groaned and bowed my head. What in blazes did this prick think I'd done to him? Maybe it was just revenge on my mother for whatever she stole from the Sirideans that night? But why? My father died saving this bastard's two sons. Was it because he couldn't save Daegal's queen?

Couldn't he look away just this once? In my father's memory?

"Okay, look—" I said with a growl, glaring at Daegal as I faced this bastard for the first time since I knew about that damned warrant. "I haven't seen my mother since I was eleven. I don't know what she stole from you but—"

"A child," said Daegal in a quiet, aching voice.

And every thought I had floated away as I stared at the king of

Rohesia. I was speechless. My mother said that my father saved both the king's sons that night. Why did she lie about that? Did he think I'd taken one of them?

"A child?" I repeated dumbly, staring at him like he'd just said I'd stolen his kid.

Daegal nodded.

"Look, your majesty," I sneered, giving this bastard who'd been trying to arrest me for a lifetime no respect. None. "I don't have your kid and I don't know squat about that. You want answers, talk to my mother. I was just a baby myself when this happened. My father died saving both your sons that night."

For a few moments, Daegal looked like he was a million miles away, flashing back to the night my father died, maybe? Maybe he was confused? Had things all jumbled up. After all, it had been more than twenty years since that night.

"Oz," said Daegal, something in his voice forcing me to shut my mouth and listen to him. "Let me tell you what happened that night. The truth. Because Tressa Tarrant has been lying to you for all these years."

My stomach did a somersault and I began to shake all over, feeling something deep in the pit of my stomach that had been buried in my head for as long as I could remember. Something I felt, but I'd been afraid to ask my mother my entire life.

Annarissa reached out and gripped my hand and I put both hands around hers, holding onto her for all I was worth.

"My mother's an expert at lying, stealing, and conning people out of their coin," I said in a tired voice. "What other lie has she been telling me?"

"That night, about twenty-five years ago, Equalizers infiltrated Mirstone Castle. In the dead of night. You father, Cedric Tarrant discovered their presence before they had a chance to carry out their assassination plan. Which was to kill me, my wife, and my two sons."

Equalizers. I wanted to rage. Those monsters had been trying to burn down Kambria forever.

I nodded for him to continue.

Daegal pulled in a breath, pain filling his eyes as he studied my face a moment.

"The guards engaged the assassins early, before they reached mine and my wife's bedchamber. Cedric lived with his wife—your mother—in a cottage just behind the castle. But that night, the only safety was to escape the grounds. Hide in the village. So, he and Tressa shepherded my family and me out of the castle along with two units of guards. Tressa had an infant in her arms. My wife and I each carried one of our babies. I carried Arence and Elise carried Roderick."

Part of me didn't want to hear this story. It couldn't have a happy ending and I didn't want to hear about my father and prince Roderick getting killed by assassins.

"But didn't my father save both princes that night?"

"Yes, Oz, he saved both my boys and we were almost over the wall to the safety of the village lights. But out of the brush emerged three assassins."

Daegal's eyes got glassy.

"One of them was at Elise's throat before we could even see them." He winced, bowing his head. "Killed her right in front of me."

I wanted to cover my ears. I didn't want to hear this, but I knew I had to listen. Had to hear it all and know exactly what happened to my father that night. Know what my mother stole from King Daegal.

Finally, Daegal lifted his head, eyes brimming with tears.

"Cedric engaged the other two assassins as one unit of guards protected Arence and me. The other guard unit rushed toward Elise and Roderick. Tressa Tarrant tried to hide in the brush, but there was a fourth assassin waiting there to strike. She fought with the assassin, but she couldn't halt the blow of the knife that slashed out at her."

Daegal's breath caught. It took him a moment to recover.

"The blow hit her in the shoulder, but it nicked her infant son. And in a heartbeat, he was gone."

I recognized and understood each word as Daegal said them, but they didn't quite register. And I couldn't quite put them together, but my heart did. And the horrible grief washed over me like a thunderstorm. Already knowing the rest of what he was about to say.

"Tressa Tarrant ran toward my fallen wife, still clutching Roderick in her arms as Cedric engaged the three assassins. That had already killed the unit of soldiers guarding my wife. Tressa fell down beside Elise as the fourth assassin attacked Arence and me. Only two guards survived that attack. Six guards and your father gave their lives to protect me that night. We took down the fourth assassin before he could kill me or Arence. But the hysterical sobbing forced me to turn around. Cedric was down, three assassins dead at his feet. With Roderick clutched in his arms. Elise lay dead in the cold grass beside Tressa's dead son and Tressa wept hysterically."

"But sire," I said, my voice so tiny I thought he wouldn't even hear me. "I'm Tressa Tarrant's son. She ran with me from Rohesia and returned to Xanthe after my father was killed."

Daegal shook his head as I knew he would, about to say the words I'd felt for twenty-five years but couldn't voice. Words I'd tamped deep down inside so I wouldn't have to think about them. Or what my mother had done that night.

"No, Oz," he said, his eyes dripping with tears. "While I fought off assassins, Tressa laid her dead son in my wife's arms and took Roderick from her. She put Roderick into her husband's arms moments after he had died, insisting he was her son. And she waited until the fighting was over. Waited for me to see my son dead beside Elise and hers alive in Cedric's dead grasp. Trying to make her switch stick and make me doubt what my heart already knew."

I winced, smashing my eyes closed. Oh, God, he was going to say it. Say the words I'd been avoiding for my entire life. The truth that I felt deep in my soul but was too afraid to face.

"Oz," said King Daegal, tears streaking down his face as he laid his hand against my cheek. "She switched her dead son with Roderick and stole him from my dead wife's arms. Claiming her husband died saving his own son. And without warning, she grabbed Roderick and vaulted over the wall. Disappearing. With my son."

I shook my head, the words all confused and not adding up in my head. But his arm slid around my shoulders as the first tear slid down my damned face. And I couldn't hold it in. Couldn't hold it back.

Annarissa gasped. "By Ereth...are you saying that—"

Daegal nodded. "Oz, you aren't a Tarrant. You're a Siridean. Prince Roderick Ballard Siridean. My son. My child that I've been trying to locate for twenty-five years. Hence the warrant."

"Hold still, princess," said Frey the healer. "The bleeding has almost stopped—thanks to your lady-in-waiting, Lady Laurel."

Annarissa let go of my hand as I turned to King Daegal, my bottom lip quivering, my eyes stinging as the truth settled against my skin, the words finally sinking into my thick head. And my heart. My mother wasn't my mother at all. She stole me from the Siridean royal family after her son died in an attack. The father I'd never known wasn't dead.

Son of a rakefire, he was right in front of me. Wanting me back where I came from.

The king threw his arms around me and pulled me into a hug. And I held the man tight. My father. And for the first time since I was a kid, I felt like I belonged somewhere. That I was wanted. That I mattered.

"Roderick," the king muttered, his voice cracking. "My son—at last."

"Father," I said and the king wept as he held me tighter.

When he'd composed himself, he let me go.

"You know," I said, "I go by Oz. My name is Ozwyn."

My father the king studied me a moment. "We'll have to change that."

I frowned. "I go by Oz," I repeated, a little surlier than I'd intended.

He chuckled. "How about Ozwyn Roderick Siridean?"

A name with promise. "Let's start with Oz Siridean and work up to it," I said.

My father laughed and patted me on the back. "Agreed...son."

But he hadn't gotten to the gold sparks business. And I was ready to fight the whole damned castle to stop this wedding to Arence.

"So what about those sparks?" I asked.

"She's out of danger," said Frey as Lady Laurel heaved a relieved sigh and sat back on her heels.

Lady Laurel wrapped a bandage around Annarissa's thin body that had been swallowed by that...that dress. That breathtaking dress that sparkled with magic.

Gently, I slid my arms around Annarissa and held her against me, cradling her. She laid her head against my chest, running her fingers down my arm.

"The sparks?" I repeated.

My father smiled as he studied me a moment and then his gaze fell onto Annarissa.

"Yes, the sparks. The first time I saw them, I had just kissed Elise in this very garden. Where there were still some roses blooming alongside purple lilies and lavender and even some sunflowers. We both were shocked when we saw the gold sparks. We rushed inside to where my mother sat writing letters. When we told her what had happened, she got this curious, knowing expression on her face. And told us it was fate telling us that we had found our mate."

My arms tightened around Annarissa.

"Is that true?" Annarissa asked in a soft, melodic voice.

My father nodded and ran his fingers through her hair a moment. "Yes, princess, Sirideans always know when they've found the right mate because fate sends up some fireworks to make it known. That's how I knew you were my missing son—because of those sparks...and the prophecy."

A sad look touched Annarissa's perfect porcelain face. "But the prophecy," she said with a moan. "I'm fated to marry Arence."

My father, King Daegal, held his stomach as a boisterous laugh rumbled from his lips. He shook his head.

"Princess, you were betrothed to Arence because he was the firstborn like you. But you aren't fated to marry him. The prophecy demands that four Thorn sorceresses must marry four Siridean princes of the blade to save Kambria."

She stared back at my father with wide eyes and a furrowed brow.

"The one you love, the one that fate sparks gold for, is a Siridean, dear girl," he said with a grin. "So, marry him. Arence loves another anyway."

She looked up at me with those burning gold hazel eyes that were filling with tears.

"Oz...?" she said in almost a whisper, staring at me in shock and wonder.

"Marry me, my princess?" I asked. "I'd hate to waste such a beautiful day for a wedding."

Her face lit up with the biggest grin I had ever seen.

"Yes, of course I will, Oz!"

She threw herself into my arms and I kissed her hard, for all I was worth. Now that I was a Siridean, I could love her and save the world.

"Can I wear my own dress?" she asked me.

"Of course," I said. "I'd marry you in sackcloth, Annarissa Ambren Maelena Thorn."

"Lady Laurel, help me get dressed again?" Annarissa asked as I lifted her onto her feet.

"Let's find something purple this time," said Lady Laurel, her eyes teary as she and Frey helped Annarissa back into the castle.

I turned back to King Daegal. My father.

"Will you marry us?" I asked.

"It would be my honor, son," he said. "Arence can be your best man." He nodded toward the musician's chairs behind the gazebo where Arence was passionately kissing some woman. "Trust me, he's never been happier to find his brother moments before he had to get married for the prophecy."

Father nudged me toward the castle. "Let's go find some more suitable wedding clothes. For your princess."

I nodded and followed him into the castle. Where I had been born. It was a strange but settling feeling.

28

A HARP LILTED A WEDDING SONG ACROSS THE GARDEN BENEATH THE ocarina's aching crystalline dance with the vielle's and gittern's emotional harmonies sweeping me toward the gazebo in a haze of lavender, roses, and sweet musky lily scent.

I still felt lightheaded from the knife wound as I nearly floated across the garden in my lavender silk gown with its beaded sleeveless bodice and flowing skirt that hugged my hips and pooled around my white silk stockings like a mermaid's tail. The sheer trumpet elbow sleeves fluttered in the breeze as I approached the love of my life who stood at the altar beside his newly found brother, Prince Arence Siridean. And newly discovered father, King Daegal Siridean.

I never dreamed that the truth about Oz Tarrant was so grand and made him a Rohesian prince, a Siridean. The mate I had been fated to marry. All along, I'd wanted to believe in the magic of those gold sparks, in our love, but the prophecy always made it impossible for us to be together.

Yet, in a breath and a heartbeat, my dreary fate became the thing I wanted most. To save Kambria and to love Oz Tarrant...um, Prince

Oz Siridean. And in a twist of fate, I had the chance to do both. And I was grabbing it with eyes open and arms outstretched.

Oz took my hand in his as I walked up the gazebo steps and knelt beside him on the cream-colored cushion. In front of the ironwood altar. Where King Daegal stood behind it, hands behind his back. His golden and ruby crown was burnished and bright, his royal red and white coat crisp and pressed like his white trousers. His tall black boots looked shiny and new. Candles burned around the altar, casting an ethereal glow throughout the gazebo, the scent of sage and lavender warm and heady. His hands shook as he held both of mine so tight. But I didn't mind. I would hold his hands for a lifetime.

King Daegal read the vows, but Oz stopped him, turning toward me.

"Annarissa Ambren Maelena Thorn, you are my love, my light, and my life. And I will protect you and our love for all of my days. You are my princess, now and always." He slid a gold ring onto my left ring finger.

My heart was almost too full to speak.

"Oz Siridean, you are my prince, my protector, and my heart's prophecy. And I will protect you and our love for all of my days. You are my everything, my forever." I took his strong, squared hand in mine and slid the gold band on his left ring finger.

"As it has been since Kambria rose above the waves," King Daegal began, "fate and love spark as one to save and protect us. And in the glow of that spark, I present husband and wife. Oz and Annarissa, kiss and seal your union."

Oz swept me into his arms with hottest kiss I had ever felt. It rushed over me in burning waves and I smashed my mouth against his, returning every rush of heat and spark of passion until we both glowed with gold light. Lighting up the gazebo and the musicians playing behind it.

And for the first time in a hundred years of sundering, Kambria heaved a sigh of relief as the sun peaked out from behind the clouds.

Softly warming the fields and the castle garden with thin, fragile sunlight. That had grown only a whisper stronger.

Knowing that one part of the prophecy had been fulfilled, Oz and I danced as husband and wife, wrapped in each other's arms, never letting go, in a haze of gold sparks.

The End of THORN & BLADE, BOOK ONE: CURSE AND CROWN

The story continues in...
CURSE AND CROWN
STEEL & STORM, BOOK TWO

This is Genevieve's story...

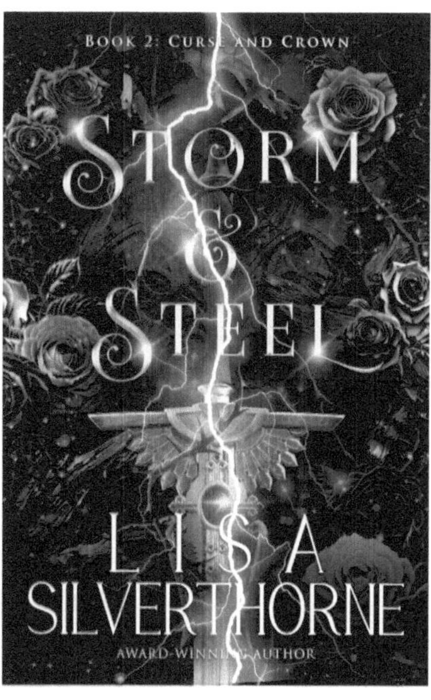

Novels by Lisa Silverthorne

A Game of Lost Souls series:
Contemporary Romantasy
THE CINDERELLA HOUR
THE PRINCE CHARMING HOUR
THE EVER AFTER HOUR
THE FALLEN HEARTS SEASON
THE RISING SPIRITS SEASON
THE ETERNAL SOULS SEASON
THE ROYAL WEDDING HOUR
THE HEAVENLY HONEYMOON HOUR
THE DIVINE NEWLYWEDS SHOW
THE CELESTIAL COUPLES SHOW
THE ENOCHIAN APOCALYPSE SHOW
THE ANGELIC ANNIVERSARY SHOW
THE PERDITION PICTURE SHOW
Complete Series!

Curse and Crown series:
Epic Court Intrigue Romantasy
THORN & BLADE
STORM & STEEL

The Spiral series:
Dark Contemporary Fantasy
BETWEEN
REPRISE
AVENGE

The Resurrectionist Papers
Supernatural Romystery
GRAVE RECKONING

Standalones:
ISABEL'S TEARS
LANDFALL
PACIFIC BLUE TATTOO

Short Story Collections
THE SOUND OF ANGELS
THE MAGIC OF ORDINARY THINGS
TIMELESS
WINTER'S EMBRACE

Science Fiction Writing as L.S. Silverthorne

Experiencing True Purple series:
RECOMBINANT, Book 1
HELIX, Book 2
SPLICE, Book 3

Standalones:
REDISCOVERY

FORTHCOMING!

Curse and Crown series:
Flame & Dagger, Book Three
Frost & Foil, Book Four
Curse & Crown, Book Five (Series End)

The Spiral series:
Ruin, Book 4
Descent, Book 5 (Series End)

The Resurrectionist Papers:
Corpses Delicti
Stiffed Again

SCIENCE FICTION WRITING AS **L.S.** SILVERTHORNE

Experiencing True Purple series:
Cipher, Book 4
Renascence, Book 5 (Series End)

About the Author

LISA SILVERTHORNE, an award-winning author, has published over 30 novels and 150 short stories and novelettes in many genres. She is the author of *A Game of Lost Souls*, *Experiencing True Purple*, *The Spiral*, *The Resurrectionist Papers*, and *Curse and Crown*.

Before you go, you are invited to please leave a **review of this book**!

Reviews are a wonderful way to help an author and share your thoughts with other readers, so **please post yours,** in as many places as possible!

 **ONLINE STORE!**

For Ebook Bundles, book swag, and beautiful **Special Edition** *hardcovers (coming soon), visit:* **LisaSilverthorneBooks.com**